Panes

splinters across the road. A tall column of smoke rose across the rooftops. Above her a head thrust out of an upper window.

'What is it? What's going on?'

'It's a practice –' someone in the street called out.

'Don't be ridiculous! Can't you see the fires? Someone's dropping bombs –' His words were lost as a salvo of bombs exploded somewhere near the centre of town.

Dust floated in the unearthly light of the full moon as the sound of screaming reached Kate. She stood shivering on the verandah, numb with shock, scarcely aware of the running figures in the street and the stunned faces of her neighbours at the windows.

'Japanese, it's the Japanese –'

The words barely entered her consciousness. All she could think of as she stood there was that this time the war had caught up with her.

WATER FROM THE MOON

Lesley Denny

G
Gainsborough Press

This edition published in 1996 by Gainsborough Press

First published in Great Britain by Century 1987
Arrow edition 1988

Printed and bound in Great Britain by
Cox & Wyman Ltd, Reading, Berkshire

ISBN 0 752 90351 9

Dedicated to the memory of my father and to the members of the Far East Prisoners of War Association for their kind help with this book.

Author's note

'Water from the Moon' is an Indonesian expression for impossible dreams

Chapter One

It was the first Sunday in December. The year of 1941, year of the Serpent.

In the dark Pacific it was December 7. Eastwards across the International Dateline the new day to come was already December 8. A day worthy of astrologers' divinations, the day appointed, the day of destiny.

The moon's round bright face greeted them as they set out, encouraged by joyous cries of 'Banzai!' from the assembled crews. Below their formation now stretched the wide expanse of iridescent sea, a glittering flight-path to their appointed target.

Before them lay the city, sweating in the tropical night. Singapore in the weeks before Christmas was ablaze with light. The municipal buildings, the law courts and Fort Canning, the military headquarters, were floodlit. Even without the full moon, the Japanese planes would have had no difficulty in finding their target. Without declaration of war, without warning, Singapore was to be bombed.

The moonlight entered the house through the wooden slats of her bedroom shutters. The night as ever was sultry and airless, strong with the scents of the city, the rich mix of spices, of fish and bad plumbing and the wet heat of Singapore.

Sleep eluded Katherine. In the white web of the billowing mosquito net the night breeze brought into the room the noises of the streets. She reached for her slippers, automatically shaking them out for unwelcome visitors, just as though she had lived in the tropics all her life.

The heat was the worst thing about Singapore. Three degrees north of the Equator, the temperature never varied much from 90°F, with humidity over 85 per cent.

When Katherine Kendall had first arrived in Singapore she thought she would never get used to the wet heat that meant the clothes on her back were permanently damp, that even at night the sweat stood out all over her body. Condensation ran down the walls of their house. The plaster had fallen and crumbled with the damp. The temperamental air-conditioning fans cost too much to run even when they did work. Her brother Tony had been out here for nearly three years and still complained he could not get used to the climate.

Katherine lifted the verandah screens, feeling the warm night breeze on her face. The moon spilled over her into a pool on the floorboards, her nightdress and loose hair seemingly colourless in the ghostly light.

Ten thousand miles from Europe, the war was another world, unreal. The Blitz in London, the bitter struggle in Russia, the horrors of Nazi occupation, all seemed so remote out here.

Even at that hour traffic still crawled its way through the narrow maze of houses and shops in the quarter. Bicycle bells on the rickshaws, taxi horns and car klaxons, laughter and drunken voices carried on the wind. Everywhere people had been out enjoying themselves, all Saturday night right into the early hours of Sunday. Troops in the uniforms of a dozen nations, an Empire. Sikhs, Gurkhas, Australians and English. Europe and the war seemed very far away.

But her complacency was soon to be shattered. At 4 a.m. the room was rocked by a deafening explosion across the town. Kate hurried back to the window as she heard the high-pitched whistle of falling bombs.

Panes of glass cracked, spraying their splinters across the road. A tall column of smoke rose across the rooftops. Above her a head thrust out of an upper window.

'What is it? What's going on?'

'It's a practice – ' someone in the street called out.

'Don't be bloody ridiculous! Can't you see the fires? Someone's dropping bloody bombs – ' His words were lost as a salvo of bombs exploded somewhere near the centre of town.

Dust floated in the unearthly light of the full moon as the

sound of screaming reached Kate. She stood shivering on the verandah, numb with shock, scarcely aware of the running figures in the street and the stunned faces of her neighbours at the windows.

'Japanese, it's the Japanese – '

The words barely entered her consciousness. All she could think of as she stood there was that this time the war had caught up with her.

It was still hard for her to come to terms with the climate. How the heat seemed to suck moisture from the very earth. How when it was dry on one side of the street, it could be raining on the other. How Manila sapped all her energy.

She had to struggle to get up in the mornings. Warren was working and most of the days were her own, to squander usually in a torpor of inactivity, a kind of limbo. The hotel was anonymous, undemanding. Since they had arrived in the Philippines, Dede had been having her first true holiday in years, sleeping almost until noon each day.

She ordered coffee in her room and stood on her balcony to watch the planes going over, probably heading for Clark Field. Manila was full of American sailors and fliers, based at Cavite, at Mariveles on Bataan, and the greatest airbase in the Pacific at Clark Field.

Down in the street people had stopped to look up at the sky, shielding their eyes, hands half-raised to wave to the planes. Then, suddenly, they turned and began to scatter, calling out to each other in harsh, high-pitched cries whose meaning did not carry up to her as she stood, rooted to the spot, on her balcony.

The silver triangle of heavy bombers overhead bore the unmistakable orange-red symbol of the Rising Sun on their wings.

Dede threw on the first clothes that came to hand and hurried out into the deserted corridor. She hit the buttons for the lifts, but the light refused to come on. In exasperation she pushed through the swing door on to the staircase, turning the sharp angles down and down into the hot well of the building until she burst out into the lobby, already packed with its lunchtime clientele.

But it was the silence which struck her at once. The

awesome, lengthening silence in the hall while from outside, on the street, came a background roar of shock and fear.

'What is it? What's happening?'

The first face turned to her was white and vacant with horror. The look in his eyes frightened her more than before. She tugged desperately at the arm of another, a serviceman standing close by the reception desk, staring at the radio behind the clerk's head.

'It's Pearl Harbor,' he said, almost choking on the words. 'Pearl Harbor's been hit.'

If you asked any American where he or she was that day in December when the first news of Pearl Harbor came, they were sure to recall it in detail. Dede knew at once the significance of the moment. She knew she would never forget it.

For more than two years America had kept out of the war that had half the world in its tortured grip. The argument had raged between isolationism and involvement. Now, it seemed Japan had made up their mind for them. It was war at last.

During the afternoon reports came in of the attack on Clark Field. The Japanese lost no time in capitalizing on their surprise raid on Pearl Harbor. The B17s at the field had taken off early in the day but had to land again to refuel later, and it was then that the Japanese caught them. Over eighty aircraft were reported destroyed. There were large-scale casualties.

Warren rang Dede to say he and his father were at the scene. Every doctor in Manila was helping out. He said that they would try to get back in time for the supper dance, even if it was only for the last waltz.

'Be sure to save that one for me,' he told her and then hung up.

The hotel housed many service chiefs and their families. General Douglas MacArthur himself had the penthouse apartment with his family. Before long many of these women and children would be evacuated. The Philippines were in the front line of the action. The Japanese held the Chinese mainland and the very planes that had bombed Clark Field had flown in from the occupied island of Formosa. In fifteen minutes the Americans lost their air cover and protection for their bases in the

Philippines, and opened up the way to the Japanese conquest of the East Indies.

That night the dance was far from gloomy. It seemed as though everyone had decided to make the best of what could turn out to be one of the last social occasions in Manila.

Dede came late to the supper room, knowing that Dr Irvine Brandon and his son, Dr Warren Brandon, were still involved in the emergency. She recognized few of the faces in the hot sticky atmosphere. Blackout curtains had been rigged across the windows, flapping ineffectually in the thick evening breeze off the bay. She danced only once, with Warren's friend Morgen from the naval base at Cavite, one of the slow-tempo foxtrots they played long into the hot night.

Almost when she had given them up, she saw Warren's father in the doorway. He was a tall man in his late fifties, broad but not heavy, a man who kept himself fit by working all the hours under the sun. He was a fine, respected physician of the old school, who had made a study of tropical diseases and had lived out East for many years.

And then she saw Warren. He came up behind his father, taller by several inches. She saw him hesitate, squinting as he searched the crowded room for her. He looked tired, his brow furrowing, his tanned face drained. Then he caught sight of her and the look disappeared as he set out to claim her.

'I'm sorry, honey,' he said softly, holding her close.

She reached out a hand to smooth back his rich brown hair, searching his face.

'We can leave if you want.' She thought he might need to talk about all he had seen, but to her surprise he shook his head.

'No, there's something I must do first. Just wait here a minute.'

Startled, she watched him cross the dance floor to the band leader. He was holding up his hands and stopping the music. The dancers came to an abrupt halt, turning to face him expectantly.

'I have an announcement to make,' he said, grinning from ear to ear. 'I'd just like to tell you all that Miss Dorothy Harriman and I will be getting married the minute we can find ourselves a chaplain. Chaplain?'

The navy chaplain led the laughter.

'Any time you're ready, Warren. I'd given up waiting for you!'

There was a general atmosphere of good-humoured surprise, but there was no one as surprised as Dede herself. She stared at Warren over the heads of the crowd as he struggled to get back to her, jostled by well-wishers:

'Congratulations!' 'Well done!'

Dede stood dazed among the grinning faces. She was looking pretty tonight, very dark and exotic in her shantung dress. Her hair was cut in a short bob and waved back from large jet beads in her ears. She was not a beautiful woman, but she was tall and self-possessed and carried herself well. Her face was agreeable in repose, arresting when animated, with fiercely intelligent, inquiring dark eyes.

Never had those eyes flashed so brightly as they met Warren's. His rash announcement had caught her completely off her guard. Was this the man they had warned her against? The man they said would or could never make an emotional commitment? The man who quipped at a party in Los Angeles, 'Honey, clever men don't become husbands!'

But he was serious. He had proved that his pledge to her that night in the restaurant in the Dilaman quarter had not been just idle words.

Since they had come to Manila they had spent most of the time with other people at clubs, restaurants or parties. But Dede found it hard going being one of the few American women left in Manila, and having virtually nothing in common with those who were.

'I hear you're still a student. Can that be right?'

'Well, yes, I – '

'But you'll be giving all that up, surely? I mean, what is the point of all that education when you're just going to get married anyhow?'

Dede gave a small embarrassed laugh. She was crazy to believe that they could understand. The women here, the army and navy wives, made a career of their marriages, which suited their men fine. They saw no need to accommodate the kind of view she represented. She was a freak to be still studying at her age.

It was a waste of time trying to explain her ambitions to any of them. Even Warren did not really understand. He was proud to show her around to his friends, telling them all about Pasadena, but what did he really know about her?

Oak Knoll, Pasadena, with half an acre of manicured garden, a piano in the music room, a library of books, that much she had told him. It was all she had ever told anyone at the university. The rest of the story of how she had become Dede Harriman was her own private concern.

Unlike these women, she had actually been encouraged with her education, even though Cultural Anthropology sounded rather remote from their own closed little world. But it was this very remoteness that appealed to Dede. Aunt Constance might not understand, but Dede knew that her father would have.

While other sophomores made the most of campus kisses and football stars, Dede made her mark by long hours of eager study, devouring every book in sight. Margaret Mead's *Coming of Age in Samoa* and *Growing up in New Guinea* set the mood for her interest in a field so new and radical that she seemed at times almost one step ahead of her lecturers. In 1935, the year Dede graduated with distinction, Margaret Mead published her controversial *Sex and Temperament in Three Primitive Societies*. Dede had made up her mind. She was going to be an anthropologist. After her Masters she was going on to write her Ph.D. thesis. She was going to travel and do fieldwork in some unknown, exotic place in the Pacific or East Indies. She was getting out. She was going to see for herself.

'Borneo? You can't be serious!'

'It's what I really want to do,' Dede told her aunt and uncle.

'How long is this going on? I don't mind paying for a good education,' her uncle rumbled, 'but what's the good of it all? Can't she teach just as well with a Masters?'

'She says she wants to travel. Borneo, she says. She wants to see how they live out there.'

'I'll tell her how they live. Savages, that's what they are. Who the hell wants to know about savages?'

When Dede found her funds cut off she suspected an ulterior motive. She knew her aunt had long been hoping she would give up her studies and find herself a husband.

From time to time there had, of course, been men in her life. Some dates had been no more than a foursome, arranged by pitying girlfriends who could not understand why fertility rites in New Guinea offered more excitement than a blind date. Even those she had selected for herself had always been supremely disappointing. There had never been anyone who came close to challenging her dreams.

Then Dede met Warren at a faculty reception. He was too old to be another collegiate drone, too flippant to be on the staff. She noticed him the moment he walked in with a stunning redhead who worked in one of the labs.

Whatever happened to that girl? He had soon abandoned her, turning up at Dede's elbow with an easy smile on his handsome face the minute her own escort went to fetch drinks.

'Don't tell me,' he said playfully, 'you're going to Washington with that high-flying creep.'

She turned to look into those smiling Irish eyes.

'No, you're wrong. I'm going to Borneo.'

'Good God! What are you going there for? The head-hunting?'

'Is the season open? Great, I'll pack my blowdarts.'

He shook his head at her. 'You know, you must be crazy – '

'If you say so.'

'I'm a doctor, so you better believe it.'

'What's a doctor doing here?'

'Getting ready to go back to Borneo.'

'You're kidding me!'

But he wasn't. She quickly learnt that it was all true. He and his father ran a medical service for one of the major oil companies in Dutch Borneo, although at the moment they were working out of Manila in the Philippines. She also learnt that he had a reputation around town, was unmarried and had every intention of remaining so. But he was fun to be with and his presence protected her from the attentions of the predatory Washington senator.

He knew he had never met anyone like her and saw no conceivable reason why he should lose her just because he had to return to the Philippines. And so they agreed to travel to

Manila together, even though she insisted on paying her own fare. After all, the Philippines were one step nearer to Borneo, and even if her savings were almost gone, she wasn't going to give up now.

As their plane circled over the San Fernando valley, she looked down on Los Angeles in the horseshoe of the San Gabriel Mountains for the last time. The huge emptiness of the Pacific lay before her and she gripped the arms of her seat and thought, I'm on my way now and nothing is going to stop me.

The Philippines only served to whet her appetite. The exotic colours, the scents of wild orchids, jasmine and hibiscus and the noise of the bumba birds at dawn: this was the East she had so long dreamt about.

The heat beat down as she discovered Manila with its Chinese shops, Spanish churches and American sailors. The women in their black and white Maria Clara skirts, the men in Barong Tagalog embroidered shirts.

Warren introduced her to his favourite restaurant in the Dilamen quarter and took her hand across the table. He knew this was the woman he wanted to spend his life with. He was in the grip of the only genuine love he had known in all his years of playing around.

'Don't you know that I love you?'

Dede looked at him with ill-concealed suspicion.

'Don't look at me like that,' he said softly, expecting the reproach.

'Why should I believe you? You had hundreds of women before I came along.'

'The right one never came along until now. I want you to marry me, Dede.'

She had been willing to fall in love. At least as far as her ambition and dreams would let her. The moment he told her about Borneo she had allowed herself to fall. She wondered if she would have slept with Warren if he had not seemed to offer her far more than other men. But marriage?

'I don't see that it's necessary. I mean, we're getting on fine, aren't we?'

'It's not enough, Dede.'

'Look, Warren, I don't think it would work. I mean,

marriage is not for me. It's not what I'm thinking of. It doesn't come into my plans at all.'

'And your plans are to go to Borneo. So are mine. So what's the problem? I'm not going to stop you from doing your work. I just want you to be happy.'

And that night it was easy to say yes to him. She liked being with him and it was increasingly harder to avoid talk of marriage. But the announcement, coming out of the blue after what had happened at Clark Field, took her totally by surprise. Perhaps it was because the war had been brought home to them that he made the announcement. Who could tell what the future held for them?

'I hate to interrupt.'

They swayed apart on the dance floor to face Dr Brandon. The three of them drew aside where they could not be overheard.

'That was quite a surprise you sprang back there.'

Warren had Dede safely by the hand.

'I hope you're pleased for us, Dad.'

'I just hope you know what you're doing.' He looked directly at Dede. 'It's no picnic being a doctor's wife, especially where Warren works.'

'I realize that, Dr Brandon, but I'm looking forward to it.' She took confidence from the pressure of Warren's hand on hers. 'I hope I can carry out research on the culture of Borneo tribes while I'm there.'

'The what?'

'The culture of the people, Dr Brandon.'

'You call that culture?'

'Well, *I* certainly do,' said Dede with dangerous sweetness. 'We could learn a lot from so-called primitive peoples about our own so-called civilization.'

Brandon's eyes glinted back at her. He was not used to being contradicted, let alone by a woman.

'I know these people, Miss Harriman, and most of them just want to be left alone. They certainly don't want any smart-arsed west-coast researcher snooping around. You'd be well advised to revise your plans if you're going to be any use to my son as a wife.'

They stared after him, stunned by the strength of his attack.

Warren squeezed her hand.

'Don't mind him, honey, he'll soon come round.'

But Dede looked after Brandon's retreating figure and knew that she had made an enemy.

Chapter Two

The Singapore River twisted and turned its way into the heart of the city. The smell of the river and the noise of the boat people was the rhythm of life here to Katherine, the throbbing, exhilarating pulse of Singapore. The straits were a forest of masts, the river crammed with sampans and the families who lived on them.

Kate never failed to be amazed and excited by the variety of goods for sale in the streets, by the riotous colours and exotic scent of cinnamon and cloves. Malays, Chinese, Tamils, Indonesians and Sikhs filled the streets with a babble of languages. Their soft muslin, brilliant silks and brocades blazed in the shimmering heat, the colours so bright they hurt the eyes. Beggars sat on the bridges, stray dogs sniffed and roamed in the narrow streets between the rickshaws; hawkers selling rice cakes cried, '*Nasi lemak!*'

Kate enjoyed riding by rickshaw in the city. Given the opportunity she would have done the marketing herself, but it was loss of face for Europeans to go to the market, everyone always sent their cookie. Not having a servant meant that Kate and her brother paid a neighbour's boy to buy for them. But no one could stop her looking at the street stalls with their bubbling vats of *nasi padang*, fish dumplings and curried eggs, and the wonderful array of strange fruit: mango, pomelo, dikku, papaya, sweet rambutans and evil-smelling durians.

She sat in the rickshaw, feeling the sweat wet through her dress and gleaming on the bare back of her coolie. The air was thick and cloying as the sun rose high. Kate saw there were still barriers in Raffles Place around the bomb damage. People stood in dazed little groups, looking at the ruined buildings and the craters in the road. The place looked as if it had suffered an earthquake.

News of the attack on Pearl Harbor had come over the radio and was greeted with a mixture of shock and elation. Shock that the Japanese could show such strength, elation that at last the Americans were in the war.

Weeks before, the Japanese hairdressers and photographers in Singapore suddenly seemed to disappear. Now, of course, people claimed to have read something into that. Everyone was talking about a fifth column of Japanese agents and sympathizers.

On the same day as the bombing, the same day as Pearl Harbor, the Japanese had landed at three points on the Malayan coast. The eastern monsoon was blowing and at first the news was treated with scepticism. They said it was impossible to land from the sea in such weather, but the Japanese outfoxed them and within three days had attacked Penang on the west coast.

Just four hundred miles now lay between the Japanese and Singapore, but people put on a good face.

'The jungle will stop them. It's our Maginot Line.'

'Yes – and look what happened to that!'

They were so blind, and yet if they had only looked around them, seen the Chinese digging trenches, preparing for war, perhaps then they would have realized –

To Kate the trenches in Chinatown brought back unpleasant memories of the summers of 1938 and 1939 in London. War fever had been at its height as Hitler took Austria and threatened Czechoslavakia. Everyone expected war to be declared at any moment and bombs to come raining down. They all expected the worst.

Had she escaped all that only to face it all again now in Singapore?

Since the time of the Munich crisis her brother Tony had been working for Beattie and Beattie in Singapore. They were wine and spirit importers, one of the giant companies of the Far East like Guthrie's or Jardine's. He wrote her thrilling letters extolling the virtues of life in the East that made her increasingly discontented with London. She was jealous of her brother and his freedom and lost no opportunity in telling him so.

Kate sailed East in 1940 only months before Dunkirk changed the face of Europe. There seemed nothing for her to stay for with all the talk of rationing, conscription and possible invasion. Kate went East rather than end up conscripted into some munitions factory back home.

Tony paid her passage on a P & O liner out of Marseilles. The voyage was her introduction to a style of life beyond her experience. She stood in awe of the glamorous women on board, feeling apprehensive about what she would find in Singapore.

To Kate it was a revelation. Singapore was a magical place of bright lights and undiminished glamour. Coming from Europe with its blackout, rationing and the threat of German bombing, it seemed like salvation.

Singapore was an oasis of old-world charm in a world gone mad. They still played cricket on the padang by St Andrew's Cathedral and crowded green trolley buses crawled along Collyers Quay with its classical white buildings. In Raffles Place the shops were crammed with luxury goods and imported food and wines such as Kate had only ever heard of and never had a chance to try. There were new best-sellers in Kelly and Walsh's bookstore, Max Factor make-up in Maynard's, and all manner of strange bargains among the tiny shops and stalls of Change Alley. After the wartime drabness of London, Singapore seemed like Aladdin's Cave to Kate.

Whether it was coffee and pastries at Robinson's, cocktails at the Café Wein or a dinner dance at the Seaview Hotel, Katherine found herself transported into a bygone era.

They were still taking afternoon tea and scones in Singapore, and at Raffles every Wednesday and Saturday there was dancing, with all the tunes six months behind those in London. In the softly-lit garden under the palms they danced until one and some even went on to the Tanglin Club until dawn. They had little to complain about. Rationing was paid only lip service. The two ordained meatless days each week conveniently did not include game or poultry in the restaurants. Oysters were still flown in daily from Sydney.

It was another world.

Only her brother's lifestyle made her uneasy. It could not possibly be maintained on a clerk's salary. Appalled by his rising debts, Kate could not shake herself of the same horror her mother had of owing money.

'Oh, come on, Kate, it's another world out here,' he chided her gently, but she could tell that underneath his nonchalance he was acutely embarrassed to be caught out.

She told herself it didn't matter. Everyone out here was doing it, and if they didn't worry then why should she? Worse than the mounting debts was the stigma of being called 'chit-shy'. Everyone they knew lived on credit.

Tony told such stories of the excesses of Harry Beattie, his employer's son and heir. Raymond Beattie had to bail him out more than once when his debts got him into hot water. The old man heard about it and smoothed it all over, pumping in fresh funds to save face at the last minute.

'Come on, Kate, it's time you started enjoying yourself. After all, that's why you came out here, isn't it?'

Singapore was a magnet for unmarried women. Girls were always in short supply, and when Kate arrived she quickly found herself included in beach parties, dances and picnics. The Beatties were an important family in the Straits and Tony had worked miracles to make his mark, getting in with young Harry Beattie and his set.

She would never forget her first sight of Harry Beattie. He strolled out of his father's office with Tony one day and her heart stood still. She knew she had never seen a handsome man to match him.

He was not tall, but he had such presence. He carried himself with a consciousness of his own worth. His clothes were well-cut, expensive if conservative. His smooth bright hair framed his head like a halo. To her he was charming, considerate, winning her with his infectious laughter.

She wondered what he could possibly see in her, although she was not at all bad looking. With her ash-blonde hair and good figure she was even striking. But never in a hundred years would he have noticed her in London. They would never have moved in the same social circles. However, here in Singapore there were opportunities for the taking. And Kate lost little time in taking full advantage of her change in circumstances.

She looked at the long line of his body on the white sheet. He had his eyes closed but she could not tell if he was sleeping. He had seemed to change towards her since that first time. She watched him through the bead curtain as she made the hot amber tea. She knew he had missed tiffin at his club to be with her.

The street outside was quiet during the afternoon heat. Kate could never adapt to the afternoon siesta, finding it made her drugged and leaden, often with a headache. She brought the tea across to the bed and he stirred and looked at his watch. The noise of the fan pushing around the hot air filled the silence in the room.

'It's no use looking at me like that, Katherine. I'm not going to change my mind. It's the wrong time to tell anyone.'

Would there ever be a right time, she wondered. He was so evasive with all his talk about romance and keeping their affair a secret between themselves. He didn't even look at her as he slipped from the bed and dressed. He kept his back to her as he sat to put on his shoes.

'Harry, I'm sorry – '

'Yes, all right, Katherine, let's forget it, shall we?' He finished straightening his tie. 'I'll have to go now. You know it's impossible to get a taxi in this district – '

He slammed the door behind him.

For a long time Kate sat on the pillows at the head of the bed in thought. She coiled her long hair up at the back of her head, feeling the sweat trickling down from the nape of her neck.

Why couldn't he understand how much she loved him? She had her dream, her secret dream for their future which she did not dare to tell him. Had she ruined everything before it had scarcely begun?

At six Tony returned with news that had stunned all of Singapore. The *Repulse* and the *Prince of Wales* had been caught by Japanese bombers and sunk. Over five hundred off the *Repulse* and over three hundred from the *Prince of Wales* had been killed. The survivors were still being brought ashore.

The news was scarcely credible. The two ships were the

pride of the British Navy. It was unbelievable that they could have been lost, that the Japanese had the power to challenge and to destroy the ships sent to protect Singapore.

Kate felt ashamed that while she had been clandestinely with Harry, men had been dying at sea.

The Japanese now dominated the sea lanes of the East. Without warning they were alone and unprotected. The danger facing Singapore was suddenly revealed.

It was an old Dodge car with running boards, borrowed from one of Morgen's pals down in Cavite. As Warren drove through Manila there were clear signs of the bombing of the day before.

The Japanese showed a distinct preference for dawn raids. They had swept in at daybreak not only to the Philippines but to other US bases at Guam and Wake Island. Reports said that Guam had been taken by the Japs in just twenty-five minutes.

They were not so fortunate when they landed at Vigan. All their paratroops were rounded up in double-quick time, even if they did succeed in gaining a foothold in Aparri in the far north of Luzon. December 10th was going down in the history books. There were simultaneous raids on Cavite, Nichols airfield and Fort William McKinley. Warren had been down at the naval base helping with the wounded right on through the night. The place was a shambles, ships hit time after time at their moorings, and the submarine *Sealion* sunk. He knew it could only get worse.

Manila had been bombed twice. Intramuros, the old town, was still burning. Many well-known baroque churches and old colonial buildings had been hit. Some parts of the town looked deserted. Refugees were flocking along the roads out, but Warren knew nowhere in the islands that was any longer safe. The Japanese had no respect even for Red Cross vehicles or hospitals.

The house he rented with his father stood on Harrison Boulevard surrounded by poinciana trees. The heat and spice scents of the district seemed homely and familiar, a million miles from the horrors he had seen overnight.

Irvine Brandon had been able to snatch a few hours' sleep after a night at the general hospital downtown. He was up and pottering around in his dressing gown when Warren arrived.

'I'm getting myself a drink. You look as if you could do with one.'

'Sure, I'll have one,' said Warren, collapsing into one of the easy armchairs, every joint of his body aching. The square blades of the fan whirred lazily above.

'About Dorothy – ' said his father.

'Dede. Call her Dede.'

'Are you sure this marriage idea is right for the two of you?'

Warren blinked at him over the rim of his glass.

'I'm not talking about the war, son. Plenty of people get hitched at times like these. I guess I'm talking about Dede. I thought she was here for her work.'

'Well, that's right, she is.'

'Look, don't take me wrong. She's a fine young woman and she shows some spirit – '

'But?'

'But she's twenty-eight, Warren. I'd say she puts her career before a husband and any kids.' He was treading cautiously. The last thing he wanted was to alienate his son. But he had seen that kind of woman before, out for themselves, usually frustrated by lack of cash, latching on to some guy to finance their career. She was close, even secretive. One day she would let fly and when she did, Christ alone knew what she would become. Hell, he didn't think that woman gave a damn for a decent home life, settling down and having kids.

'If she was my girl I'd soon put her in line.'

'Well, she's not, is she?' Warren retorted, suddenly very angry. His shoulders tensed as he leaned forward, glaring into his glass.

'I'm only thinking of your own good, son. I'm just telling you what other people are saying.'

'Oh yeah? And what are they saying?'

'That she's not right for you, that she's just using you. She latched on to you back in the States and she's not going to let go – '

'Well, that's as much as you know! Don't tell me what people say, Dad, I don't want to know. Don't press me too hard. I have made my own choice. It's got nothing to do with anyone else – not even you.'

Brandon stared at him, taken aback by the passion of his anger.

'Are you sure? Are you sure it's really what you want?'

Warren gave a deep sigh. He knew he could never explain to his father how the night he met Dede had changed his life. The old man would never understand. The countless girls passing through, that he had understood. But finding one woman, Dede, with whom to share his life, that would make no sense to his father.

'You don't believe I can make it work, do you? But I tell you, Dad, I've never been so sure of anything in my life, and that's an end to it.'

Chapter Three

Black December cast its shadow over Manila. The Japanese already had air superiority thanks to their pre-emptive strike at Clark Field. On 20 December a new force landed at Davao in the southern island of Mindanao. The Japanese were trying to cut off access to Manila from American allies and shipping in the south. Time was running out.

On 22 December the heroic defence of the US Marines on Wake Island came to an end. Morale in Manila was low, but worse was to come. That same day the Japanese landed 100,000 men and tanks from Lingayen Gulf on Luzon. The defenders who had fought back the invasion of 10 December were now strained to the limit. The fighting was fierce, but the Japanese 14th Army was clearly under orders from Tokyo to seize a foothold. They pressed their advance regardless of the cost. Men too wounded or too weak to keep up were simply abandoned. They continued to advance.

The Japanese needed the Philippines. Not just for its own strategic interest but for access to South-East Asia and the islands of the Dutch East Indies. America had cut off oil supplies to Japan, and the British had cut off supplies of rubber. The Japanese war machine was going nowhere without them. But in Malaya, Java and Sumatra there was enough rubber and oil to take them to the very shores of Australia, perhaps even to the gates of San Francisco.

'But can the Philippines be defended?'

'That is the sixty-four dollar question,' said Morgen at Cavite. 'The Man says yes.'

'Then he's crazy,' said Warren. MacArthur had not a hope

of defending the Philippines group without air support. 'And you're crazy if you believe it.'

'I'm not arguing with you. I was off sick when the decision was taken. Don't blame me.'

Warren quirked an eyebrow. 'A diplomatic illness? Don't you care that he's gambling with thousands of lives?'

'Well, he reckons he can do it – from Bataan.'

'Bataan?'

'Withdraw into the peninsula. Defence lines at Limay and Lamao. Keep the sub base open and the harbour at Mariveles. And in the event of trouble there's always Corregidor.'

'Corregidor?'

'Do you have to echo everything I say?'

'But Corregidor's a sitting duck.'

'He says it's Gibraltar. He's already given the order. And the Malinta Tunnel is being packed with supplies. Oh yes, and he's setting up field hospitals there and on Bataan.'

'Hold on, hold it, now we're getting to it. You expect me to go along with this?'

'I don't have to tell you, Warren, your skills are at a premium just now. You're in the Volunteer Force, you know what's happening. We will never hold Manila, but there's still a chance if we can hole up in Bataan.'

Warren frankly doubted it. The Japs weren't going to stop at the Philippines. They had landed in Malaya and Sarawak already. If help was going to come through to bail them out, then it certainly wasn't coming out of Singapore or the Dutch East Indies. They had enough trouble of their own. So that left Australia, and that meant a long wait for reinforcements. Just how did he rate their chances of holding out on Bataan against a flood tide of Japanese?

'They'll bomb the shit out of us.'

'Except for those lucky bastards in the Tunnel,' said Morgen sardonically. 'You did say "us", didn't you? I can't promise you won't regret it. But at least the four-eyed little bastards won't be able to pick us off piecemeal. You heard what they did to our boys in Luzon?'

Warren nodded. He had heard enough about the mutilated American and Filipino bodies to know how they would be treated if they did not fight on.

'There's really no choice, is there?'

Warren arrived back in Manila just as his father was finishing breakfast.

'You look all in,' Irvine said as he drank the last of the coffee. 'But I've got some good news for you. There's a boat to take us on to Borneo. If we're ever going to get out, then it's got to be now. We'll have no second chance.'

There was an ominous silence as Warren met his gaze.

'I'm staying behind, you know that, don't you? They need me here.'

His father took time to digest this. And then he said, 'And Dede? She'd be better out of here.'

'I know it and you know it,' said Warren. 'The problem is how to persuade her that it's true.'

'She's got less than twenty-four hours.'

A Jeep dropped him off right outside the hotel. The lifts were not working – as usual – and he was breathless as he arrived outside Dede's door. In the room the blinds were drawn against the savage midday sun.

'Time has run out,' he told her, leaning with his back against the door.

'For God's sake, Warren, don't try to persuade me,' she said flatly, turning on him. 'I'm staying.'

'Like hell you are!' he exploded. 'Don't you see this place is expendable? There's absolutely nothing we can do about it.'

That made her stop. Expendable?

'I do believe you're serious.'

'Look, I don't want you to go, you know that. But I do want you to be safe. Go to Borneo and when all this is over, we'll be together again.'

'Borneo?'

'Sure, Borneo. You'll go with my father down to Sandakan. It won't be a pleasure trip, but at least I know you'll be safe.'

She paused and gave him a long hard look.

'Okay, you win.'

'What?'

'You heard me. You win.' She saw that her sudden capitulation had taken him by surprise. She shrugged and said she didn't know what would happen to her Ph.D. thesis.

Warren produced one of his dazzling smiles. 'Ah, quit complaining. You're going on the greatest field trip ever.'

By Christmas Eve the evacuation to Bataan was in full swing. The Japanese had taken Rosario and there was no time to be lost. Day and night supplies had been moved from Cavite to Mariveles on the peninsula. Ships and barges carried men and supplies back and forth in the brilliant moonlight.

Warren was organizing a general hospital at Limay, with plans for a second unit as well. The gaudy Philippine buses were commandeered to carry supplies, but everyone knew it was a belated and disorganized withdrawal. The Japanese were making no effort to prevent refugees flooding into Bataan. There would not be enough food to feed the servicemen, let alone the influx of civilian refugees. Bataan would have rations for barely one month. Even if they drastically cut the rations, how long could they withhold a siege?

The last two destroyers had already left for Java. That afternoon President Quezon left Manila in his wheelchair, deeply distressed, complaining that the Americans had let him down, for a last stand on the island of Corregidor.

Soon there would be no possible retreat. Those who remained behind on the mainland had to face the threat of internment and occupation. The Japanese were on the road to Manila.

It took a powerful mental effort to come to terms with the situation. Dede saw the dazed, shell-shocked expressions on faces all around. No one could believe this was really happening. They were losing the war.

MacArthur had declared Manila an open city. Notices went up on the main streets into the capital: OPEN CITY! No Shooting! But no one denied that Manila was being abandoned, offered up to the Japanese like a sacrifice.

The Americans were destroying anything that might be of use to the invaders. On Christmas Eve the oil dumps were set alight. A dense pall of black smoke hung over the city as the precious fuel was deliberately destroyed. The moon was totally obscured. Dede stood at her window as the smoke belched skywards.

'You have very little time.'

She looked at Warren's father almost with exasperation.

'All right,' she said, 'what am I to pack?'

Warren was to meet them at the docks. As they crossed the city it did not seem like Christmas Day. The baroque churches were deserted. The Misa de Gallo, the masses of Buena Noche to herald Christ's birth, had been banned for fear of air raids in the early morning, the Japs' favourite hour. By the time Dede and Dr Brandon made their way to the port there had already been an air attack on a passenger train and bombs on San Pablo. The streets were littered with Japanese leaflets demanding surrender.

'Let them wait,' said Brandon in disgust. 'They'll have it all soon enough.'

Down on the wharf men were walking around with loaded rifles. Dede hardly recognized Warren in a pair of overalls and a tin hat. He wore a Red Cross armband on his sleeve and looked as though he had been working all night.

'Thank God you're here,' was all he said.

Dr Brandon led the way down into the boat, a fast light tender. He stood there fastening the waterproof belt that had pockets for his money and identity papers.

Warren held Dede back, his grip so strong and possessive that it hurt her.

'You're leaving and we may never see each other again.'

She stared up into his face, wanting to say something to contradict him. But the pain and fear in his face stopped her. This was no time for false sentiments and lies.

'I'll watch you,' he told her. 'I'll be watching, even though you can't see me.'

He pulled her to him and his mouth crushed hers with such terrible desperation and despair that tears sprang to her eyes. Reluctantly he let her go and she stumbled her way into the boat.

Warren was everything she could ever want in another human being, and yet – why could she not love him?

She supposed she had never really fallen in love. Not what they meant by love. There had always been something holding her back. Her independence, for instance.

Love implied the sacrifice of free will, of freedom. Even with Warren.

Tears rolled down her cheeks as she looked back at the land.

He's so good, she thought. I'm not the one for him. I don't deserve him.

The figures on the wharf became more and more distant. She could no longer distinguish him from the others left behind to continue their hopeless struggle. She stared hard at the disappearing landscape until there was nothing more to see.

A wave of irrepressible relief washed over her. Warren was gone. Her life was hers again.

Chapter Four

Everyone who was anyone went to the Tanglin Club on Sundays. There was bathing and the usual tiffin dance. On Sundays the winding tree-lined streets near the golf centre were always crowded with cars. But for Kate it was her first visit to the clubhouse, and Harry's suggestion.

'You look wonderful.'

She had put up her hair under a big picture hat, one of the last things she had bought before leaving London. She knew she looked as good as any of the other girls who made a play for Harry. She stood there pulling on her little white gloves, aware of his admiring gaze. How much she was looking forward to today!

Beside him in his car she felt so proud. For the first time everyone would see them together at the club, a real couple at last.

'Have you told anyone? Have you told them that you're bringing me?'

He gave her an odd glance. 'What for?'

'Well, I just thought – '

'I know what you thought, Katherine, but let's drop all this, shall we? Don't you see how it spoils everything? Christ, I thought we were going to enjoy ourselves for once.'

'I'm sorry, Harry. I didn't mean anything by it. I just hate hiding the truth.'

'You just like to stir it, you mean. I can't even have a peaceful Sunday with you, can I? Christ, I can't stand people who fuss.'

'I'm sorry – '

'So, let's drop it, shall we? I came out to enjoy myself today.'

She turned her head aside so that he would not see how much he had upset her. The slightest negligence on Harry's part caused her misery. Of course, she knew that she loved him far more than he loved her. She wasn't sure he really knew what love was. He had been spoilt by too much love, by his mother and his sister as well as the other women in his life, and now he thought he could always get just what he wanted.

Perhaps that was the trouble. He had got what he wanted from her too easily. She had given in to him willingly because she loved him, but now he seemed to have changed towards her.

At the beginning they had been delighted with each other. He had been happy, she knew it. But with the war everything began to get more complicated and before long it had all started to go wrong.

War might swamp all her hopes at the moment, but surely it could not last? In Singapore there was still a semblance of normality. Tony went to the office every day. Tin and rubber were booming. Business life went on almost as usual. Tony had never been busier, at Beatties' all day and taking on new ARP duties two nights a week.

Christmas had brought a lull in all the talk of war. Once again Kate had to get used to turkey and Christmas pudding served in a temperature of almost 100°F. The Christmas tree, of course, was a casuarina, but it was almost as good. There were dances and beach parties and some time alone with Harry, but all that was spoilt by Singapore's second air raid on 29 December.

The banner in the clubhouse might proclaim 'Welcome to 1942' but the situation up country seemed more serious than anyone was admitting.

They were still serving a curry tiffin as Harry took her inside. The chicks were lowered to keep out the searing sunlight. On the verandah those who had already eaten were relaxing, calling the Chinese boys to bring another Tiger beer or gimlet.

The constant babble of conversation ceased for a moment as Katherine walked in on Harry's arm.

'Who's that striking girl with young Beattie? Don't recall seeing her around and about – '

Phyllis Beattie was in no doubt about the identity of her son's companion. She was sitting in her favourite chair, away from the noise of the dance floor, where she could survey the clubhouse and everyone who came in. She was a handsome woman in her fifties, well corseted despite the heat, with a discreet string of pearls and matching ear-studs that set off her cream silk dress. If she was surprised at the sight of Harry and his companion in her absurd picture hat, she was too well bred to show it openly. She sat and watched as her son steered Tony Kendall's sister through the dancers in her direction.

'Mother. You know Katherine Kendall, don't you? I'm meeting Tony later and as Katherine was rather at a loose end, I thought I would ask her to join us.'

'By all means,' said Mrs Beattie graciously, but she wondered at the lengthy explanation. 'And how do you find Singapore these days, Miss Kendall? I fear the war has changed everything for the worse.'

Katherine found herself blushing under her scrutiny and was furious with Harry for not warning her that his mother would be there.

'Oh, come on, Mother,' said Harry, 'the war hasn't changed a thing.'

'Not for you, Harry. You never take anything seriously. But I understand that Miss Kendall's brother is making some contribution to the war effort, isn't that so, Miss Kendall?'

'Oh yes,' said Katherine. 'He's joined the ARP.'

'There you are, Harry, I knew I was right.'

'Ah, it's all just a passing storm. Believe me, if things ever got really serious then I'd join up like a shot. As it is, essential war work, you know – '

'In Australia they say women and children are being evacuated from Sydney and Melbourne.'

'Panic merchants! Don't they trust their own chaps over here to do a decent job? Can you imagine us evacuating Singapore? Packing you off on the first ship out, eh, Mother?'

'I would refuse to go,' said Mrs Beattie. 'Singapore is my home.'

Well, I wouldn't, thought Kate. If it really came to that, I wouldn't hesitate to get out. I've done it once before.

'Oh God, it's Suzy!' He was on his feet.

'Harry!'

He bent to peck her cheek. Suzy Beattie was the replica of her brother, with the same sleek golden good looks and egoistical temperament.

'Get me a drink, darling, I'm fit to burst.' She collapsed into the nearest chair. 'God, how can they dance in this heat? I'm absolutely dead – '

Harry ordered a pink gin for his sister before he remembered to ask Katherine what she wanted. Kate felt a sudden flash of pure jealousy.

'It's no fun living here any more,' Suzy complained. 'No races. All these ghastly soldiers everywhere.'

'Well, darling, there is a war going on,' said her mother.

'Don't talk about it. It's simply too awful.'

'Why don't you come along with us?' suggested Harry as Kate cringed. 'We're picking up Katherine's brother and going for a spin – '

'How dreary, no, darling, I couldn't bear to spoil your little outing.' Her eyes met Katherine's briefly over the top of her pink gin. 'Anyway, how far can you get on the beastly petrol ration?'

Kate looked at her obliquely. Did Suzy realize how much Kate hated her? She had come out here to get away from people like that, but now she found herself trapped in the midst of a colony of the very worst type of English expatriate.

'Well, we must be off.'

'Oh, darling, must you? Well, have fun.' She bestowed her famous smile on them both. 'Do be careful, won't you?'

'What was that all about?' Mrs Beattie asked her daughter.

'Couldn't you tell? She's had her eye on Harry for months past. That kind can always smell money.' She laughed. 'Poor Harry had better watch out for himself!'

Mrs Beattie stared at her, wondering. The little Kendall girl? She had the kind of tense uncertainty associated with the lower classes. Here she was certainly out of her depth. The Kendalls were not the sort of people one would invite to dinner. The brother, well, Harry had a wide range of peculiar friends, but surely Harry would not contemplate – no, it was clearly ridiculous!

'The trouble with you, Mother, is that you don't want

anything unpleasant to disturb your cosy way of life.' Suzy shook her head at her mother. 'You would far rather bury your head in the sand than see what is staring you in the face.'

'Please don't be trying, Suzy.'

'Well, don't say I didn't warn you. I just hope Harry has the good sense to avoid a scandal, that's all.'

Jolo had been taken on Christmas Day and there was heavy fighting over the Miri oilfields.

When Dede and Dr Brandon landed south of Sandakan they were barely one step ahead of the Japanese. Brandon's base at Sandakan was a prime target and it was obvious that if they went into town they would be walking into a trap.

Dede was too interested to be really frightened. She was finally in Borneo, the land of her dreams, even if it seemed to her now that she had stepped out of the frying pan into the fire.

They travelled south into the mountains, avoiding the coast and its dangers. Their Murat guide took them as far as Dutch Borneo, into the land of the Kalabit people. As she followed Brandon into the village of longhouses, she was entranced by the proximity of the people and delighted by the sensation that she was creating.

Brandon paused before the longhouse and spoke in a solemn voice that carried to the crowd:

'*Haman ma 'Un Uma?*'

Dede knew he inquired if there was a taboo on the house that would prevent strangers from entering. It was traditional politeness to the religion of Apau Lagan to obey local law, or *adat*. They were soon assured that there was no taboo, and were made welcome inside.

Dede stared with unreserved curiosity at the Kalabit chieftain with his long pigtail and body adorned from legs to shoulders with intricate tattoos. Brandon was offered *tuak*, the strong rice wine of the area, as he questioned the chief about the possibility of transport south. Dede had only seen flimsy canoes with outriggers on the river, but Brandon had hinted at a sea-going *prahu* manned by the Dyaks, famed for their sailing as much as their head-hunting. All her life Dede had been fascinated by stories of the Borneo head-hunters. At university she read many accounts and papers on these people.

She knew that tattoos on hands and fingers indicated the number of heads taken from their enemies. Heads were an expression of manly valour and brought good crops.

Looking up, Dede saw the circular frame hanging from the rafters of the longhouse. Dr Brandon sat in the place of honour under the smoked and shrunken heads which protected the house from evil spirits. She felt a shiver – of excitement, not fear. She could scarcely believe her luck in reaching Borneo. She envied Dr Brandon his knowledge of local languages. If she could only persuade him to let her stay, she might still collect enough material to write her thesis, war or no war.

That night she slept in the women's house on a rush mat on the wooden floor. The Kalabit women with their enlarged hanging ear lobes weighted with gold discs stared at her and giggled like schoolgirls. Dede could not understand a word but she felt safe and slept that night like a baby.

Next day Kalabit guides took them down to the river delta. Among the maze of tiny islands stood a small outpost, now abandoned and deserted by the Dutch who had evacuated to Tarakan, the island centre of the oil industry.

As night fell Dr Brandon and Dede stood on the verandah of the cabin and watched the torches of the Kalabit guides like fireflies in the valley. The night air was full of the scents of the tumbling green forest and frangipani from the garden. Since the monsoon it was no longer well tended. It was wild and overgrown, halfway back to jungle. Jasmine, yellow canna lilies, blue bougainvillea and scarlet-leaved creepers ran over the walls in a riot of colour.

Brandon said very little. They ate frugally of smoked fish, sweet rambutans and star-fruit. Dede noticed his fingers stained by cigarette smoking as he ate. He seemed sullen, almost antagonistic towards her. When she summoned up courage she asked,

'Will we go to Tarakan when the boat comes?'

He looked up, startled, and it seemed the skin grew taut across his face. 'No, we shall not,' he snapped. 'Do you think the Japanese won't try and take Tarakan any day now? That's what they're here for. Within weeks they'll be crawling all over the island – '

'Then where will we be safe?'

He laughed derisively, echoed by the piercing and strangely human cry of a chik-chak. Dede saw the pale little lizard dart across the ceiling.

'My son put me under an obligation to you,' said Brandon, 'and I'll do my damndest to see you safe out of here. As far away as it's possible to get, believe me.'

That night Dede found it difficult to sleep. She was filled with resentment against Dr Brandon and it was hard for her to remember he was Warren's father, they were so different. Warren had followed his father's profession, had followed him out to work in the East, so they were close, perhaps as close as she and her own father had been.

She took a cool bath using the huge Dutch jar, ladling water from the jar over her like a shower. Somewhat refreshed she lay in the dark heat of the room, listening to the sounds of the forest at night. For the first time in months she allowed herself to think of home, her first home, the real one so long ago. Not Pasadena, that was never home to her, even though she owed her aunt and uncle so much in material terms. Her real home was close to the ocean, close to her father's work out of Balboa and Catalina Island.

How she loved to hear him talk. Even now she could remember vividly sitting on the wharf waiting for him to come back from some long voyage, eyes fastened on the shimmering horizon for the first sign of his ship. Before his marriage he had travelled even further afield. He knew the islands of the Pacific like the back of his hand. She would ask questions and he would talk. Talk far into the night or until her mother got angry. He never talked to the boys like that.

With a stab of pain she still remembered the day he sailed out of Balboa for ever. She saw him off from the pier, never dreaming he would not be coming back. The storm had come so suddenly, unexpectedly.

It was a bad time to be widowed. The Depression struck hard in California. Her mother had three kids to think of when she wrote to her sister. The offer to take one of them to bring up as her own was a godsend. The boys were older, tougher. It was her daughter she sent away, just nine years old, a little girl for her sister's childless marriage. Overnight Dorothy

Delaney became Dorothy Harriman, spoilt little rich girl in Oak Knoll, Pasadena.

No one knew the pain and resentment she felt. She had been chosen, the boys stayed behind. She was the one her mother chose to give away.

Of course, looking back on it, she could see other reasons for her mother's decision. But nothing could ever compensate for the sudden loss of not only her father but her whole family at such a vulnerable age.

She supposed it coloured her life. It certainly channelled her interests, those that marked her future career. She shut herself off from other children. She became a voracious reader and buried herself in books. In her aunt's home there were plenty of those and more to be had for the asking. Bright heaps of yellow *National Geographic* grew over the years. She read under the bedclothes with a pocket torch. She longed to travel, to go to the romantic, remote places her father had known. She devoured the articles and photographs of explorers' expeditions in the *National Geographic*. She wanted to see the world, to see how others lived.

She did well at school. She was working towards a goal. Her aunt and uncle gladly paid for her place at university. Dorothy Harriman took back her father's name and became Dorothy Delaney Harriman, D.D. Harriman the scholar, or Dede to her friends.

When the expedition from Oxford University in England went up the Baram-Tinjar River in Sarawak in 1932, she knew what it was she wanted to do. Borneo became her fantasy.

On each bank of the river the nipah palms and mangroves grew down into the water. They stood watching the *prahu* as it rounded the bend in the river.

Their goods were quickly loaded, there were so little. In other days Dede had been known as a snappy dresser, smart and fashion-conscious and able to afford the best. She was scarcely recognizable as the same woman in her shabby clothes and broken-down shoes, but she did not care.

She was here in Borneo fulfilling her dream. Come what may, whatever the danger, she was living out her adventure at last.

The Borneo twilight fell like a curtain over the land. The deep purple and violet hues of the evening sky and the pinpricks of lamplight from the village reflected in the mirror of the river.

It was late when Amy left. Grandmother scolded her, warning that she would not keep supper. She knew she had to hurry to water the goats and feed them before Grandfather found out. It was not her fault she had forgotten. Father's letter had come and she had to read it once, twice, secretly up in the attic room over the shop before she could bear to share it with her grandparents, translating from the English. They were proud of her, proud of her education. Adrian Meadows had left his daughter to go to the war, sending her back to her mother's parents. She had reluctantly returned to the village she had not seen since her mother's death. She feared she would lose too soon the English and the carefully absorbed manners that had made her almost forget her mixed parentage. Amy Meadows. Nothing could be so English.

She felt lost and alone without her father, without his world. She wished he could have taken her with him, but he was going to Australia to join the army. The war that was so incomprehensible to her had divided them, leaving her stranded in an alien world.

The shadows lengthened as she left the village behind, treading the cool earth down towards the river. The wind had risen, shaking the high palms. It seemed suddenly that a storm was developing and she turned her head, quite unprepared, despite the droning overhead, for the sight of three planes skimming over the rooftops.

She stood there transfixed by the sight of the orange-red sun on the dipping wing tips. Their shadow passed over the night-blue meadow as the whining scream of their bombs hit the houses.

Amy ran back screaming towards the village. The explosions created a shockwave that brought her to her knees, hands in the earth as it vibrated under her body. Looking up she saw figures running in and out of the smoke and flames that engulfed the street. Their screaming reached her even at the distance.

She entered a world that was no longer recognizable. The

single street was awash with lurid fires and thick, choking smoke. She ran through a tunnel of flames as red-hot shrapnel rained out of the sky. Underfoot earth and rubble from the explosions half buried human bodies sprawling in death.

The rumble and hiss of collapsing buildings engulfed the street in rising walls of flame. The palms burnt like obscene candles in the smoke-blackened sky.

She fought her way past the blast-shocked woman who tried to block her way, her straight black hair scorched, her feet bleeding. Amy came at last to the shop, or where she believed that the shop had stood. The whole area had received a direct hit.

Amy was shaking, suddenly cold. Around her and before her the village lay buried under smoking rubble and blistering wood. She threw back her head but her scream caught in her throat. She ran forward and started digging away at the debris, scrabbling with her bare hands in the rubble of her grand-parents' home. She tore at the charred timbers and red-hot stones, her hands blistered, her chest heaving painfully with the foul air and with exhaustion as she desperately searched on. The tears dried on her cheeks in the heat. The ruins were still smoking long after the fires had been put out.

As she knelt over the lifeless limbs, yellow with blast dust, she knew she had no one and nothing left to stay for. Her father had wanted her to remain in Borneo, but events had overtaken them all. She looked up at the drifting smoke that half obscured the sickle moon.

No, it was not an idle dream. It was not 'water from the moon'. She would leave here to find her father. She would reach him in Australia or England, wherever he was. Even if she had to walk there. Nothing was going to stop her.

Chapter Five

The windows in the clubhouse were shuttered in the blackout for protection against flying glass. Inside, candles flickered in storm glasses on their table.

The men she judged to be planters. They wore khaki-coloured jackets and shorts and hung up wide-brimmed hats just inside the door. The taller of the pair surveyed the room and then came directly across to their table. He was an ape of a man, the dark hairs bristling on his well-muscled arms and sprouting from the neck of his sweat-dark shirt.

'Cees de Vek.' He held out his hand.

Introductions were made all round. De Vek called for a beer and sat heavily in the cane-backed chair, his knees two damp globes in the candlelight.

'Thank God you both arrived safely.' His English was excellent, if heavily accented. 'Did you know Heimie de Vere? He was killed in Sandakan, yes, in the bombing. The news grows worse by the hour. You were very lucky.'

As they arrived in Balikpapan, the great oil port in south-east Borneo, Dede and Dr Brandon had heard the news of the fall of Tarakan. The Japanese had landed in the north on 10 January, laying siege to Sandakan and the offshore island of Tarakan. The Dutch had held out for three days before sabotaging the famous oil installations to prevent them falling into Japanese hands. It was a valiant, last-ditch act by brave men who knew the vengeance the Japanese would enact upon them.

It was vital that the Dutch East Indies oilfields should not be taken intact. Women and children had been evacuated, leaving only local officials and experienced oil men behind to set up the explosive charges to destroy the oil wells and storage tanks. The whole Japanese offensive depended on the capture of the oilfields intact.

When Tarakan surrendered on 13 January the Japanese took a terrible revenge. The entire white civilian population was massacred on the beach. Local leaders had first been savagely mutilated, their limbs struck off by swords.

The Japanese were set to unite all Asia under the flag of the Rising Sun. The Year of the Serpent was drawing to an ignominious end.

'How long do you think we can last here?' asked Brandon grimly. The question was disquieting.

De Vek turned to look at Dede. 'This is no place for you now.'

A group of women and children had escaped from Sandakan in three ships. Another group got away safely from Samarinda as the Japanese arrived.

'We are organizing a final evacuation,' said the Dutchman. He saw Dede look across at Brandon and abruptly added, 'For women and children only.'

Brandon said quickly, 'I would stay in any case. I'm a doctor. You'll need me.'

De Vek nodded gravely. 'Yes, whatever happens I will stay, too. This is my country.'

That night refugees were still pouring into Balikpapan. An exhausted flood of humanity, barefoot and ragged, with terror in their eyes. Many had been walking for days to escape the Japanese.

Among them, her legs leaden with exhaustion, every muscle in her body stretched and aching, came Amy Meadows. She looked small and vulnerable among the ragged band of refugees, her eyes huge in her delicate face as she looked about her.

She had reached her goal. Balikpapan was as far as she could go in Borneo. If she was ever to fulfil her dream and find her father again, then somehow she had to find a boat to get out of here.

In Singapore the *Straits Times* had carried an optimistic editorial on New Year's Day:

'Goodbye to the year 1941 and good riddance! We enter into a new year in local conditions that are simply fantastic . . .' It ended, 'We shall be rejoicing before 1943 comes round.'

That same day Kuala Lumpur was attacked by Japanese bombers. In the three weeks since Pearl Harbor the Japanese had taken more than half Malaya. Underlying the New Year festivities there was a prevailing sense of impending disaster.

The Kendalls lost their landlords in January without warning.

'They're leaving,' Kate told her brother. 'They don't care about the house. They just want to get away from here.'

'That's ridiculous – '

'Is it? They say the war is spreading out of control.' She searched Tony's face. 'It's true, isn't it?'

But he was evasive. 'Look around. How many people we know are going? No one to speak of. It's crazy, alarmist – '

She had to admit he was right. No one among the Europeans they knew was openly talking about getting out.

'We must put up a good front,' they said, and read the war news with an outward show of calm. Reports of defeat up country were 'an exaggeration' in spite of the all-day battle at Kuala Lumpur and the destruction of rubber stocks. In mid-January the ships leaving Singapore were still half empty.

But ominous messages began to appear in the newspapers for missing people:

'Mrs Granger seeks news of her husband W.B. Granger, last heard of in K.L.'

'Paul Lorimer is inquiring after the whereabouts of his wife and daughters. Contact c/o Maynard's.'

Among the advertisements for life insurance and Greta Garbo's *Mata Hari* at the cinema, the *Tribune* and *Straits Times* carried a sudden flood of houses for sale. Secretly, it seemed, people were thinking of getting out.

Around-the-clock air raids became a fact of life. It was no longer just the dock areas under attack. There were heavy raids on Tanglin and down around the shops on Beach Road. The whole atmosphere of Singapore had changed. Supplies grew short, the Cold Storage stopped baking white bread. The hospitals were filled to overflowing with air-raid casualties, often hundreds each and every day. Refugees and bomb victims choked the streets. Telephones to the front line were cut by the post office and the golf club refused to allow anti-aircraft guns to be mounted on the links. On top of everything, the monsoon rains did nothing to ease the terrible humidity.

Kate no longer knew what to think or who to listen to. There was a black joke going around that the rate of the Japanese advance could be gauged by the daily newspaper announcements of the Hong Kong and Shanghai Bank branches 'closed until further notice'.

They were fighting and falling back all along the line. The Australians' fiery commander Gordon Bennett could do little to halt the rapid advance of Yamashita's forces down the spine of Malaya.

'Two more towns lost. How could they have come so far in just one week?'

'Christ, what a farce.'

Kuala Lumpur, Malacca, perhaps even as far as Johore. What was happening?

Percival was saying nothing, apparently consulting no one. He was not a man to inspire confidence. His appearance, with strange protruding teeth, was even sinister. There had been talk of over-enthusiastic interrogation and summary execution of prisoners when he commanded the Black and Tans against the Irish. He was not the man they needed in command of Singapore at such a time.

Word went round that the Naval Base – the raison d'être of Singapore – was to be abandoned. Rumour was rife in the face of official censorship, but there was no censoring the constant stream of terrified refugees pouring on to the island, full of horror stories of Japanese atrocities, to overturn the certainties of their sheltered world.

Chinese heads on stakes in the streets of Ipoh and Kuala Lumpur, some of them children. Malay women rounded up for Japanese brothels. The rule of the sword over Malaya.

The backwash of wounded troops did nothing to raise sinking morale. General Percival attacked the rumour-mongers, saying they were 'the enemy within our gate', a Japanese fifth column to undermine resistance.

But the ever continuing retreat down the length of Malaya could only reinforce the belief that Singapore itself was a city under siege, with time running out.

'We've pulled right back. We've abandoned the high country to the Japanese.'

Did they still believe that the island could be defended? By the end of January no one seemed to believe it any longer. The country that had appeared so beautiful and glamorous on arrival to Katherine now seemed to change, revealing a sinister face of terror and inconceivable cruelty. For the first time she felt alone and at risk among the unfathomable and alien crowds in the street. The Japanese were infiltrating everywhere. She felt she had to get out.

No arrangements had been made for the evacuation of women and children, the 'useless mouths' as Churchill called them. At the end of January the demand for passages out exceeded all expectations. The government finally centralized all bookings through P & O in an agency bungalow in Cluny, five miles out of town.

Kate made her way out to the office, walking the last part of the way there, up the steep hillside off the Johore Road. Parked cars lined the grass verges and the grinding heat beat down on the heads of the slow-moving lines of women and children queuing to get into the bungalow.

As Kate arrived the heavy sky throbbed to the rhythm of enemy bombers. The crowd scattered as, with a piercing shrill whine, the first bombs began to fall. Car windows shattered, showering the women huddling in the ditches with deadly spinsters of glass. The earth shook, vomiting up gouts of stones and soil.

Casualties were few although several of the cars were write-offs. Deep craters pitted the road and the clipped lawns up to the bungalow had been trampled into a sea of mud by the crowds seeking shelter.

The house had once been beautiful with a wide verandah shaded by rattan chicks leading down into the garden. Inside it was now a stage for harrowing scenes of panic and bitter arguments over nationality, entitlement and who would pay the passage money. At two trestle tables marked 'UK' and 'Colombo' Kate saw the fortunate ones receiving scraps of paper in lieu of real tickets. The overhead fans turned monotonously, stirring the hot air.

When she reached the table, Kate was finally told that priority was being given to women with children, but that it would help if she could pay her passage in advance without a government loan. After queuing there all day, she was turned away.

It was galling therefore to learn later that Raymond Beattie, by a simple phone call, had secured passage for his wife and daughter on a ship outward-bound soon for Australia.

How blind and stupid she had been, how complacent! Why hadn't she sought Harry's help, swallowing her stupid pride and forgetting their arguments?

The Japanese sent two Dutch prisoners of war taken in northern Borneo to Balikpapan. They carried with them an ultimatum for the surrender intact of the oil installations in return for the promised wellbeing of its citizens.

In Balikpapan they were sceptical. The dreaded Japanese Kempei Tai were not known for their humanity. The Japanese had little or no pity for the weak and wounded, including their own, and none at all for those who surrendered without honour.

The Dutch were under instructions to blow up the oilfields to prevent the Japanese getting their hands on them. This had been carried out at Tarakan in spite of Japanese warnings, and Tarakan had paid the price.

Now Balikpapan was faced with the same dilemma. If they obeyed the enemy ultimatum they would betray thousands of lives at risk from further Japanese expansion. If they followed Tarakan's example, then they would face a fate equal to, if not worse than, theirs.

As the tropical night enveloped Borneo, the Japanese made fresh landings on the coast. The future survival of Balikpapan and its people could be counted in hours rather than days.

Chapter Six

The night was full of explosions and the noise of dogs barking. Dede followed Dr Brandon through the black smoke drifting along the wharf with the stench of burning rubber. Men with rifles ran in the opposite direction, their shirts dark with grime, their faces running with sweat.

It all seemed like a horrible nightmare repetition of all that had happened in Manila.

A burst of blinding white light filled the night as another oil tank exploded a mile away. Torrents of vivid sparks shot skywards against the dense black smoke rolling above Balikpapan. Dede choked and wiped her streaming eyes, temporarily blinded by the light and the acrid stench.

Down on the wharf she saw Cees de Vek and a crowd of women and children going down towards the boats.

'What about the walking cases?' asked Brandon.

'They'll manage. We have put the others on board already.'

Brandon looked at the huddled mass of frightened refugees, desperate to get away.

'All these women are just a burden here at a time like this.'

De Vek looked at Dede and seemed about to speak when another deafening explosion split the night. He rapped out a series of commands in Dutch and the rush of refugees separated them, hurrying down to a large boat manned by a dozen Dyaks. Black silhouettes scuttled about in the pale light of the lanterns hanging on the boats.

'Don't waste time,' Brandon hissed in her ear, his hand on her elbow propelling her forwards.

She saw at once that there would not be enough room for all

of them. The Dyak boat was already full to overflowing, barely leaving room enough for the men to move their oars. The other boat was a wooden *prahu* with strange paintings on its pointed prow, its stern high and square. It had two tall masts and two steering rudders like enormous paddles in the glassy water.

'Bugis from the Celebes,' said Brandon, enjoying his superior knowledge. 'You'll be all right. They're noted seamen.'

The Dutch women and children were already surging aboard, stoutly ignoring the explosions. The Bugis tried to direct them but they would have none of it, brushing aside all advice with typical arrogance.

Cees de Vek had been intercepted by a young Chinese woman in a torn western-style dress and bare feet. She tugged at his sleeve, imploring.

'Who is that?' asked Dede.

'Just some woman from the kampong.'

De Vek came over to them, but the Chinese girl still followed him. At close quarters, Dede saw that she was Eurasian, not full Chinese. Her striking beauty was enhanced by the bluest of eyes, now desperate as she argued with the Dutchman.

'What's wrong?'

The girl looked round at Dede with a surprised and tentative smile. 'I was wondering – I was hoping – '

'It's no use,' said de Vek, 'Australia won't take her, even if she gets that far. They have quotas for Asians, you know.'

'But I'm not Asian,' said the girl. 'I want to find my father. And he's British.'

'What's that? British, you say?'

'Don't believe a word of it,' said Brandon flippantly. 'These Chinese will say anything to get a passage out.'

'I'm British,' the girl insisted. 'My father's British.'

'Well, now, what proof have you?' said de Vek. 'There's just no room to evacuate anyone who comes along. The Japanese won't be troubling about you, my girl – '

'Oh no?' said Dede, coming swiftly to the girl's rescue. 'Didn't you hear what the Japs did in China? There's no love lost between the Japanese and Chinese.'

'But I'm not Chinese!' cried the girl. 'I'm Adrian Meadows' daughter Amy. My name is Amy Meadows and I'm British.'

Cees de Vek looked down at her, noting the obvious traces of European blood in her face and the shape and colour of her eyes.

'Adrian Meadows is your father?'

'Yes, yes,' cried Amy desperately. 'He went to Australia to join the army.'

'Do you know her father?' Dede asked de Vek.

'He's an oil man, based up country normally, but he passed through here last year on his way – '

'To Australia? She's telling the truth, isn't she?' Dede was conscious of the Eurasian's emaciated little face turned to her in astonishment. 'Then let her come with me.'

'Now, look here.' Brandon caught her by the arm and swung her about to face him. He looked right into her eyes, belligerent and hostile. 'I've bust a gut to get you out of here, for Warren's sake, even though I know you don't really give a damn for him at all. So I'm not going to take any nonsense from you now. Get yourself on that goddamned boat right now!'

Dede was stung by this unexpected response and tears came to her eyes, tears of anger and remorse.

'You know very well what he means to me.'

Dr Brandon looked at her with unconcealed disgust.

'Don't give me any of that crap. You used my son to get yourself a meal ticket.' He gave a short laugh. 'Well, I don't give a damn. Give your place in the boat to the Chink for all I care.' He turned abruptly on his heel and stormed back down the quay into the enveloping black smoke.

Cees de Vek stared at her, stunned and embarrassed by the scene he had just witnessed, but if he was expecting some kind of explanation he was disappointed. Dede grabbed Amy by the arm and pulled her along the quay with her towards the *prahu*.

The boat was already crowded with women and children and piled high with luggage and rolls of bedding. The sails were old and rotten, the wooden hull patched and possibly unseaworthy. The whole structure rode only three feet above the water. If Dede had ever seen a boat likely to sink it was this one.

But this was no time for hesitation. As they reached the *prahu* another enormous explosion rocked the town. Whorls of dense black smoke belched from the ruptured oil tanks above wild flames. Dede brutally pushed Amy into the boat as she saw the Celebes seamen begin to cast off. Ignoring the cries of the women already safely aboard, she jumped the growing distance between the dock and deck and fell into Amy's arms.

The two women stood in silence looking back at Balikpapan. The sky was lurid with sickly colour. Darting black figures were silhouetted against the fires. The vital oil that could have serviced further Japanese conquests was burning in a foul sump of choking destruction.

The people of Balikpapan had shown their contempt for the Japanese ultimatum. Now they would have to bear the consequences.

Chapter Seven

The night they sailed, they were so exhausted and distraught with all that had happened that they huddled together in a desperate silence and tried to sleep.

The wooden deck of the *prahu* was jammed with bodies lying or sitting in whatever space was available. A disproportionate amount of room had been wasted with luggage. The Dutch women had insisted on bringing aboard suitcases, hampers and even their handbags, as though this was some pleasure trip, not a flight for their lives. Dede and Amy had only the clothes on their backs, nothing else with which to make a new life.

The mountains of Borneo showed a deeper black on the horizon where fires still marked Balikpapan. Amy had fallen into a fitful doze, clearly exhausted. Who she was or what her story had been, Dede could not guess. She only knew she felt sorry for her and was pleased with herself for getting the girl out of Balikpapan. But they were all on their own now.

The two boats were within sight of one another, aware of the notoriously capricious currents of the Makassar Strait. The crew went about their business with calm professionalism. Clearly they knew these waters well. But as the night continued and the distant outline of Borneo was lost to sight, the boat began to roll in earnest in the swell.

Amy woke with a start, looking at Dede in dismay as the *prahu* creaked alarmingly in the rising sea. Several people were suddenly sick and the smaller children began to cry. They felt the rush of hot wind that signalled bad weather and they were frightened.

There were no longer stars visible as the sky turned a threatening metallic purple. The boat dipped into the waves and up again, and began to ship water. The Bugis shouted and hurried between the terrified women and children up and down the tilting deck.

The ragged sails were hauled in and secured with ropes as they prepared to ride out the storm. The wind had risen to a violent shriek so loud that it was impossible to hear the sailors' cries of warning. Before anyone could act, a great pile of luggage tipped over the side of the boat, bobbing away on the huge grey-green waves. The women were white-faced and frightened, clutching their children to them and grasping anything solid to keep their balance in the swaying boat.

The lurid sky turned yellow and malevolent with a violent heaving, rent suddenly by a dagger of lightning. Thunder cracked overhead and all at once the rain hammered down in vertical rods, striking the metal sea with electric splashes.

Dede clung to the side, her arms and face soaked. She looked in vain for the Dyak boat but the waves were now so high there was nothing to see but water. At her side Amy was whimpering and shivering as though she had malaria. Dede forced her to take hold of one of the ropes, gripping with her small frozen hands to avoid going over the side.

The decks were now half under water, the crew frantically baling out with whatever came to hand. The boat was rocking wildly under the impact of the rain and high seas, taking in water faster than it could be baled out.

Dede suddenly knew fear. She felt the deck below her tilt wildly, she heard the roar of the waters and she saw the terror of the women and children around her. She saw, too, the look exchanged between the men in the crew. A look of desperation, of despair, as hope slipped away from them.

The sky opened again with a jagged strike of lightning, searing the sea with a deathly white light. Dede waited, her breath shallow, for the mighty blow to come. The air was dense with electricity. The thunder came at once with a deep-throated rumble and the very sea seemed to tremble and erupt.

The tiny ship shook and hung suspended on a mounting wave as on a yawning precipice. Their screams were swallowed in the engulfing roar of spray as the wooden vessel toppled sideways in a fierce whirlpool of tormented water and was sucked beneath the sea.

Total blackness shrouded everything. Dede surfaced, gasping in the air between each wave, feeling herself grow weaker and weaker. The bar of wood to which she clung was barely strong enough to bear her weight, a mere matchstick tossed on the mighty sea.

Had she been weak-willed, she might have given up, her grip slipping away from the wet plank inch by inch. But something inside her made her cling even tighter to the wood, regardless of the sharp splinters in her hands.

Above the sea noise she believed she could hear human voices. How many others had survived? The darkness added to her terror at finding herself in the sea. She knew these waters were infested with sharks. As the storm died they would seek pickings among the wreckage. How far were they from land? How long could she survive?

In the swell of the sea she clung to a suitcase which offered more buoyancy than the plank of wood which had saved her. Drenched and shivering, she was swept by the rolling waves closer to the wreckage. The sea was cluttered with floating obstacles, barrels, pieces of luggage and the limp limbs of the drowned tangled in the flotsam. Dede could hear someone crying out and suddenly she saw a head bobbing away among the debris on the water. It was a woman, dark hair plastered to her white face, arms flailing as she desperately sought some lifeline in the fierce swell. But as Dede tried to call out the restless current dropped her down again and she lost sight of everything except the glassy wall of water.

Clinging to the piece of luggage she gasped for air, shaking the seawater from her eyes as she was lifted up again on the wave. She searched the sea around her, uncertain now of her direction, but there was no one there, no one where the woman had been, as though she had been a mirage.

The sky was now clearing, the waves suddenly less violent. The storm had gone now, leaving a terrible vacuum. The sea settled, showing a widely scattered trail of wreckage over its deep green surface. Dede hung over the suitcase, exhausted and filled with despair, unheeding where the current took her.

It was growing lighter with every minute. The sky had cleared and the edge of the enormous pale disc of the sun rose above a deeper green on the horizon. Had she dreamed? Was it her imagination? She looked up, her face colourless and drawn against the water. Shock and a desperate joy came into her eyes as she heard Amy calling to her.

With an effort that made the sweat break out on her face, she pushed herself forward. Tears ran down their sea-drenched faces as the two women swam together, clasping one another among the wreckage that held them afloat.

'All gone, all drowned.' Wild despair filled Amy's face.

'No, no, we're alive,' gasped Dede. 'We'll find a way.'

The two women lay in the water, moved by the current towards the breaking day. The horizon took on shape and form, the sea flecked with white foaming surf over shallow water. They were drawn and sucked over a hidden sandbar and into warm green waters off the coast of an island.

The dark outline of a range of mountains tumbled down to the sea. Walls of white foam battered the sea-carved cliffs. The land, the sea and the sky were tinted with warm amber in the dawn light, rippling gold as the surf rolled in.

They fell together in exhaustion and relief where the water deposited them in the warm shallows of the bay. Amy was sobbing, on all fours in the water, gripping the white sand of the shore in both hands. Dede was crying, shaking with emotion, knowing that now they were both safe.

They lay back on the beach above the water line, feeling the sun already hot on their skin. Their clothes were torn and saturated, their hands and arms bruised and bleeding from cuts and gashes. Dede sat up and tried to pick the splinters from the palms of her hands, while Amy stared at the beauty of the brilliant green mountains that rose above them.

'Where are we? What is this place?'

'I don't know. I don't even care. We're safe, aren't we? That's enough for now.' She looked around them. 'I guess it must be part of the Celebes. That's the nearest land to Balikpapan.'

'You know, I don't even know your name and yet you saved my life in Balikpapan. Are you American?'

'That's right. You can call me Dede.'

She rolled it around her tongue. 'Dede? Dede.'

'You speak English very well.'

'My father sent me to English school. He wanted me to have education.'

'Well, thank God we can speak the same language! I tell you, Amy, I think your Chinese may come in handy with the people here. You do speak Chinese as well, don't you?'

'Of course I do.'

She gave Dede a trace of a smile, but she still seemed uncertain. The conversation had drained them both and they sat for a long time in silence, trying to get their strength back.

Sooner or later they would have to move away from the beach and this temporary haven. They had come through the storm together, but they did not know where they were or if the island had yet been occupied by the Japanese. Their escape was far from over.

Chapter Eight

On the morning of 5 February the *Empress of Asia* sank off Singapore Island in just fifteen minutes.

Katherine Kendall and her brother stood on the quayside as men were rescued from the ship. They stepped ashore, soaked to the skin, lucky to escape with their lives. Many of them had been travelling at sea for months, first by Atlantic convoy through the icebergs off Greenland, then down the coast of South America and back across the Atlantic to Cape Town and on to India to pick up the *Empress* for this final fateful journey. They had no experience or training in jungle warfare, they were not even acclimatized to the conditions they were expected to face, and the weapons and the artillery, which the 18th Division so desperately needed had all gone to the bottom in minutes.

The strains of 'Land of Hope and Glory', played over the radio every hour on the hour, now began to sound hollow. The 'Dig for Victory' campaign only served to show that Singapore could never hope to feed itself. By the end of January the population had almost doubled. Refugees, most of them Chinese, flooded into Singapore.

Air raids continued to wreak havoc. On 30 January the docks had been attacked from ten in the morning until late afternoon with incendiary bombs. In the attack four ships managed to leave, the *Westpoint*, *Wakefield*, *Duchess of Bedford* and the surprisingly named *Empress of Japan*. When Kate heard that those ships had sailed to safety she was sick with envy.

The strain had long ago begun to tell. You could see the

signs on faces in the street. The fall of Kuala Lumpur marked a turning point. Somehow until then none of it had really struck home. It was impossible to believe they were going to lose the war, that Singapore would fall.

On the last day of 1941 the retreat down the length of Malaya came to a sudden end. The last men of the Argyll and Sutherland Highlanders crossed over to the island and blew up the causeway behind them. The impossible had happened. Singapore was under siege. But like Hong Kong, Singapore was defended only from the sea.

Hong Kong fell on Christmas Day but news of all that had happened there did not reach Singapore until February. Singapore was stunned by the atrocities committed by rampaging Japanese troops, suddenly aware of the danger that now faced them.

After the news Kate found she was terrified of being alone at night. Tony was often on ARP duty and she had not seen Harry for weeks. There was no one she could talk to or confide in. At night in the blackout the thick heat cloaked the island. In the damp, close bedroom Kate slept fitfully. The mosquito net seemed to suffocate her. Drunken Japanese troops ran riot in her nightmares. She saw them coming, crashing into the hospital in Hong Kong, bayoneting the sick and wounded, while screams rang in her head.

She twisted from side to side in her tormented dream. The hospital rang with screams as patients were murdered in their beds without mercy. The Japanese were outside in the corridor. They were here, now. They would burst into the room at any moment. She was trapped. Any second now they would be breaking down the door. Where could she hide? She could hear their bayonets smashing the wood. . . .

The cupboard – there she could be safe, inside, in the dark, listening, watching. The Japanese were here! She could hear them searching the room, searching for her . . . God, oh God, they were opening the door, letting in the light – they would find her and kill her!

The light exploded in her eyes and she abruptly sat up. Sweat was streaming down her face and she broke into desperate tears of relief as she realized she was safe home in Singapore.

She was still shaking when Tony arrived home later that morning. He did his best to comfort and reassure her, but his words rang hollow.

'Tobruk held out for months before help arrived. London won't let us go under. We'll hold out as long as it takes.'

'Don't try to butter me up, Tony, I'm not a child! What are we doing out here? Why didn't we get out while we could?'

Tony tried to hold her in his arms but she broke away roughly, angry tears on her cheeks.

'I came out here because I thought it would all be different. Better than back home. I wanted a new life, a better life. The kind of life you had out here, the kind you wrote about.' She pulled free and shook her head. 'But it's not better, Tony, it's far worse! At least they're fighting back home. Even in the worst of the Blitz they didn't give up, they didn't stop fighting and surrender – '

Tony grasped her by the shoulders but she was sobbing bitterly, hysterically, beyond any reassurance.

'I've got to get out! Tony, you've got to get me out of here!'

Tony was just leaving his desk at the office when news came through that the Japanese were storming the broken causeway.

'By morning they'll be on the island. This is it, old chap!'

During the night the Japanese crossed the mile-wide strait separating Singapore from occupied Malaya. Tony was with Raymond Beattie when he heard that three ships would be sailing early – for those with valid tickets.

'Be a good chap, Kendall. See that my wife and daughter get the message, and send the car over to the house to collect them. I'll do my best to get down to the dock to see them off.'

Tony took Katherine with him to collect Mrs Beattie with all her luggage in a company car.

'I'm sorry to say you have just ten minutes to pack,' he confronted her at the door. 'I've come to take you and your daughter to the docks. Your ship is leaving in an hour.'

'But, surely – '

'Your husband sent me, Mrs Beattie. I'm afraid the balloon's gone up.' He saw that she was still prepared to argue. 'The Japanese are on the island, Mrs Beattie. They crossed over last night and have pledged that no ships will be allowed to leave. "There will be no Dunkirk in Singapore," they said. If you don't go now, Mrs Beattie, you may not get out at all.'

He saw that he had made his point, but still she hesitated.

'Shouldn't you start to pack now? Time is very short.'

'I have been packed, young man, for a week past. That is not the problem. It's my daughter Suzy, she's not here.'

'Not here? Where is she then?'

'She went with Harry to a supper party in Changi village last night. Some friends of Harry's, I don't remember their name – '

'Oh I know who you mean,' said Tony eagerly. 'Would you like me to telephone them and find out if they are still there?'

Mrs Beattie's face cracked into a spontaneous smile.

'That's very good of you, young man. Do try and get Harry to drive her straight to the dock.'

She directed him to the telephone and left him to make the call while she went to organize the servants to load the luggage.

'Was she there? Did you find her?'

'Yes, yes, it's all right, Mrs Beattie. There's nothing to worry about. Harry is driving her to the dock now. If you are ready then we had better be on our way.'

Mrs Beattie hesitated only a moment longer, taking one long last look at the house where she had lived all her married life. The servants watched her climb into the car without a word and drive off.

Kate sat sullenly in the car among the luggage, scarcely able to bring herself to be courteous to Mrs Beattie ensconced in the back seat. How she resented the Beatties at that moment! To see them off to safety while she was left to face the Japanese was more than Kate could stomach.

Wild orchids still bloomed along the roadside amid bomb damage and deep craters. Broken pipes and mounds of rubble caused them to make several detours on their way downtown.

Suddenly they found themselves caught in a bombardment. A low distant whine signalled the beginning of a mortar attack. The shells screamed overhead in a piercing crescendo, so loud they seemed about to fall on the very next house. The explosion sent a tremor through the earth as screaming crowds pushed and stumbled their way for cover. Thick dense smoke hung between the buildings, so that Tony had to use his horn to clear the street. He had to be careful not to run into the monsoon drain at the side of the road.

The city centre was in chaos. Every street was a struggling bottleneck of people and vehicles. Fires were burning in the downtown tenements and the godowns at the dock.

Time was already short when they finally arrived. Rickshaws threaded a path among the crowd but Tony had to use his horn to force his way through. On the wharf thousands of desperate men and women, Europeans, Chinese and Malays, fought to push their way through to the gates where armed guards and port officials checked tickets.

Tony edged the car forward, ignoring the insults and screams on every side. The distorted faces pressed against the closed car windows, venomous and threatening. Tony sounded his horn, waving the Beatties' tickets at the stern-faced guard on the gate, and drove through on to the dock as the gates were slammed behind in defiance of the furious crowd.

Katherine sat in the car as the luggage was unloaded. She stared at the ships, reading some of the names, *Devonshire* and *Felix Roussel*. Mrs Beattie had got out to look for her daughter. She came back to Tony, her face red with the effort and the heat.

'She's not here yet. She'll miss the sailing! I don't understand where she can be – '

I don't care if she never makes it, thought Katherine bitterly.

More cars arrived bringing passengers but there was no sign of Harry's car. After a quarter of an hour one of the ships unroped its gangway and prepared to sail. The Japanese mortar attack continued and now they were finding their range. If the ships did not leave soon, it could be too late.

The crowd beyond the gates roared their anger as another car was let into the compound. One of the guards fired a warning shot to force them back. Katherine saw no white faces among them any longer. They, like herself, had no influence and no money to buy their way out.

Mrs Beattie had recognized her husband's car and left Tony's side to tell him that Suzy had not arrived.

'Where the devil can she be? They've had ample time to get down here.'

The ship's hooter sounded for another departure. Panic seized those remaining on the wharf. At the gangway officials were scrutinizing tickets and a fight broke out. Only those with valid documents would be allowed aboard.

Raymond Beattie stood with the tickets flapping the palm of his hand impatiently. The second ship cast off and followed the others out into deep water. Only one now remained at its moorings to take his wife and daughter to safety.

'After all we've done for the girl!' he exploded bitterly, not caring who heard him. 'If she doesn't come now the damned ship will sail and she'll be left behind. Where is the little fool?'

Chapter Nine

Women and children swarmed up the last gangway. The piles of luggage had vanished from the quayside.

Mr Beattie paced backwards and forwards, barely able to contain his anger, while his wife saw that her luggage was put on board. Kate had got out of the car in the shimmering heat. The air on the wharf stank of smoke and oil fumes but at least there was a breeze off the sea. She saw Tony watching her anxiously but before she could say anything, he was off to join Raymond Beattie, talking earnestly with short glances from the gate to the ship that was about to leave.

The ship's horn sounded a warning. Mr Beattie delayed no longer. He marched across to his wife and Katherine, looking very pukka, the Tuan Besar himself.

'There's nothing else for it,' he declared. 'If the stupid little bitch can't get here on time then there's no sense in wasting her place.' He turned to Katherine. 'You must go instead.'

It was difficult to say who was the more surprised by his suggestion. Mrs Beattie stared at her husband askance and was about to protest when the ship's hooter cut short all further conversation with its last warning. Kate looked from the Beatties to her brother, wondering if she had imagined it or if it was some kind of sick joke.

But Mr Beattie was propelling his wife towards the gangway, commanding the over-eager ship-hands not to cast off until Mrs Phyllis Beattie was securely on board. Without warning, Kate found herself in a fierce brotherly hug and pushed towards the barrier as Mr Beattie handed over the precious tickets.

'Oh, Tony – '

'Get aboard now, miss,' said the sailor at the gangway, 'or we'll sail without you.'

She needed no further encouragement. She followed Mrs Beattie on to the ship and watched, still stunned, as the ropes were cast away and the figures of Tony and his employer stood far below with their hands raised.

She was leaving Singapore! She raised her gaze to the dark pillars of smoke rising above the bombed city. She was getting out after all! Suzy Beattie was staying and she was getting out. It seemed incredible. If she had not come to the dock, if Tony had not insisted that she came –

Suddenly a strange thought entered her head. She stared at the tiny diminishing figure on the wharf. Had he known? Had Tony somehow contrived to get her on board? It scarcely seemed credible and yet –

Yet here she was, with only the clothes she stood up in. No bags, no luggage at all. Running away, just leaving everything to get out whole.

Around her the ship was a scene of indescribable confusion. Countless children of all ages ran up and down the deck while women were dragging suitcases and bundles, some calling out for non-existent porters or stewards, some complaining bitterly that all the first-class cabins had been taken.

'No cabins?' Mrs Beattie's indignation drew Kate's attention back again. 'But this is intolerable. I had a cabin reserved.' She saw Katherine standing there and seemed suddenly to remember that they were in this together. 'Katherine? It is Katherine, isn't it? Do go and look for the reservation, won't you? Look, A Deck – it's here on the tickets.'

'I wouldn't waste my time, if I were you,' said an elegant woman with a double strand of pearls and two small children. 'The whole ship is upside down, if you ask me. A Deck is down in the hold – with no beds, no chairs, absolutely nothing at all! These continental ships number their decks in reverse order. It's simply too awful!'

All around them women were now sitting on their suitcases on deck, silent, full of tension and dreadful apprehension as they looked their last on Singapore.

For twenty or thirty minutes they watched, taut with fear as the noise of the shelling grew louder and they sailed out past the burning godowns.

How long before the city fell? What would happen to their husbands, brothers and sons left behind?

A whistling shell struck the sea just yards off the bow of the ship in front, sending up a fountain of salt water. As the convoy left the burning city behind, their thoughts were filled with fear for their own safety as they headed out into the unknown.

As the ship pulled away from the dock Raymond Beattie and Tony got back into their cars on the wharf. Mr Beattie called out, 'I'm pleased I could do something for your sister, Kendall.'

'I'm very grateful to you, sir. I'm just glad that Mrs Beattie and my sister are safe.'

'Can't imagine what happened to Suzy and Harry. They got the message all right? Well, I suppose it was the roads. Chaos, absolute chaos. I'll have to try and get the girl another passage out – if there is another.' He grunted, settling himself in the passenger seat of his car next to his syce. 'Well, let's get out of here. Follow me back to the warehouse, will you? There's something that must be done.'

Tony reversed his car and followed Beattie's limousine out of the gates. The crowd had dispersed in sullen desolation as the ships had sailed. They drove to the Beatties' massive warehouse.

'I always meant to attend to this the moment I put Phyllis on the ship.' Raymond Beattie led the way into the vast cavern among row after row of bottles. 'It seems like the final gesture somehow.'

After the horrors of Hong Kong, no one in their right mind would leave alcohol stocks for the Japanese to raid. Tony knew that all over Singapore, at John Little, at Caldbeck McGregor and Robinson and Co., stocks of millions of bottles of whisky, brandy, rum and other spirits, including *samsu*, the Chinese firewater, would be systematically destroyed.

Tony watched Raymond Beattie as his workers smashed bottle after bottle against the high brick walls of the warehouse. His face remained stoic and seemingly impassive as thousands of pounds' worth of stock went flooding over the cobbles and down the drains. The fumes were an intoxicating gas in that confined space. Before they were done, they were all more than a little drunk.

'I couldn't see it all go, all my life's work,' said Beattie, 'without saving this for us now.' He produced a bottle from behind his back and dusted it off. A vintage Napoleon brandy to drown their sorrows.

As they all stood around and drank to their health and future survival, did Tony Kendall feel just a qualm of guilt for what he had done – or rather for what he had failed to do? Where Suzy Beattie and her brother were, he had not the least idea, nor had he ever known. His phone call at the Beatties' house had been a sham, a splendid piece of improvisation to get Katherine out of Singapore, whatever the cost.

He knew he would have to pay for this deceit before long. The Beatties would turn up and there would be all hell to pay. But it was worth it. Worth it to know that Kate was safe. They were all going to the devil here anyway, it was just a question of time. But Kate was beyond the reach of the Japanese and just knowing that would keep him going, no matter what happened in Singapore.

Chapter Ten

The Japanese shelling was left behind as the little convoy sailed out of the Singapore Strait. Attack by air was the fear as they passed Batam, Bintang and Mâpor islands heading for the open sea. The captain took a zig-zagging course that avoided the narrow waters of Banka Strait. Sumatra was not their goal, but Australia via the Java Sea.

Two days out from Singapore found their ship among the islands of the Dutch East Indies. They had lost contact with the other ships during a squall at night and now steered a lonely course, the southern coast of Borneo away on the port side.

The evacuation had thrown together women from all walks of life and the confusion over quarters had ensured a genuine mix. Here there were no privileges. The war had reduced everyone to a state of near destitution, sharing the same cramped conditions, the same meagre rations. On campbeds and mattresses in the lounges and on deck, the women made the best of it, many gladly sharing what they had managed to bring out of Singapore.

Mrs Beattie had been eminently practical in her packing. Unfortunately for Katherine, Suzy Beattie had been less discriminating. Katherine discovered Suzy's suitcase to be crammed with the vanities that marked her social round in Singapore. It was tough on Kate. Three evening dresses, a swimming costume, a rope of jet beads and two jars of French cold cream were going to be of little value where she was going.

However, she was not alone. Many women with babies had come away with bags full of nappies and little else. The children had their favourite teddy bear but mother was lucky if she had a toothbrush and a change of underwear. The girl who had cunningly packed a hatbox full of sanitary towels was soon the focus of envious droves of women eager to barter.

The woman who had talked to Kate and Mrs Beattie on the first day took the precaution of wrapping her pearls in a silk scarf around her five-year-old daughter's head.

'Then, if anything should happen to me,' she told Kate, 'at least Chloe will have something to keep her going.'

Mrs Beattie gave a terrible sigh, casting a jaundiced eye around the ship.

'What a sorry sight we are without the trappings of civilization.'

'It won't be for long,' said Kate. 'It can't be for long.'

The surprising lull after the frenzy of their last weeks in Singapore left everyone rather shell-shocked. A kind of apathy took over. They sat or lay around, lacking all energy or sense of purpose, waiting, just waiting.

Only the children seemed to be unaware of the danger. They began to enjoy themselves, catching the sun as they played or raced around on the deck. There was great excitement at the sight of shoals of flying fish, flashing in the fierce sunlight over the water.

As the ship left the lee of the land the currents of the capricious Java Sea caught them unawares. As night fell the swell took over, making the vessel roll wildly. The women cleared the top decks and packed the inside lounges and staterooms. Many were soon taken sick and a melancholy line formed outside the toilets, but for some it proved too late.

Katherine sat with her head pressed to the back of her chair, the room swimming before her eyes. But when she closed them it was even worse. She fought valiantly to control her nausea but she truly thought her last hour had come.

'You don't look too good, Katherine. I do hope you're not going to be sick.'

'I'm sorry,' she gagged, stumbling to her feet and staggering her way across the swaying room to the nearest bucket.

Mrs Beattie watched her progress and shook her head. She pitied the girl, thinking she looked thin and exhausted. She was greatly changed from Singapore. How Suzy could ever have imagined the girl was a gold-digger! But the thought of

Suzy induced a tear or two as she remembered, and wondered where her daughter was now and what was going to happen to her.

Kate wiped her face and scraped back her damp hair into a knot on top of her head, loose tendrils clinging to her neck in the heat. She was aware that she had let Mrs Beattie down. She had behaved impeccably since they were thrown together. It was certainly less trouble to agree with her than not. But that was not the only reason, and she knew it. She felt guilty that she was here instead of Suzy Beattie, but that was only part of it.

In Singapore her relationship with Harry Beattie had been a secret. Perhaps, if things had worked out differently, they would have broken their news together to his mother. But for weeks past Kate had schooled herself not to think of Harry, not to recall those hot afternoons in the room above the street, not to remember the touch of his hand and the soft cries that had filled the afternoon. She must not think of him. She must not remember what was lost or the crazy dream which had once fed her days.

Here, adrift in this no-man's-land, miles from anywhere, Kate knew that secret would have to be kept even longer. There was no way that she could shrug off what had happened in Singapore, even if she wanted to.

This was the first time Mrs Beattie had seen her being ill. She would assume it was nothing more than seasickness. But she had not seen her every morning since their journey began, hurrying out on deck to ease the queasy feeling. She had not commented on her lack of appetite. She had not guessed that anything was wrong. And if Kate had her way Mrs Beattie would never guess that she was pregnant, pregnant with Harry Beattie's child.

Makassar was sweltering in the heat after the mountains. As Dede and Amy entered the city they found it quiet and virtually deserted. The Europeans had been evacuated long ago and the occasional Japanese air raids, firebombing the godowns on the docks, had frightened away most of the local population.

On their journey across the mountains of Celebes Dede and Amy had passed refugees fleeing in the opposite direction.

Makassar was being bombed but the Japanese had already landed near Menado in the north, didn't they know that? They had heard the trap was closing – Amboina, Rabaul, Hollandia – the Japanese were everywhere.

It was two weeks since they had started their journey from Majene. The Toraja people had found them, fed them and set them on their way. With very little communication – Amy's Chinese was less than useless – but with Dede's respect for taboo and local customs, they soon won new friends. They found the people gracious, welcoming. They were happy to help the two strangers on their journey, even if they did not understand the reason for it.

Their language problems did not improve when they reached Makassar in the south. For a port of its importance on the East Indies sealanes, Makassar was smaller than they imagined. The town was full of attractive colonnaded buildings in the colonial Dutch style around a high fortress wall. All the street names were Dutch. Dutch was the lingua franca of everyone they met, from a Salvation Army worker to the nuns at the new Roman Catholic hospital. In the end there seemed little to do but get down to the harbour and hope and pray for a ship to come in.

In normal times Makassar was a magnet for Dutch liners and mail boats ploughing between the islands. The harbour would have been full of schooners, fishing smacks and tramp ships. But by the second week of February 1942 all that had changed. The last scheduled ship had long gone, and every other available craft had been commandeered. When Dede and Amy arrived they found the harbour deserted.

The silence among the burnt-out godowns was uncanny. The mild sea stretched to an unblemished horizon, devoid of life. Had they come this far only to reach the end? The Japanese would take the town very soon now. Without a boat of some kind, any kind, they would be caught in the trap, all their efforts at escape come to nothing.

Back in the town they prepared to wait it out, anticipating the worst. The well-meaning but incomprehensible Dutch-speaking Salvation Army assistant gave them a place to sleep and a free meal. When Dede pointed out the route they had come on a child's school atlas, she was met with incredulity.

In other days Dede would have been scrupulous about the clothes she wore, but when they were offered their choice from the second-hand charity collection, she and Amy were like children laughing and playing at dressing up. The local Celebes women wore elegant black sarongs and tight black blouses, but they found their new clothes had been donated by wealthy Europeans. Amy found a sleeveless silk dress that seemed almost new, and although it hung rather loose on her, in the heat of Makassar she was glad of it. Dede was less fortunate. Her height meant that every dress she held up seemed stranded somewhere around her naval. Somehow she did not see herself facing the Japanese in any of them. She knew that whatever she picked might well have to last for years. The thought of internment terrified her, but the thought of having to survive wearing the frills and bows of a Dutch housewife terrified her even more. In the end she selected sensibly, finding a pair of white ducks that fitted well, with the bottoms turned up, and a loose white shirt that kept her cool and protected from the sun.

When Amy saw her she collapsed into the first laughter that Dede had heard from her.

'Oh come on, it's not that bad.'

'You look very nice – you look very – Chinese!'

Before dawn on the Friday they were woken by a wildly excited native boy sent by the assistant superintendent. He kept shouting at them, gesturing downtown, pulling them outside into the half-light. The only word they could decipher was 'Port, port' as he insisted they climb aboard his *beca*. The tricycle was one of the rickety taxis widely used around Makassar in former days. They got behind him, unable to understand the rapid commentary the boy gave them as he pedalled furiously through the sleeping town.

Down at the harbour they saw the reason for his excitement at once. In the dock stood the ghostly white form of a huge liner.

'My God!' cried Dede. 'My God!'

The boy was delighted that they were so pleased with his news. They kissed and hugged him and then ran screaming down the dock, waving their arms and shouting out to the women and children who crowded the rails of the ship.

The ship from Singapore had made the unscheduled stop the night before to refuel and take on fresh food. In fifteen minutes they were about to sail, the last ship out of Makassar.

As the two refugees were taken on board, Katherine Kendall watched them from the boat deck and thought that they at least had good fortune on Friday the 13th.

Chapter Eleven

'A Chinese woman?'

'Not Chinese, Eurasian. You can always tell by their chichi accents.'

'Well, I don't think it's right,' Mrs Beattie said firmly. 'If we stopped to take on every little halfcaste we would never get anywhere.' She stared around at her fellow passengers. 'I mean to say, they're two a penny out here. Malays, Chinese – '

Katherine knew that many European men had native wives before their real wives or fiancées came out from home. The Malay or Chinese girls were then sent back to their own people, and if they were lucky the man would pay something towards the upkeep and education of any children.

'They do all right for themselves,' Mrs Beattie was saying.

Kate's stomach turned over. The thought struck her that she was like one of those native women, taken up by a European of wealth and position and then discarded, forgotten and unwanted, sent home with a child that would never know its father.

She watched as the Chinese girl and her odd-looking companion in men's clothing were brought into the lounge.

'Thank you very much for making room for us,' Dede said enthusiastically. 'We have never been so pleased to see anyone before in all our lives!'

'An American,' groaned Mrs Beattie under cover of the noise in the room. 'I might have guessed!' Her indignation turned to horror as she saw the two women shepherded in her direction.

'They tell us there's room for us here. I hope you don't mind if we join you.'

Mrs Beattie stood up, drawing herself up to her full height. 'But I do mind. I'm afraid all these chairs are taken.'

'We don't mind the floor,' said Dede. 'After all we've been through, the floor will suit us fine.'

Mrs Beattie's colour was high with nervous excitement.

'Well, I'm afraid it will not suit us, Miss – ?'

'Harriman, Dede Harriman. And this is – '

Mrs Beattie cut her short. She clearly had no interest in discovering Amy's name.

'Well, Miss Harriman, we may all be in danger, but there are certain standards to be maintained.'

Katherine wished Mrs Beattie would stop. Everyone in the room was looking at them now. She was being unfair, ridiculous.

'I have no objection to *you* staying, of course, but – '

Dede began to see the light.

'But you don't like my friend, is that it? I don't believe this! What do you think this is? A Sunday school outing?'

There was embarrassed laughter on all sides now. Kate looked at Mrs Beattie in despair. Didn't she realize she was alienating everyone?

'How dare you talk to me like that!' Mrs Beattie was red-faced in outrage but she had lost the support of the other women.

'She thinks she's still at Raffles!'

'You come over here, dear, and never mind that old bitch – '

'This is quite intolerable!' Mrs Beattie stormed. She stared at the ring of hostile faces and then at Kate, who looked quickly away.

Dede and Amy were made welcome in the opposite corner of the lounge, where they were given a spare mattress to sit on. Amy seemed shaken by the scene with the Englishwoman and sat sullen and quiet. After a while Dede took her out on to the deck to watch the last of Makassar.

'How she despises me.'

'That woman? She's just plain ignorant, honey. Forget her.'

'No, its true, I don't belong with her sort. I never knew where I belonged – '

Dede saw that she was deeply disturbed but she did not

know what to say. She wondered what it must be like for Amy to be neither British nor Chinese.

'All my life I have wanted to go home.'

'Home?'

'To England. My father told me he would take me to England one day.'

Dede felt pity for her but it was tinged with just a little exasperation or annoyance. She had never been given to easy confidences herself. Amy's trust embarrassed her and only served to remind Dede that the girl looked up to her. She knew that under normal circumstances they would never have met, never been friends. But these were not normal times. She saw that Amy had come to depend upon their friendship. Suddenly Dede saw that her responsibilities to Amy had doubled.

The old sailors' superstition came true. They had sailed from Makassar on a Friday, and Friday the 13th at that. The day lived up to its evil reputation.

Across the Flores Sea the captain set a zig-zag course. The sea was calm, untroubled. There was no sign of danger. At noon a meal was served of riceballs and fresh fruit. The heat of the day made everyone drowsy and it was late afternoon when Dede woke from a light sleep.

As she went on deck a member of the crew came rushing past and knocked her flying. She fell heavily on to her knees and had to be helped up again. It was Katherine Kendall who helped her, looking at the sailor racing down the deck.

'Say, don't mind me!' Dede got to her feet, wiping her hands and the front of her trousers.

'What's wrong? What's he shouting?'

Dede followed Kate's anxious gaze. Panic seemed to have seized the men on the bridge. Two of the crew suddenly appeared with rifles. Dede saw her assailant pointing back to the sea and looking round she for herself the dark form which had appeared out of the heat haze. Kate met her eyes and then looked back towards the plane that was now zooming in on the ship. It was unmistakably a Japanese Zero.

'Get down! Get down!' The warning was not just for them but for the women and children who had flocked to the rails at the sound of the Zero's distinctive engine.

Screaming broke out even before the plane moved to attack. The spectators scattered as the Zero came in a low dive, roaring down on the ship at deck level. The women ran, helping one another to cover. A stream of tracer bullets strafed splinters out of the deck, cutting down a woman stranded at the ship's rail.

Kate stood rooted to the spot, mesmerized by the sight of blood on the white wood. It took Dede to move her away, pushing her violently down the nearest companionway as the plane swooped past.

The ship swung to starboard as the men with rifles opened up and the plane spun away. Dede and Kate ran down the stairs to the lower deck and stepped into a scene of carnage.

Women on the exposed port side had been machine-gunned without mercy. More than seven women lay over the deck, limbs twisted into unnatural positions. Kate knelt at the nearest figure, trying to turn her over on to her back, but a voice behind her said it all:

'I'm afraid it's no use. She's bought it.'

A terrible scream cut the growing silence. They turned to see the Zero, accompanied by two dove-tailing torpedo bombers, moving back towards the ship. The Zero's pilot had obviously radioed to its base on a nearby island or perhaps even an aircraft carrier for bomber assistance.

Dede and Kate scuttled into the nearest doorway for cover and found themselves in a small stateroom. The cabin that had originally been intended as a single bedroom was now shelter for a dozen women and children. They sat on the edge of the bunk and the floor, moving up without a word to accommodate the newcomers. Dede and Kate stood one side of the door, aware of the roar as the planes dived into the attack.

The young girl opposite was white-faced and shaking, on the verge of hysteria. She sat twisting a handkerchief over and over in a ball in her hands, never still. Next to her a woman in her twenties held a baby on her lap and a small boy with a shock of blond hair by the arm. Her middle-aged neighbour tried talking to distract him.

The first torpedo struck the ship with a powerful explosion at the stern. Vibrations rocked the ports and threw the women off the bunk and on to the floor. The baby wailed, the nervous girl screamed, and an elderly woman hit her head going down. While she was being helped to her feet the small boy broke free from his mother and ran out through the door before he could be stopped.

'David! David!'

His mother screamed and the woman who had been helping with the boy suddenly ran after him on to the deck.

Dede ran after, crying out for her to stop. On deck she saw the woman running after the child and heard the drone of the Zero behind her. Her warning words were drowned in the stutter of bullets that took the woman full force in the back and legs and sent her spinning down to her death.

Dede collapsed face down on the deck, protected by an unknown corpse which was struck again by a burst of machine-gun fire as the Zero swooped in. She kept down, half stunned by the blast of another explosion near the bridge as a second torpedo struck amidships. The deck trembled beneath her and the sound of screeching metal grated her teeth. As she lay there it seemed that the ship was listing, the deck tilting, threatening to send her rolling down into the sea.

She looked up sharply and dragged herself back along the deck towards the flapping cabin door as it swung drunkenly on its hinges. Only when she was sitting up near the doorway did she look back along the deck and see the woman and beyond her the broken body of the child.

'David? David!'

Dede's face told the story as she was dragged into the cabin by willing hands. She sank down on to the bunk, her head spinning, the room filled with tension and tears, not least of all her own.

The white-faced girl next to Kate suddenly lost all control. She leapt towards the cabin door, eyes fixed with a glassy stare, and had to be forcibly restrained.

'We'll die, we'll all die,' she screamed, fighting to escape. 'The ship will sink and we'll all be drowned.'

'Shut up, shut up!'

'We're all going to die, don't you understand?'

'Can't you make her shut up?' demanded the elderly woman who had taken the wailing baby. She was trying to coax the child's mother to hold him, but she just sat there staring blankly through the metal door as though she could see the body of her son outside on the deck.

Half of the women still crouched on the tilting floor on hands and knees. Beyond the walls of the cabin came the noise of children crying and the distant drone of the aircraft. They waited, intently attuned to the sounds outside, eyes meeting with the same desperate fear. Would the planes attack again? Had they more torpedos to sink the ship?

The sound of weeping filled the tiny airless room. Kate looked at Dede and saw the sweat running down the American's face and neck. Her once-white trousers and shirt were blotched with grime and what must have been blood.

'Are you hurt?' she asked anxiously, met with a chorus of hushing from the tense women. But Dede shook her head and gave a small smile of reassurance. Kate liked her and admired her but she knew there was little chance of them ever becoming friends.

Her own hair had come loose and hung hot and damp to her skin. Even the hysterical girl was now quiet, feeling the silence growing and enveloping the whole ship.

'They've gone!'

They all sat, listening to the silence.

'They've really gone!'

The other women turned drained faces to Kate, unable to take in anything more.

'It's all right now. We're going to be all right.'

As they emerged from the heat of the cabin the women stared in horror at the havoc that had been wreaked upon the ship in barely fifteen minutes.

Fires had broken out on the bridge and down near the stern, belching dark smoke and leaving buckled metal girders and blazing wooden rails flashing sparks. The crew were fighting the flames which shot skywards like a beacon, an invitation to all enemy bombers. The shell-shocked and wounded moved like phantoms out of the drifting smoke, sidestepping the corpses.

Kate and Dede were anxious to return to the upper deck where they had left Mrs Beattie and Amy. The companionway down which they had come was now a red-hot tangle of twisted steel. They had to manoeuvre their way round the deck to find another way up. Eventually they came to an inside staircase and went up on to the boat deck, finding lifeboats charred and splintered by shrapnel and the scorched deck littered with glass from the windows of the staterooms.

A fire which had broken out in one corner of the huge lounge had been doused with buckets of water and sand passed hand-to-hand by a chain of women organized by Mrs Beattie. She barely looked up to acknowledge Kate's return as she busied herself issuing instructions to all and sundry. Kate saw that nothing ever seemed to touch the woman. She was more than capable of looking after herself and everyone else on board if necessary.

Dede located Amy after a longer search. She found her attending to a woman who had been badly cut by flying glass, her face and hands a mass of lacerations dribbling blood. Amy got Dede to help her to pick splinters of glass from the cuts, an interminable and delicate process that went on as long as daylight lasted.

The crippled ship had staggered into the lee of Kamba Island, but as night fell it was decided to try to struggle on with whatever power remained, putting as much distance as possible between themselves and the Japanese.

That night they cried their last tears. After a day of fearful terror they knew the worst that could happen. No one held out hope of escape any longer. They had all been on the run too long to fool themselves. The ship would never make Australia in its condition.

As morning broke the extent of the damage became apparent. The ship listed badly as it cut through the smooth turquoise seas north-east of Alor. The dead had been removed to the holds for identification and one of the staterooms had been turned into a sickbay. During the day three more women and one child died. They knew the end was coming quickly for all of them now.

In the tense afternoon the captain announced that the war was over for them. He would try to reach the neutral port of Dili on Portuguese Timor. There they would be safe for the duration. Portugal, like Switzerland and Sweden, was not in the war, and they might even find another ship there that could take them on to Darwin in Australia.

As the rugged island loomed up on the southern horizon, the

women and children crowded the rails of the ship to watch. The mountains were visible even at that range, enormous desolate peaks against the faultless sky. The women stood in silence as their ship with its dead and wounded limped in to Timor, barely one step ahead of the Japanese.

The Year of the Serpent had given way to the Year of the Horse.

Chapter Twelve

Dusk was falling among the islands. From Sumatra to Bali Admiral Ozawa's ships of the Imperial Japanese Fleet lay in wait.

The great aircraft carriers and destroyers of the Japanese battle fleet entered the narrow straits of Ombai, closing on their target. The island of Timor rose dark and peaceful against the dying light of day. Its soaring green-backed mountains darkened into silhouette as the sun slipped into the sea beyond Kambing island.

The swift onset of the equatorial night found the Australian camp in the coconut groves in the last throes of activity before settling down for sleep. Crouching around a scattering of fires between the trees, men of 2/2 Independent Company in drill shorts and boots ate their Meat and Vegetable with the usual grumbling. Night did little to ease the steaming heat of the Dili lowlands. It was a godforsaken malarial wasteland at the world's end and no one knew any longer why they were there.

Two months before, in the week before Christmas, the Diggers found themselves transported from Koepang in the Dutch half of Timor, north to Dili. No Maoris' Farewell for this departure. Their mission to defend the island from Japanese attack may have been accepted by their Dutch allies, but Dili was the colonial capital of neutral Portuguese territory and the governor made it very clear that they were not welcome.

Waiting offshore while negotiations went on, Jack Ford had had his first view of the island, his eyes drawn to the mountainous heartland over the water. The wild blue distances beyond the lowland haze drew him as though he had some sense of precognition, as though he knew that one day soon those mountains would claim him.

Now, squatting on the hillside above Dili with sweat running down his back, he ruefully reflected on the deal that had salvaged the honour of the Portuguese and yet still permitted the Australians' 'friendly invasion'. The men of 2/2 were a specialized force of volunteers, trained commandos, better armed than the handful of Portuguese officers and native soldiers of the island's defence force. It did not take long to change the governor's mind.

But since they had come ashore just before Christmas it had all gone from bad to worse. The Portuguese made it very plain that they did not want them there, the Dutch contingent of Sparrow Force continually fell out with their Australian colleagues, and meanwhile, malaria picked off the men one by one.

Looking around him in the camp, Jack knew their numbers were still short. Many men from his section were still in hospital or recuperating in the foothills near Tibar. With such a shortage of able-bodied men it had been a long hard haul to bring their supplies up from the coast. The Dutch were less than helpful, choosing to set themselves up in Dili, throwing the Japanese trading company out of their palatial building into an internment camp, and strutting the streets of the capital with their smart green uniforms and curved swords while 2/2 Company moved to occupy vantage points around the city, sending out scouts to map the rugged countryside and to transport ammunition to secret stores in the hills. Their officers took the Japanese threat seriously, believing that Timor would be the springboard for an attack on Australia, but as weeks went by disillusion set in among the men.

Jack had been no exception in volunteering for a bit of action. Most of the 2/2 volunteers were countrymen, accustomed to hard physical work and living off the land. They had been trained on Wilson's Promontory, a tough and relentless course which called for high levels of fitness and endurance. Jack had not joined up in order to sit on his backside under a palm tree on some far-flung speck in the ocean, eating bully beef and staring at the stars.

Perhaps things were finally hotting up. Jap recce planes had been in the area for weeks past, triggering air-raid alarms. Some Portuguese property had been damaged in a brief shooting match and what a row that had caused! No one was allowed to forget that East Timor was still neutral in this war. The rest of the world could go to hell, it didn't worry the Portuguese.

The men were growing sluggish with the continued inactivity. They were irritable and argumentative. Fights broke out, often for no reason at all, especially with the smarmy Dutch who seemed to have got the better deal.

The climate down at the coast had got to Jack. The damp heat seemed intensified by the night. Sweat still rolled down his back and the mosquitos were having a field day. His thin sunburnt face was gaunt, his dark hair limp in the wet heat. He sat on the hillside, a figure of dejection and fatigue, without noticing the sergeant who came up at his side.

'What's up, Jack? Feeling crook?'

'Just sick of this place, that's all. How much longer are we going to be stuck here?'

The sergeant shrugged and scratched his swollen mosquito bites. 'Don't ask me, mate. No one ever tells me a bloody thing. The mosquitos are picking us off one by one. At this rate the whole bloody company will be crook before we ever see a bloody Nip.' He mopped his expansive sweating face, squatting in the dust. 'Could I do with an ice-cold beer, mate.'

'Too right. I bet those Dutch bastards down in Dili – '

The incoming shell that whistled out of the sea mist took off the top of the palm trees only yards away. The earth shook with the force of its impact, showering earth and splinters of tree trunk and leaves in every direction.

'Holy Christ – '

His words were drowned by the crump of another shell landing on the far side of the camp. The air was full of the sound of whistling shells coming out of the darkness.

Plates of food went flying as the Australians scattered and dived for cover, their ears singing from the explosions. The coconut trees showered down debris and dust as the men buried their heads in the earth. The whining of the shells could be heard clean across the hillside, echoing in the valley where searchlights from the sea cut through the drifting mist and the obscurity of night.

A thick pillar of dark smoke rose in the valley as the shells found their mark. Jack had flung himself headlong as the hillside erupted around him. The ammunition dump had received a direct hit, searing the grove with a ball of light and engulfing the whole area in sheets of vivid enveloping flame.

Hot splinters rained out of the burning trees. Swirling blackened embers of scalding ash billowed through the acrid air. Jack turned his head from a wave of flame that shot through the clearing. In between mortars the birds went on singing in the trees.

Craters pitted the ground and he stumbled, falling over the body of one of his comrades. The bottom half of a torso had tripped him up, but of the head and arms there was no sign. He gagged suddenly at the sight, recognizing the mangled corpse of the sergeant in the very place where he had been sitting himself only moments before. Some kind of anti-personnel bomb had been dropped, like the infamous 'daisy-cutter' that the Japanese used in China to cut men into horizontal slices of flesh.

His breath shallow with fear, Jack began to edge his way through the grove in search of safety. He wanted to get out of the range of the Japanese warships in the fog.

The whole area was littered with burning corpses and the smashed branches of the broken-backed trees. The palms were on fire behind him. He could hear the rush of flame together with men screaming in the distance, but there was one thing he could no longer hear. The shelling had stopped.

It took him a few minutes to realize it. Beyond the fierce crackling of the fires that had broken out all across the Australian camp down the length of the hillside there was now silence. He knelt, hands in the earth, listening. He was dizzy and his throat burnt. He drove all thought of the horror around him from his mind. All his senses were alerted. It seemed to him suddenly that the silence was more sinister than the shelling had been. He knew that the danger was far from past.

He turned his back on the valley, sure that the coastal targets would draw the Japanese fire. If he could reach the main road on the far side of the hill he was sure to join up with the main body of Australian forces. Soon the whole area could be crawling with Japanese.

Among the drifting smoke the stark skeletal remains of the shattered forest loomed up around him. His head was pounding, every step an effort. The smoke, wraithlike, appeared to hang in the air like slow-motion phantoms, sinister and silent. Jack stared ahead through the smoke and he thought he dreamed. He thought he imagined the white images floating down through the trees. But ten paces further on he knew it was not his imagination but dreadful reality.

He saw the figures in the bush away to his right and then heard a single shot. In the ringing silence among the trees he saw the mushroom outline of a Japanese paratrooper descending only yards away.

Others had arrived before him. Crouching low in the grass, breathing heavily, Jack stared with burning eyes at the wilderness about him, seeing Japanese behind every tree. Scarcely daring to breathe he lay prone in the grass, watching and waiting, all his nerves afire as he heard the sounds of movement coming closer.

Two men broke cover of the plantation, hurrying wildly in the direction of the main road. He saw that they were Australians at the same moment that he heard the crack of sniper fire from the trees opposite.

One lay prone in the dust. The other had fallen forward on to his knees, caught in the stomach. Behind them came a rustling in the bush and two other Aussies appeared out of cover. Bravely grasping the wounded man under the arms, they tried to drag him off the exposed ribbon of road, but he began to scream, blood pouring from between his fingers.

The next minute the silence was shattered and all hell broke loose. There was wild firing and bullets erupted in the dust for yards around the three men. They stood no chance at all in that storm of fire. Their bodies bounced on the flat road surface, struck time after time. Yet, astonishingly, Jack saw that there were two not dead. The wounded man who had inadvertently brought about the death of his friends lay twisted in a pool of his own blood, groaning softly. One of his would-be rescuers was trying desperately to crawl back towards the long grass, dragging his right leg in the dust.

Jack willed him to make it, although he could see figures moving among the trees on the far side of the track. Perhaps the man heard the Japanese coming for him because he frantically redoubled his efforts to pull himself along, his face a sweating mask of agony.

Unarmed, Jack could do nothing to help him.

Behind him Jack saw the Japanese appear out of the bush. They walked with a strange rolling gait, their legs encased in old-style puttees. They carried gleaming bayonets fitted to their heavy stock rifles. They were the first Japanese Jack had ever seen in his life, and they were too damned close for his liking.

With his head buried low between his arms, Jack felt rather than saw their approach to the wounded men. They moved with caution, their light footsteps rustling the grass at the side of the road. Jack lay still, hardly breathing, listening to them hunting, not daring to move.

He knew that the Australians must now be dead. The sound of moaning had ceased. There was only the soft shuffling of the Japanese as they wiped the blood from their bayonets.

Did they suspect he was there? He knew the slightest noise would give him away. They were so close now, he could almost imagine he could smell them. He lay in the wavering grass, listening, able to see only a matter of feet. In the thick night all his senses were alive to the danger facing him.

Suddenly one of the Japanese called out from the far side of the road. His words were alien, harsh, but Jack thought they were his salvation.

But what was clearly an agreement came from somewhere alarmingly close at hand.

'*Hei!*'

The grass moved, brushing the side of Jack's face. He saw the oiled bayonet carried a few inches above as a pair of strange canvas boots trod through the undergrowth. The long blade bore a notched runnel down its length, still marked with blood. Jack stared, mesmerized, his life in the balance.

Then the boots turned, stalking back towards the roadway, crushing the grass underfoot. Jack could hear the Japs' staccato talk some distance away. He permitted himself the luxury of several long deep breaths.

He had burning cramp all along one leg down to his foot but he willed himself to bear it just a while longer. He lay there sweating, attentive to the sounds of the Japanese troops moving away.

How long he lay there he could not judge. Darkness and the sounds of the night closed about him, reassuring in their very naturalness: cicadas and tree frogs, undisturbed by the death around them.

He stretched his leg, gritting his teeth against the stabbing sensations, yet knowing he had to move. He began to crawl painstakingly forward through the bush. He pulled himself into the undergrowth beneath the trees, closing the thick foliage around him.

Exhausted and drenched in sweat he curled himself into a tight huddle, feeling protected by the friendly forest, waiting for the Japanese to move on.

Chapter Thirteen

He was being violently shaken. Blindly he struggled out of a deep and exhausted sleep, struggling to sit up but feeling the thick bush close about him.

In the dull grey light he was startled to look into a human face, lost in a dazzling sea of whiteness. As he tried to focus he felt a hand reach down to touch him, the flesh startling in its warmth. The hand restrained him, cautioning silence, and Jack saw a smile on the face of the white-coifed nun.

He looked up into her face, shielding his eyes.

'Are you real?'

She wore white from head to foot and for a moment he almost convinced himself that this was no mortal woman. But a faint smile touched the nun's lips and her smooth, curiously unlined face leant over him.

'You must come with me.'

Her voice was little more than a whisper. All his fear vanished as he met her resolute grey eyes.

'Come, come,' she demanded, grasping him firmly by the wrist with a grip that was far from illusory. 'No talking now.'

He stumbled blindly after her through the bristling undergrowth as though still half asleep. She moved swiftly, sure on her feet as she led him in and out of the trees, keeping well away from the road. For an old girl she could certainly move. She clutched the cumbersome habit away from her feet, exposing a pair of well-worn leather boots that could almost have been army issue. Jack gratefully accepted her rescue. She clearly knew the area like the back of her hand, and that she was here at all was little short of a miracle. Jack was left in no doubt that his luck had held.

'Over here.'

She had not come alone. Jack bent his head as he stepped under the covering branches of palm frond. The man stood in the shadows, dark and watchful.

'Are you injured?'

'No – no.'

'Then we must get out of here. There are Japanese everywhere.'

That news overrode all the other questions that Jack wanted to ask. He moved closer to his rescuers, looking from one to the other.

'So they've invaded?'

The dark man was about five feet nine and with a lean intelligent face. He gave Jack a penetrating stare. He had the strangest pale eyes.

'First you,' he said softly, 'now the Japanese.'

He was half-smiling and yet there was something in those eyes that was a little ruthless. Not a man to dismiss lightly.

For Jack it was like a dream, stumbling along between the white-robed nun and the surly Portuguese. Their fierce breathing was the only sound as they wove between the trees at the outer edge of the coconut plantation. Acrid smoke still hung in the air, masking their progress and turning the crippled forest into a lost wilderness.

They had almost strayed into the clearing before they saw the Japanese. Jack pulled the nun down into the undergrowth as the sentries snapped out unintelligible orders to a group of shambling Australians tied together like cattle in a line. At that distance their faces were indistinguishable. Jack turned to find the Portuguese watching him, warning him to keep silent. It was almost more than Jack could bear. He saw the Japanese tie their prisoners to the trunks of a clump of coconut trees. He saw them take up their rifles with the bayonets fitted. He knew at once that he was helpless to prevent what was happening. There was nothing he could do to save them without betraying their own presence to the Japanese. But as the soldiers struck at the Australians, their dying shouts of defiance made him sick with guilt and despair.

The Portuguese laid a steady hand on his arm and Jack became aware of the nun softly murmuring prayers for the dead. He could not look into the clearing but the distant laughter of the soldiers reached into his heart.

The little nun was anxious to be away. She led them as before, pulling Jack along in her billowing wake through the fringes of the plantation. The Portuguese brought up the rear. As they set off Jack had noticed the revolver he carried in his hand.

Moving through the bush they travelled without talking within yards of the Japanese silhouetted against the fires in the old Australian camp. Jack saw that the bodies of his mates were still scattered across the open space. The Japanese moved between them, picking over the corpses for wristwatches and other loot.

The little group started downhill into a scrubland gully that hid them from view. In the half-light before the dawn the spare eucalyptus savannah was still and melancholy. From the low-hanging branches of the trees flying foxes glided silently. The air was cold.

After another twenty or thirty minutes they reached the far side of the gully, climbing out beyond a line of tall white arekas and through a belt of wild bananas bordered by a cultivated garden. Jack was automatically on his guard but their pace continued unabated. He followed silently around a wicket fence on the edge of the hillside where a red-roofed bungalow stood among hibiscus and bright yellow cannas.

The nun moved swiftly up to the bare-boarded verandah which ran around two sides of the house. She signalled impatiently for the men to follow her. Whatever Jack had been expecting, it was not this.

'My home,' came the accented English of his escort. He stood close behind him, putting away the revolver and, noticing Jack's hesitation, added brusquely, 'You better get inside now.'

From the verandah Jack caught a glimpse of the green tracts of paddy fields gleaming in the early sunshine. The fog had lifted from the valley as the day's heat broke through. Everything looked fresh and translucent.

Inside, Jack found himself in a long, low-ceilinged room

lined with bookshelves, rattan furniture and vivid native rugs. The nun had opened one of the green-painted shutters to let in the morning light, moving about the place as though she knew it well.

'The road to Remexio lies below.' She stood at the open window which overlooked the back of the house.

Jack joined her, catching his breath at the beauty of the scene. Far below the sea emerged from the mist, a smooth band of turquoise below banked coral clouds in the morning sun. All around the hills rose sharply in banks of luxuriant vegetation, rich emeralds and blue-toned jade.

'It's so peaceful here,' he said at last.

The nun turned to face him, her face soft with compassion. 'You're in a great deal of danger, you know.'

The enormity of what faced him could no longer be evaded. 'I have to try somehow to join up with any others, the rest of my team. Don't think I don't appreciate your help but it seems to me now that I'm here on the coast and my blokes are up there in the hills, with the whole bloody Japanese army in between.'

'Don't go losing your head now,' snarled the Portuguese. 'Sister Eulalia risks her life for you – '

'Yeah, I know. And you too, mate. Don't get me wrong, Sister, I just think the sooner I move out of here, the better it will be for us all.'

Sister Eulalia talked rapidly to the Portuguese in their own language. It was very different from what he had imagined. He found that he could barely make out a word of it.

'I'm certainly glad you two speak English,' he said with a forced laugh.

'We have decided that Daniel will take a look around,' Sister Eulalia told him. 'He will find out what is happening.'

'Is that wise? I mean, I don't want you getting yourself killed on my account.'

'Don't trouble yourself, *senhor*,' came the cool retort. 'We Portuguese are neutral in this conflict, don't you remember?'

Jack stared at the retreating figure and groaned. 'I put my foot in it there.'

'I'm sorry?'

'I mean I put his back up. Daniel, is it? – he doesn't think much of me.'

'Daniel Letria. He is a good man. Please do not worry. God will provide.'

Back inside the house, Jack took his chance to ask some questions. Sister Eulalia gave the impression of being a woman of some spirit and education, while Letria was the mystery man, scholarly, moody, perhaps with a chip on his shoulder.

'How come you were there, Sister? Isn't it pretty dangerous to be wandering around?'

Her smile was indulgent. 'I would not say wandering exactly. I go where I am needed. I am – how do you say? – a medic – *enfermeira*.'

'What's that? A doctor?'

'Not so grand, not so much education. I do what I can – where I can.'

'And Letria?'

She seemed to hesitate. 'That you must ask Daniel himself.'

Sister Eulalia insisted upon cooking for Daniel's return.

'I don't know when we may get the opportunity again.'

The kitchen was the only part of the house Jack had seen with no books around the walls. He had taken a look at Letria's expansive library shelves, turning a book or two over in his hands. Barely a handful were in English anyway and those that were might just as well not have been. *The Accumulation of Capital* by Luxemburg, *Ten Days that Shook the World*, Reed, and Thomas Paine. Jack had never heard of him.

'What's that?' Jack tensed at the sound, ready to make a run for it. But Sister Eulalia moved quickly to the door.

'Don't be afraid. It is only Daniel with the car.'

'You have a car?'

'Come and see.'

From the window they saw Letria get out of the hybrid automobile drawn up in front of the house. It was like no other car Jack had ever seen. He recognized part of a Chevrolet, part from a Buick, but the result was a mongrel crossbreed of extraordinary flair and design. It must have been a good ten years since it had seen a coat of paint and rust had claimed a victory, pitting the chassis with pockmarks, but the wheels looked almost new.

'That's some car.'

'Over the years people have contributed – to keep us mobile. She can do sixty,' added the nun with the sin of pride. 'You shall see.' Jack didn't know if that was a threat or a promise.

Letria got out of the monster and came across to join them.

'Did you see any of our blokes?'

'Australians? None that were alive.'

From what he had been able to discover the Australians had succeeded in holding off the Japanese at the aerodrome for several hours in the night before having to withdraw. They had set off explosive charges before abandoning the airstrip to the invaders.

'That will stop them landing supplies and reinforcements,' Jack said with satisfaction.

'For a while, perhaps.'

'Were many killed?' asked Sister Eulalia.

'*Sim, os nipões –*'

'In English, Daniel, please.'

'The Japanese are certain to take Dili,' said Letria. 'Where do you think your people will go?'

'Into the mountains. That's where we set up temporary headquarters – what with the opposition we met from your people.'

Letria raised his chin warily. 'My people?'

'The governor, you know. It wasn't exactly a secret we weren't welcome here.'

Letria shrugged. 'The governor is Lisbon's man. He does not speak for all Portuguese.'

They ate in a rather subdued atmosphere. Letria produced a bottle of some kind of liqueur distilled from mandarins. What he had seen that morning made him drink deep.

They ate a dish of pork and rice, well-spiced. Jack found himself suddenly ravenous, mopping up his plate with the coarse white bread, unaware of the amused expressions on the faces of his hosts.

'I'm really grateful, you know, for everything you've done for me,' he said sincerely.

'It is not over yet,' Sister Eulalia reminded him. 'But at the convent you will be safe. For a time, at least.'

'We ought not to delay,' said Letria in his coldly precise

English. Jack made a mental note to ask him where he had learnt the language.

'I will drive, with Sister Eulalia next to me. You will be here,' he told Jack, drawing back a rough tarpaulin that covered the floor in the back of the car. 'It will not be a comfortable journey. I cannot say how long you must be there.'

Sister Eulalia drew Letria aside, speaking to him in rapid Portuguese. Her face was strained and anxious beneath the nun's wimple, tight around her face in the intense heat. Daniel was shaking his head, stiff with insistence, his dark beard bobbing. He walked round to the driver's seat, casting Jack a look of stern impatience.

'Get in, please. We do not have all day.'

'What's the matter? What's up?'

'Nothing, nothing.'

Sister Eulalia stepped in front of him, exasperated. 'I have told him he must not come back here.'

Jack was astonished to discover Letria's intention to return to the house. 'You're not coming with us?'

Letria turned his strange pale eyes upon him. 'I have nothing to run away from.'

'The Nips don't give a monkey's, mate. You stay here and they'll soon find out about you.' His words came out with more aggression than he had intended. 'How long d'you reckon your famous neutrality is going to save you?'

'He's right,' said the nun severely. 'You would be a fool to stay here. And perhaps,' she added firmly, 'it is your chance to get off the island.'

Letria gave her a sour grin. 'All these years I have waited to go back. Now I ask myself what there is to go back to.' He saw Jack's confusion. 'Didn't she tell you about me? I am what they call *deportado* – a prisoner of the government, sent here from Portugal. I do not belong here. That is my home, there in Portugal. Not this place at the end of the world.'

Jack was shaken by this admission. He suddenly saw the Portuguese in quite a different light. 'Christ, mate, what did you do?'

Letria shrugged it off, unwilling to go further. 'It is political.'

Jack was out of his depth. 'I don't know a thing about politics, mate.'

'Then what are you doing here?' asked Letria pointedly. He turned sharply away but said a few words with the Sister in passing. From the smile that spread across her face, Jack knew that they had convinced him after all. He had hurried back into the house, returning with a small leather case, a bundle of books and a hunting rifle.

'It is strange,' he said softly, looking back at the red-roofed house that had been his home in the islands, 'but I shall miss this place.' He caught Jack's eye. 'It was safe here. Too safe, perhaps. We can all grow soft.' He drew himself up. 'But now we go into the unknown, my friend, and who can say what fate awaits us?'

On the bouncing floor of the old car, Jack felt every rock and pothole on the track as they made their way up the hillside to join the main road. Occasionally Sister Eulalia would make a comment and then Jack knew it was safe, but when she fell silent he tensed, sensing that the Japanese were nearby.

The sounds of fear and panic reached him even before Letria slowed down the old car. He sounded the horn again and again at the throng of ragged refugees blocking the road ahead. Unable to see with his own eyes, Jack was well aware of the tide surging about their vehicle. Sister Eulalia made appeasing noises at the crowd pressing near. They had slowed almost to a standstill and Jack could feel the violence tangible in the air. One false move and the crowd could seize the car, perhaps even murder its occupants. The sight of his Australian fatigues would start a riot. If the natives didn't finish him off then the Japanese certainly would.

Suddenly a great wail went up from the mob. Under the cover of screams and the noise of running feet, Sister Eulalia was able to lean back and whisper urgently to Jack.

'Keep very still. It is an army convoy.'

Her words were barely audible above the new sounds of approaching vehicles. As Letria had reported earlier, truck-loads of Japanese marines were converging on Dili.

'Here they come!'

Jack lay still in the space behind their seats, listening as Letria pulled the car over to one side of the road, giving the invading army room to manoeuvre. The car ticked over, waiting.

Sister Eulalia gave the Japanese soldier one of her best smiles. He strode up to the car, his flat dank face shiny with sweat. He bent to look in at their faces and to her surprise spoke in passable Portuguese.

'Where do you go?'

'Dili,' Letria answered briskly. 'We have urgent business there.'

'No, no,' the sentry contradicted. 'No one must go to Dili. You go back now.' He subjected them to closer scrutiny, his eyes betraying nothing. 'You both Portuguese?'

'Yes, both of us.'

He gave a little grunt. 'Well, you go back. Dili is a closed city now. By order of Imperial Nippon Forces. All roads only for Nippon Forces. You must go back.' He stood aside, waving his arms at them, waiting for Letria to put the car into reverse gear.

On the floor Jack felt the vehicle slowly grinding back on the uneven surface of the road. He wondered what Letria would do now. The whole venture seemed crazy but he was struck once again by the danger that they were running for his sake.

'It's all right now,' came Sister Eulalia's gentle voice. 'We are safe for the time being.' But Jack heard her say three Hail Marys under her breath just in case.

A little further on she conferred with Letria and then switched again into English.

'We have taken a side road and are climbing the mountain. Daniel says all is well. It is as we wanted.'

Jack hoped Letria knew what he was doing. The island seemed to be crawling with Japanese troops. How many had they landed? How far could they get?

But in the event the Portuguese proved a cunning tactician. Twice more they were stopped by patrols all heading down into Dili. Each time the Japanese, seemingly acting on instructions and showing enforced restraint with the white Portuguese neutrals, set them on a fresh course inland. Step by step they worked their way across country on the rough side roads, steadily climbing all the time.

Once they were in the open countryside Jack was able to

remove the tarpaulin and sit up in the back.

'That was one hell of a risk you took.' Jack was full of admiration for the Portuguese.

'Sometimes it is better to do the obvious thing.' Letria pointed ahead. 'That is the way we must go.' The high mountains stood out stark against the deep azure of the afternoon sky. 'Only there in the mountains can we be safe.'

Chapter Fourteen

Silence had fallen over the burning city. Daylight brought a respite from the shelling, but half-demolished buildings were still smoking on every side. Cracked timbers groaned and finally gave way, crashing into the rubble in the street with a flare of shooting sparks. The large wahringan trees on every street corner were showered in dust and embers.

Through the drifting smoke and choking dust, Jaime Macedo walked as if in a dream, shaken to the very core by all that he saw. He had spent an anxious night with the rest of the guests at the Hotel Portugal cowering from the Japanese attack. Halfway through dinner they had flung themselves to the dining-room floor, crouching beneath tables to hide from the terror of the night outside. Scarcely able to understand what the bombardment could mean, they waited for some word of explanation as the terrified hotel manager tried to reach the governor's office by telephone.

After the first shock had worn off, anger replaced it, jostling with fear, sweat and muttered prayers of those on the floor. Macedo himself had little doubt that the Australians were to blame. No one had asked their troops to come to Timor in the first place. It was their high-handed takeover which had provoked the Japanese response.

It was unthinkable that Portugal should be dragged into someone else's war. Had not Salazar struggled for years to keep them out of it? The cunning old fox had trod a delicate path of neutrality between the Axis and Allies in Lisbon. It was intolerable that Portuguese citizens, even in this far-flung corner of the Empire, should be made to suffer such an indignity.

Dili was his home. It was the town where he had been brought up and educated. Its burgeoning streets were as familiar to him as the *posto* in the hills which had become his home. On his frequent trips down to meet the govenor's administration staff about business, he always took a day or two for himself to renew his bonds with the old town. But stepping out in the uneasy morning after the Japanese bombardment, Macedo felt a stranger in the streets he knew so well.

The waterfront was normally a meeting place for the people of a score of different races and colours – Timorese, Chinese, Dutch, Malays, English and, of course, Portuguese. It was uncanny to find the empty spaces, to hear the beat of his own footsteps on the worn cobblestones of the quayside. Fishermen and tradespeople alike had abandoned the town centre, leaving it deserted, lost. The Chinese stayed behind their boarded-up shopfronts, shutters firmly closed against the shimmering heat and a city under siege.

Macedo moved cautiously, feeling the tension as heavy as the humidity. His shirt clung to his back already as the sun rose in the sky. He longed suddenly to be back in the hills with his family where the heat was tempered by off-shore breezes and rain from the high mountains. Tomorrow he would go, God willing, but today he had to know the worst for himself.

The new cathedral stood intact after the shelling, dazzling in its pristine whiteness in the fierce sunshine. Its twin towers soared above the dripping condensation of the low buildings which flanked it, a landmark and yet, miraculously, unharmed. It was reputed to have cost more than a million petaccas from the treasury of the Holy Fathers in Macao, to be a symbol of Portugal in this small outpost of her Empire.

Alone in the square Jaime Macedo felt unsteady on his feet. Was he sickening for something? In the dense humidity of the islands the seasons merged into an uncomfortable sweat all year long, but he was no stranger to the Dili climate. He knew his fever must have another cause. Was he a fool to be out risking his life when even the lowliest of native Timorese shut themselves away?

In the commercial quarter the wide streets were also deserted. Near the barracks there were fresh signs of the night's bombardment. It seemed that the Japanese had known their targets. A gaping hole had been torn out of the roof, with rubble and charred timber blocking the street. The Japanese spies had done good work before their internment by the Dutch at Christmas. They were not to know that Captain da Costa had removed all Portuguese troops from Dili after the fiasco of the Christmas invasion by the Dutch and Australians, unwilling to be associated with a governor who had betrayed Portuguese interests. In any case, the local troops with their ancient Winchester rifles and half a dozen Vickers machine guns were hardly a match for the forces of Imperial Japan.

Overnight there came word that Japanese paratroopers had landed along the coast. By morning it was evident that all roads out of Dili were blocked. The Japanese were said to be landing north of the capital and it could not be long before they arrived. By mid-morning they had all known it was over and Dili prepared to meet her new rulers.

Gradually more adventurous souls emerged on to the streets to join Macedo, curiosity overcoming fear. Across the square he suddenly caught sight of Sassoon, one of his shipping contacts, hurrying away through the hesitant gathering. There was no mistaking his neat white ducks and slicked-back hair.

For a Jew he had done very well for himself, getting in thick with the governor's staff, utilizing his special gift for native languages which made him the obvious choice as middleman in a hundred deals. Sassoon had once had extensive dealings with the Japanese investment company which had been shut down by the bombastic Dutch the minute they landed in Dili. By keeping his head down, Sassoon had got away with it, using his acquaintance with Ross, the Australian-born British Consul, to appease the Australian colonels.

Sassoon moved on quickly between the trees. Macedo set off to follow him, eager to learn what had been happening. Sassoon always managed to know the latest news.

'Don't go!' He caught the dapper little man by the sleeve, forcing him to turn round.

He was dressed in his usual style, as though the events of the night had not troubled him. From the shiny patent leather shoes to the diamond pin in his perfect cravat, he was the picture of sleek assurance.

'Oh it's you, old man! Still in Dili then?'

He appeared less than delighted to see Macedo there.

'Not much choice now, I'm afraid,' Macedo replied, somewhat shamefaced. 'I understand that the Japanese have us surrounded.'

'It seems that way.'

To Macedo he seemed curiously evasive and he could not resist asking, 'Have you no news? What has happened to the Australians?'

'Well, there was a spot of bother up country. Some problem at the airport, I understand. Quite a bit of damage there. Could take weeks to repair – at this season, too, as if there weren't enough to do – '

Macedo wished he could take two invasions in two months as calmly. But at least Sassoon was talking.

'What of the Japanese?'

'Oh I shouldn't worry too much, old man. Things will soon settle down now. Anyway, *you* won't have to worry. And how are things at the *Posto*? Your wife? She's keeping well?'

'Very well.' Macedo was irritated. What did he mean *he* didn't have to worry? 'Look, what I mean to say is what is going to happen when these Japanese arrive here?'

'Oh yes? Well, it won't affect us, will it, old man? I know these people. They're a civilized race. They understand business matters and while we are here to oil the wheels we should all get along pretty well, I would say. They need us.' He shared a slight smile, showing a glint of gold teeth. 'I fear the same cannot be said for our Australian and Dutch protectors. Now that Singapore has fallen – '

'What's that? Singapore, did you say?'

'Surrendered, old man. Just like that.' He paused reflectively. 'Curious, isn't it? One little push and the whole British Empire just came tumbling down. India will be next, they say.' He gave Macedo an indulgent pat on the shoulder. 'We live in interesting times, my friend. We must all learn to swim with the tide now.' He cast a swift glance at his gold fob watch and made his apology. 'Must dash, old man. Van Straten the Dutchman is waiting for me. Though what I can do for the fellow now – well, even I cannot be expected to work miracles!'

Macedo remained standing in the street, the sun beating down on his neck and shoulders. He removed his panama, pushing back his lank hair, still taking in the news about the fall of Singapore.

Now, certainly, there was nothing holding the Japanese back. They must surely have swept through all the Indies to have reached Timor. The British had not even put up a fight, they had surrendered. And what of the Dutch? Their Empire in the islands was almost as old as Portugal's. How could the work of so many centuries crumble overnight?

Sweat began to roll down his back and legs as he walked in the direction Sassoon had taken. There were more people in the square now, sharing the same anxious, excited air of anticipation. He found himself swept along, hearing the commotion at the crossroads that could only mean one thing: the Japanese were coming.

He tried to get through the crush of Timorese but he was jostled and elbowed in the ribs as the crowd surged forward, eager to see the victors for themselves. It was an extraordinary thing for Macedo to find himself buried among the sweating, straining masses of natives. On their gleaming faces he saw for the first time a chilling disregard for all he represented. In their dark eyes he saw a message he feared to interpret.

A fever of anticipation seized them as the sound of grinding armoured cars grew louder. Around the corner there appeared a convoy of troop carriers. It was Macedo's first sight of the Japanese who had conquered half of Asia. Like the crowd straining for a better view, he was disappointed.

Such little men. There was little of the heroic or revolutionary in the squat, khaki-clad figures clutching bayonet rifles almost as tall as themselves. They were untidy and sweating in their coarse puttees, web-toed canvas boots and criss-crossed belts. Their pudding-basin battle helmets had dangling neck flaps, hanging like the lank ears of a listless puppy on to their shoulders. But these flat moonlike faces betrayed nothing. Sweat-drenched, sallow-skinned, their faces half shadowed by their combat helmets, they were alien.

There was a great deal of shouting as erratic figures moved behind the front ranks. The local crowd stood in silence watching everything, watching and waiting. Asia for the

Asians. That was their message, wasn't it? The Japanese were here as self-styled liberators to crush colonial power and expel foreign, that is, European, armies. If the Dutch and Australians had kept out of Portuguese Timor the Japanese would have had no reason to invade, would they?

The leading armoured car arrived at the crossroads. It crashed its gears, smoke belching as it came to an abrupt stop. The flat-footed Japanese moved towards the crowd with their curious rolling gait. Using their rifles with a display of indiscriminate contempt they beat them back about the heads and shoulders, forcing a path for their officers. And the crowd took it, for what else could they do?

Macedo, clutching a bruised shoulder in the crush, found himself looking into the eyes of his neighbours. They too had received blows from the liberators, but used as they were to beatings from their white masters the light in their eyes was not of resentment. It was pure exultation.

They were delighted to see him, one of the great *tuans* in his so-smart white suit, cradling a blow delivered by an Asian. He saw in their faces triumph and a burning hope. Then he knew that they believed it all. Asia for the Asians. This was how empires fell.

An uneasy calm settled itself on the town. In the next few days the Japanese High Command came to some formal agreement with the Portuguese governor. He was becoming expert in accommodating invading armies who vowed they would not trespass on Portugal's neutrality.

The rigid formalities and contorted niceties of the Japanese negotiations amazed even tradition-bound Portuguese bureaucrats. They were under no illusion that they were dealing with unyielding veteran troops, the marines of the Japanese 38th Division who had taken Hong Kong, and everyone knew what had happened at Hong Kong.

There was little they could do in the face of sweeping new changes in everyday life. Japanese time was to be introduced throughout the Co-Prosperity Sphere, one and a half hours ahead of local time. Not only this, but the very year was to change. No longer was it 1942 but the Japanese year 2602. All newspapers, all official documents would bear this date, as all business transactions would be affected by the introduction of Japanese currency.

When the Japanese brought forward their dead from the initial battle at the aerodrome, Macedo heard how their ideology infected even their attitude towards the dead. While their own troops were accorded a massive funeral pyre flanked by an honour guard, and later sent home to Japan in little white boxes, the six corpses of the Australian casualties must still bear the weight of their enemy's contempt. The bodies were laid out for cremation but soil was then carefully arranged to leave the heads, arms and legs uncovered.

'Then only those parts which burn will ascend to heaven,' said an eye witness. 'They believe that in the next world the Australians will be less than men.'

'Barbaric!'

'It is their belief,' affirmed the bystander simply. 'They are very different to us, after all.'

The liberators of Timor soon made free with the more material aspects of life in Dili. Protected only by diplomacy, the Portuguese could only watch as Japanese troops looted the houses of less fortunate Dutch and English neighbours which had been left abandoned. Some Europeans had vanished overnight into internment, herded into the backs of lorries or force marched into some unseen prison camp. The lucky ones had fled into the hills just in time.

The Japanese made no pretence. Trucks were driven up to the wrought-iron gateways, the Japanese loading everything that took their fancy, from the heavy velvet curtains to ornate ladies' dressing tables. Though what use the marines might have had for abandoned dress suits three sizes too large was beyond the furtive audience watching from behind half-closed shutters.

'It will be us next,' said a guest at the hotel.

'Nonsense! We have come to some arrangement. They will respect our neutrality.' But although he hotly denied this prophecy in public, Jaime Macedo had seen the underlying depth of nationalism among the people that only waited to be tapped.

There was evidence all around. The Asians were all too willing to ingratiate themselves with the new masters by denouncing their old masters. People were arrested or shot as they ran down the street. The foreign enclave was in a state of hysteria, of infectious panic. Outside the Hotel Portugal a body lay in the gutter for a week, face down in the dust.

The streets were lined by jeering crowds whenever Dutch prisoners were marched off to internment. Some waved Japanese flags in their faces, fickle opportunists for the most part. The more ardent nationalists watched the Japanese with cynical detachment, thinking their lot little improved.

In the end it was Sassoon who helped Macedo to leave. As *chefe do posto* it was argued that his presence was essential at the plantation to ensure law and order among the native workers. A travel warrant was issued promptly. The Japanese had concentrated their forces on the narrow coastal plain, only tentatively venturing into the high hill country. The mountains beyond were unknown territory, possibly swarming with dangerous retreating Australian troops.

'They need someone they can trust up there,' Sassoon explained, 'but our work must continue as usual. You have to understand that they would be most displeased if your production figures dropped because of trouble with your native labour. But as I told them, that Macedo is a good sort. He knows the tribes up there. He's used to handling them. You won't have any trouble if he is allowed to go home, I said.'

Macedo swallowed his pride and took the warrant eagerly. There was nothing for him in Dili now among such clever men.

He prudently found himself a pennant flag of the Republic and flew it from the front of his car with conscious ostentation. He saw no shame in his neutral status, only safety. He drove out of town past the deserted, looted villas of former friends without a backward glance.

At each and every road block he faced the close scrutiny of the Japanese sentries with tolerance and growing courage. Sassoon's papers passed the test time and time again. The Japanese cordon was left behind as he climbed beyond the belt of garden resorts in the cool hills above Dili. The pastel flower-fronted villas with their red roofs and delicate wrought-iron balconies seemed too comfortable to be true. Here among the mellow brickwork, the vines and potted plants, the governor had his villa. Here the diplomats of the old order had come to recuperate and escape the Wet down in Dili. Among the greenery white gum trees stood sentinel above a dazzling vista to the sea below.

With the fresh breeze in his face Macedo turned his car on to the mountain road. For half an hour he climbed, the setting sun hastening his approach to the convent. With panic-stricken Australians wild in the countryside, probably in fear of their lives, it was no time to be lighting up the roads at night.

Macedo was sure of a warm welcome from Mother Teresa. She had known his family for years and he had made it his habit to call in whenever he made the journey to Dili. He wished this time he had brought something other than war news.

As he alighted he stood a moment to breathe in the scents of the evening. The church and convent buildings stood in the shadow of the vast ridge of mountains, wrapt in a blue embrace. Frangipani trees spouting red and pink stars grew in abundance and in the terraced gardens were white oleanders and purple and orange bougainvillea perfuming the rising wind.

The buildings were more than two centuries old, the walls a honeyed hue, with tiny balconies and dark green shutters. The tinkling bells of the wind chimes drifted across the yard to draw him in. Nothing had changed, then. All was as it should be.

One of the native women fetched him to the Mother Superior. In those calm precincts he felt an intruder, treading in the dust of his journey and bringing with him the odour of conflict.

Left in the hallway scented with beeswax, he waited impatiently, pacing the tiled floor until a footstep made him turn.

'Jaime!'

Cushioned in the soft embrace, he slipped once more into the blissful security of childhood. Mother Teresa was his guardian, his protectress. She never changed.

'Eva and the children?'

He told her how eager he was to be back with them, how much he longed to be home. He wanted to have simple things to tell her, all the ordinary everyday tittle-tattle that amused her on other occasions. But, as if she caught the tension in his manner, she went straight to the heart of affairs.

'Will they occupy the whole island, do you think?'

In her bright eyes there was no denying the real state of things. They sat down together, his voice dropping to a whisper, straining as he related all he had seen in past days.

'It is very good that you are going home,' she said at last, taking his brown hand in hers. 'Eva should not be alone just now.'

'Yes, I fear the Australians. Have you seen anything of them here, *Māe?*'

She looked at him from beneath hooded eyes, eyes of a soft grey and vivid clarity. 'The Australians were very sick with malaria, you know. Their Major Spence brought many poor men into the hills to get well again.'

She paused significantly and Macedo's heart leapt within him with fear.

'But not here? Surely not here?'

'Of course, when we heard that the Japanese were landing, those fit enough to travel made their way to join the rest of their forces, going deep into the mountains.' She saw the fear on Macedo's face begin to fade. 'But,' she added, increasing her pressure on his hand, 'but not all were well enough to go.'

Macedo pulled his hand free and stared at her. '*Māe*, what are you saying?'

'Upstairs I have two Australian officers and one other soldier who came later. The officers were too sick to be moved with their men.'

'You mean that they're here now?' He was on his feet.

'And the English ladies.'

'*What* English ladies?'

'The refugees from Singapore,' she reported in her most matter-of-fact style. 'Now you see why we need you here so much, my son.'

Chapter Fifteen

'*Estás doido?*'

He had forgotten himself. One look at her face showed that he had overstepped the mark this time.

'*Desculpe, Mãe*, I'm sorry. But I can't believe it. How could you do such a thing? Don't you realize the danger? How could you be so – so stupid?'

She had turned her back on him, standing still and silent before the shuttered window. Her white robes hung like long folded wings.

Macedo sunk down on to one of the heavily carved Chinese chairs that graced the mother superior's study. He had never felt so old and exhausted. He ran a hand through his lank dark hair, resenting bitterly this unwanted extra burden. Hadn't he enough to worry about? His wife and two small children were up there in the hills, alone except for the servants, and those Australians were on the run. Who knew what was happening at the posto without him? And now Mother Teresa wanted him to sort out these problems, all of her own making.

He realized all too well that she had shared her secret with him for one reason only. She wanted his support with the government authorities.

'The Australians pressured you into this.' He spoke his thoughts out loud. 'The rest of their army has disappeared and those who remain must follow them, and quickly.'

'That may not be possible. One of the officers is still very sick – '

'I wouldn't give five *escudos* for their chances if they remain here.' He looked round at her in exasperation. 'You don't seem to understand. The Australians and Dutch are defeated.

They have been run out of Dili by the Japanese and they will be thrown off the island. You cannot harbour them here, don't you see?'

'But the women refugees – '

For a moment he had forgotten the women.

'This is ridiculous. How on earth did they get here?'

Mother Teresa spread her hands as if the fault was not all hers. 'The ship that brought them from Singapore was attacked by Japanese aircraft at sea. It had to put into Dili for repairs. All the passengers were sent ashore. The authorities would not allow them to stay in Dili. They were sent to various places – the four here were sent to us, and we had to take them in.'

'What happened to their ship?'

'I don't know. It was in very bad condition. The women hoped later to find another ship to take them on to Australia or even back to Singapore.'

'Singapore has fallen,' said Macedo.

The Mother Superior drew in her breath. He saw her quick glance across the courtyard, no doubt towards the rooms where the Englishwomen lay. How was she going to break the news to them?

'There is no stopping them, you see,' said Macedo sullenly. 'We must accept the fact and come to terms. They will be here soon enough.'

Mother Teresa stared at him, her eyes widening. 'But surely they will respect God's mission?'

'Their god is not our god, *Māe*.'

She took a moment to digest this most unpalatable information.

'But we are Portuguese,' she reminded him. 'We are still neutral in this dreadful conflict, are we not?'

Macedo sighed deeply and looked troubled. 'From what I have seen in Dili, the Japanese have little respect for foreigners. Any foreigners. And when they discover you have their enemies hiding here – '

'But how should they learn that, my son? Who is going to tell them?'

He felt her hot eye of suspicion on him and shuffled uncomfortably. 'Not I, certainly,' he said swiftly. 'But you have many native servants here.'

'Whom I trust, my son.'

'You are too trusting, *Māe*. I know these people. You are in very great danger, please believe me.'

From the first he had known they would not get on together.

'Ford? Irish, isn't it?' the officer had asked, his soft pink face expressionless.

In the sudden silence the overhead fan clicked round remorselessly, shuffling the stale air.

'My grandfather was Irish, yes,' said Jack, ready to make something of it.

'Yes,' said the officer, 'I thought that was it.'

Jack waited, expecting something more, but Captain Robert Fielding hardly looked at him. Since his bad bout of malaria he had seemed distant and preoccupied, his mind wandering. Jack had never really had a chance to talk since his arrival but now he thought Fielding would open up to him. After all, there had to be a good five years' difference in their ages.

'Robert, is it?'

Fielding looked over at him, his blue eyes round and childlike with surprise. He always seemed to have a look of slightly anxious intensity, pushing back his pale yellow hair from his forehead.

'Call you Bob, do they?'

The captain was startled into response. 'I don't think that – '

'I'm Jack to all my mates, never John.'

Fielding took in this information with a solemn nod. His thin, long mouth compressed into a stubborn line. He looked uncomfortable in his crumpled uniform as though it was not his but borrowed. Dark patches of sweat stained the jacket although it was now a lot cooler. He still showed signs of the malaria.

'Yes,' he murmured, 'yes, but of course our situation here is somewhat changed. We cannot forget that we are at war,' he added, drawing himself up. 'Whatever our circumstances, we're bound to maintain some sense of discipline, some formality – corporal.'

Jack swallowed down his natural response. If that was the way he wanted it, right enough. He'd seen that type before.

Among the Australians sheltering at the convent Jack had soon discovered that he ranked last.

Originally, it seemed, there had been a major commanding the contingent left behind. Mostly they were malaria cases, brought down with the illness in the foul swamplands outside Dili. But through some complication the major had died – as it happened on the very day of the Japanese invasion – leaving just two officers behind at the convent: the delirious Lieutenant Davison and Captain Robert Fielding of Headquarters Staff, aged just twenty-three, in charge.

It was an exhausting, irritating place, so different to Singapore. The heat and the effort required to do the least little thing sapped all energy. Phyllis had lost her appetite and spent nearly all her time in the small cell-like room she shared with Katherine.

The people meant well, of course, but really, they had no idea. Imagine even suggesting that all the women should sleep in the same room. Before she could speak out, the Chinese woman herself had pointed out the problem. She gave her credit for realizing her position at last.

'It is for her own good,' she announced as Amy departed. 'She will be better off away with her own kind.'

It was quite a surprise therefore when the American woman packed up her things and left after her. It wasn't as though they had even known each other very long. But then Americans were always behaving in such eccentric ways – and besides, it left all the more room for Katherine and herself.

How long would they remain here? The pace of life was so different, far worse than Singapore. Always *amanhã*, *amanhã*, and no one told you anything. What was happening?

The nuns crept about the place in summons to the endless bells, twitching their rosaries, moving like silent giant moths in the shadows. The Mother Superior had not been to see them for days. She sent instead that knowing little native woman with her food on a tray.

Mrs Beattie had long ago given up eating with the rest of the guests at the convent. Of the Australians only the captain had made any impression.

'You can hardly tell he is Australian,' she told Katherine

approvingly. 'He has almost no accent at all.'

The other Australian, who was only a corporal and should not have been eating with them at all, she described scathingly as 'little better than a navvy'.

But Katherine's loyalty to Mrs Beattie was strained almost beyond limit by her self-imposed segregation. She tried her best to try to convey her desire for friendship, hanging around the American woman and trying to strike up conversation. But everyone seemed to regard her as 'one of the Englishwomen' and her resentment against Mrs Beattie grew.

Although Lieutenant Davison was still very sick and confined to his bed, the captain was on his feet again and could be found often sitting on the verandah in the inner courtyard, reading. Kate admired his gift for languages. There was nothing among the sisters' meagre collection of books in English. Once or twice she asked him to read aloud to her, translating as he went along. It was amusing for a while, but he soon grew tired, smiling up at her in apology.

When she went looking for Fielding the evening of Macedo's arrival she found him in the company of Corporal Ford, the Portuguese who had arrived with him, and Dede Harriman.

Letria had brought the news of the night's new arrival. He had the facts from one of the native nurses with whom he had struck up some kind of friendship. That way he had more chance to learn what was going on in the outside world.

'Who is this Macedo?'

'It seems he's a *chefe do posto* up country somewhere.'

'A *chefe* – ? What's that, some kind of native bigwig?'

A faintly derisive smile touched Letria's lips. 'He would not be amused to hear you, my friend. No, he is Portuguese. He runs a plantation up in the mountains and looks after native affairs in the district for the governor.'

The captain seized upon this piece of information eagerly. 'So he's going up into the mountains? Surely he could act as guide for us at least part of the way?'

'Certainly that is what the Mother Superior will be asking him now,' confirmed Letria. 'She has a persuasive tongue, by all accounts.'

'Your little nurse is a mine of information,' grinned Jack.

The warmth fled from Letria's face and he looked around the circle of attentive faces with apprehension. 'I'd better tell you.'

'Tell us what?'

'I didn't mention it before – '

'What are you talking about?'

'They are saying that Singapore has been taken.'

There was stunned silence in the room. Only the noise of the whirring overhead fan punctuated speechless horror. Dede knew what the news meant to the others. She had felt the same way herself as one by one the islands had fallen into Japanese hands. But Fielding was unwilling to take the news at face value. He turned with sudden anger on the Portuguese.

'No, you're wrong. It can't be true.'

'Surrendered, they say,' Letria insisted.

'Surrendered? Never!'

'Perhaps it's a mistake. Your friend got it wrong.'

But Letria shook his head. 'The *chefe* brought the news himself. In Dili the Japanese were boasting of it.'

'Ah, well, that's it,' said Jack. 'The buggers are just trying to rile us. It's all lies.'

'Propaganda,' added Fielding.

'No, I don't think so.' Letria almost wished that he had kept his bad news to himself. 'The British have surrendered in Singapore and the Dutch in Batavia. The Miri and Lutong oilfields must all be in Japanese hands now. They have it all.'

Dede knew there was no point in arguing. Amazing as it seemed, she had seen the collapse of the Dutch in Borneo for herself. Then there had been no time to stand around arguing and now she knew there was only one priority.

'When do we get out of here?'

Fielding turned and looked at her with his startled blue eyes. 'Look, Miss Harriman, I know that the situation seems pretty grim at the moment, but this is just a bad phase we're going through, that's all.'

Letria was exasperated. 'Dili is in Japanese hands,' he announced bitterly. 'They have a firm hold on the capital and look set to move up country at any moment.'

'Then she's right,' Jack declared, with a quick sideways

glance at Dede. 'The sooner we get out of this place the better. All of us.'

'I agree,' Dede added. 'I don't want to get caught here. I've run enough already but I'm damned if I'm going to give up now.'

Kate looked at her in admiration, wishing that she had enough courage to speak up for herself like that.

Finding himself outvoted, Fielding accepted the inevitable.

'Then we must move directly. Perhaps I should talk to Macedo myself. Try and convince him – '

God forbid, thought Jack.

'I don't think that's a very good idea,' said Letria pointedly, coming to the rescue.

Fielding's look of reproach confirmed Jack's earlier impression that the captain somehow resented the Portuguese's presence.

'What I mean,' Letria continued, 'is that we should leave this matter to the Mother Superior. She knows Macedo. She's known him for years and believe me, she will be as anxious as we are to get us away from here.'

Dede stood outside on the verandah, breathing in the cool night air. The lilting sounds of the wind chimes and the soft scents of the waxen frangipani did little to soothe her anxiety. She had to get away by herself, with time to think. She felt trapped and claustrophobic, almost on the verge of panic.

Whatever happens, I must get out of this place, she told herself. She knew that the Portuguese authorities had sent them to the convent because they did not know what to do with the women refugees. They could expect no help from the Portuguese. If they wanted to get out of here, they must do it themselves.

She turned sharply, startled by a footstep behind her.

'I'm sorry if I scared you,' said Jack Ford.

He leaned against the mellow wall, watching her. He wore his faded greens with the sleeves rolled up above the elbows, long-limbed and casual. His bright eyes met hers and when she said nothing, he took it as an invitation to join her, leaning over the rail of the wooden verandah.

'Don't worry. We won't let the Nips catch us. You'll be safe enough.'

She turned to face him and a slow smile took him by surprise. There was something about her that had made him follow her. He liked the way she had spoken up for herself back there.

'Well, thank you,' she said, looking up at him with her fine dark eyes. 'Thank you very much, Corporal.' The way she said his rank ought to have warned him. 'It's very reassuring to know that you'll be there to rescue the women when the time comes.'

'Look, I – '

'But I hear that when your life was on the line back in Dili, it was Sister Eulalia who came and saved you from a fate worse than death.' She looked up and saw the confusion on his thin, handsome face. She gave him a crooked smile. 'I guess I'll just look after myself, if you don't mind.'

And with that she turned and left him standing there in the dark, stunned, wondering what he had said that was wrong.

'There is only one solution as I see it,' said Macedo. 'Those who are fit to travel must leave. The others' – he shrugged – 'they must take their chance.'

'But where can they go, my son?'

'They must try to find the rest of their countrymen. They have taken to the mountains somewhere, trying to escape the Japanese.'

Mother Teresa looked doubtful. 'The mountains are dangerous, even if you know them well. How can they go there without a guide? They do not even speak Portuguese or Tetum.'

Macedo was becoming more and more irritated. He did not want to be rude to the Mother Superior but his patience was wearing thin.

'No one asked them to come here. Let them find themselves a guide, someone who knows the mountains, who knows the trails – '

'As you know them.'

She saw at once that her inference had horrified him, but she could not afford to let that deter her. 'You could guide them,

Jaime. You are travelling there yourself. You know the area well and all they need is some guidance. Set them on their way, that is all I am asking you.'

But he was shaking his head violently, up from his chair and pacing the room. 'What you ask is impossible.'

She saw she was in danger of losing him. 'Please, Jaime, listen to me – '

He turned to face her, his eyes small and bitter behind his steel-rimmed spectacles. 'You don't know what you're asking.'

'Should we stand aside with our arms folded and do nothing to help them?'

'It is not our war.'

She saw then how much he had changed from the young man she used to know. Had Father Jacinto been there he might have moved him. He had always been able to persuade him, ever since he was Jaime's form teacher so many years ago. But Father Jacinto was up country buying new pack animals from the mountain people and no one could say when he would return.

God give me strength to convince him, she prayed, turning her eyes upon the ivory crucifix washed red in the light of the dying sun.

Outside, a native woman moved along the verandah and lit a paraffin lamp in the hallway. She moved soft-footed as a cat, her silhouette molten in the lamplight, her hair secured by a high comb, wearing a long-sleeved *kebaya*, graceful and silent. The night was perfumed with heavy blossom. The rising wind stirred the curtain at the window where they sat.

After a long moment he said quietly, 'Do you realize the danger you put me in?'

'I pray you will change your mind, my son.'

Macedo threw her a look of bitter reproach. 'I have my family to think about.'

'And these men and women, they too have families.' She rose to her feet, fighting down her anger and disappointment. 'Sleep well tonight and think on it, Jaime. I know that God will guide you to do what is right. We will talk again in the morning.'

As the door closed behind her, Macedo sat hunched and

solitary in the shadowed room, weary and racked by doubt.

So, Singapore had gone. It was really true then, despite all their proud protestations that it was the invincible island fortress. Even in those last days, with the bombs raining down like a monsoon, that surety, that sense of superiority had hardly been dented.

Looking in on the sleeping figure of Phyllis Beattie behind her protective wall of netting, Kate wondered if the shock would kill her.

Throughout their flight south between the islands, through bombing and shelling, as their own fortunes had gone from bad to worse, the thought of her family safe if besieged in Singapore had kept Phyllis Beattie going.

She had been Kate's anchor in a sea of strange fears and uncertainties, even here in this remote and alien island a thousand miles from civilization.

As she sat by Phyllis's bedside wondering if she should wake her, Kate found it hard to imagine that the Singapore life style was lost for ever. Hard to imagine the pint-sized men she had seen on the China newsreels riding their bicycles down Battery Road. Hard to believe that the Rising Sun now flew above Raffles Place and that the men who had so confidently sent their wives and children away could now be prisoners of an Asian empire.

What had become of them all? Of Raymond Beattie and Suzy, whose place she had taken? It could have been her there, prisoner of the Japanese – and pregnant.

She shivered with terror at the thought. And what of Harry? For so long she had denied herself all thought of him, afraid to open up the floodgates of despair. But she could not imagine Harry Beattie a prisoner of anyone. How would he ever survive?

Tears pricked at the corners of her eyes but she fought hard not to give way. She thought of her brother, poor Tony who alone had predicted disaster. If he was with Harry then they might pull through together.

But I'm still free, she thought. The Japanese won't get me or my baby. I won't give up hope now.

She looked down at Mrs Beattie, suddenly full of

resentment. She had been protected, cushioned against the real world. Perhaps she had had it all too easy.

Not like me, thought Kate. She seemed to have spent all her life running away. Running from poverty and the London Blitz, running from Singapore. And now, it seemed, running here on Timor to escape the Japanese.

When would the running finally stop? And how much longer would the luck that had brought her so far last?

Chapter Sixteen

Fielding entered the breakfast room with a brisk step, ready to get right down to business and prove his leadership to the others. He looked straight at Letria.

'Where is the mother superior? I ought to see her at once to put our point of view.'

Dede noticed that Letria was less than enthusiastic about Fielding's plan. He remained sitting in his wicker chair, his dark face surly and sceptical.

'I don't think that will make a lot of difference – now,' he said slowly, waiting until he had the attention of everyone in the room. 'He's gone.'

'*What?*'

Letria's sharp pale eyes flashed in the captain's direction. 'Macedo was up and away while they were all at mass. He obviously didn't want to face the old lady.'

Jack swore and was rebuked by a stern look from the captain. He looked round and saw Kate and Dede standing there and quickly apologized with a sheepish smile. 'G'day, ladies. Didn't see you there.'

'Thanks a lot.' Dede turned her back on him and looked back to Letria, surprised by his quiet acquiescence.

But the captain was far from acquiescent. His soft young boy's face had flushed an unhealthy red as he confronted Letria.

'Did you see him go? Didn't he leave any word behind?'

'It's clear that he wanted no part in this business.'

'Whose side is he on?' Fielding exploded.

'His own, clearly.' Letria shrugged. 'There's nothing we can do about it.'

'But surely – '

The Portuguese was on his feet, suddenly irritated beyond measure and impatient with Fielding.

'Fear can change a man, Captain, don't you see that? Why should he put his life in danger to help us? The Japanese would take revenge on him and his family.'

'You mean he saved his own skin,' said Jack.

'How can you blame him?' Letria demanded. 'You saw what the Japanese did to your own people, unarmed and surrendered. They roped them together and bayoneted them to death – ' He heard the sharp intake of breath from Mrs Beattie and Katherine close behind him. 'Yes, ladies, I am sorry to be the one to make you face the truth. The Japanese do not play this war by the rules.'

'It's true that Japan is not a signatory to the Geneva Convention,' said Fielding, 'but – '

'So the little rat ran away,' Dede interrupted. 'Surely the question now is how the hell we get away from here?'

'Thank you very much, Miss Harriman!' Fielding said in fury, 'What we decide to do is my responsibility. I have to consider all our safety – '

Dede was ready to argue with him. She did not want any army officer telling her what to do. And he wasn't even an American. He might well outrank Jack Ford, but she wasn't about to forget that, except for Kate and Amy, Fielding was the youngest of them all.

The uncertainty of their position was written clearly on Mother Teresa's face as news of Macedo's hasty departure was made known to her. With bowed head she said softly, 'I would never have believed it of him.' Looking up, she added with unconcealed desperation, 'If only Father Jacinto had been here. He, of all people, could have made him listen.'

They were forced at last to realize the very real danger they now faced.

Ironically, the very day that saw Jaime Macedo slip away at dawn saw the return of Father Jacinto at sundown.

As the priest rode into the yard with a string of pack ponies and a number of native boys, the nuns and their unquiet guests came out on to the open verandah to watch. Their eagerness must have conveyed itself to the elderly priest as he saw their craning figures. He sat his pony with his long white soutane tucked up about his stout boots for easy riding. He was shaded by a large-brimmed straw hat that framed his weathered face like a halo. His long thin legs almost brushed the ground on either side of the sturdy little Timor pony, and his height was apparent as he dismounted, stretched, and then strode purposefully across to the mother superior.

Close to, his lined brown face gave little away about his age. He could have been anything from forty to seventy, although everyone knew he had been a teacher in Dili for years before he came to the mountains. He stopped to talk to Mother Teresa and shared a quick word with Sister Eulalia, looking across at the group of Europeans with his bright shrewd gaze.

When he marched across to meet the strangers who stood together and silent at the far end of the verandah, they were surprised to find he spoke English very fast in a heavy Portuguese accent.

'I am sorry to find you here,' he said bluntly. 'We must do our best to get you away as soon as possible.'

Fielding exchanged a look with his fellow Australian and Jack knew that their presence there was the source of danger.

Seeing the Mother Superior's and the priest's anxious deliberations that evening made Dede all the more aware of their danger. She realized for the first time that the convent's very existence was at stake because of their presence. Fear struck her with an almost physical sensation. She felt sick to her stomach and Amy watched her with anxious concern.

'You're not ill are you? I couldn't bear you to be ill now, Dede. You're my only friend here.'

Dede looked down at the beautiful face and saw she was on the verge of tears. Amy needed her, looked up to her. She couldn't let her see how frightened she was herself. She had to try to be strong for both of them.

'No, I'm not ill, Amy. It's all right,' she reassured her. 'It's just my time of the month, I guess.' She gave a faint laugh. 'Trust me to pick a time like this.'

She put an arm around the frail shoulders of her new friend and hardly knew whether she was supporting Amy or the girl was supporting her. They were so different, from such dissimilar backgrounds, and yet now perhaps they needed each other in order to get out of the trap that was rapidly closing about them.

Father Jacinto himself insisted on taking them south into the mountains to search for the remnants of the main Australian forces. Since Macedo had left them high and dry there was simply no one else capable of leading such a party into the high vastness of the central massif.

'But we must not delay our departure any further,' he told the collected refugees the next morning. 'The Japanese may be here any day now.'

'We realize that, Father,' said Fielding, 'and yet I am reluctant to take the ladies along with us.'

His objection surprised and alarmed the women, whom he had not consulted. Dede shared a look of furious reproach with Katherine who was obviously of the same mind.

'It will be a long hard journey in this heat,' Fielding added hastily.

'It will be harder still to leave them here,' said Letria acidly.

'You can't leave them for the Nips,' Jack added, leaning over the back of Fielding's chair. 'We can't cut out and leave them here.'

'I thought perhaps they would be better off without us, Corporal. The presence of the army could make the convent a target, but without us – '

'Yes?' Dede demanded. 'What do you think they'd do with us? Remember I saw what they did to civilians in Borneo.'

'And we all know what happened to the women left in Hong Kong,' said Kate with horror. She turned to look at Sister Eulalia. 'Including the nuns.'

'She is right, my son,' said Sister Eulalia. 'This is not for you to decide. If the women choose to go, how can you deny them?'

Everyone turned and looked at Phyllis Beattie. She had been sitting listening to the argument with an air of detachment, as though the problems that were facing everyone else in the room somehow did not apply to her. But now she was aware that she held centre stage and seemed determined to make the most of it.

'I assure you,' she said calmly, 'that we are all very well aware of our weaknesses. We may be women, young man,' she told Fielding, 'but we are not prepared to give up without a struggle. I did not come all the way from Singapore' – as she said the word she seemed to hesitate slightly as though remembering the dreadful news – 'from Singapore,' she continued, her chin a little higher, 'in order to give in to the Japanese here. Nor am I willing to sit out this war in some dreadful internment camp. It is quite out of the question.' She gave him a condescending smile. 'I think you have your answer.'

'Yes, indeed, ma'am,' the captain replied, showing his admiration for her spirit. 'If that is the decision of all the ladies, then of course I will abide by it.'

Father Jacinto looked around the group, his mind already calculating and planning for the journey.

'We will be a large party, will we not? Sister Eulalia has agreed to accompany us as she is a trained nurse and may help.'

The news was greeted with enthusiasm by everyone.

'Good on you,' said Jack warmly, beaming at the sister. He had been concerned about her staying behind at the convent, her future in the balance. After all he owed her, he wanted to see that she got safely away.

Kate was equally pleased. She did not expect for one moment that they would still be on the island when her time came. She hoped and prayed that no one would ever have to know about her condition, especially Mrs Beattie. She had pushed the thought of it to the back of her mind, but it was certainly a comfort to know that someone with medical expertise would be with them on the journey.

'Yes, it will be difficult,' Father Jacinto was saying, 'but we will have our guide, Moita-Ka, with us as far as his village.'

'Motor Car?' laughed Jack as the priest brought the native boy forward.

'*Tabe, tuan.*'

He could not have been more than twelve or thirteen years of age. He was short and thin as a rake, with angular narrow shoulders and awkward elbows sticking out of a western-style vest. He had wild frizzled hair and a most engaging grin, showing reddened lips and teeth stained black from chewing betel nut.

'Moita-Ka is the son of a mountain *lirai*, one of the senior chieftains. He comes here to mission school, isn't that right, Moita-Ka?'

'I talk English fine. *Português*, Tetum, some Malay. Everything people talk I talk.'

'*And* he knows the mountain trails,' said the priest. 'Don't be under any illusion that the way is not difficult. There are no roads where we are going. Although Timor is only a small island, perhaps sixty miles to the coast, between us and the south are mountains more than ten thousand feet high. We shall try to go round, but where it is impossible, then we must climb.' He paused and then, just when their spirits were at a low ebb, he added jauntily, 'Just thank the Lord that it is the dry season. In the Wet we should be cut off by many dangerous rivers.'

'Sixty miles,' said Jack as the group split up. 'It's not so far. We're bound to find our blokes before then.'

'Yes, it sounds pretty hopeful, doesn't it?' Fielding agreed. 'Even with the ladies along, I expect we shall be safe in, what? – a month at the most?'

'Well, six weeks at a stretch,' said Jack. 'Won't that be something?'

But listening to the Australians, Sister Eulalia knew they had a lot to learn about Timor. She gave Letria a wan smile.

'You know the saying, Daniel? "Pray to God but keep rowing to the shore." We'd better keep rowing.'

With the assistance of the nuns the pack ponies were made ready for the exodus. The Timorese used horses on the high mountain trails, riding skilfully on the narrow ridges without the use of saddles or bridles, hanging on to the stringy manes, their legs straddling almost to the ground. The sturdy little ponies were the only means of reaching some of the distant mountain districts. Father Jacinto was an expert rider, travelling often into the remote interior on mission business. There were few other white men who dared to venture so far.

He displayed his particular flair for management as he took charge of the preparations for departure. He devised reins and saddle-cloths for the ponies, issuing instructions to Jack and Letria. He soon discovered that Jack knew as much about horses as he did himself and was pleased to use his expertise to pick out rides for less experienced members of the party.

'Don't tell me,' Jack said quickly before Dede could speak. 'You know all about horses. You were born in the saddle and don't need my help.'

'What's the matter with you? Do you imagine all Americans are still cowhands, or what?' She actually made him blush. 'Let me tell you there isn't much horse-breaking going on in Pasadena any more.'

He didn't have the faintest idea where Pasadena was or what it was like, but he did know a put-down when he heard it. Clearly she was used to much better things than he would ever know, and how was she to guess that a cowhand was exactly what he had been in Australia?

'I'm sorry, I'm sure,' he snapped back, feeling a fool. 'We can't all be so clever. I'll leave you to it.'

Damn, damn, damn, thought Dede as she watched him walk away. Why do I always open my big mouth? She was left facing the rogue eye of her selected mount, wondering how to show him who was boss.

'Here, horse. Nice horse!'

The Mother Superior found the young captain hunched over the bedside of Lieutenant Davison. The air in the room was stale with sickness and sweat stood out on the neck and face of the sleeping patient.

Fielding turned sharply, aware of her presence close behind him. He got quickly to his feet, full of rash, nervous movement.

Again she thought that he was little more than a boy, really. Too young perhaps to bear such responsibility. She knew what he was doing here. She read the doubt in his eyes before he looked back to the bedside.

'Lieutenant Davison is too weak to make the journey.'

'But you must know what the Japs will do if they find him here? They will hold you responsible, Mother. Don't you realize? And look what they did to the wounded in Hong Kong.'

Meeting her eyes he saw the first signs of fear and uncertainty as he pushed home the point. He told her how the Japanese had overrun the Crown Colony at Christmas, bayoneting the sick in their beds at the hospital, raping and killing the nurses, and at Eucliffe Castle they forced the men of the Royal Rifles over the cliffs on to rocks hundreds of feet below.

'They were drunk. They did not spare anyone.'

'That may be so, my son. But I am too old to be killed. I will stay with Lieutenant Davison. We are all in God's hands. He will protect us.'

Fielding looked at her doubtfully but she took pity on him.

'When God gives hard bread, He gives sharp teeth too.' She sent him away with more pity for his youth than fear for her own future. 'A word of advice only. Do not think too much about the dangers ahead. It is best not to be too prepared for matters of this kind.'

Fielding arrived back in the courtyard after his guilty farewell with Davison. He was deeply troubled in spite of the Mother Superior's kind words. He felt that the decision to leave Davison behind had been thrust upon him and that it was not the right thing to do. He felt responsible for what might happen to Davison after they left him behind.

He watched the others loading the horses with medical supplies, food and water, but his mind was still back in the sickroom. Sister Eulalia quickly noticed the distracted look on his face and joined him under the shade of the verandah. 'It is very hot.'

'Yes, indeed.' His eyes wandered across the men working in the yard. 'Though Letria scarcely seems to feel the heat. I suppose he must be used to it.' His pale fingers toyed nervously with the rim of the slouch hat in his hands. Of all the company, he alone had turned out in his full uniform. 'I hear that he did not come to Timor willingly.'

'That is true.' Sister Eulalia looked narrowly at him. 'In all these years he has dreamt of going home again. So I said to him, why should you stay now when you can go?'

She saw that the captain was convinced that Letria had been sent to the island as a criminal. No doubt he seemed uneasy to be facing the prospect of a journey across the island in the company of a condemned killer.

'Why do you not ask what he has done?'

'Perhaps he would not tell me the truth,' said Fielding.

The nun's eyes were shrewd. 'Then I will tell you.'

They had drawn away from Mrs Beattie and Katherine Kendall on the verandah. Sister Eulalia did not want what she knew to become common knowledge.

'You will not have heard of Marinha Grande, Captain? It is only a small town back in Portugal. It is Daniel's home town. They make glass there. Glass that is famous.'

Fielding said impatiently, 'I don't see – '

'I want to make you understand, Captain, to see what kind of man is Daniel Letria.' Ignoring the irritation on the young man's face, she said, 'In Portugal, you see, it is possible to go to jail for what is normal in your country. That is what happened to Daniel. When he was only a little older than you are now, the soldiers were sent into Marinha Grande to put down a strike among the glass workers. The town was subject to military law.' She met his eyes, trying to make him listen to her. 'The army had just put away the government of the Republic. It was a time of troubles, of bombs and assassination.'

'And Letria? He killed someone?'

'The leaders of the strike and all their families were taken away. They had killed no one. The strike was enough. Many were transported to colonies overseas – to Angola, to the Cape Verde islands – or Timor.'

After a moment Fielding asked, 'For how long?'

'Captain, he will never return to Portugal unless he leaves now, with us.' She followed Fielding's gaze across the yard to where Letria carried another heavy load. 'He is a remarkable man, a learned man who has suffered much. We may yet be thankful to have him with us.'

Before them lay the rugged highland interior, their destination. For the most part it was an unmapped wilderness of steep, twisting gorges and hidden tribal villages. Somewhere out there were the Australian forces and the possibility of rescue and a way off of the island.

Behind them lay the entire sweep of the northern shoreline with Dili far below. The sea was vast and smooth like burnished silver as the sun hung high over the horizon. But as the small train of refugees pulled up their horses to catch their breath, it was not the city that held them in such desperate silence, but the spectacle in the straits between Dili and Kambing island.

On the beaten silver waters lay the entire Japanese Fleet, victors of the East Indies.

As they watched more than twenty warships steamed south after their sweeping successes in the Java Sea, slow-moving and stately with assurance: cruisers, destroyers and the threatening aircraft carriers. There was no danger to them now. From Manchuria to Mandalay and from Shanghai to Dili, the Rising Sun flew supreme in an awesome Japanese victory which even now seemed to threaten Australia itself.

Chapter Seventeen

Father Jacinto and the captain set the pace at the head of the column with Moita-Ka.

A heavy heat hung over the island. They could hardly breathe in the fierce afternoon sun, climbing, always climbing towards the wall of cobalt-blue mountains on the horizon. In the stifling heat every step was an effort for those on foot. Even those sitting on horses were bathed in sweat streaming down their skin.

Dust veiled everything. The men were leaden-footed, raising dust clouds of red mist in their wake. The air shimmered in a haze over the circling mountains. They wound on up the track in the fierce heat, already doubting.

Mrs Beattie was clearly exhausted. Affected by the heat and the dust, she drooped on horseback, letting Jack take the bridle and lead her forward. The movement over the uneven terrain was tiring enough. There was no disguising her distress as red-faced and winded she wiped her face and clung on to the rocking pony. Fielding had been most attentive to her, giving her more than her fair share of their water ration and calling frequent stops in an attempt to give her some privacy.

'At this rate we'll never make it,' Letria declared harshly. 'The Japanese cannot be so far behind.'

'That's not your problem,' Fielding retorted instantly, giving him a stony look that conveyed all his distrust and suspicion. He had not forgotten Letria's troublemaking in Portugal where he had rebelled against authority.

Letria stared after his retreating figure and understood very well. 'So that's the way it's going to be.'

He had not noticed Amy who stopped nearby, overhearing every word that passed between them.

She had been walking, like the American girl, so that the Englishwomen might ride the horses. She had accidentally witnessed Fielding's assertion of authority and felt she had to say something to Letria.

His dark scowl vanished at her words and he gave her a quick smile, for the first time taking notice of the girl's delicate face and soft almond eyes. How was it that he had never noticed the girl's gentle beauty before? She had the grace and elusive attraction of many mixed-blood women. Her oriental blood enhanced her western attributes. He did not think he had ever seen a woman with such a delicate beauty as she possessed.

He abandoned his place in the line and fell into step beside her as they continued their journey.

As the sun hung high in the faultless sky they were silent, saving their breath for the painful struggle. Every mile seemed like a mistake. Sweat ran down their backs and down their legs into their boots and shoes. Dust stung their eyes. Their feet swelled. They limped. They moistened their cracked lips and longed for water but knew they had to conserve their supply. They were short of breath and their tongues seemed stuck to the roofs of their mouths, painfully dry.

The stamina of the women amazed Jack. He knew that Dede and the half-caste girl had not ridden at all. He admired their courage and determination and the way they stuck together in the face of Mrs Beattie's prejudice.

That night as they made camp Jack saw that the Englishwoman was insisting on separate sleeping arrangements, with her own bedroll as far as possible from the Chinese girl's. He watched as Dede pulled her own bed across to keep Amy company, her loyalty tested yet again. There was going to be trouble between them before long, he thought, if someone didn't pull that woman down a peg or two.

Katherine woke in the middle of the night, stiff and cramped from the position in which she had slept. For a moment she could not remember where she was. She wondered where the mosquito netting had gone and why the bed was so hard. And then she sat up and suddenly she remembered everything and the weight of misery hit her again.

She leant forward on her knees and looked around her at the sleeping camp. The darkness pulsated with the noise of cicadas. The sky was full of stars.

Her body was wet with sweat. The temperature had hardly dropped at all with the darkness. She felt sticky and dirty, her long hair limp and dull. She longed for a cool bath or a deep pool in which to lie. How long would it be before the rains came?

She knew that her health had deteriorated since she had come to the island. The food did not agree with her and the journey had only made things worse. She knew she was losing weight instead of gaining it and her back and legs throbbed with pain.

She had not undressed to sleep, although modesty had been one of the first casualties on the journey. The lack of privacy had worried her more on the ship than here in the open countryside. There was no water to wash with in any case, but she was afraid to let anyone see her without the shapeless cotton dress in case they managed to guess her secret.

She knew she must be at least four months pregnant now. It was hard to be sure of dates after all that had happened, but she knew she could not hope to hide her changing figure from the others much longer.

How was she supposed to tell them the truth? They were all sure to think badly of her. How was she supposed to tell Mrs Beattie? She would never forgive her. She would certainly put the blame on Kate, imagining that she had trapped Harry into the whole affair. She would think she had hoped to trap him into marriage. A real catch for the sister of a shipping clerk!

What could she say to make them all understand that it was not like that? An unmarried girl with a baby! There were few liberal enough to understand her point of view. Anyone in their right mind would say it was stupid and self-indulgent to bring a child into a world at war. She was putting all their lives in danger. Although there was no doubt at all that they would be off the island and safe when her time came, the fact that she was pregnant would seem to put them all in danger.

It's not fair, she thought desperately. I never wanted it this way! What am I doing here?

She looked around at the sleeping figures of the women, wishing that one of them at least would be her friend. She did not notice Sister Eulalia lying on her side watching her in the night.

The sun had risen. In the trees surrounding the little wooden house the birds were singing. Breakfast was being prepared for the officer in charge.

He emerged from one of the inner rooms of the house, still wearing the regulation white *yukata* from the night. He sat on the rush matting to eat, and as he reached for the chopsticks the Australian shot him with a single bullet in the base of the skull.

All hell broke loose. Harrison and his men had taken out the sentries posted on the perimeter fence, allowing his sergeant to move in close to the house. Swift and silent as a cat, Seaton skirted the wooden outpost looking for victims, ending their day which had scarcely begun.

The Japanese had only moved into the district the day before. The house had been abandoned, the valley silent. The commander had immediately sent out a patrol to scout the area, remaining behind himself with a small contingent, unsuspecting.

Counting the corpses, Harrison frowned, suddenly alert. He was anxious to be away before the patrol returned from the hills. There could only be a little time left to them.

'*Tuan, tuan* – '

The native guides were restless, as sensitive to the danger as he was. Where the hell was Seaton?

Stepping over the Japanese sentries face down in the dust, Harrison was heading for the house when the sergeant suddenly appeared.

'Come on,' Seaton shouted hoarsely. 'Let's get the hell out of here.'

He had hardly started down the wooden steps from the verandah when another figure appeared behind him wielding a short sword.

'Look out!'

The sergeant swung about, firing automatically. The Japanese seemed to stop instantly, caught in the chest and throat. Then he spun backwards out of control, the sword still gripped in his hand.

Harrison ran up to Seaton and seized him protectively by the shoulder. 'Jesus, mate, that was close.'

'Too bloody close. Let's get a move on.'

Bending low into a run, the two Australians collected the Timorese boys who had been helping them and moved quickly back towards the scrubland that surrounded the house.

The plain led through a maze of dry bushland running up through a valley between the hills. The ground was so parched underfoot that it crackled. The native guides led the way, using a dried watercourse as a track into the hills. Red dust swirled around their knees as the sun rose behind the clinging hillside.

Harrison brought up the rear, cradling his Owen machine gun. The metal casing had grown hot, forcing him to shift position every few yards. Seaton was still having trouble with his boots. His feet had been so swollen the night before that he dared not take them off for fear he could not get them back on again. He picked his way painfully through the sharp brittle scrubland, his face dripping sweat.

The silence of the valley was suddenly shattered by the piercing scream of the young Timorese boy at the head of the gully. He plunged forward into the air, falling heavily on to his knees, his mahogany skin fresh printed with scarlet.

Again the Japanese machine gun stuttered. The second boy was down in the scrub, moaning and writhing. Blood pumped from the shattered flesh of his stomach.

Seaton had thrown himself to the ground, his face on the burning stones of the dry riverbed. The stunted growth of the little gully gave virtually no cover. He lay there stock still, head spinning, listening for any movement in the sharp silence between shots.

'You there, mate?'

Harrison heard the sergeant's voice with sharp relief. 'For now, I am. What about the boongs?'

Seaton looked at the figures that lay prone further up the track. 'Copped it, I reckon, or good as, poor sods. Looks like we're on our own.'

Harrison began to edge his way like a lizard on his stomach over the rough ground to join his comrade. He was only three yards away when the machine gun opened up again, showering the two men with gouts of dust erupting all around.

'We're sitting ducks here. Can you see the little bastards?'

'Somewhere among those crags, over on the right.'

Seaton struggled to look into the sun, but sweat ran into his eyes. 'Shit, we'll have to make a run for it.'

'A crawl, you mean. And keep your bloody head down.'

It was hellish moving inch by inch across the sharp rocks of the riverbed and brittle scrub. The Timorese boys were both dead. One had slumped forward, his forehead to the earth as though in prayer. The other lay on his back, his head twisted to one side, his eyes staring up towards the sun.

Brushing the flies away as they settled on the corpses, Harrison went from one boy to the other, pocketing their sharp-bladed knives and taking a water bottle that was still quite full.

On the hillside the Japanese machine gun started up as soon as he moved. Harrison lay still, watching the dry scrub and stunted trees on the edge of the gully, seeing their range was short. He heaved himself up and in a running crouch made for the bush, the water bottles clanking.

At the edge of the hot eroded valley bed Harrison made the low cover of the bush and collapsed on to his stomach, his face gleaming and his chest heaving with the effort.

'Be careful, *tuan*,' came a voice at his ear.

Harrison almost jumped out of his skin, but the small brown hand held him down.

He looked up into the genial open face of a Timorese boy, a stranger. As Seaton came up on all fours to join them he was too out of breath to talk, so Moita-Ka did all the talking necessary.

'You come with me,' he grinned, clearly enjoying his adventure. 'You come. No danger now.'

Obediently they launched themselves in the dust behind him as he set off up the steep hillside. The dry bush crackled in their wake. With blood-scraped knees and hands they reached the rise, aware of the Japanese on the opposite side of the valley.

They thankfully slipped down into the cool shade of the far slope among the stunted pines.

'You're safe now.'

The Australians laughed with relief at the familiar sound of their own tongue spoken in their own accent. There was no mistaking the identity of the two men crouched before them.

Seaton looked up at Jack and the grin nearly split his dirt-caked face.

'G'day, mate, am I pleased to see you!'

Chapter Eighteen

'That's a smart little bloke you've got there,' said Harrison, slapping Moita-Ka on the back.

'We heard the gunfire,' said Fielding. He looked them over curiously. 'How long have you been on the run?'

The rescued men exchanged a look that did not pass unnoticed.

'Hell, mate, we're not the ones who've been running. We must have hit more than thirty bloody Nips in the past few days.'

'No offence, mate,' Jack put in quickly, recognizing a temper when he saw one.

They were certainly a curious sight. The only remnants of their army uniform were the dogtags, khaki shorts and heavy army boots. They looked fit and muscular but their brown bodies were caked with dust and dirt.

The one with the temper had a shock of dirty blond hair over his eyes and a good four days' growth of beard. He had good features but a sullen look and suspicious eyes. His companion was dark and wiry, sporting a heavy Owen gun and two water bottles. His short fringe of beard made him look like a Turkish bandit.

'If you mean the beards,' said Seaton, scratching the blond hair on his chin, 'we swore we wouldn't shave again until we're back home in Sydney.'

'Is that blood yours?' Jack asked Harrison, noting the fresh stains on his shorts. 'We've got a nurse with us if you need help.'

'No, no, mate, I'm fine, it was just one of the boongs. He caught one back there.'

Down in the steep gully behind the hill they joined the rest of the convent group. When the newcomers caught sight of the priest and Sister Eulalia they passed a few acid comments which Jack alone overheard.

'Don't go underestimating the sister, mates,' he warned them. 'She saved my bacon back in Dili. I reckon I owe her.'

Looking around at the other women, the sergeant asked, 'All them Poms?'

'And a Yank. She got out of Manila, the others from Singapore – '

'S'truth, reckon they've had a crook deal then.'

'A bit rough on the old Sheila,' said Harrison, looking at Mrs Beattie.

Father Jacinto strode across the gully when he saw them.

'Do you know anything about horses?'

'Everything,' said Harrison.

Jack and Letria laughed outright, but the smiles died on their faces as Harrison, red-necked, swung himself on to the back of the nearest pony with supreme ease.

'D'you want to bet on it?'

'I wouldn't waste my money.'

Harrison trotted the small horse in and out of the scrub, a handful of mane in both fists and his legs almost brushing the ground on either side. He looked down and called out, 'Hey, who cut the poor mutt's legs off then?'

Seaton looked on hesitantly. 'I'll walk if it's all the same,' he volunteered.

'No, give it a go, mate,' said Harrison slyly, dismounting but holding the horse steady for his partner.

The sergeant kept his composure with difficulty as the women gathered round to watch. He managed to hoist his leg up and over, but as his feet left the ground the pony suddenly took in into his head to set off, making an eager run towards the almost vertical drop into the valley on the other side.

With a strangled cry Seaton clung on to the pony's neck, seizing the thick stringy mane. The pony tried to knock him off under the low bough of a tree, leaving Seaton hanging with one leg around its neck while Moita-Ka led the others in shrieks of laughter.

'S'truth, mate, what d'you feed the little buggers on?' the

sergeant demanded, his pride badly bruised.

The Timor ponies were adept at removing their riders if given a free rein. Jumping from rock to rock with the agility of mountain goats, they trotted at high speed among the maze of dry, twisting tracks. They approached all obstacles with malicious glee, delighting in finding new ways of unseating their unwanted passengers.

They made quite a procession, strung out along the rise of the mountain as they climbed, always climbing up into the soaring crystal air.

They made camp before dusk on the edge of a ravine, well screened by stunted gum trees. From the wooded ridges all around came the sounds of the night, of cicadas and tree frogs. The short twilight of the tropics brought night like a curtain, the darkness obscuring everything. By the light of two camp fires they moved in silhouette, preparing food.

Dede had moved away into the bush to find a bit of privacy but as she made her way back to join the camp she encountered Seaton waiting for her.

'Are you the one who's a nurse?' he asked ingenuously. 'I need some help to get these boots off.'

'No, I'm not the nurse,' said Dede, 'but I'll give you a hand.'

He sat on a rock and let her unlace the boots, watching her all the while.

'You're the Yank, then? How the hell did you get here?'

'The same way you did. By everything going wrong.'

He winced as she managed to get one boot off. 'Not a pretty sight.'

'I hope you're not going to faint at the sight of blood – '

Dede looked up, annoyed with herself for not suspecting his motives earlier. She saw a chance to embarrass him and took it.

'Well, I guess not, sergeant. If you saw as much blood as women see every month, perhaps you'd understand why.'

She tugged off the other boot and let go of his foot.

'You've been walking on stony ground, Sergeant. I should tread more carefully in future, if I were you.' She got to her feet and called back over her shoulder, 'I'll send you Sister Eulalia. She'll know just how to handle you.'

Seaton stumbled his way barefoot back to join the other Australians by the camp fire.

'No go there, mate,' said Harrison with a wry smile.

'Smart-alec bitch,' Seaton muttered half under his breath. 'Bloody Yanks. I've got no time for them.'

Jack couldn't help smiling to himself, pleased that a chancer like Seaton had fared no better with the American than he had.

Fielding joined them for the bully beef and weak tea, eager to learn any fresh news from the newcomers.

'Singapore and Sumatra are lost.'

'That much we knew.' The young captain could barely conceal his disappointment.

'At least Australia's free.'

'For the time being.' Fielding sat back on his haunches, staring into the embers of the fire. He moodily stirred the twigs with a branch. 'We will head for the border. Head for Koepang. There we can join up with the Dutch forces.'

'Koepang?' Seaton stared at him in disbelief. 'You haven't heard then?'

'Koepang fell weeks ago, mate,' said Harrison. 'No one there stood a chance. Our blokes are all gone. The Dutch caved in and the bloody boongs went over to the Nips.'

'Bastards,' swore Jack softly.

'The Dutch went and surrendered straight down the line – '

' – and those who did make a run for it were turned over to the Nips by the boongs.' Seaton flashed a glance across at Moita-Ka and Amy. 'You don't want to let them get ideas.'

Fielding shook his head. 'There's a world of difference between the people here and those on the Dutch side of the border.'

'Yeah? Well, if the Nips get the upper hand here,' sneered Seaton dangerously, 'I wouldn't give a toss for our chances.'

Jack looked across at Fielding, but the sergeant continued, 'I'd say the best bet is to head south. McMaster's group have got to be down there some place.'

Jack looked at the surrounding mountains bleakly. 'Some place out there? How big can this bloody island be?'

Seaton and Harrison had been part of McMaster's group, carrying out a number of raids against isolated Japanese units outside Dili. Although the commando raids were small scale, their effect on morale was staggering. They harried and menaced the Japanese at every turn. The Japanese in Dili were blaming everything that went wrong on the phantom Australians.

'We had some good blokes,' said Seaton. 'When we got separated we were trying to make for a base that was being set up in the highest mountain range. I wonder if they made it.'

'The people back home will write us off. They won't even know if we're dead or in the can.'

They shifted uncomfortably, all thinking of home.

'My bit won't give up on me,' Seaton said, pulling out a tiny snapshot tucked in the belt of his shorts. 'Isn't she a bloody miracle?'

Her proportions were certainly miraculous. Jack grinned at Harrison and then passed the picture on to Fielding. The captain made a polite noise and passed it straight back to the eager sergeant. 'Isn't that Sydney?'

'Dead right it is. Martin Place, matter of fact. The very day I signed up.' He kissed the picture before slipping it back out of sight. 'You from Sydney, Captain? Isn't that something?'

Jack looked at Fielding's face and thought the sergeant optimistic to think he had anything in common with the captain.

'Know the Cross? Some beaut little bars there where we used to hang out.'

'No, I don't think so.'

'Aw, go on,' Seaton persisted. 'You must know Bluey's – '

'No, I don't believe that I do,' said Fielding abruptly and got rapidly to his feet and walked off.

Stunned, the little circle looked after him. Seaton's disgust was written clearly on his face, his second rejection of the evening. His cigarette dangled out of the corner of his mouth, forgotten.

'He's full of himself, that one,' said Harrison.

'He's top bloody shot, mate,' Seaton grimaced.

Fielding took himself off down the hillside. The night was thick and close about him, full of soft scents and the noise of insects. He could still hear the others talking at the firesides and a wave of intense desolation swept over him.

He sat down on a ridge of red soil, staring into the night. He felt isolated and remote from the others, unable to share their easy banter. Their good humour sat uneasily on him. He thought of Seaton's photograph almost with revulsion. Passing that picture around among the men. He could never have shared Miriam with anyone.

Here in the hot pulse of the hills, the memories of that last summer at Mosman and at Chinaman's Beach were with him again, a nostalgic sweet longing.

Looking out into the short Sydney twilight towards Castle Rock. Sitting together on the front porch with the fragrance of the garden trees, the familiar sight of the white picket fence and the scarlet poinsettias. And Miriam.

His hand found the picture, where it always lay, next to his heart. The sight of her was a private treasure that he could not have brought himself to share with anyone.

She stood on the porch, black against white in the monochrome picture. Her dark dress and dark hair framed a face of such sweetness that he had to look away for a moment to take a grip on himself.

She stood on the porch with the labrador at her feet. Miriam and Lara, both looking out of the picture directly at him, their love locked for ever in time.

What was he doing here, so far from everything that he loved? What had made him agree to come out here? He was appalled at his own lack of purpose. Such a waste, so much lost opportunity. It had all been delusions of grandeur – he had to see himself in uniform, eager to be the hero, with empty words like duty and honour echoing around in his aching head. Perhaps only to die now in this God-awful place in a thankless *Boy's Own* adventure. What a waste.

Without Miriam what was there to keep him going?

In the pool of dying firelight Sister Eulalia sat watching Katherine Kendall as she laid out her bedroll. The girl was still following Mrs Beattie's diktat that a semblance of segregation should be observed between the white women and those contaminated by native blood.

Over the past few days the nun had thought she observed a change in the girl's attitude, an unwillingness to blindly obey the tyrannical English memsahib any further. She seemed to regret their alienation from the American woman who, in normal circumstances, might have been a friend to her. She did not seem to follow Mrs Beattie out of conviction but from some sense of propriety or service. What was the relationship between them? The nun sensed an air of fear or guilt in the girl's attitude: treading delicately, trying not to offend the woman who seemed to control her life.

Sister Eulalia had her own ideas about the reasons for Katherine's air of guilt. She had been watching the way the girl kept herself to herself, guarding her privacy. She had also taken note of the way she held herself, the care she took, as though for all the world she was carrying a fragile parcel that must not be damaged. Sister Eulalia knew that look. She had seen it countless times as a nurse. She did not flinch. She had dealt with situations similar to this over many years. She went over to Katherine, touching her lightly on the arm, drawing her a little way from the fireside where they would not be overheard.

Kate looked at her with that pinched anxiety she had seen the night before. On top of everything else that was happening, the girl was worried sick about her pregnancy. Sister Eulalia had to reassure her. She was not there to judge, she was there to provide counselling and consolation.

'There's something wrong, isn't there? You can tell me, child.' She was kind but direct.

Kate stared at her with a kind of horror, realizing at once that the nun knew everything. 'I don't want to talk about it.'

'But I'm afraid we have to,' the nun said gently. 'You cannot go on pretending that it will go away.'

Kate knew that Sister Eulalia was right, but she still feared to face the consequences of bringing her secret into the open.

'Please trust me. I want to help you.'

'I know you do, but – '

'You're afraid? Afraid of Mrs Beattie?'

Dumbly, the girl nodded, on the verge of tears. 'I don't know how to tell her. She'll never forgive me. She'll cut me off and then I'll be all alone.'

'No, no, child, that's nonsense. We are all your friends. Don't be afraid.' She had a strong arm around Kate, warm and comforting. 'How long has it been?'

'I'm not sure. Four months, perhaps more.'

So far along, thought the nun. She had not thought her so far advanced. She scarcely showed at all.

The two women looked at each other and seemed to share the same thought: when would they be off the island? When would they be safe?

'It will be all right,' said the nun, thinking that they still had four or five months' leeway, but in the back of her mind was still a nagging doubt. The unexpected was now normal. Every day brought new surprises, new dangers. Who knew what would happen before the birth was due?

'Will you forgive me if I offer you some advice, child? Don't tell the others yet. There is no need for them to know just now.' She saw the relief flood back into the girl's pale face. 'When the time comes, I will tell them.'

Kate saw that the nun was a woman of the world after all. She was tough, resilient, coping with all kinds of hazards from day to day, but she was also a woman of compassion and understanding, a friend to whom Kate knew she could turn.

'What's the matter, child?'

'I'm sorry, Sister, it's just that I seem to have spent all my life running away, keeping just one step ahead of disaster – '

'You make it sound almost personal.'

'But that's how it seems to me!' cried Kate softly. 'I got away from Europe just in time, but then it was Singapore. And now it's all too late. The war has caught up with me at last. It's my turn now.'

'No, you're wrong. It's all of us now. We must try to find strength within ourselves. In some ways you are the lucky one, Katherine. You have your child to live for.' Within the white coif, Sister Eulalia's face was calm but determined. 'There are some who cannot learn to be strong. They give way too easily, and I say to myself, well, that one will not make it – ' She looked up suddenly. 'But you are not like that, Katherine. I saw that at once.'

Kate stared at her, thinking she would never have suspected that a nun could talk so plainly.

'A time of our lives is ending,' said Sister Eulalia. 'The world is changed and we have to survive. The faster we accept that this is so, the easier it will be for all of us.'

Chapter Nineteen

They were higher now, climbing the steep rock, their breath hammering in their ears. The horses picked their way over the stony ground with their rocking, swaying burdens. The afternoon was filled with the thick perfume of the forest, the air alive with the hum of insects and birdsong. Bright sunshine fell in shafts through the branches overhead, lighting dust motes against the field of green and scorched brown.

They stopped frequently to rest and catch their breath. Katherine gave Phyllis Beattie her water bottle but there was a troubling, distant look in the woman's eyes.

'Do you ever think about the boys?'

Kate looked at her sharply, worried by her wandering mind.

'Do you ever think they could still be alive?'

'Yes, I'm sure – ' She stopped, seeing the vacancy on Mrs Beattie's face. She was no longer listening. Her mind was far away, her eyes glazed from exhaustion. Kate knew that the heat and exertion of the journey were taking their toll on all of them. She was finding it hard just sitting her horse, but Dede and the Chinese girl were walking. Kate felt guilty but she could no longer keep up the pretence that she was a normal fit and able woman.

'Is she all right?' Dede was at her side, seeing that something was wrong.

'We can't go on like this. The captain must be told we can't go on indefinitely at this pace.' Kate looped her hair back behind one ear, wiping the sweat from her forehead with the back of her hand. 'It gets worse the further we go. It was a mistake ever leaving the convent.'

Dede looked doubtful.

'We would have been safe there,' Kate insisted.

'All right,' Dede agreed, 'no need to worry yourself. I'll go and talk to the captain.'

She caught up with Fielding at the head of the trail, trying to get him to stop long enough to hear her out.

'They're both so tired. They can't keep going at this kind of pace. They've had enough. More than enough.' He didn't seem to hear her. 'Look, how much further must we go?'

He flashed her a bitter look of reproach from his blue eyes. 'As far as it takes to be safe.'

Heat and stubble covered his face, changing his appearance dramatically. Only the eyes that met hers seemed the same any more.

She saw that he could not give way. There was no other alternative. In her heart she did not believe that they would have been safer at the convent. That was just wishful thinking. They were free up here in the mountains and there was still a chance they would escape. That was the thought that drove Fielding on. While there was still a chance of escape they had to keep on.

She nodded abruptly, taking his point, and went back to Kate and Mrs Beattie to try to explain it to them.

All the men were now growing beards, as water was at a premium. Fielding had caught the sun in particular. His fair skin was reddened and sore where the golden stubble along his chin ended. His hair was sun-bleached paler than ever and even his eyebrows were turning white.

Jack Ford thought he looked no fitter for being outside at last. He looked haggard and had lost a lot of weight. They were all leaner, of course, but there was something sickly still about the captain's appearance.

Had he been down in Wilson's Promontory during training, or as a headquarters bloke had he got away with all of that? Had he been there when they rigged that pontoon over the Goulburn River? This country was little different, just as rugged and remote. If Fielding had been there with them he should have been accustomed to it all, showing less signs of physical exhaustion, more acclimatized. Yet Jack thought he looked worn out, older and more anxious than ever. His mouth was a thin, stern line of resistance and grim endurance as he moved on up the path.

'Something up?' Jack asked as he came alongside.

Fielding stopped a moment, wiping the sweat from his round pink face. His blue gaze turned on Jack with false bravado. 'Slight touch of malaria, that's all. It will pass.'

Jack had to admit he had never felt fitter in his life. Away from the dense humidity of the Dili lowlands he seemed to have found a new strength.

Among the curiously familiar scrubland and wild hill country he felt that he was in his own environment, able to cope. It was not so very different from the bush back home. The mountains heading their steep trail reminded him of the promontory where 2/2 Company had done their training, only he knew that these ranges were higher than any he had seen in Australia.

The ridges and barren hills soared into the desperate blue sky. Sparse cover from the fierce heat was provided by gums or eucalyptus. Only the valleys were green and productive with sandalwood trees or plantation crops of pineapples and coconuts, or prized and valuable coffee.

They emerged from the trees to a discovery that took their breath. Before them on the floor of the valley was the pale ribbon of a road. Not a track through the bush like the one they had followed for safety, but the white sandy stretch of a main road linking a village or a town with Dili.

'What is it? Do you know?'

Rising in the saddle the old priest searched the valley floor. The others came to a halt around them while Father Jacinto conferred with Moita-Ka in what Jack assumed to be Tetum, the language of Timor.

'The *postos* are linked by roads like this,' Sister Eulalia explained to Dede. 'If we are near one then perhaps we can get help.'

'But is it safe?'

No one could answer that question. After a short conference between the priest and Captain Fielding, Father Jacinto put the proposal to seek out the nearest *posto*.

They were all weary, hungry and dehydrated. The prospect of a night's lodging and a real bed perhaps was enough to sway them, however much they feared the Japanese.

As they wound down into the valley the landscape changed

as the light altered. The orange sun rolled down the sky, casting a pearly haze over the cultivated fields bounding the road to the south. The plantation was part of the administrative area under the control of the local Portuguese *chefe do posto*. Beyond the neatly kept fields rose ordered ranks of sandalwood evergreens.

'The Tree of Destiny we call it here,' said Father Jacinto. 'It has made many a fortune in these parts.'

'Oh yes,' said the cynical Letria, coming up behind them. 'Some of our countrymen have their fingers in every pie.' He turned to Dede. 'Did you know that every native has to give one month of compulsory unpaid labour to the *chefe*? Forced labour, as in feudal times.'

'You mean, like slaves?' asked Dede in horror.

'They are treated little better than slaves and flogged with the *palmatora*.'

'What's that, for God's sake?'

'God has nothing to do with it,' said the priest. 'It is a round piece of wood with holes drilled through it, so that it lacerates the flesh when used on hands or the soles of the feet – '

'You can't be serious, Father?'

'These things must change one day,' said Father Jacinto.

'Your bishops do nothing,' Letria retorted. 'The Portuguese who came out here with their boss mentality were nothing in the old country. Here they behave like petty tyrants. You had trouble enough, Father, for attacking them in the past.' He glared at him. 'Don't you change sides now.'

Dede and the priest looked after him as he stormed off.

'You must excuse him,' said Father Jacinto. 'He feels these things too strongly. He is impatient for change.'

'Impatient?' Dede said in astonishment. 'The rest of the world abolished slavery a century ago! How can you call him impatient?' Letria had gone up in her estimation and she began to see what Amy had meant when she talked about him so enthusiastically.

The valley was a magical place after the harsh barren scrubland. The small outpost of whitewashed houses lay behind white walls in a garden planted with lemon trees, hibiscus and scarlet and orange cannas. In the centre of the compound, surrounded by a wicket fence, stood a large villa in the Portuguese style, with an airy verandah dripping with cascades of purple bougainvillea from the red-tiled roof.

A notice at the entrance to the garden warned, 'No Natives and No Dogs' in Portuguese.

Fielding moved on inside, oblivious of any restrictions. But their arrival had attracted the attention of a group of native women working in the outer compound, and Father Jacinto halted the group under a spreading banyan tree just inside the gate. There was a pond with giant waterlilies of various shades of pink and salmon with thick fleshy stems. Mrs Beattie and Katherine sank into an exhausted huddle against the tree trunk entwined with creepers and Sister Eulalia brought them water.

Amy had seen the notice at the gate and her uneasiness was quickly noted by Letria. He moved to her side, as though to offer her his support or protection if she should need it.

Fielding frowned when he saw the men who were now under his command stretched out in the shade. Only Father Jacinto came across the garden to join him, striding towards the front steps of the *chefe do posto*'s house.

A five-year-old white girl was playing among the stiff Dutch chairs on the verandah with a young Timorese houseboy. Behind them stood a Timorese nursemaid carrying a white child in her arms. He was strong and sturdy, almost eighteen months old, shouting happily to his sister on the floor.

The amah tensed, catching sight of the strangers, her dark eyes startled, like a doe poised for flight. The houseboy stood up, hesitated a moment and then fled into the house calling, '*Patrão, patrão!*'

They halted at the foot of the steps among the scarlet zinnias as a Portuguese in a gleaming white shirt and highly polished leather boots emerged from the villa, shading his spectacles from the high sun.

Both Father Jacinto and Fielding recognized Jaime Macedo at the same time. They exchanged a quick glance of apprehension as Macedo strode to the top of the steps in astonishment.

'Why, Father, what are you doing so far from home?'

'Jaime! You look well.'

Macedo's eyes flicked over the Australian without recognition. He had not been aware of the captain watching his arrival that evening at the convent.

'Is he an Australian?' Macedo demanded of the priest in Portuguese, his tone far from hospitable.

'You know very well he is.'

'And the others under my tree?'

'We have travelled a long way. They are all exhausted and need your help, Jaime.'

But Macedo had caught sight of Amy and Moita-Ka. 'Did you not see the notice? I can't have these *macacos* here – '

A cold anger entered the priest's lean face. He was about to reply when Fielding stepped forward, oblivious to the turn the conversation in Portuguese had taken.

He held out his hand and said civilly in English, 'If you will let me explain our position, sir – '

But Macedo did not take his hand. Fielding stood there with his arm outstretched a moment longer and then let it drop, suddenly aware of the Portuguese's hostility.

'Will you not invite us in from the sun, Jaime?' asked the priest, this time in English.

Macedo stared from one to the other and then clicked his fingers over his shoulder, ordering the children and servants inside. He looked at the priest with unconcealed resentment but nodded his head curtly and with an ironic sweep of his arm motioned them into his house.

The large sitting room was darkened, the chics pulled down because of the heat. The sound of the overhead fan cut the silence. Across the room Fielding saw a European woman stretched out full-length on a sofa with cushions at her back. She did not look Portuguese, she was too fair for that. She had been reading a magazine but looked up in surprise at their entrance.

'Dona Eva.'

She sat up abruptly and stared at the priest with hard eyes, recognizing him with obvious lack of enthusiasm. She pushed back her waved hair, jet earrings catching the long light filtering in through the slats of the shutters. As she got slowly to her feet there was about her an elegance that even this remote outpost could not quite diminish. Then she saw that Fielding was watching her from the doorway in his khaki uniform and her eyes widened.

'He can't come in here!' she exploded in her husband's

language. 'You know who he is! I won't stand for it!'

Fielding stood mute, tight-lipped, aware of feeling an outcast as the flood of Portuguese filled the room.

'What are you thinking of, Father, bringing these people here?'

'My God!' cried Eva. 'How many are there?'

'We have women in our party,' replied the priest. 'They are sick and need your help – '

She turned her back on him. 'The world is large enough. What have they to do with us?'

Macedo took his old tutor firmly by the elbow. 'You know how it was at the convent,' he said in a low voice. 'They must have told you. Why did you come here?'

'We had no choice.' Since Seaton and Harrison had joined them, they were very short of food. 'We need supplies. We need food and water. What do you have that you can give us?'

'For them, nothing.' Macedo's Dutch wife was desperate to preserve her food stocks. She glared at her husband, urging him to take some action and throw out the stranger in the dangerous uniform.

Macedo dutifully went across to Fielding. 'I don't understand your people. The war is over for you now.'

'I'm afraid we don't quite see it that way.'

'The Japanese have proved victorious. They are the conquerors of Asia now. There's a new world now. You will have to learn to accommodate yourselves to work with them. Why don't you see reason and give up your arms?' He pointed to the service revolver that hung from Fielding's waist.

'Turn ourselves over to the Japanese? Is that some kind of bad joke, *Senhor* Macedo? Perhaps you haven't heard that Japan is not a signatory to the Geneva Convention?'

Macedo shrugged. 'It is not my problem, Captain. Nor yours, Father. Portugal is a neutral country.'

The priest looked around the room with slow deliberation, letting his gaze rest on the fine porcelain, the leather-bound books, the silverware.

'It is possible that the new authorities will find a reason to take over the *posto*.'

Macedo took instant offence. He turned on the Australian, as though he blamed Fielding for corrupting the Portuguese priest. 'You are to blame for all of this. It's because of your foolish terrorist antics that the Japanese are behaving this way. Some of your people destroyed the bridge over the river in the valley. It took my natives six months to build it. It took two of your terrorists to blow it up.'

Fielding seemed unimpressed. 'We are at war, *senhor*.' He looked at Macedo sharply. 'But you seem very well informed. Is there a radio transmitter here?'

'You know that there is. That is why you came here.'

'Ah!' said Eva, staring at Fielding with a consciousness of her own superiority, smiling almost with satisfaction. 'So you expect us to put our lives in danger for you and your friends?'

'She's quite right,' Macedo told the priest. 'Did you never think of the burden you are imposing on us?'

Fielding turned abruptly on his heel and went into the garden again to summon Jack Ford. Together the two men made their way towards the compound buildings housing the radio, only to find the door locked. The captain ordered Jack to break down the door.

Macedo hovered in the doorway as the two Australians examined the radio, their blond and dark heads together. Jack had pulled a chair over to the transmitter and began to tune and dials while Fielding grew impatient.

'Will it work?'

'Get out of the light, will you?'

Watching them together the *chefe do posto* was aware of the undercurrent of tension, almost of antagonism, between the two men. He was astonished at his discovery. He had imagined that the rebel Australians who had taken to the hills in guerrilla bands were united in their objectives. In comparison with the Portuguese and native units on the island, they appeared disciplined, with high morals. But the look that passed between the officer and the corporal left him in little doubt that the two men kept their hostility barely concealed beneath an outward show of rank.

Jack started to tune the radio, moving the dials back and forth with patience. There came a faint crackling of static and a trace of distant voices.

'What's that you're getting?' Fielding stood at his shoulder.

'Some lingo. It's not English, I'll tell you that much.'

Macedo came over from his place by the door. 'You won't get anything outside the island,' he told them derisively. 'We can barely get Dili in the dry season.' He saw that he had their attention. 'It's the mountains, you see. It needs a high-powered set. There's nothing you can do.'

Jack turned back to the radio, pressing the headset close on one ear. 'Shut up, will you? I think I've got something!'

'What? What is it?'

'It's English, but it doesn't make any sense – '

'Here, let me listen.' Fielding snatched the headset away from Ford, ignoring his furious glare. He listened for a few minutes before speaking. 'No, it's no good, I can't get it.'

Jack exploded with exasperation and took the headset back.

'How do you make this switch work?' He wanted to be able to transmit as well as receive.

'It won't work,' Macedo answered bluntly. 'Hasn't worked for months.' He saw the suspicion on their faces. 'I'm telling you the truth.'

Fielding looked sceptical, watching Jack struggle with the wiring of the switch to no avail.

Macedo watched the young captain and envied him his youth. What had he been at twenty-three or twenty-four? More than a decade divided them and suddenly he felt old. Where had all his years been spent? And why? All he knew was the island. Surely that had never been his only goal in life? Once he had strength and conviction. Yes, once he had been that sure of himself, too.

Fielding's eye caught sight of a faded map of the island pinned on the wall. It had the Dutch-Portuguese border clearly marked and main towns ringed in red. His sunburnt face glowed with excitement and he quickly drew the pins from the wall, pulling down the map.

'Give me some names. What was that they mentioned, Ail – Aila – ' He looked round at Macedo for help, but the Portuguese was polishing his spectacles, feigning indifference.

Jack listened in, calling out whatever place names he overheard, while Fielding knelt over the map in the dust and tried to make out Australian positions. The lack of roads was plain to see but native tracks through the mountains were ominously missing. Fielding stabbed the map, finding the names that Jack dictated.

'Ailalec, Bobonaro and Ainaro.' He grinned. 'However you pronounce them. And Hatu something – '

'Hatu Builau? That's way up in the mountains. Must be nine or ten thousand feet. What's the name of the mountain, Tata Ma – '

'Tata Mai Lau,' Macedo corrected him sardonically.

'Tata Mai Lau.' Fielding rolled the name on his tongue, getting used to it. 'Is it far?'

The Portuguese shrugged. He obviously had no inclination to tell them anything that could later be held against him.

Fielding rolled up the map and took it with him. 'Let's clear out now, Corporal, while we can.'

'What about him? We don't want him spilling the beans the moment we've gone. Better smash the radio – '

'But it doesn't work!' Macedo objected.

'Better safe than sorry.' Jack tore the radio from the wall and sent it crashing to the floor, coils and wires spilling out of the box like entrails. 'At least that bastard won't be able to shop us,' he said with satisfaction.

Outside in the yard under the banyan tree the rest of the group wilted. Sister Eulalia and Father Jacinto came up to Fielding and Jack Ford, anxious about their plans.

'The women cannot keep up this pace,' said the priest. 'I tried to persuade *Senhora* Macedo to permit Mrs Beattie and the young Englishwoman to remain behind, but she would have none of it.'

Fielding looked over to where the Englishwomen lay in the shade. 'Well, there's nothing we can do about it,' he said lamely. 'If they stay here their lives are in danger.'

Sister Eulalia touched him on the arm. 'There is something you don't know, Captain. I'm forced to tell you that Miss Kendall is expecting a child, and if we go on into the mountains she will be an increasing problem.'

A crease of pain crossed Fielding's face. Jack thought he was suddenly disappointed in the young woman, that she had dropped in his estimation.

He walked briskly over to Katherine and before anyone could stop him, he was asking, 'Is it true, Miss Kendall? You should have told us before now. It is very irresponsible of you.'

Kate flashed a look of pure terror from Sister Eulalia to Mrs Beattie behind her. Everyone was watching her.

There was more than a hint of defiance in her eyes as she stood up. 'Yes, it's true. I'm pregnant,' she announced.

Behind her Mrs Beattie let out a little choked gasp. She stared at Kate as though the girl had struck her. 'Oh yes! I see it all now!'

All the hints and allegations made by her own daughter back in Singapore came flooding back into her mind. She saw again the Kendall girl in her absurd picture hat walking into the clubroom on Harry's arm. The brazen, conniving creature had deceived all this time! She had even taken her own daughter's place on the ship out of Singapore, inveigling her way into Phyllis's confidence all this time! How dare she stand there so brazenly confessing in front of them all? Had she no shame?

'I will never forgive you, never.'

Dede saw the tears begin to well in Kate's eyes and leapt to her defence, taking Kate by the shoulders.

'Shut up and leave her alone, will you?' She saw that Sister Eulalia looked distressed but that most of the others were simply embarrassed. 'What's it got to do with you, anyway? Mind your own business.'

'Well, really!' Mrs Beattie was outraged. 'I won't be spoken to in this way – '

'Aw, dry up,' said Jack brutally, shocking her into silence. 'We're just wasting time here.'

'He's right,' said Letria. 'If the people here won't help us then we must leave. There's no alternative.'

'Yes, but now that we know about Miss Kendall – '

'I'll manage,' said Kate quickly. 'Don't think you can leave me here.'

'Leave you? Who said anything about leaving you?'

'I can keep up. Just don't leave me behind for the Japanese.'

'No one is being left behind, Miss Kendall,' the captain repeated, his thoughts full of Davison who had been left behind at the convent. He took up the map and turned his back on the women, calling Father Jacinto and the native guide Moita-Ka to advise him.

'Old bitch!' said Dede, looking back at Mrs Beattie.

The old order of polite manners had been broken at last. The pretence that their lives were unaffected by their deteriorating situation could now be dropped. The things that had mattered back in Manila or Singapore were not the things that counted out here. For survival there was a different set of values. Perhaps now they would find out who their real friends were.

Dede caught Jack's amused smile over Katherine's fair head. Suddenly she realized that he had been the only one to back her and wondered if she had misjudged him. She saw him in a new light, looking at his thin face with its light brown fuzz of beard emphasizing his long jawline, his full lips grinning at her. His lively green eyes held hers until at last she was forced to laugh too, her anger subsiding rapidly as she was suddenly able to laugh at herself.

Chapter Twenty

The priest stood at the outer edge of the plantation and lifted his eyes to the southern hills. 'We must keep off the road.'

Leaving the *posto* behind, the fear of being betrayed was in all their minds. In the mountains they would be safe. They could lose themselves in their vast embrace and perhaps find their way to the main Australian base.

'We have to keep heading south.'

'There are no trails marked on this map,' Fielding complained.

'But they do exist,' Father Jacinto affirmed. 'Moita-Ka will help us to try for his village. It is the only way.'

'Unless you'd care to chance your luck on the main road?' Letria added sardonically.

'What luck?' asked Fielding, and the rest stayed silent.

Before them rose the angled cliffs of the Ramelau Plateau. The Ramelau and Cablac central massifs rose ten thousand feet between them and the south coast and any hope of rescue. In the heartland of the mountains rose Tata Mai Lau, over nine thousand feet of almost perpendicular ridges of rock in sharp folds backing one upon another, cruel to climb.

If they were to keep ahead of the Japanese patrols they had to keep to the mountain trails, relying on assistance and guidance from the people of the interior. At all costs they had to avoid the few roads that crossed the island, for these would be the main arteries by which the invading Japanee could take over the whole island.

When the rains finally came the going would become doubly hazardous. Flash floods and landslides could wipe out the mountain passes, mud destroy the forest paths overnight. There was no time to be lost.

The giant trees gave them occasional cover from the sun as they continued to climb. Below them the neat rows of the plantation diminished into miniature. Down through the screen of trees with their fat leaves the valley was perfect. The ribbon of a road drove straight and dust-white through the plantation until lost in countless variations of colour.

Jack Ford followed Dede up the steep trail through the overhanging ferns, around them the incessant hum of insects and the raucous cries of unseen birds. She did not stop for him to catch up or come alongside her. She moved steadily on, following the footsteps of the Chinese girl who walked ahead with Letria.

Jack focused on the shape of her shoulders and neck as she bent slightly forward with the exertion of the climb. The delicate skin at the nape was turning red and tender and he wanted to tell her about it, tell her to protect herself from the sun, but he knew that if he did she would see it as another intrusion. She was such a strange mixture of assertiveness and vulnerability. Back there at the *posto* he had seen the hurt in her eyes when Katherine was being attacked and no one seemed to take her part. She had come to her defence, but he guessed that it had cost her a lot to push herself forward again. He didn't think that she was as tough as she seemed to be.

Dede was aware of the Australian coming up the trail right at her back. He had never been very far away since the incident at the plantation.

She paused for a moment, looking out across the dust-brown hills parched for rain. Her heart soared as a large hawk, all russet gold with a proud white head, floated on an air spiral. She almost felt that by stretching out a hand she could touch its feathers, but it was a free spirit and glided down in a dazzling arc towards the buried valley floor.

'So you're not afraid?'

His face was half concealed by the dusty branches of a tree as she turned and looked at him in surprise.

'Afraid? No, not here. I was afraid before, down there. Those people at the *posto* – '

'Good types, eh?'

He was staring at her, thinking she had a compelling face and fine eyes. She seemed to have softened suddenly in his eyes.

'At times like that you begin to see – well, see that they really do believe people are just so much trash.' Her eyes held his. 'You realize what people are really like.'

His green eyes flicked open. 'Bit of a shock, was it?'

Dede took instant offence. She began walking, her brisk pace telling him more than her angry words. 'Don't think you know anything about me. I'm not part of that damned Singapore set. In fact, I doubt if our backgrounds are so very different.'

He looked sceptical. Her world was so much more than his could ever have been. 'Aw, come on. I don't have your fancy education. I've never been out of Aussie before this picnic. I'm just a bloody ringer, lady.'

'Don't underrate yourself. Maybe you're not as dumb as you'd like to be.' She gave him an enigmatic smile before turning her back and setting off to catch up with the others.

As they moved into the mountains the countryside seemed almost mystical to Dede. Ahead lay the central massif with its secret interior high among the clouds. From what she had seen of Borneo her ambition had been whetted. She no longer resented being in Timor. She was stimulated and excited at the prospect of being in the mountains and meeting the mountain people.

The trail they were following doubled back on itself with maddening frequency, cut in knife-folds on the cliffside with barely enough room for both feet. Only the local Timor ponies could successfully manoeuvre the rugged ledges, moving with alarming speed but thankful accuracy. The drop below was terrifying.

As they climbed higher their ears popped in the thin air. They formed a straggling line along the side of the mountain. There was little talking as they concentrated on the next step, the heat of the day beating down on their heads.

Beyond the sharp rise they came out on to a forested plateau where they stopped briefly to rest. The cobalt shadows were a brief pleasure, but they knew they could not stay long. Beyond the trees the land descended into a shallow gully. Among the spare outlines of waif-like eucalyptus, the lalang grass grew parched and brown in the open sun for want of rain.

As they moved through the high, weaving pasture Dede thought the crackling noise they made was loud enough to announce their presence across the island.

Ahead, the others were looking nervously about, aware of the strange silence of the gully.

'Don't go near!' Moita-Ka's voice cut across the open land as he hurried across to Kate where she stood under a tree.

'What is it?' she asked the Timorese boy.

They both looked up into the high branches of the tree as the others came running to join them.

'Stand back,' said Moita-Ka. 'Is a nest.'

They stared up at the metre-wide construction that was suspended from the overhanging branch.

'Wild bees,' explained Father Jacinto. 'The local people come to smoke out the bees and collect honey and beeswax. It is an important source of wealth for the people here.'

Dede looked around, meeting Jack's eyes. 'Perhaps there is a village near.'

They had not gone another half-mile before the group stopped again. Father Jacinto raised his hand to stop those behind him, and they all stared in trepidation at the sight of two natives who had appeared at the rise of the track.

The young men were hunters on horseback carrying wooden bows and long, feathered arrows at the ready. They were without doubt as astonished to see them as the party was to be found. Their dark eyes traced the whole group as eagerly as the foreigners stared at the tattoos, the amulets and flashing gold chest plaques of the tribesmen. They were mountain people, from some of the oldest of the island's races. Short of stature, darker than the lowland and valley people, they were older versions of Moita-Ka, except for their finery and wide bushy hair trailing feathers from exotic local birds.

Dede looked towards Fielding and Father Jacinto, but it was Moita-Ka who took control of the situation.

The Tetum language was based on Church Latin and very melodic to the ear.

'What are they saying?' Dede asked Letria.

'I have no idea. They speak Tetum and something more. There are so many local dialects. I have never been so far inland.'

'The one with the feathers is apparently nephew to the local chief, who is Moita-Ka's father,' Father Jacinto explained. 'I think he has invited us to the village.'

'Is that wise?' asked Fielding.

'We all need food and rest,' said the priest. 'And we may hear some news there. The chief is cousin to Dom Aleixo Corte Real.'

'And who is he?' Dede said lightly.

'Dom Aleixo is a great leader. He has been honoured by Portuguese governors since the native rebellion of 1912.'

'He can be trusted?' asked Fielding.

'Captain, no one comes into the mountains without the knowledge of Dom Alexio. Even the Japanese.'

'How much further?'

'Not far,' Moita-Ka replied, but the trail they took led along the steep hillside and then down again. Wading through gullies and climbing back up the dry dusty side of the mountain, they despaired of ever reaching the village that was Moita-Ka's home.

'*Pigi-pigi*,' said their guides. No one was allowed to rest.

'Come on,' said Father Jacinto. 'It cannot be so far now.'

'That's what you said an hour ago.'

'I live in hope,' said the priest with a weary smile.

About a mile further on Sister Eulalia came back to join Katherine, Amy and Letria.

'Are we there?'

'Yes, at last. I expect there will be quite a lot of excitement. The people here rarely see white people, especially women. Do not be offended if they want to touch you.'

'I don't think I'm going to like this,' Kate said as Dede caught them up.

'Don't worry, honey. There's nothing to be scared of, really. They're just people, like you and me. Only, just watch what you touch. We don't know what taboos or local customs they have. It's all too easy to give offence.'

'I forgot that you knew all about these things.'

'Hardly,' Dede laughed. 'But I'm really interested to learn.'

'You're so bright. I really envy you the chance to go to college and everything. I never had that kind of chance back in London.'

It was the first time that Katherine had opened up to anyone. Dede had not even known that she was originally from London. But since Mrs Beattie's bitter betrayal, she had been on her own. Dede was not sorry that Kate had left the isolationist camp and now wanted to be friends with the other women. The only thing Dede regretted was that, like Amy, Kate seemed to look up to her as some kind of leader and expect too much of her.

Beyond the forest they entered a clearing and saw the tall thatch of houses on enormous stilts almost ten feet from the ground. There were various shapes and styles, with some houses much taller than others, with platforms around the bases and ladders up to the higher storeys. Dede had never seen anything like them before. They were quite unlike the long-houses of Borneo, far more exotic and eccentric in design.

The village seemed prosperous and so far untouched by the war. Outside the bamboo stockade and palms were cultivated fields. Inside, in the centre of the village, stood strange poles with a table for offerings, entwined with flowers and vines.

'I know what that is,' Dede told Kate as they passed into the village. 'They make offerings to ward off evil.'

It was quite a large settlement, with well-fed people, and a great many pigs and chickens rooting around between the stilts of the houses. As they passed the tall beehive huts, women stopped pounding sago to stare at them. The children eyed the strangers with huge round eyes, running towards them from every direction, scattering the chickens. Laughing and shouting, they were eager to touch the white-skinned strangers, pawing their clothes and seizing their hands. Any trace of fear quickly dissolved.

As they were ushered through to the central square by the children and barking dogs, they came before the poles Dede had seen before. She saw now that the altar was topped by the horns of a buffalo, dressed in flowers.

'*Lulic* poles,' said Sister Eulalia. 'To ward off evil. Many villages combine old ways with the new. We have a saying, "Religion comes in from the sea, but customs come down from the mountains." '

There was a commotion in the crowd and they drew aside to make room for their chieftain. He was obviously a person of great age and authority. The crowd fell silent out of respect. Chief Sha Nana was dressed in a draped sarong and *tais*, with a decorated skin belt and a pectoral necklace of beaten gold and quartz. He carried the staff of his authority, his arm jangling with many bracelets. His face was proof of long years of experience, finely etched with lines and scars. His bald head was smooth and polished like old mahogany, his eyes were bright as buttons as he saw Moita-Ka, his son.

'*Pak!*'

The boy ran to his father and fell at his feet. The old man raised him, his affection showing in his face. He heard his son explain their arrival and then turned to greet Father Jacinto, of whom he knew much but whom he had never met. He looked around the group, his liquid eyes fixing on the burly Australians, repeating some phrase over and over.

'*Tuan cataus*,' said Father Jacinto. 'It is their name for Australians.'

'Have they seen any of our blokes?' asked Jack.

'Or any Japanese?' asked Fielding.

Their questions were translated but Sha Nana seemed either unwilling or unable to provide the answers.

'There are formalities we must go through first,' said the priest. 'Later he will talk to us, but first we must follow the local custom. They want to show us their hospitality.'

Fielding drew himself up. 'Tell the chief we are most honoured to be here in this village – among allies.'

'S'truth,' said Seaton out of the corner of his mouth, 'he's treating the old boy as if he were bloody royalty.'

'That's what he is, I daresay,' said Jack, narrowly watching the chief summon his family to greet the strangers.

The chief's wives and Moita-Ka's sisters appeared, all ten of them. They made a bright array with their patterned *tais* and heavy gold necklaces. Dede noticed that the chief's head wife wore a rosary among the many beads at her throat.

A great meal was being prepared to honour the guests. The central square was spread with mats and flowers. According to the laws of hospitality, guests were to be treated to everything the village could offer. Fortunately Sha Nana's people had food in plenty, but even if they had not it would have been their duty to give what they had to their guests.

'*Adat*,' said Sister Eulalia, realizing Dede's interest in everything around her. '*Adat* law covers every aspect of their lives from the cradle to the grave. For instance, do you see those stones on the roofs of the houses? They are to keep bad spirits from harming the people inside.' She lowered her voice. 'And in some districts it is the custom – God forgive them – to build each house over the body of a child. One under every support.'

'How horrible,' said Kate, looking at her neighbours with less confidence.

'Don't be alarmed,' said the nun. 'It may not be so in this area.'

In a special ceremony of welcome the chief offered the men of the party a strong alcoholic drink called *tuaca*. There was some ritual attached to the way the liquid had first to be sniffed and then offered to the other men before drinking. Father Jacinto performed the traditional rite with due solemnity.

As if he were at mass, Dede thought, with a quick look at Sister Eulalia.

The women all sat together on the woven matting with the Timorese wives and daughters. They sat gracefully, legs tucked to one side, or with one knee bent, resting on an elbow. The women with babies were kept to one side.

Father Jacinto took a deep draught from the cup but his composure was soon shattered as the fiery liquid struck home. He passed the cup quickly over to Fielding. The captain took a delicate sip but then spluttered and grimaced, much to the amusement of their hosts.

'He won't like that,' Seaton predicted, but to the surprise of the Australians Fielding broke into a wide grin that was infectious, breaking through that stern and formal mask of authority he had adopted, laying bare a buried youthfulness.

Plates of food were laid before the guests. Dede knew the taro and sweet potatoes that accompanied rice dishes of pork and roast goat. There was also *tempi* and papaw.

As Kate reached towards a dish that was offered to her by one of the chief's daughters, Dede warned her to eat only with her right hand. The left hand, she quickly explained, was commonly regarded in the east for use for more intimate bodily functions.

The others showed little hesitation, reaching out for

whatever they wanted, grinning at each other as they ate. Father Jacinto tried to express his appreciation to the chief and looked around for confirmation.

'Best tucker we've had in weeks, Father,' was the cheerful Australians response.

The evening proved a success. As they picked at the dishes with their fingers there was much laughter. It was almost possible to forget that they were in the middle of a war and that the Japanese were daily moving further into the heart of the island.

As the party began to break up and the pungent smoke from the cooking fires faded, Fielding asked the priest to try to discover any news about the Japanese. Father Jacinto went with Moita-Ka and conferred with Sha Nana, coming back looking pale and troubled.

'They have seen no one here,' he told them, 'but Dom Aleixo has made contact with some officers of your army. The problem is that they are very far from here.'

'What about the Japs?'

'There was a raid on Dili. The Japanese blamed everything on Australians and have called special troops to come to the island. Remexio has been attacked with artillery.'

Letria looked at Sister Eulalia, full of apprehension for his old home. Even the neutral Portuguese would not have been safe in an artillery bombardment.

'And here?' asked Fielding. 'Is there news of any Japs operating in this district?'

The priest looked away. He paused only a second longer before producing a few crumpled sheets of rough paper from behind his back.

'These were found in the valley,' he said ominously.

The papers were passed around the inquisitive group but their interest turned to silent suspicion. Dede took one and saw it was some kind of leaflet, crudely printed in a lurid colour with tight rows of black characters. She shrugged, passing it quickly over to Amy, who turned it around in her hands.

'Is it Japanese?' asked Jack, clutching another of the leaflets. 'Does the chief know what it says?'

'No,' began the priest, but he was interrupted.

'Roughly translated it says, "We are waging war against the

White Devils",' said Fielding, shocking them all into a tense silence.

'You speak Japanese?' asked Dede in astonishment.

'Bloody hell!' said Seaton. 'He speaks Japanese!'

'And Dutch. That's why I was sent here.' Fielding stared back at them defensively, acutely aware of their surprise and hostility. 'They needed language experts. They came recruiting in the university – so I volunteered.' He looked down again to the Japanese leaflet in his hands and continued with his translation. 'It goes on to warn any Asian servants who stay to help Europeans that they will be found and put to death.'

The little group looked at each other, knowing that the villagers were now at risk for helping them. But more than that, they now knew the Japanese planes had been in the area very recently.

'Well,' said Father Jacinto. 'There's nothing we can do tonight. I suggest that we all try to get some sleep.' He offered to show the men to the house that had been given over to them for the night.

Fielding was uneasy. He watched as the men and women began to move away to their separate quarters. He wondered if he had imagined it. But as he saw Amy hesitate, then turn her head and look back at him, he knew he had been right.

Chapter Twenty-one

At the entrance to the women's house Dede and Sister Eulalia were stopped by Kate. Her face was pinched with anxiety as she prevented Dede from climbing the ladder into the hut.

'Wait a minute, please. Is this the only place where we can sleep?'

Dede looked up at the hut, noting its size, and then looked back at Kate, clearly puzzled. 'Oh yes, I know it's big enough,' Kate said quickly, 'but you try telling that to *her*.'

Dede was in no doubt whom she meant. Only Mrs Beattie had gone ahead of the little group.

'Well, tough,' said Dede. 'Tonight she's going to have to share and like it.'

Sister Eulalia grinned ruefully. 'She'll have something to say about that.'

Amy had caught up with them and immediately assumed that she was the reason behind the conflict.

'Please don't let there be trouble. I'll find somewhere else to sleep – '

'You stay right where you are, honey,' Dede told her. 'I'm sick of that woman throwing her weight around.'

'It's not you,' Kate said anxiously. 'I'm afraid it's me, too. She hates me. No, it's true, you've seen the way she looks at me.'

'To hell with her,' said Dede.

'That *is* one solution,' Sister Eulalia remarked drily. 'Come with me,' she told Dede, 'we're going to have a little talk with the senhora.'

Dede was surprised to find such an ally. Kate's pleas seemed to place even more responsibility on her shoulders. But the nun had shown surprising strength and leadership. Dede was only too pleased to follow where she led.

Inside the hut they were in for a shock. Mrs Beattie had finally unpacked the contents of her precious luggage, revealing an undreamt of hoard of treasure and comforts spread around the wooden hut as if it had been her own private first-class cabin. She was brushing her hair, using a matching silver-backed brush and mirror, and looked up with some surprise at their entrance.

'Yes?' she inquired, brush raised.

Dede was about to jump in with both feet but Sister Eulalia cut short her hot-headed biting rush of words.

'Why, Mrs Beattie! What wonderful things you have here.' The nun moved silently, for all the world to Dede like Little Red Riding Hood approaching the wolf in its lair. 'And to think you have brought all this with you so far only now to leave it all behind – '

Dede blinked as much as Mrs Beattie.

'Leave it behind?' echoed the Englishwoman.

'Oh yes, didn't you understand? Father Jacinto has given the horses to the village in exchange for food and for help. You will not want to carry all this yourself – '

'I don't understand! What on earth are you talking about?'

'Ah, my English is so bad!' the nun lamented soulfully. 'I try my best, but I am not a good – scholar, do you say?' She looked at Dede with a plaintive expression that almost disguised the glint of mischief in her grey eyes.

'What is the woman trying to say?' Mrs Beattie demanded of Dede in exasperation.

'But don't worry,' Sister Eulalia continued breezily, bending down to pick up things from the floor, 'I will see that these get a good home. The villagers will be delighted when they see what you are giving them. Such charity!'

'But I'm not – '

'No, please! Such modesty!' She looked at Dede. 'Help me move all this to one side. In the morning I will give them to the chief.'

'Oh no you won't!' said Mrs Beattie in horror.

'Ah, you want to give them to him yourself? Of course, of

course I understand, but first of all let us make room for the night. After all,' she added with a determined glint in her grey eyes, 'there are *five* of us in here.'

Dede went out to tell Kate and Amy that they could go inside now, there was room for all of them. Amy climbed the ladder but Kate still seemed nervous and reluctant to face Mrs Beattie. Dede touched her lightly on the arm, remembering the scene back at the *posto*.

'Don't be afraid. She's shocked, but so what? It's none of her damned business.'

'You don't understand,' said Kate. 'The father of the baby is her son.'

'Oh my God.'

Kate grimaced, a mixture of pain and shame, distressed to have to talk about it.

'I try so hard to forget him. But I think of him all the time.'

Dede shifted uncomfortably, aware that the girl was watching her expectantly. Expecting what? Sympathy, reassurance? Perhaps even shared confidences?

'I dream of him,' said Kate in a small voice. 'I have these terrible dreams – ever since Hong Kong, you know. But now, of course, it's all about Singapore. About what's happened to Harry.'

'Harry?'

'Oh, Dede, he was so handsome, so – '

Oh God, thought Dede, she's going to cry!

'Mrs Beattie didn't know, you see. It was all a secret, our secret. And I didn't know, I never dreamt – when I left Singapore, I mean – '

'Yes, I can see it must have been some kind of shock,' said Dede gently.

'She was my last link with all that, Singapore, I mean. Mrs Beattie kept it all alive, real, you know. But now – ' Kate broke off, desperate to make Dede understand that now Mrs Beattie's hostility had robbed her of her last link with everything she had known before. Singapore was gone and fading in her memory where only the day-to-day struggle to survive now had any significance. 'I can't cry, Dede. All my tears have been used up.'

'That's okay, honey – '

'No, you must think me so selfish. You never talk about your fiancé – '

'No, I don't.'

'But it must be just as awful for you, too.'

Dede gave what she hoped would be a reassuring smile. How to explain that it all seemed so far away? That Manila was like a dream, and Balikpapan a nightmare? That if she ever thought about Warren at all, it was with regret – not for what might have been, but for the hurt and disappointment she knew she would have brought him. In a way, the war had intervened and saved them both.

'I just hope he makes it through alive,' said Dede. Then, perhaps, he would get the second chance he deserved, without her.

In the dark shadows of the women's house the moonlight filtered in thin shafts through gaps in the thatch. When Sister Eulalia made ready to extinguish the coconut-oil lamp between their rush-mat beds, she gave a noticeable shudder.

'What's the matter?' asked Dede.

'Listen.'

The extinguishing of the lamp was the signal for an onrush of feverish activity in the thatch.

'What the hell is that?'

'Rats!' came Amy's distinctive voice in the darkness.

'Put the lamp on again, quick!'

Sister Eulalia struggled to light the oil just in time to see a column of grey furry rats scatter away down the wooden joists, twittering in high-pitched squeaks. One, more adventurous than the others, leapt four feet from the wall, its thin long tail brushing Kate's bare legs. She leapt to her feet, screaming, but the rat disappeared.

'Please can we leave the lamp on?' she pleaded.

'Yes, please,' croaked Dede, sitting hunched up in a corner, revealing that she was really no braver than any of them.

Hours later she woke from a fitful sleep to find herself surrounded by a ring of faces staring back at her. It seemed that the whole female population of the village had turned out to wake them up, eager for a closer look at their curious guests.

Mrs Beattie was still asleep, snoring hoarsely, her face turned away. But of the others there was no sign. Dede hurriedly shook out her shoes before putting them on and ran her fingers roughly through her hair, much to the amusement of her audience. A grinning six-year-old offered her a tree orchid for a hair decoration.

She left Mrs Beattie still sleeping and went with the village children outside, climbing down the notched ladder into the compound. The bright morning sunshine seared her eyes as she stared about her. Even at this early hour the village was a hive of activity, boisterous with noise. Walking with her escort of gaily chattering children, Dede finally caught up with the rest of her group outside the chief's house.

Fielding appeared dishevelled and vulnerable, as if he, too, had only just been woken.

'There is nothing else for it,' he explained to the others, 'we have to move on. We can't expect the villagers to put themselves at risk for us.'

Dede saw that Seaton and Harrison were restless. They made no secret that they saw this development as a betrayal. In spite of last night's hospitality, they were still racists. What they had seen and heard of the Timorese in Dutch Timor continued to colour their view of all natives.

'They'll sell us to the Nips the minute we shoot through.'

Fielding was holding one of the Japanese leaflets. 'Then why did they show us these? They wanted to warn us of the danger.'

Jack came forward, his green uniform jacket still undone, revealing a broad expanse of tanned chest.

'Won't they help us any more?'

'No,' said the captain, 'they are very willing to help.'

'But you said – '

'They just will not let us stay in the village. But they have agreed to show us a safe place further up the mountain. They are giving us food in return for all but one of the pack horses.'

'Hey, hold on, mate,' said Seaton, 'we need those horses ourselves.' He shared a glance of open resentment with Harrison. It was just one damn thing after another. Would their luck never change?

The whole village turned out to see their departure. The people had seen bad times come and go in their history. Now they had come again.

There was genuine warmth and regret in their farewell. Moita-Ka stood at the boundary with a raised hand.

'May the mountain spirits guide your steps.'

Father Jacinto looked back at the boy with an indulgent smile. It seemed that all his mission education still could not compete with his true cultural heritage.

Their local guides set off at a great pace, full of vitality at their venture as the rest of the group struggled on behind. Father Jacinto led the heavily burdened pack horse and all the men and some of the women carried supplies. Mrs Beattie, for the first time, had to walk.

'What is this place they're taking us to?' asked the captain between breaths as he climbed beside the priest.

'It's an old Portuguese villa. There used to be a small village there for hunting, but now it's abandoned. We will be safe up there for a while.'

'Why was it abandoned?'

'Oh, the local people have certain taboos. They hold the villa in superstition. They never go up there. They won't even take us all the way.'

They made a fast march, trying to keep up with the guides. A haze hung over the mountain, a warning of the terrible heat to come. The way was increasingly difficult, even for the fittest of the party. The line straggled out down the hill as they climbed, stumbling and slipping, but the boys would not slow down.

There was a growing uneasiness about them that soon made itself felt among the rest of the group. The boys would talk together and then change direction, hurrying onwards with nervous looks back over their shoulders.

'Why are they so nervous?' Kate asked Dede, pausing for a moment to get her breath back. Her legs were swelling and the pain in her back had never been worse. She stood, arching her back, her hand on her hip.

'I guess they're afraid of the spirits. Father Jacinto said something about the place being full of taboos. I saw something like it in Borneo. They believe there are spirits in trees, rocks, anything. If they take the wrong path then the spirits may take revenge on them.'

She saw that her little lecture had been overheard by Seaton and Harrison. Seaton's mouth twisted with coarse scepticism and she fell silent, her mouth closed in a sullen line, not even looking at Jack who had come up to join them.

As the shadows lengthened, the forest was full of birdsong heralding dusk. The edge of the enormous crimson disc of the sun peeked behind the mountain. It would soon be dark.

'How much further?' asked Fielding. They had been walking all day, with few rests for he had been afraid of losing their guides.

'They say they will leave us soon,' said the priest.

'I'm worried about Mrs Beattie,' Fielding told him, glancing back down the trail in the half-light. 'She won't accept help from anyone. I'm afraid if we have much further to go, we may have to carry her.'

Ahead of them on the path were gigantic standing stones. For a moment Fielding thought they must be part of some ruined building half-overgrown by the forest, but as he drew closer he saw that they were not man-made at all.

'*Fatu*,' said their guide, keeping his distance.

'They will go no further,' said Father Jacinto. 'They believe the spirits of the dead come and gather at such rocks.'

In the humid shadowland the place seemed strangely silent. No one mocked the natives' beliefs. They looked about them, a little wary of the strange grove.

'But where is the villa?'

'Very close now. They are telling us to go up the hill.'

'Won't they show us the way?' Fielding asked, turning back to where the guides had been standing, but they had vanished. 'Where have they gone?' he asked in amazement.

The strangers found themselves alone and deserted, standing before the high stones. The skyline of the mountains had turned a threatening purple, heralding a storm.

'The rains,' breathed Amy, her eyes meeting Letria's.

With no other alternative they took the path the boys had indicated, moving ahead cautiously. The track was barely visible in places under the long grass. The overhanging branches brushed their faces as they passed, oddly silent. The villa was isolated halfway up the mountain, in the middle of nowhere. It was a place of thunder, cool among the pines.

The small group moved through the wild grass, what was once the garden overrun by a jungle of trees and flowering shrubs. Grass had almost devoured the villa, abandoned under the hill, with crumbling pillared verandahs thick with wild figs and half-buried by vines. In the waning light it looked desolate and mysterious.

'So we're here,' said Jack. 'What d'you reckon?'

Flame trees glowed in the lengthening shadows. The jacaranda and weeds choked the wooden steps of the verandah. A lizard ran as Fielding's boots vibrated on the hollow boards. He tried the door, almost lost behind a curtain of vegetation, but a window proved easier. The diseased wood of the frame soon gave to pressure and he forced the sash up and free of the trailing vines.

The house reeked of decay. How long it had been abandoned was anyone's guess. Once it had been a family home, with some aspirations towards modern comforts. Passing from room to room they stepped on a carpet cloaked in dead leaves and grasses, staring at the faded photographs of long-lost hunting parties still hanging on the yellowed walls in their cracked frames.

'It's amazing,' said Dede.

'Look, there's still some furniture in here.'

'It's like the bloody *Marie Celeste*,' said Jack, scratching his beard. 'What d'you think happened to them?'

'Christ, mate, I don't want to think about it.'

Sister Eulalia stood in the doorway. 'Can someone please help me with Mrs Beattie?'

She was exhausted, her legs unable to support her as they carried her through to one of the bedrooms. They let her down gently and put a pack under her head. Her face was scarlet, beads of sweat stark on her brow.

'She has a high temperature,' said the nun, kneeling at her side. She saw Katherine standing in the doorway. 'I don't like the look of this.'

Lightning split the dense sky, promising the advent of the rains. As Jack stared out through the broken lattice of the wooden shutters he heard the crash of thunder and saw the first heavy drops of rain splatter the dust. In the fitful night the room was lost in darkness, the air thick and oppressive. The sudden downpour of violent rain came as a relief.

Jack alone among the men could not sleep. Australia was still there on his mind. Home and the sight and smells of the outback. Standing at the window he was racked by thoughts of home and half-forgotten memories. He was full of sudden bitterness at the fate that had delivered him here for no apparent purpose.

The wind rose, slamming shutters and shaking the window frames. Leaves and petals swept across the garden. A flash of lightning lit up the room. He looked back at Fielding, curled up on his side, dead to the world, and envied him.

He went and stood outside, hearing the fierce patter of the rain all around him, feeling the warm thick splashes soaking his back. The night was full of the scent of the pines and damp earth. The first brief squall had turned the fine dust of the track to bronze mud. After the rain the earth steamed. He heard the sound of a rushing stream through the hazy trees.

As he walked towards it he caught sight of something extraordinary, a flickering light that drew him nearer. At first he thought it was a fire started by lightning among the dry grasses, but as he moved into the light he saw it was not a fire at all.

It was a firefly tree. Hundreds of the little insects hovered about its branches in the dark, so that the whole tree seemed afire.

'Isn't it wonderful?'

He had not heard her approach, his very rigidity made that clear.

'The rain woke me,' said Dede. Her dirty white shirt was patterned with rain splashes spreading out across the fabric.

Jack searched his pockets for cigarettes and then remembered he had run out. His thoughts were very far away as he stared at the firefly tree. There was a lost childhood wondering in his eyes as she looked at him.

'This place up here, it's more like Arnhem Land.'

'Where's that?'

'Back home,' he told her. 'It's completely wild there. Just as hot. Up to fifty degrees in the summer, our summer, I mean. The rivers there are full of crocs.'

'Crocs?'

'You know, crocodiles.'

'Yes?' She wanted to hear more.

'Used to be abo land once. You still see some of them going walkabout. There are these caves full of paintings they did thousands of years ago.'

'Is that where you come from? That part of Australia? It must be very different from here.'

'No, it's not at all. In fact the minute we started up into the mountains I thought how much like home it was. We did a lot of our training in land like this down around Katherine.'

'Katherine?'

'It's this station south of Darwin. All gums and scrub. We could live off the land there, no problem. But down around Tennants Creek, well, that's different, dry, you know.'

She was looking at him, intrigued by his nostalgia, almost a kind of homesickness. A new side of his character was revealed, a side she had not guessed existed.

He stood silhouetted against the firefly tree brightness, with a hardness of outline that belied the look in his eyes. His strong almost stocky build gave him the outward appearance of someone who could handle himself, a bruiser of the outback. His almost classic nose close up was revealed slightly crooked, broken, perhaps in a fist fight. But the green eyes were a revelation.

He grinned suddenly, disarmingly. 'You ought to see Arnhem in the Wet. There's this gorge and the river right down the bottom. Some sight.'

She noticed a scar on his lip from some accident long ago. He seemed suddenly vulnerable.

'You miss it?' she asked softly.

He looked away, but she had seen the laughter lines around his eyes that were proof of earlier, easier times.

'There's nowhere like it. It's a new land, you know. You feel you can start out fresh, do anything.'

Like the pioneers, thought Dede, like America used to be.

'I joined up looking for a bit of excitement, you know. To

see a bit of the world.' His green eyes caught and held hers. 'Like yourself.'

'Yes,' said Dede slowly, 'like me.' He had taken her by surprise. She had not thought they would be alike in any way, but she saw that she was wrong. 'You know, when I was a kid I used to dream about getting away, travelling to remote exotic places. Like this.' She laughed and he joined in. 'Well, at least I was prepared,' she added. 'I was brought up in a real rough-house with my brothers, both older than me. I guess I was a tomboy. I was always in hot water. It's not so different, is it?' She shrugged. 'When this war is over, I don't know what I'll do, but I still want to travel, see places – '

'When the war is over, if we come through, I'm going to do something with my life.' He seemed suddenly self-conscious, glancing at her sideways. 'Maybe that's dumb, I don't know, but I don't want to be pushed around all my bloody life, do you see?'

'Yes, yes I see,' said Dede.

They sat on side by side in comfortable silence, the darkness around them, the air rich with humidity. Strange to share the night in such a place, at such a time, having come so far, without knowing the future.

Chapter Twenty-two

Mrs Beattie was ill, there was no denying it. She had a high fever and at times was delirious, calling out in the night for her husband, for Harry and Suzy.

'I've done all I can for her,' said Sister Eulalia, 'but I don't have the right medicines. I don't even have herbs to bring down the fever.'

'Could the villagers help us?' asked Father Jacinto.

'They have helped us enough. We cannot put them in danger when what we need could be found on any market stall.'

Father Jacinto told the assembled group that he intended making a journey into the nearest town in the valley that Sunday.

'There will be a bazaar. If any village has food to spare I will try to bring some back, for they will surely try to sell it there.' He claimed he would not attract suspicion if he travelled alone. The sight of a Portuguese priest on a pony would not cause comment if seen by Japanese patrols or their local agents. On Sundays there was a tradition of freedom of movement. The former Portuguese administration had controlled the movement of natives. They had to have written permission to leave their own districts, but on Sundays there was unrestricted traffic to and from local markets and bazaars.

'It's a chance worth taking,' said Letria thoughtfully.

'Nothing doing,' Seaton retorted.

'Surely it's dangerous, Father,' said Dede.

Fielding knew that as an officer he must give the lead. The others surely expected it of him. He saw they didn't like the priest risking his neck on their behalf. He would have to come up with some argument to keep Father Jacinto where he belonged – with Sister Eulalia and the other women.

'You can't go down there,' he told the priest in front of the listening audience. 'It's too dangerous, I'm afraid.'

The priest turned, a little surprised. 'I was not asking your permission, Captain,' he said with maddening patience. 'We are already – how do you say? – beyond the pale? Even before you came here we had become outcasts.' He smiled to see Fielding's confusion. 'We decided we must stay and continue our work as long as possible, in spite of the war situation. The bishop wanted all nuns and priests to return to Dili. He said the Japanese would guarantee our immunity, our neutrality, do you understand? But we decided – Sister Eulalia and myself – we decided we would go with you into the mountains. Here, with our people, because they need us.'

'What about the bishop?'

Father Jacinto spread his veined knobbly hands. 'We cannot always please our superiors, Captain. Down in Dili things are very different, I daresay. The bishop has to please the governor and the new Japanese administration. Down there people will be afraid. Afraid to lose the things they have.' He looked up sharply. 'Here, Captain, the people have nothing to lose. That is why they will fight.'

There was a stunned silence. Who among them had guessed that Father Jacinto and Sister Eulalia were as much outlaws as themselves?

'Once the father makes up his mind,' said Sister Eulalia, 'nothing can stop him.' And she gave a resigned smile.

With the single pack horse Father Jacinto set off down the mountain as the mist lifted in the valley. It had rained overnight and the low leafy path downwards now glistened in the early sunlight. The air was rich with the cloying sweetness of moist earth and the smell of resin from the pines.

Travelling north he found a countryside in turmoil. The main valley road was flooded with refugees in flight from the Japanese advance. Many families were in a desperate plight, without goods or money, their children badly malnourished.

Through the hot dusty noonday he passed flocks of peasants walking in the opposite direction.

'You are going the wrong way, Padre,' he was warned time

and time again. 'The Japanese are coming.'

As he approached the little market town nestling beneath the hills he met a family driving a buffalo cart laden with their household possessions.'

'*Makan angin kah?*' They asked him if he was out riding, as if for pleasure, here in the midst of a war.

'*Selamat datang*,' he returned. 'Are there Japanese in the town?'

'Not yet, Padre.'

'They were seen on the Ermera road,' another passerby contradicted.

He found the town ready to burst at the seams, swollen to three times its limits by the influx of refugees down from the north. In the streets there was a sense of undeniable panic. As Father Jacinto led his horse among the surging crowds, the heat and the smells made the town seem like a cauldron about to burst.

In the market place he was alarmed at the feverish activity. The sense of danger and panic was infectious. He could read the fear in the eyes of the motley crowds, feel the tension as they jostled each other. The whole area was a polyglot of races and colours, some from the towns in brightly dyed sarongs and turbans, others in native *tais* with tattooed skin marking them as mountain people. Women in vivid colours carried pots on their heads and babies on their backs.

Everywhere the business of the day was buying and selling, with the refugees frantically disposing of whatever they possessed for food for the hard journey south. Leading his pony between the assorted goods spread out on stalls or rush mats on the ground, he saw rice from Ainaro, salt and pineapples from the coast and coffee from local plantations. There were round white mangosteens halved in their thick purple skin, long dried chillis, green and local red-skinned bananas and other fruit. There was a rich smell of spices in the heat, overpowering the scents of food. There was a constant hubbub of conversation shouted in a dozen dialects and accents. The village people from miles around sold their produce direct, haggling and gesturing as they chewed the habitual betel nut, their mouths red and stained.

Father Jacinto could see no livestock, no chickens, no pigs, not even eggs. When he asked he heard the news that the Japanese were seizing animals wherever they went, including all available horses with the clear intention of making a push south into the mountains after the Australians. The Timorese were very willing to sell the Japanese as many horses as they needed, as often as they needed them. They were expert horse thieves and could easily sell the same animal twice over, given the chance, as Father Jacinto knew only too well. He had to smile, thinking the Japanese stood little chance against the cunning of the local people.

But he found the news disturbing. From refugees he learnt that the Japanese were conducting ruthless campaigns to drive out the *tuan cataus*, as they called the Australians. They were also attacking any Portuguese or native Timorese who helped the Australians.

Such was his distraction that he was almost knocked down by a Moslem on a bicycle who turned to shout abuse at him. Father Jacinto watched him drive off, honking the horn as his bicycle swerved through the crowds.

Wandering through the displays of batik and woven fabrics, Maubisse pottery and baskets, he wondered at the high prices being demanded because of the crisis. He wondered if he would be able to buy medicine with the money at his disposal, let alone any food. And what reaction would he find when he produced some of the Australian money he had been given?

'Father, Father! You don't remember me?'

He turned to find a Chinese trader at his side dressed in a distinctive white linen jacket with brass buttons high to the neck.

'Lu Shan! What are you doing here?'

'Ah, Father! Now we all serve new masters.' He gave an ironic shrug, his bland face crinkling in a grimace. 'I was sent out from Dili to fill the bellies of our new gods.'

Like the rest of his race Lu Shan did not disguise his loathing of the Japanese.

'But I am a businessman, too,' he added, 'and when food is like gold dust back in Dili I accept the safe conduct to fetch in supplies.' He pressed the side of his nose with a tobacco-stained forefinger. 'Be a bamboo, bend with the wind and you will never break.'

'As always, Lu Shan, you are a born survivor,' said the priest. He took his old friend by the arm and spoke softly. 'Tell me, what news have you heard? It is many weeks since I was at the convent – ' He stopped short, recognizing the look in the Chinese trader's eyes. 'What is it, my friend? You have heard something? Come, tell me everything. Hold nothing back.'

The Chinese shook his head, his mouth tight with emotion.

'What I have to say will bring little joy or comfort, Father. First you must believe I have not seen these things for myself. I saw only what happened in Dili and on the road here. Many arrests, many things stolen for new masters. They are rebuilding the aerodrome.' He met the priest's eyes. 'They blame the *tuan cataus* for everything. They call them devils. There is now one hundred pataccas for each head. A thousand pataccas for their leaders.'

The priest digested this news solemnly. He wondered what would be the reaction of Fielding, Jack Ford and the others.

'But what of the convent?'

The Chinese looked about him and then called out to the boy who was guarding his supplies to wait a while and guard the father's horse.

'Let us talk then, Father,' said Lu Shan. 'I will tell you what I know. Of the convent, yes, and of the new camp at Liquissa, too. Come with me.'

The bright sunshine was incongruous to the darkness which had suddenly descended. Weighed down by the fresh burden of his news, Father Jacinto leant heavily on the crupper of his horse in a cold sweat. Alone among the rushing throng, he could not move a step. The horse bore his weight patiently, head held low in the dust of the market place.

With the heat and the noise he was unsteady on his feet. The persistent clamour of voices and the ringing of bells made his head swim. Men and women knocked into him and the sudden surge of panicking bodies struck him unexpectedly, as unexpected as the wild tolling of church bells over the square.

Father Jacinto jerked up his head, caught by the urgent alarums scattering the crowd all around him. He looked out across the market place and saw the planes as they appeared skimming the rooftops.

'Run, run!'

The air was full of the sounds of fear and panic. The streets of the little town rang with screams and cries as the crowd began to thin and scatter, knocking over the piles of produce in their terror to escape.

'Run, run!'

Father Jacinto stared in mesmerized horror at the sight of the Japanese bombers droning in for the attack.

The sound of firing reached him as he turned to run. He was caught in the crush of panic-stricken people trapped in the narrow streets leading off from the central square. Their fear was contagious, spreading through the crowd as the planes groaned overhead. Two Zero fighters dipped in low, spraying bullets into the white plasterwork of the houses. Here and there someone went down, almost under the stampeding feet of the crowd as the bullets erupted across the street.

Those who could got inside the houses and shops down the side streets before doors and windows were battened against them. Those left outside in the open hammered frantically on the shutters, crying and cursing. Others crouched in the gutter, huddling low together against the walls for protection. Only the children, open-mouthed at their first sight of aircraft, seemed without fear.

Overhead the Japanese twin-engined bombers moaned as they released their load on the tiny town.

There was no shelter as the buildings surrounding the market place were struck. The white tower of the church received a direct hit. It cracked all along its length, sending the alarm bells tumbling in a roar of furious sound down among the debris of masonry into the street.

All around people were thrown off their feet by the blast wave of the explosions. Father Jacinto lay with his face in the dirt, feeling the very earth shudder from the impact. The air was dense with dust and red-hot ashes as lethal shrapnel ricocheted between the buildings. The smell of burning timber and thatch reached him as he tried to struggle to his feet. Clouds of swirling dust and choking smoke cloaked the full horror of the scene about him.

He stumbled across the rubble in the street as the ground began to shake again. Suddenly he felt the earth tilt. He crashed headlong to meet the moving wall as the whole street caved in to engulf the huddling masses.

The town was on fire. As the Japanese aircraft circled to off-load their bundles of circulars, a pall of dense smoke blotted out the noonday sun. The drifting white papers scattered over the ruins as they turned and flew north once more.

By the time Father Jacinto struggled free from the debris of the streets, the planes had disappeared. He stood up unsteadily, unaware of the blood that ran down his arm. He was caked in thick plaster dust and gasping for air. The taste of bile was his mouth.

One side of the entire street had been demolished. Flames snaked through the broken masonry, the heat fierce in his face. It seemed to scorch his skin as the wall at right angles sagged and crumpled in upon itself, sending showers of fiery splinters across the street.

The priest struggled to pull people from the ruins. He was the only one among the shell-shocked, weeping survivors to think about those trapped. He tried in vain to get others to help him, met only by blank, uncomprehending stares.

What reason could they have had for such an attack? The town was not a military target. It was not even strategically important. His brave words to the captain back at the villa seemed so hollow now. Sheer boasting to talk of resistance and the will to fight. The sin of pride. Foolishness. What hope had these poor people of ever opposing a technological power like Japan? Armed only with stone axes, bows and arrows against the bomber and heavy artillery?

He stopped to pick up one of the leaflets which lay like obscene confetti over the broken town. The printing seemed familiar as he turned it over in his hands, and then realized he had seen something similar in Sha Nana's village. The only difference was that the Japanese had learnt to print their propaganda messages in the language of their enemies. These leaflets were in Portuguese and Tetum.

One hundred pataccas were offered for the head of each Australian caught or handed over to the Japanese authorities. Lu Shan had not lied. He had not lied about the Japanese rewards, he had not lied about the mindless brutality of the new masters of Timor.

Bombing first and then coercion. Those who survived to crawl out of the ruins of their devastated towns were now expected to collaborate or die. The Japanese were ready to bribe them with their hundred pataccas for men like Seaton, Harrison and Jack Ford, and a thousand pataccas for an officer like Fielding. The stark print in his hands proclaimed their message:

'The time of liberation has come! Peoples of Timor, Japan has sent her bravest soldiers to help you overthrow the tyranny of the white man! A new dawn comes to Timor! Act now!'

Chapter Twenty-three

'Are you still here?' Dede stood in the doorway looking down as Kate sat beside Mrs Beattie.

'There's no change. She doesn't even recognize me. It seems so strange. She was always so strong, so much in charge – '

Dede sank on to her knees at Kate's side.

'I thought,' Kate continued, 'I thought she was having a heart attack. She couldn't stand the heat. She was exhausted.' She looked up sharply, her face drawn and pale. 'Do you think – she'll die?'

Dede took her hand and squeezed it. 'She just needs rest, I guess. If you don't come away and get some sleep now you'll be falling ill too, and you've got the baby to think about.'

Kate placed a hand on her stomach and gave a pained smile. 'She hates me, she hates the baby. And yet if she only knew – '

'Don't think like that. It doesn't matter what she said. Nothing matters now, don't you see? We've got to put the past out of our minds. The future's what counts. Getting out of here, being safe.'

Kate looked up at her, full of admiration. 'You're so strong, Dede. Nothing ever seems to get you down. You keep us all going.'

Dede thought ironically, 'That's all you know! You don't know how I long just to run off, to get out of here and save my own skin. I'm not strong, she thought, I'm weak and scared. I no longer know who I am or where the hell I'm going.

As darkness fell over the valley, fires continued to burn in the town. Dark silhouettes moved against the flickering orange light among whorls of grey smoke. The rubble-strewn streets rang with the wailing of those still searching the ruins for their dead.

The smell of dust and death were all-powerful. Bent figures, scarred by the experiences of the past twenty-four traumatic hours, scrabbled with bare hands in the rubble, pulling the dead and dying from the ruins. Red-eyed from weeping and fatigue, they were filthy with blast dust and splattered with blood. There seemed no end to the line of sprawling corpses being laid out. Father Jacinto moved softly among the wounded and dying, giving the last rites to those who called out to him.

Many had not stayed behind to face the full horror of destruction. Throughout the long agony of the night small groups of terrified townspeople fled the ruins of their homes, taking with them whatever they could carry. They fled the town in a state of shock, moving ever southwards.

Only those with relatives wounded in the raid remained. Their stooped figures moved like scavengers among the shattered smoking buildings, searching for food and any medical supplies by the flare of the fires.

In the fitful dawn a fresh tremor of panic ran round the town. Father Jacinto was in one of the houses that now served as a temporary first-aid post when they brought him the news. Eyes wide with stark terror, barely able to mouth the words, they pointed back along the north road.

'*Djepang, Djepang!*'

The priest stood up among the wounded. They had lost no time then, following up their terror tactics. He moved outside among the panic-driven Timorese. The Japanese convoy was already on the valley road, clearly visible between the flattened buildings.

In awed silence the survivors of the town gathered around him in the ruins of the market square to watch the arrival of the armoured vehicle at the head of a column of horsemen and infantry. Many had never seen such a motor vehicle in their lives and took a step backwards as the car ground to a halt in the square. Behind stood the first of the Japanese, carrying rifles with bayonets at the ready.

What Father Jacinto saw was primarily a peasant army, men of the fields thrust into shabby, mass-produced uniforms, flap caps protecting their heads and necks from the sun, ancient rifles in their hands. They were as small as the Timorese, but alien, their blank faces communicating little. Uneducated men perhaps, but blooded by long years of savage warfare in China, brutalized, unquestioning.

What were their thoughts now as they entered this pitiful town and saw the handiwork of their brave fliers? Saw the pathetic line of men, women and children laid out in the sun, already drawing the flies?

Behind them came outriders and pack horses loaded with weapons and supplies. As they drew aside the people saw for the first time the Japanese allies massed a hundred strong in their rear. The priest felt the increase in tension in the crowd as they saw their Timorese brothers in arms for the Japanese invaders.

So, it was true then. All that they had heard was now confirmed. The sight of the Dutch-area natives put more fear into the survivors than even the armoured car of the Japanese. The Dutch half of the island had gone over to the invader, creating a division among the Timorese that was tantamount to civil war.

The warlike band stood in an undisciplined huddle, wearing a strange combination of traditional native dress and donated Japanese accessories, their faces and arms still bearing the painted designs and tattoos of previous victories. Father Jacinto knew the old rivalries and feuds that had threatened the peace of the island over many generations. Now he saw that the coming of the invader had drawn these internal hatreds to the surface once again and harnessed them for the Japanese' own purposes. But the weapons borne by the Dutch natives were all of local manufacture, stone axes and spears. It seemed that the Japanese did not trust their new allies sufficiently to arm them with rifles.

The motorized vehicle had come to a stop well away from the site where the dead lay. The Japanese officer never even glanced in that direction. He was a *shosa*, a major. He stood up in the car and adjusted his white gloves before climbing down.

His eyes moved across the pathetic, cowed crowd before him. He carried himself with exaggerated pride and conveyed a sense of limitless authority to the crowd. There was no doubt that this man carried the power of life and death over them all.

The contrast between his cold precision and the barely controlled wildness of the native contingent at his back did little to reassure Father Jacinto or the people about him.

The officer raised one white hand. A *gunso* stepped out from the ranks of Japanese troops and moved quickly towards the crowd, drawing his sergeant's short sword threateningly. The crowd drew back before him, silent with trepidation, but he still struck those nearest to him in an arbitrary fashion with the flat of his sword, making way for his officer.

A man ran forward from among the soldiers and made a deep bow of obeisance before the *shosa*. He was an Indonesian by his distinctive style of dress but he wore a Japanese armband to show that he was a member of the new police. He moved with rigid staccato movements, bowing again as he received his instructions. He stood forward and began to speak to the crowd in a heavily accented Tetum dialect.

'The major demands to know who is your leader here.' He looked archly around the crowd. 'Step forward at once and show proper respect.'

Afraid to speak, the people hung back, sullen and silent. They looked with barely concealed hostility at this foreigner who spoke their tongue in such a strange manner. Father Jacinto saw that their silence only served to anger the Japanese officer, who clearly did not care to be kept waiting. His eyes were sharp and dark, missing nothing.

Quickly the priest stepped forward, aware of all eyes turned in his direction.

'The local leaders have been killed. Yesterday.'

Translated, this news seemed to interest the officer.

'*Ah so-ka?*' He bent to his translator, his words soft and unheard.

'The major demands to know your nationality,' said the Indonesian.

The priest replied unwillingly. 'I am Portuguese,' he answered, having little desire to draw further attention to himself.

The officer continued to stare at Father Jacinto without blinking. There was nothing in his eyes to suggest what he was thinking or planning. It was the Indonesian who spoke for him.

'Major Shimada has decided to give his assistance to the town to show the spirit of generosity and friendship between the Imperial Japanese Forces and the people of Timor. The major appoints for you a new headman to direct the work of reconstruction and give guidance for the New Dawn of co-operation between the peoples of the Co-Prosperity Sphere.'

The flood of highly stylized language washed over the heads of the traumatized people. Faced with a barrage of bombs and rhetoric it was little wonder that they were shell-shocked.

The newly appointed headman stepped forward, another Indonesian wearing his own national dress and a headband. In his heavy accent he announced to the crowd that his name was Jalan and that in future all decisions relating to the town would come directly from his appointed police agents.

Father Jacinto had noted the deference he and his fellow Indonesian paid to the Japanese. A level of discipline and strict hierarchy existed between them, reminding the priest of the medieval philosophy of feudalism and rule by the sword. Indonesians had always been unpopular in Timor and it seemed an act of mindless bureaucracy to place an Indonesian in charge of these captive peoples. He wondered what would be the role of his own people, the Portuguese, in such a ruthless system.

The *shosa* began a diatribe on the benefits ahead for Timor as part of the South-East Asia Co-Prosperity Sphere. The correct precision of his Japanese was rapidly translated into a minced concoction of local dialects. The crowd listened in silence as they were promised a new world of opportunity.

Following the line taken in the leaflets showered over the valley, the Japanese extolled Asian cooperation. For too long, the translator told them, the East Indies had been dominated by degenerate European powers. Timor had been sold as a colony to the Dutch, the Dutch who were all cowards and without honour, surrendering rather than seeking an honourable death.

This part of the speech went down particularly well with the native contingent from Dutch Timor, who were in full agreement with the Japanese and still full of their victory over Dutch forces in Western Timor. But Father Jacinto noticed that no direct condemnation was made of the Portuguese in Eastern

Timor. For the time being, at least, it seemed that Portugal was still neutral in this war.

'You have been misled by degenerate and deceitful leaders,' the translator told them. 'All this is now changed. The peace and prosperity of the New Dawn bring liberation to Timor. The leaders who have betrayed you will be punished.' He added ominously, 'Be loyal to the new order and denounce the traitors.'

Father Jacinto and the rest of the townspeople waited in trepidation for the full meaning of the major's statement. With solemn intensity the Japanese stared out across his audience, pausing between his clipped sentences for the Indonesian to translate.

Some Portuguese, he continued, had wickedly assisted in acts of terrorism and sabotage against Timor by the *tuan cataus* guerrillas. These terrorists threatened the peace and security of the island and must be eliminated.

'For the safety of the people of Timor, all Portuguese must return to Dili. A neutral zone has been created. All Portuguese must return to this zone. Portuguese not returning after the time given are classified bandits, no better than terrorists.'

He indicated an official proclamation which Jalan, now headman, ordered to be nailed on the doorpost of one of the few houses still standing on the square. He waited expectantly.

'Any person with information will come forward.'

The *shosa* and his interpreter studied the crowd for a long moment. But no one stepped forward. They watched with growing fear as the officer suddenly grew apoplectic with rage. He turned abruptly on his heel, casting a final scathing look over the crowd, and snapped out fresh orders to the *gunso*.

'*Hei!*' The sergeant bowed low and then turned and rasped out the command at full volume. It seemed that the Japanese could do nothing without screaming.

The Japanese troops moved quickly to his direction. They began a search of the town for suspicious signs of the elusive *tuan cataus* and their allies. They thrust the people brutally out of their path, swaggering with their rolling gait through the ruined streets, all the grandiose talk of Asian unity seemingly forgotten.

The blatant racism of their ideology had shocked Father

Jacinto, but in practice it now filled him with a new fear. The arrogant Japanese were worse than the colonial whites they had replaced.

'*Gaijin! Kura!*'

Father Jacinto took not the slightest notice of the fierce command, unaware that it was directed at himself. The furious *gunso* strode across and seized him, savagely beating him about the head and shoulders. It seemed that he had been summoned to talk once more to the major.

Bringing him before the Japanese officer, the *gunso* thrust down the priest's head into the subservient position they clearly considered showed proper respect. The *shosa* barked an order and the sergeant fell back into line with the automatic response, '*Hei!*'

The priest slowly raised his head and looked the *shosa* straight in the eyes without flinching as the translator spoke for the Japanese.

'The major demands to know what you do in town. Your church is destroyed, finished.'

With reluctance Father Jacinto strived to explain. 'I am here to offer help to the people. They are now homeless and starving.'

It was a mistake. Even as he saw the translator mouth his reply he saw the change come over the face of Major Shimada. The calm mask of detachment had gone. The *shosa*'s face contorted with unseemly emotion as a wave of fierce rage took hold. His eyes fixed upon the priest with the opaque gaze of a serpent holding its intended prey with its mesmeric stare.

'Old man, there is no one starving here,' came the stinging rebuke in a flow of unexpected but competent Portuguese. 'Some of them are even fat,' he added blatantly pointing to the terrified local children with their distended swollen stomachs.

Father Jacinto had to swallow back his shock and natural anger at the malicious reply. He felt that the Japanese officer had been playing with him, speaking Portuguese but choosing to use the interpreter in Tetum in order to intimidate the townspeople. He saw the major watching him and thought he detected a gleam of anticipation in his narrow eyes. But the priest had already learnt that a show of anger was rash and even dangerous. He forced himself to control all outward signs of what he was thinking. He bowed his head in apparent acquiescence, refusing to rise to the bait, and almost felt the wave of disappointment in response. Now there was no easy scapegoat for the Japanese.

The officer soon grew bored with him and turned away with an acid comment in Portuguese supposedly to the Indonesian about the Catholic Church.

Taking his chance to draw away, Father Jacinto felt the almost tangible smell of fear among the crowd. The Japanese were looking for victims. He knew and they knew that their new masters needed to make an example.

A hillman chewing betel nut on the edge of the crowd was suddenly seized by the *gunso*, seen as insolent, lacking in respect.

'*Misu-wa-nei!*' bellowed the *gunso* and hit him with the side of his sword.

The native doubled up, falling to his knees from the force of the blow. He screamed in fear, terrified that worse was to come. His teeth and lips were a livid mask stained scarlet with betel juice and blood.

No arms were found in the town and there was no sign of any Australian presence. But as Father Jacinto had suspected the search party were afraid to return to their commander empty handed. He was distressed but not surprised to see the crowd part as a solitary prisoner was brought forward.

The priest recognized the man who had almost ridden him down on his bicycle the day before. The soldiers thrust the prisoner forward, his arms cruelly trussed up behind his back with wire. He fell in the dust before the Japanese officer as the troops reported their discovery of the bicycle. The offending vehicle was proudly brought forward, in much better condition than its unfortunate owner.

The translator announced that all bicycles were to be regarded in future as war transport. All vehicles should have been handed over at once. To withhold any transport was regarded as an act of sabotage. Such criminality could not be condoned.

Almost beside himself with fury, the *gunso* ordered the helpless victim to his feet. He was half dragged, half carried across to the open doorway of a bomb-damaged house by two of the Dutch native recruits. The watching crowd knew at once what they intended to do with him.

A dread silence fell over the market square as they watched the rope being made ready, but no one dared make a move to stop them. The priest knew that by using the Dutch natives against the local people the Japanese were using terror as another weapon. The continued resistance of the Australian commandos and their supporters in the mountains was a thorn in the side of the island's new rulers. The Japanese saw that the only way of putting an end to guerrilla activity was to eliminate local support for the Australians. To the Japanese all Timorese were potential guerrillas and would be treated as such. It was a chilling omen for the future.

As Father Jacinto watched with the townspeople, the Moslem was hanged from the lintel of the ruined doorway. As he crossed himself and began a prayer, he feared for the survival of them all.

Chapter Twenty-four

While the Japanese searched the valley for fresh horses to carry them into the mountain districts, Father Jacinto contrived to slip away from the town. With his single pony, well hidden from the troops, and the little food he had been able to find, he stole away into the night, never resting until he was already deep into the mountains.

By the time he was sighted at the villa, the priest was exhausted. Pleased as they were to see him back safely, his appearance spoke for itself. His soutane, once white, was stained and caked with dust and dried blood. He shook off Sister Eulalia's attempts to clean his cuts, accepting only as much water as he could drink before collapsing against the wall. They helped him inside just as the first thunder of the evening announced the onset of the rains, and sat with him in apprehensive silence as the brief storm beat about the little house.

After a while he began to talk, watching their faces in the yellow light. He described the air attack first because it was so incredible, because he wanted them to know at once the full meaning of the news he brought.

A ripple of shock went around the room. Sister Eulalia crossed herself and he saw Katherine look at Fielding, as if the captain could confirm or deny it. Fielding sat with his head bowed but his fellow Australians were less reticent.

'Bastards,' hissed Seaton between clenched teeth. 'Savages, that's what they all are.'

Fielding's blond head flicked up and he turned to look at them. Only Jack Ford was silent, his green eyes attentive, missing nothing.

'I cannot understand,' Sister Eulalia began bleakly. 'How can they behave like this?'

'They're not human, Sister,' Katherine retorted.

'No better than bloody animals,' said Harrison.

'Sadists,' said Dede.

'Give me a chance to get at the little bastards,' Seaton threatened vehemently. The colour had risen in his face and his eyes were bright with violence. Father Jacinto saw the danger and found himself stepping in swiftly.

'I do not believe they are all sadists,' he told them in a quiet, controlled voice. 'They are under orders. Their whole system is different.'

In the sudden silence Fielding looked at the priest and spoke out at last. 'That is true. Their code of honour is very rigorous. If you like, they are indoctrinated, brainwashed. The individual must submit himself to the national good. He does not count. Every Japanese recruit says farewell to life at a shrine when he enters the service. He believes he has given up his own life, and he will do whatever he is ordered to do for his nation.'

Harrison was really interested. 'So that's why the buggers are so crazy in a fight,' he said. 'Sometimes you'd think they were all trying to get themselves killed.'

'Their military code is very harsh.' Fielding looked at his fellow Australians. 'You wouldn't last five minutes.'

Jack had been watching but now his eyes narrowed. 'You admire the bastards, don't you, Fielding?'

'Well, I wouldn't say that – '

'Aw, come on, don't give me that. You learnt their bloody language for some reason, mate.'

Fielding was under pressure. He saw the fierce resentment on the faces ringed about him. The only sympathy was on the face of Sister Eulalia. Father Jacinto looked puzzled. There was only open contempt on the faces of the Australians and Fielding knew he had surely confirmed all the doubts that had been growing about his capability to lead them.

His eyes met Jack Ford's and the look that passed between them was noticed by the priest. He saw that the young and inexperienced captain thought of Ford as a troublemaker. It was only a matter of time before things came to a head between them.

'I have not told you everything,' Father Jacinto said quickly. 'I have news of the convent.'

He told the story simply, without waiting for comment. He told it just as Lu Shan had told him. The Japanese had moved south from Dili, arriving at the convent only days after their own group had got away. He saw the pained look of anticipation on the face of Sister Eulalia, but there was no way he could soften the blow.

'The sisters were all ordered out while the Japanese made a search of the buildings. The Mother Superior approached the officer to ask that the sick be allowed to remain, but – ' He paused, very grave now, facing the prospect of breaking the worst to them. 'But Mother Teresa was driven off at bayonet point.' He ignored the nun's sharp intake of breath. 'The troops then entered the convent and remained there a day and a night before moving out. When Mother Teresa and the sisters returned they discovered the corpses of the sick and wounded. They had all been badly mutilated.'

Fielding was quiet, too quiet. Father Jacinto was disturbed to see the effect his news had on the captain. He knew that Fielding had a tendency to avoid the others, keeping himself apart. There was a sense of isolation about him. Something that marked him out from the rest. He knew that he blamed himself for the death of Lieutenant Davison left behind at the convent. But Fielding would not talk to him. With a mumbled excuse he moved away to find a place where he could be alone with his thoughts.

Amy too was moved by the priest's news. She stood on the verandah feeling the fresh breeze after the rain. She was quickly joined by Daniel Letria and was glad to see him.

'Don't be afraid,' he said gently. 'We'll get away. The Japs won't find us here.'

She looked up at him, her eyes large, expressive and beautiful. 'Oh Daniel! You and Dede are my only friends.'

'You're thinking about Mrs Beattie again. She's ill, Amy, she can't hurt you – '

But Amy twisted away. 'You don't understand, Daniel. You can't understand.'

He took her face between his hands, trying to fathom the

look that haunted her eyes. 'I want to understand everything about you, Amy. I want you to trust me.' He bent his head and suddenly he was kissing her, kissing her with all the hidden passion of his being.

In the faint light of the rising moon Fielding sat overlooking the valley trail. He felt the wave of guilt wash over him, appalled by the knowledge that he had been responsible for leaving Davison behind.

If only, he thought, if only there had been some other way. If only he had decided differently. And was it true, as Ford had suggested? Did he still admire the Japanese in spite of all they had done?

He understood the codes by which they lived, Shinto, Bushido and the battle code Senjinkin. Emperor Meiji had decreed to his troops long ago, 'Honour is heavier than the mountains, Death is lighter than a feather.' They believed above all that with honour they could – as the words of one song put it – 'Die without sorrow: do not think of yourself but of the nation.'

The Japanese had not been signatories of the Geneva Covention. They subjected prisoners of war to their own laws. Here on Timor they were the laws of the Imperial Japanese Navy. Troublemakers would be treated as mutineers. Perhaps it was better not to be taken alive.

The air was humid, the trees still dripping from the rainstorm. The warm earth steamed. He dug his fingers deep into the soil, pressing the clay into a rich mud. Alien earth, what was it to him? Poor Davison, never to see his home again. Had he been married? Someone would have to tell his family one day when they all got home. *If* they got home.

Inside the house Dede had to break the spell the priest had cast over them all in her usual way, through action. In the confusion over his news they had forgotten the medicine he had bought from Lu Shan. Now she took the packet into the room where Mrs Beattie lay and lit the tiny oil lamp at her side, kneeling on the faded ancient carpet.

She opened the paper packet and discovered a quantity of dried brittle leaves. They were dark and smelt pungent. Perhaps they were herbs of some kind. She turned the paper over and found a brief prescription in Chinese characters written on the back. Scooping the leaves on to a plate, she took the paper and immediately went outside to find Amy.

She found her with Letria on the verandah. Kate and Fielding had both been in the garden but were now returning.

'Amy, can you translate the instructions on this packet for me? It's the medicine for Mrs Beattie.' She handed it to her.

Amy looked down at the paper and her thin face was pinched with anxiety. She was aware of Kate and Fielding suddenly close behind her.

'What's the matter?' asked Dede. 'It is Chinese, isn't it?'

'Oh yes, it's Chinese,' answered Amy in a small voice, her hand seeming to tremble on the paper. She was aware of the young captain regarding her intently. There was a terrifying sinking feeling in her stomach.

Fielding's strained voice was barely audible as he spoke.

'A Chinese girl who can't read Chinese?' He swung her round to face him. 'I think we all deserve an explanation, don't you?'

Chapter Twenty-five

'What are you getting at, Fielding?' Letria's fury showed in his face.

'Perhaps you had better ask Miss Meadows,' said the captain, still looking straight at Amy.

She appeared too stunned by what had finally happened to move. She seemed unaware of Sister Eulalia, the priest and the Australians who had come to see what was going on.

Dede went to Amy and put a protective arm around her shoulders. 'I don't know what this is all about,' she said to Fielding, 'but can't you see that you're scaring her half to death?'

'You'd better have a bloody good reason, mate,' said Jack.

'No, no, hold on,' Seaton interrupted. 'I want to know why she can't read her own bloody language.'

'Christ, mate, there could be a dozen reasons – '

'Then why doesn't she tell us?'

'Well, Amy?'

Fielding turned to them in the lengthening silence. The muscles in his shoulders were rigid with tension.

'I've known for some time. She's not Chinese, she's Japanese.'

A shock wave rippled around the circle. Dede and Jack exchanged a look of total surprise. Letria felt the blood drain from his face.

'It's a mistake – ' He looked at her for guidance, for some denial that would reassure them all.

'No,' said Amy in a choked voice. 'No, it's true.' She let her self-control slip. Silent tears spilled down her cheeks.

'Japanese?'

'S'truth, mate, a bloody Nip!'

Jack turned on Fielding. 'You've known about this? What the hell did you think you were playing at?'

'She could read the Japanese leaflets back in the village. I saw her,' said the captain. 'She knew I saw her.' Amy turned frightened eyes towards him. 'I thought she might come clean to me.'

'Confess?' said the priest. 'The poor child must have been terrified all this time.'

All this time, Dede thought to herself. She felt let down, betrayed and foolish. The girl had deceived her ever since they met. No! Even before they met – back there in Balikpapan. And again in the Celebes, never denying, never contradicting their assumption that she was half Chinese. Dede had treated her like a friend, but she had never really known her at all.

'She could be a bloody Nip spy!' Seaton railed, only partly serious. 'She's been making fools of us.' With his flippant tongue he was insidious, dangerous.

'Yeah, if it came to the crunch,' said Harrison, 'she'd know which side her bread was buttered on.'

'Now, wait a minute – '

'Oh sure,' sneered Seaton, glaring at Letria, 'you'd support her right enough. You've got a good thing going there, haven't you, mate?'

Fielding had to intervene to prevent Letria throwing a punch at the pugnacious Australian sergeant.

'That's enough,' cried Sister Eulalia, distressed by the whole situation, as Kate was.

'We can't trust her,' Harrison protested. 'We can't let her stay on.'

That silenced them all. Amy stared in numb horror around the circle of faces, some full of hate and suspicion, some hurt or anxious.

'I'm British,' she announced, her voice barely above a whisper. 'My father was British.'

'Yeah, but your mother was Japanese,' said Harrison, 'and that's all that counts.'

The night had brought a weary respite from the weight of tragedy and suspicion. Amy was left shamefaced, afraid to join Dede in the room they shared.

She stood in the darkness at the window knowing that her whole future hung in the balance. Would they decide to throw her out of this haven? Cast her out like a leper to fend for herself? What could she say to make the others believe that she presented no danger to any of them? Nothing she could say or do would make any difference now. She had lied, or at least kept the truth from all of them, even Dede. They would never believe her. Not even Dede. She had seen the look in Dede's eyes, hurt, betrayed, and knew she had lost her one good friend.

'Amy – '

She turned, her hair swinging in front of her face.

'Don't stay here, don't be alone,' said Daniel.

Looking at his dark troubled face Amy knew she had been wrong. She may have lost her only friend, but now she had found one.

Safe in the room where she slept alone, Kate could not sleep. She had hung up her dress, washed so often that now its colours had faded almost completely away. The night was humid, oppressive. Sweat soaked her body as she lay restless, hands on her belly.

'How long has she got?' she had heard them ask, thinking she could not hear.

'Seven or eight weeks, it's hard to say. Time is running out.'

Yes, she knew time was running out for her. Japanese or no Japanese, there was no escape, no avoidance of the grim ordeal to come. Seven weeks? Yes, at the outside. She did not look big enough. Perhaps she could still convince them, persuade them to let her go on with them.

She felt a qualm of terror as the baby kicked, a stranger inside her, keeping her body prisoner. If it wasn't for the baby, there would be no danger. They couldn't treat her like Amy, threatening to throw her out, leave her behind.

How could they do that to her? It just showed what people were capable of. They were soldiers, of course. No time for women holding them up. Only women, after all. One half-caste, Japanese, a liar, a possible spy. The others, an old woman, heat-exhausted, sick, and a girl stupid enough to fall for a baby, a cheap gullible girl who deserved all she got . . . .

The sharp low pain came again. For a moment she found it difficult to breathe and a note of panic sounded inside her head.

No, it couldn't be. Not yet, surely not.

She lay there drenched in sweat, waiting, waiting. Fifteen minutes she lay there and then the pain came again, a stabbing, searing pain that made her gasp out. She was panicked, terrified. It could not be happening. Not yet, not now, not here.

She got to her feet and pulled on the dress. Another pain caught her, surely less than fifteen minutes this time. She walked up and down, trying to convince herself that she was mistaken, but the pain did not go away.

She staggered outside into the long narrow corridor of the villa, deserted now in the slanted light of the moon between the shutters. She walked up the corridor, holding her aching back, in search of Sister Eulalia to break the news.

Chapter Twenty-six

'But she can't have the baby here.'

'There's no "can't" about it, Captain,' said the nun bluntly. 'She'll have the baby some time later today, God willing. There's nothing you can do about it.' She gave him a rather indulgent smile. He was, after all, so very young.

'It's no big deal, is it?' Seaton demanded. 'The boongs have their kids in these conditions all the time.'

'Kate's hardly a native woman,' said Dede sharply. 'It's fine for you to talk! What do you want? The place fumigated to keep away demons, like they do in Borneo? Why don't you just go and get lost?'

The men took the hint and made themselves scarce. Fielding still looked very troubled about the whole business. He couldn't bear the unexpected.

Dede walked with Kate up and down the long corridor. 'Okay, kid, you're doing fine.'

'I'm sorry, Dede. I'm causing everyone so much trouble. If it wasn't for me you would all be out of here.'

'And what about Mrs Beattie? That Chinese stuff didn't seem to do her much good. She's still lying there. She won't eat, she hardly even takes a drink. So, you see, we're not going anywhere in a hurry.'

Kate kept on walking. It was less painful than trying to sit or lie down. She was restless and had to keep on the move. Thank God that Sister Eulalia was a trained nurse. At least she would know what to do.

Would it be a girl or a boy? This unwanted child who had ruined her life? Would it look like Harry? She had tried to picture Harry's face, and failed. It was ironic after so many weeks trying so hard to forget him.

It all seemed so long ago now. She no longer felt the same person. How gullible she must have been! She had mistaken Harry's ruthless self-interest for strength of character. The traits so obvious in his mother had shown her the true quality of the son.

They were on their own now, in more ways than one, she and the child.

Amy lay in Daniel's strong arms as the morning light flooded in through the shutters of his room. The fear and guilt of the night before had brought them together and she clung to him like a rock in a storm. He was her lifeline, her one hope for the future. Only with him did she feel safe from the hatred she had seen in the others' eyes.

She had never known anyone quite like him before. He did not seem to be aware of the difference in colour between them. Like her father, he treated her with respect and with love. He loved her. His love reassured and absorbed her, and almost made her forget the trauma of the night before. Almost, but not completely.

The tears ran back into her hair as she remembered. Even Daniel's love could not save her from the confrontation that was bound to come. They would never allow her to stay with them, never.

'What's wrong?' Letria stirred and leant on his elbow above her. He brushed away the tears and stroked her long bare throat. Her mouth hung fascinated and entranced by his powerful and ardent kisses. All too easily she could have succumbed to the spell he wove, but her fears had been revived. She gently pushed him aside and sat up, her black hair falling back over her shoulders, the sunlight turning her naked body to liquid gold.

'I have to face them, Daniel. I cannot let them see I am afraid.'

'Then we'll face them together,' he said. 'From now on, what affects you, affects me.'

As they stepped from Letria's room Seaton turned round and saw them. An amused smile played about his wide mouth and his eyes were insolent.

'Oh yeah, I see I was right,' he brayed for all the world to hear. 'How was she, mate? Your "sleeping dictionary"? I heard they've got some pretty neat tricks, these boongs. If you don't get the clap, that is.'

'Why, you filthy – '

'You want a fight, mate? I'm ready! Come on, then, you bloody Nip-lover – '

'What the hell's going on here?' Fielding demanded, but it was Jack who broke up the fight, thrusting Seaton back against the wall.

'What is all this?' said Sister Eulalia, emerging from Kate's room. 'Don't you know the poor girl is trying to have her child in there?'

Daniel and Amy looked stunned by the news. Amy in particular felt guilty for not knowing what had happened to Kate.

'Can I do anything, Sister? Can I help?'

The nun looked at her gently. Although there was little room for the girl she did not want to turn her offer down in front of the others.

'You certainly can. Come with me now. And you,' she added, looking at the men with stern grey eyes, 'can be of some use, too. We're going to need some water.'

By the afternoon the men were quietly sunk into gloom as there seemed no end to Kate's labour. Every time the door to the room opened, they started up, all eyes turned eagerly for news. But each time it was a false alarm.

Inside the room Kate sat upright against a bank of pillows. She was in a torment of heat although Amy kept on fanning her and Dede pressed a cool cloth to her shining forehead.

Kate's face was marked with fatigue. There were deep shadows under her eyes, which had a hunted look as she tensed with each wave of pain. She groaned, gripping Dede by the hand as the pain quickened, and Sister Eulalia did her best to encourage her.

'Don't cry, child. You're doing so well. Just think of the baby you will soon hold in your arms.'

But Kate was almost beyond the point of thought. She moaned, rocking back and forth, unable and unwilling to lie down as Dede thought she must for the birth. But both Kate and Sister Eulalia were at ease with her more natural position. With no drugs or sedatives to help, Dede could only pray that everything would come right.

'Come on, Kate, come on, honey, you can do it.' Dede held Kate's hand in both of hers, trying to give the girl some of her own wasted energy. Even as she spoke she heard Sister Eulalia gasp with delight as a little red face appeared.

'Kate, Kate! You're nearly there!'

'One more push, child, once more – '

'Oh Kate!' cried Amy. 'Kate, how wonderful!'

There were tears in their eyes as the baby slipped free and gave a plaintive wail.

'It's a girl, it's a girl,' said Sister Eulalia and lifted the baby, still attached by its cord, for her mother to see.

'Well, what d'you know!' grinned Jack. 'A little girl, eh?'

'Good on her,' said Harrison. 'Pity we don't have any hooch to celebrate.'

'How about going down to the village? We could get some of that firewater the old chief had there,' Seaton suggested. With an eye on the priest, he added artfully, 'Could pick up some milk for the kid at the same time.'

In the end it was Father Jacinto who went down to the village with the sergeant. The others were anxious for their return, afraid of possible Japanese patrols in the district.

Dede left Kate sleeping with the baby at her side, her tiny fingers curled in a tight little ball as she slept.

'So, no Japs yet,' Fielding was saying, standing with the others in the main room.

'But the news isn't too hot,' said the sergeant. 'The place was buzzing with stories and rumours of what the Nips have been doing.'

'The *chefe do posto* of Maubisse was in hiding in a local village,' said Father Jacinto, 'but someone betrayed him – '

'Yeah, and the Nip bastards – sorry, Sister – well, they messed the poor bugger up before killing him.'

'He was tortured then killed,' confirmed the priest.

'He was Portuguese,' said Daniel. 'So much for our neutrality.'

The priest looked at him, his sharp bright eyes full of anger. 'The Japanese have new laws about that. They have set up a camp at Liquissa on the coast. It used to be a pleasure resort,' he added with a sour smile, 'a place where administrators and bankers took their wives and children. And now women and children are being sent there under guard. All Portuguese are being rounded up. The Japanese want them all under their "protection". But some have already escaped the Dili area. The valley roads are choked with Portuguese refugees as well, but they are easy prey for rogue bands of Dutch Timorese recruits working for the Japanese. The bands are lawless, drunk. They have taken women as well as food. No one is safe.'

Sister Eulalia crossed herself.

'There is little doubt, my friends. The Japanese intend to control the whole of Timor – whether the Portuguese like it or not.'

Fielding looked at the priest solemnly and then said, 'I think we should warn the Macedos at the *posto*. We should tell them of the danger they're in.' He looked around the group. 'Someone has to go back down there.'

Chapter Twenty-seven

The others looked at each other, taken aback by the suggestion.

'Your idea,' said Letria, 'is very humanitarian, Captain, but going there will put us all in danger.'

Fielding shook his head, not even looking at him. 'I feel we are responsible. After all, we smashed their radio, so they might not get to hear about the ultimatum before the Japanese deadline expires.'

'That's their hard luck,' said Jack.

'There are women and children at the *posto*. Will you see them sent to this concentration camp at – where was it?'

'Liquissa,' said Father Jacinto.

'Liquissa.' Fielding was staring at the others. 'We have a duty to warn them.' He became very matter of fact as though the whole thing was now agreed and only needed organizing. 'I suggest we make a start first thing in the morning. With luck, with a quick march all downhill, we ought to reach the *posto* this time tomorrow.'

Jack laughed. 'That's funny.'

Fielding tilted his head, as though he had not heard him correctly. 'It's no joke, Corporal.'

The grin died on Ford's face. 'Then you're a bloody lunatic, mate.'

Fielding was deathly still. His soft boyish cheeks were flushed with indignation. 'You don't speak to me that way, Corporal.'

The others remained silent, aware of the animosity that already existed between the two men, waiting to see what happened.

Fielding eyed the renegade, his face set. He had recognized him as a potential troublemaker all along. If Fielding did not bring him down now he knew that he would lose the others and their support altogether.

'Right,' Fielding retorted abruptly, 'then I'll go alone.'

Jack turned aside, making a pained face. 'Oh Christ! Just what we need – another bloody hero.'

The captain tensed, his arms down at his sides, fists clenched.

Jack thrust his face forward, the strength of his anger marked in the line of his jaw. 'Nobody's going to make *me* go down there. I'm not getting my head blown off for some bloody heroics so that you can get yourself a gong, Fielding – '

'Christ, mate – '

'You blokes go if you like,' Jack retorted, 'but I've got no interest in committing suicide.'

Seaton intervened, 'Come off the boil, Jack – '

'No one is asking you to go, Corporal,' Fielding told him. 'Don't you stick your neck out for anyone.'

Jack was going to take a swing at the captain but Letria caught him with a restraining hand. He went to Fielding himself.

'Look, Captain, you need someone with you who can speak Portuguese. I will go with you.'

'No – ' cried Amy softly, but then became nervous of the attention she had attracted.

'You come if you want to, Daniel.' It was the first time that Fielding had called the Portuguese by his name.

The two men went out together and Dede found herself looking at Jack, but he had settled back in a chair again and shrugged.

'Let Fielding handle it – if he can,' he said derisively.

'I think perhaps I should go with them,' Father Jacinto remarked. 'I know Macedo, after all, and he is a Catholic. Perhaps he will listen to me more than the others. If I can get him to evacuate the children at least – '

Jack's watchful eyes turned on him. 'You watch your step, Father, if you go with Fielding.'

'You are hard on the captain, my son.'

'Don't you be fooled. Just because Fielding has grown a

beard doesn't make him Jesus Christ.'

To his surprise the priest laughed.

'Ah, yes, the golden beard. Just like the romantic paintings.' He turned with a calm smile towards the corporal. 'I will be cautious, I promise you. And I will rest easier in my mind to know that you are staying here to protect the women.'

Sensing the atmosphere in the room, Sister Eulalia followed the priest outside. She found him standing among the trees near the monolithic stones that so frightened the villagers. The sun was already dipping behind the mountains, heralding night.

'You are exhausted,' she told him, standing like a white ghost in the twilight. 'You ought to rest.'

He gave her a look that she had learnt to recognize long ago. In all the years of their friendship, she had never been able to dissuade him from any project once his mind was set on it. But the times and the circumstances had changed.

'I don't want you to go,' she told him bluntly. 'Why does it have to be you? You have done your share.'

He frowned, his face grey, and then shook his head a little, as though disappointed. 'How can *you* say that to me?'

'What's the matter with you, Jack? We don't need your protection. You should go with the rest of them.'

He looked at Dede with shrewd green eyes, his pugnacious chin giving a hard line to his face. 'It's a fool's errand. Do these people at the *posto* deserve it? Risking our necks to rescue them? Putting everyone here in danger? They've done their dash.'

'No, but – '

'So let Fielding get himself a gong. Let him play the bloody hero. I'm playing safe. I want to get out of this war alive – '

She lost her restraint, her eyes bright with anger and sore disappointment. 'He's right then, you are a coward.'

Jack stared at her, meeting her accusing eyes without flinching. 'You can think what you like,' he said bitterly. 'I wouldn't want to disturb your rosy view of the world. When have you ever had to fight for anything? You've had it all. You don't know what it's like to have to fight and struggle to pull yourself out of the gutter inch by bloody inch – '

Dede tried to protest, bright tears of anger in her eyes, but he was persistent.

'You think what you like, but come hell or high water I'm not going under this time.'

As he slammed out of the room Dede's calm dissolved and all her pent-up feelings of disappointment and injustice gave way to tears.

The party set out at dawn with backpacks, leaving the pony behind. Fielding was intense and quiet and had barely exchanged a word with the others all night. Father Jacinto looked weary, his cheeks hollow with fatigue, but he could not be persuaded to stay behind.

'We should be back in the morning, God willing.'

'We will pray for you,' said Sister Eulalia, fingering the beads of her rosary.

Jack went over to Letria and slapped him on the shoulder. 'Watch yourself, Dan.'

Letria grinned at him and raised a hand in farewell to Amy in the doorway. They set off down the mountain in single file.

'Don't worry, Amy, they'll be all right.'

Amy turned to find Dede at her elbow. 'Dede – I wanted to tell you, to try to explain to you – '

'Please, Amy, there's nothing to say.' Dede hid her embarrassment, her tone rather brusque, but it did not put Amy off.

'No, I know the wrong I did you. Lying to you, not trusting you enough to tell the truth about my mother and who she was. I knew you thought she was Chinese, but I said nothing. We were friends and yet I did not trust you.'

Dede saw the tears starting in the girl's bright eyes and knew she had to say something to reassure her. 'We're still friends, Amy. I understand, believe me.'

Amy seized her hand and the tears began to fall. 'Oh yes, I hope so, Dede, I do hope so.'

'Come on and see the baby,' said Dede quickly. 'Kate's waiting to see you, too. No more tears, all right?'

Now the rains had set in much of the countryside was greatly changed, as Father Jacinto had warned them it would be. Mudslides and rockfalls had made many of the forest paths impassable. They stopped to eat briefly at noon although they were nervous and without appetite. Every step beyond the village meant danger. All of them were eager to get down into the valley and observe the situation there for themselves.

From the mountain the valley and its plantation had seemed almost close at hand, easily visible from the treeline. But as they descended they found the valley floor partially flooded by the swollen river as the late-afternoon deluge drenched them. Soaked to the skin one minute, they were dry again as soon as the sun broke through the cloud layer, shivering slightly at the change in climate.

It was almost night before they approached the plantation and the entrance to the *posto*. Even as they entered the compound Father Jacinto became aware that all was not well.

He sensed the change there, the same smell of fear he had known in the town. It was clear that the charged atmosphere meant that panic had seized the people here, too, that their news had travelled before them.

At the entrance to the *posto* his fears were confirmed. A notice had been hung on the doorpost warning all Australians to keep away.

'I see we are expected.'

'That? Oh, I daresay that is for the Japs' benefit,' said Fielding, lifting off his pack.

'Then it seems they intend to stay.'

Fielding looked at Letria. 'If you don't want to come inside then stay here.'

'I didn't say that. No, I want to see the *chefe do posto* for myself.'

The captain found something ominous and unsettling in Daniel's words, but Father Jacinto was already striding towards the house ahead of them.

Macedo himself came to the door.

He angrily accused them of trespass and was clearly terrified to see them there again.

'Go away, Mother of God, go away.' But he saw the look on their faces and resorted to his natural authority as a bureaucrat. 'I will file a complaint.'

Letria suggested he file it with the Japanese in that case, as they were right behind them.

Macedo's eyes opened with wide shock. Fielding saw there was trouble brewing between the two men. Remembering Letria's particular history, he was not greatly surprised.

'Will you not invite us inside, Jaime?' asked the priest. 'The whole world can see us here.'

Nervously, Macedo ushered his uninvited visitors inside, securely fastening the door behind them. The wide drawing room was soft with lamplight. Macedo led the way through a maze of heavy furniture, carved in the colonial style. They entered what was obviously the dining room, where Eva Macedo was standing at a table laid with silver and fine Macao china, preparing to eat. She looked round at their approach and her face twisted with an unattractive mix of fear and loathing.

'Get out! Get out! I won't have you here in my house – '

'*Senhora* Macedo – '

She sobbed, 'You must go, you can't stay here.'

'Eva – '

'Why have you, a priest, brought this man here?' She stabbed an accusing finger in Fielding's direction, her face betraying her disgust. 'I don't want him here, don't you understand?'

Her anger had alarmed the children upstairs. They began to cry, the little girl calling out for her mother. Eva looked at the intruders with venom.

'You see what you have done? Now I must go to my children.' She turned on her husband before she left the room. 'Get them out of here! Now!' she hissed bitterly.

Macedo looked at the three men. 'You're fools, coming back here.'

'We heard a large Japanese force crossed the border. They have many native troops recruited in the Dutch sector.'

'Do the natives there support the Japanese? Well,' he shrugged, 'they do things differently over there.'

Father Jacinto looked intently at him. 'Unless we all leave now, Jaime, we could be caught between two Japanese armies.'

Fielding said, 'Many natives here are working against the Japs.'

'Then they are fools. Don't they understand that the Australians are defeated?'

Fielding's blond bearded jaw jutted aggressively. 'Defeated? Your natives are wiser than you, friend. The war here is just beginning.'

'I have nothing to say to you,' Macedo told them.

'But we have plenty to say to you,' said Letria.

Fielding followed Macedo's wife, leaving behind a heated discussion in Portuguese which he could not understand. The rest of the house was ominously silent and he wondered suddenly why they had not seen a servant anywhere since their arrival. Had they already heard the news and taken flight?

He came to the nursery door and stood a moment watching the Dutchwoman with her two children. The girl was four or five years old, the boy darker and little more than eighteen months.

He coughed a little self-consciously.

'What do you want in here?' She had the boy in her arms, her face pale in the shuttered nursery.

'Don't be frightened,' he told her in Dutch, waiting in the doorway, watching her reaction.

She stood rooted to the spot, staring at him with her enormous eyes. 'You speak my language.'

'I was once in Holland. Just before the war broke out. I had friends in Rotterdam.'

'Rotterdam?'

Did she know the city or was she thinking of the German firestorm blitz that had wiped it out?

'Do you know it at all?'

She shook her head, biting back a response. She busied herself with the child, fussing as she laid him back in his little bed, avoiding Fielding's eyes.

'I thought perhaps you had been there. To Europe.'

She shook her blonde head and he was shocked to see that her reaction was not one of anger or aloofness at all. There were bright tears standing in her eyes as a wave of emotion took over. He had never thought to see this woman cry.

She said in a small choked voice, 'Always, always, I longed to see Europe. From the books and magazines, the newsreels – it was always where I wanted to be.' She stood up, brushing away the tears as though ashamed to let him see. 'My family lived here. I was born here, you see, in this place.' Her words dropped like acid; it was still an open wound.

Fielding said softly, 'If you came with us now, we could get you there. With your children. To Europe.'

She stared at him as if he were a madman.

'We're leaving,' he repeated. 'We're going to get off this island before it's too late. Don't you know the danger you're in?'

She shook her head, her eyes never leaving his face. 'No, no, you're wrong. It's safe here. Safer to stay where we are. Jaime said so. No one will harm us.' She looked away towards the shuttered window. 'Out there – ' The thought of the wild fastness of the mountains clearly terrified her even more than the threat of the advancing Japanese. 'You're wrong,' she insisted, her voice gaining more confidence. 'We will be safe here. Only *you* put us all in danger.'

Downstairs Father Jacinto was telling her husband of the Japanese ultimatum and the camp at Liquissa.

'We are going to try to reach the south coast.' The old priest leant forward urgently, trying to rouse his former pupil to action. 'Don't you see what will happen if you stay here? Do you want Eva and the children to starve in some concentration camp?'

Macedo turned his head away, exasperated by the onslaught. 'Portugal is neutral. We have not declared war on the Axis powers. We have no quarrel with Japan.'

Letria snorted. 'Don't be a fool, man.'

Macedo turned resentful eyes upon him. 'What do you understand about anything? You're a foreigner here.'

'No more than you,' said the Portuguese with undisguised contempt. 'This island will one day belong to the Timorese.'

'I've no time for your revolutionary nonsense! The Australians are to blame for all this trouble. No one asked them to send troops here. It was a violation of our neutrality. No one wanted their protection.'

'I'm tired of hearing this,' said Letria scathingly. 'You know full well that Lisbon would deny neutrality at once if they thought the Axis were winning. It's all a game, a sordid game of politics.'

'I know nothing about politics,' said Macedo.

'That much is obvious,' sneered Letria bitterly. 'Men like you are responsible for all that is sour and rotten in our country.'

Macedo gnawed his lip, shifting uncomfortably under Letria's clear gaze, aware of what they thought of him.

'You think it's fear, don't you? You think I'm afraid. Can't you see? I can't put my family at risk. My wife and children. If the Japanese hear you have been here! For Christ's sake go away and leave us alone!'

Letria leant over the back of Macedo's chair menacingly, his voice dangerously low. 'As far as the Japanese are concerned you *have* helped us. It's too late now to be neutral.'

Fielding appeared in the doorway and looked at Father Jacinto for news.

'We're wasting our time here,' Letria intervened, turning his back on Macedo in his chair. 'Let them stay and see what happens. It's not our concern.'

Father Jacinto caught Fielding by the sleeve of his faded army jacket. Out of Macedo's hearing he told the captain, 'I think I have a chance here. He will listen to me in the end. All he needs is time.'

'Time is what he hasn't got, Father.'

'You two go back to the others. I know what I must do, believe me. I will stay here and bring them all on later.'

Chapter Twenty-eight

As Letria and Fielding panted up the final rise of the hill towards the villa, it was Jack Ford who came forward to meet them.

'Dan,' he said, seizing him roughly, 'tell me what's happened.'

Letria stared beyond him to where Sister Eulalia looked anxiously for the priest. 'Father Jacinto decided to stay at the *posto*.'

'He what?' Jack turned hostile eyes on Fielding. He had no doubt whatsoever where the blame lay.

'He wanted to stay down there. He thought he could persuade – '

'And you let him?' Jack swung him round furiously until they were face to face. 'What the hell were you thinking of?' But Fielding moved on past him. 'Hey, I'm talking to you – '

Fielding turned back with a pained expression, aware of his anxious audience. He looked exhausted, haggard and drained. His remnants of uniform were filthy and sweat-stained. His lips were parched.

'There was nothing we could do,' he told them. 'He was so sure that he could make them change their minds. He said he would bring them here within two days.' He looked again at Sister Eulalia. 'He had made up his mind.'

She nodded, forced to accept that the captain had no greater powers of influence with the priest than she had. But she was still deeply troubled. In the depths of her heart she felt a sudden chill, a dread sense of impending loss.

She almost collided with Seaton and Harrison in the doorway.

'Sorry, Sister!' Harrison apologized, setting her to rights. 'Hey, what's going on? Where are they, then?'

'They couldn't persuade the Macedos to leave.'

'No? Well, I reckon that's their hard luck, then.' He scanned the group. 'Where's the Father then?'

Jack glared at them, his strong jaw emphasized by the line of his beard. 'Our brave captain left him down there.'

'He's quite safe,' said Fielding quickly. 'There were no Japs in the area.'

'Not yet, you mean.'

'He'll be all right,' the captain insisted.

'No thanks to you, mate.' Jack stood his ground, wide-eyed, his mouth slack with rage.

'No thanks to you, either, Ford. If you cared that much, then you should have been there.'

'Why, you – '

At that Letria intervened. His voice was cold and sharp, cutting through the poisonous atmosphere. 'That's it, Jack, you weren't there, so you keep your mouth shut. We'll do what the Father wanted. We'll wait two days. If he's not back then I'll go and fetch him myself.' He brushed past them all. 'Now I'm going inside and I'm going to sleep, if that's all right with you.'

Sheepishly Jack moved aside for him. He stood apart as the others went back into the villa, all except Dede.

'Don't take it out on Fielding,' she told him. 'He's been through enough.'

Jack looked round at her and his frowning brow seemed suddenly menacing. 'That's right, you defend him,' he said bitterly. 'You swallow everything he tells you.'

She stared at him, her hands clenched, her nails biting deep into her palms.

'It's good of you to let me stay.'

'What do you want here, Padre?' asked Macedo levelly, very controlled and very cautious. 'There is nothing you could say that would make me change my mind.' He raised heavy-lidded, weary eyes, blinking behind his spectacles, but the priest seemed undaunted.

They sat on after eating, sharing a pot of thick dark coffee, grown locally. Dona Eva had left them behind in the lamplight and no sooner had she gone than Macedo produced a stone bottle of Dutch gin.

'She doesn't like me to drink,' he said, splashing the scented liquid into two tumblers. 'But I think I have cause enough, don't you?' He gulped down his gin, emptying the tumbler in one draught. 'The servants have fled. The whole country has panicked. What's the matter with the people in Dili? No one has consulted me. I'm left completely in the dark. I'm left to my own devices here. No thought at all of the proper channels, not now. No one seems to care. I have my duties to perform – '

'All that is meaningless now, don't you see?'

'I am responsible for this *posto*. The governor said – '

'As far as the Japanese are concerned there is no governor any more.' He leant forward impatiently and prevented Macedo from pouring another drink. 'Why don't you come away, Jaime? You've done more than your duty here, God alone knows.'

'I don't believe in your God, Padre. Don't include me in your flock.'

'I'm not shocked, Jaime. But that way won't work.' He sat back in his chair, shrewd eyes watching Macedo. 'Once a Catholic, always a Catholic. The Church is stronger than your despair.' He looked at him intently. 'You say you want to help the people who are your responsibility and yet you sit back and do nothing. The Japanese will not respect your authority here.'

'No, it's you who are wrong, Padre. I know these people. Unless they are controlled they will run wild like dangerous children. I have worked with them all my life. They need a strong hand.'

'The Japanese will give them that.'

In a chilling voice the priest began to recite the series of horrors he had seen and heard about. He spoke of the bombing and the Japanese officer at the town, of what had happened at the convent, of the camp at Liquissa and the death of the *chefe* at Maubisse. As he spoke he saw Macedo shift uneasily in his chair, trying to shut out the death and despair of others. Mother Teresa's brush with the Japanese at the convent affected him most, but the *chefe do posto*'s resistance to the

Japanese at Maubisse made him hesitate. This proof that other Portuguese had made a stand threatened his neutrality. Must he, too, take a stand?

'I can understand that some are vengeful. Some whose relatives have been taken to Liquissa or killed,' he conceded.

'But it doesn't affect you, is that it?'

'Of course there are many injustices, but it really cannot be as terrible as you try to make out.'

'No?' Father Jacinto was furious. He looked at his old student and wondered just what was left of that friendship that he should risk his life for him now. 'These are not isolated crimes, Jaime. You know Martins Coelho, who was decorated as a hero in Flanders in the last war? The Japanese killed him. Killed him and the women and children at the *posto*.' He saw Macedo's face blanche. 'Yes, and sent the Dutch natives in to slaughter all at Bazar-Tete and Aileu – '

'Aileu?' It was only the next valley.

'Your wife and children. Why must they be punished for the sake of what you see as your duty? Will you not send them away with us to safety?'

But Macedo shook his head, sick to the very heart.

The dead sky was yellow and luridly lit. Eva Macedo was closing the shutters upstairs against the coming storm. Macedo showed Father Jacinto a spare room, but he had no intention himself of going to bed. He needed time to think, to be alone. Back in the empty drawing room the lamps burnt low. He sat there with a fresh bottle, listening to the advancing storm hammering on the wooden shutters.

Behind the public facade there was a different Jaime Macedo. He knew what it was to be trapped between two worlds, to be disappointed. Nothing had worked out the way he had wanted it. Not his work, not his marriage, not even the home he had made. The plantation was his home, the island all he knew. How could he ever leave it?

Had all that Father Jacinto told him been true? He thought he was outside the war and all the suffering that others must go through. His country was neutral. It was nothing to do with him. But Liquissa? Liquissa was a place of dreams, of long childhood summers in finer days. Liquissa was his memories.

Was it the drinking that had made him remember? The creak-creaking of the see-saw in the park, lost laughter on summer breezes. Gone now for ever. And yet he could remember. He saw himself, an adult, incongruous in the childrens' play park, moving solemnly between the swings and roundabouts, still now, past the little pond with its ornate fountain, dry now, all deserted in a nightmare image, with only the cold wind stirring the poincianas.

It was late indeed when he finally stirred himself, stumbling to his feet. The room was close, foetid and stale with tobacco smoke. The rain still beat upon the closed shutters. His head ached and he was weary, weary. He longed to sleep, to shut it all out, but the thoughts inside his head were crowding in upon each other and would not let him be.

As he reached the door he thought he heard a noise. He stopped to listen, certain that it came from outside.

Was it imagination? A head befuddled from smoking and gin? He went out to the servants' back kitchen, strangely deserted, unfamiliar, and found the Dutch *mandi*. The deep stone tub was full of cool water. As he poured a ladleful over his sweating head and shoulders he heard the noise again. He straightened up from the *mandi*, the water dripping down the front and back of his shirt, certain now.

If he had been drunk, it was not the water which had cleared his head. He dropped the ladle and moved swiftly back to the hallway, making for the stairs.

Father Jacinto lay awake on a couch in the upper room, his head settled back against the wooden panelling, and watched the moths dance in the candlelight. He blew it out and lay in the darkness, listening.

Yes, there it was again. He lay tensed. A footstep on the stairs? He watched the door of his room slowly opening, pushing forth a finger of light into the shadows. He saw the silhouetted figure and sat up abruptly.

'Jaime!'

'Padre, wake up, but speak quietly. I don't want to disturb Eva and the children.'

'What is it? What's happening?' He saw with alarm that Macedo was still dressed.

'There's someone moving around outside. No, don't say

anything. Come on, get out of bed and I'll show you.'

He drew back the shutters, letting in the grey night. Father Jacinto looked down into the rain-lashed compound across the flat outlines of the outbuildings. He saw nothing for a moment and then a sudden movement between the buildings caught his attention.

'But who – ?'

'Let us go downstairs.'

'No, look.' The priest seized Macedo by the arm. He pointed to a figure scurrying across the yard. 'I know that man. There, the one with the headband.'

Rain patterned the window.

'I saw him after the bombing. He's the new headman.' He turned to face Macedo, his voice barely above a whisper. 'The Japanese made him headman. He has their backing for everything he does.'

'Including stealing my livestock?'

Food must have been very short for the Japanese with all their native recruits. The Indonesian headman Jalan and his Dutch natives were ransacking the *posto* for whatever they could find. He stood apart, marked out by the red headband, rain lashing his face as he rasped out orders.

After Father Jacinto had dressed he followed Macedo down the dark stairs, watching as the Portuguese *chefe do posto* pulled back the bolts from the front doors.

Light flooded out into the dense night warm with water. The oil lamp in Macedo's hand wavered. Father Jacinto could see his hand trembling, though whether with fear or anger he could not tell. The raiders were caught in the light like moths in a flame. Their faces ran with rain.

'I'll settle this,' Macedo declared bitterly.

'For God's sake, Jaime! You'll get us shot!'

The headman Jalan came over to where Macedo and the priest stood on the verandah sheltered from the worst of the rain. Very insolent, his dark eager eyes took in the size of the house behind them. He seemed surprised and curious to see Father Jacinto there. As his eyes met the priest's, he smiled.

Behind him stood the Dutch natives, some with weapons. One wrong word and the priest knew they could ransack the place and murder them all.

'*Selamat datang*,' Father Jacinto said quickly.

'*Selamat*.' The thin layer of courtesy did nothing to hide the Indonesian's menace. His dark eyes flicked over the silent Portuguese at the priest's side. 'This is *Senhor* Macedo?' His voice was a sneer. 'I have written authority, *senhor*, to collect supplies here for the Imperial Japanese Forces.'

'That must be very reassuring for you,' said Macedo cynically.

'But I want to know – do you have medicine, medical supplies? *Di-sana taxan* malaria – ' His arm encompassed the whole of the valley to the north.

'No, nothing. We have nothing for malaria.'

Jalan's eyes narrowed. The rain dripped down his face, plastering his hair beneath the headband over his forehead. He slowly looked from one man to the other.

'*Tuan cataus* – they have been here?'

'We have seen no Australians.'

Jalan's face betrayed open suspicion. In his eyes he showed clearly his contempt for the Europeans. Deliberately he turned aside and spat into the mud, then walked back to join his men.

Father Jacinto felt Macedo relax beside him, but he doubted that was the last they would see of the Indonesian. He knew that men like Jalan came into their own in such times. The war bred the little men who filled the ranks of police and bureaucrats. Bloated with sudden power, they were able to remove rivals, settle old scores, to make their own laws and line their own pockets.

Helplessly the priest and Macedo watched as the night raiders seized the few goats and pigs remaining at the *posto*.

'*Canalha*.' Macedo quivered with frustrated rage.

As the raiding party withdrew into the driving rainstorm, Father Jacinto turned away. His wet cassock slapped at his knees.

'Thank God that's over.' Macedo moved back into the house, relief written all over his face.

'Perhaps it is not over,' said the priest.

Macedo looked at him, a ghost of doubt in the small eyes behind the spectacles.

'Why will you not believe me?' Father Jacinto was deeply irritated, leaning back against the wall of the hall, shivering.

'This was but a warning. I know that man, Jalan, from the town. I told you that the Japanese put him in charge there. The people are subject to his every whim.' He angrily brushed past Macedo. 'How far is it to the town from here?'

Macedo looked confused. 'I don't know. I mean, the valley road has been cut by flooding – '

'What about the hill road?'

'I don't know. I haven't been in that area for weeks.'

Father Jacinto was exasperated. 'You're a fool, Jaime, and I'm a bigger fool to stay here. We could all have been out of here long ago. How long do you think it will take Jalan to raise the alarm?'

The priest knew they had been granted but a brief reprieve. There was no knowing when Jalan would send the Japanese. He knew only that their danger was very real.

Chapter Twenty-nine

The priest felt the pent-up tension of some evil about to descend upon the house.

'Is it really serious?' Eva asked.

She was still in her dressing gown, clutching the material about her as though the night was cold. The expression in her eyes troubled Macedo.

'Don't be afraid,' he said. 'It is nothing for you to worry about.'

She looked beyond him to the priest, avoiding her husband's eyes. He had told her all was well but she knew he was lying to hide the truth. Through all the stormy years of their marriage, years of conflict and resentment, he had always told her the truth. Until now.

Surely he could not have smiled like that if there was anything really to fear? Or could he? Yes, he could, and now, as she looked at the priest, she knew it.

'I believe,' said the priest, 'that the Japanese will be here any time now.'

Eva's eyes widened in horror. The enormity of her husband's deceit appalled her.

'It can't be true. Jaime said – ' But the look in Father Jacinto's eyes stopped her. She clutched her dressing gown at the neck, pale and sick. 'How could this happen to me?'

'It is happening to all of us,' her husband cut in. 'They don't even know you are here.'

'You care nothing for us, nothing!'

Father Jacinto was unsettled by the clash between husband and wife. He had long since suspected that all was far from well between them. The frosty looks over the dinner table, the way she had withdrawn from him in the evening – all these indications had disturbed the priest, adding to his sense of disquiet.

Now he intervened, saying irritably, 'We are wasting valuable time with all this arguing. We must leave at once.'

But Macedo stood unmoving at the window.

'Surely there's a back way out of here?' said the priest.

'It's too late now. Come and look.' From the window he showed the priest where one of Jalan's men stood posted under the banyan tree at the end of the garden. 'We are being watched.' He turned aside, pulling off his spectacles. 'It's all my fault. I am to blame – '

'A fine time for talk like that!' retorted his wife.

'Perhaps we can talk to them, make them see reason – '

Father Jacinto could have smiled hearing that, knowing what he knew of Japanese methods in the town.

'All my things!' cried Eva, her face newly animated. 'We must hide everything at once. Those barbarians will steal all my things! There will be nothing left.' Her eyes shone with inspiration. 'The cellar. Everything must be taken to the cellar.'

'How can you think of things like that?' Macedo railed. 'It's not just our things they want – '

The priest put a cautionary hand on his arm. She was frightened enough as it was.

'It's too late for that now,' Father Jacinto told her softly. 'We must think of escape for you and the children.'

Outside in the compound there was a sudden flurry of activity that cut short their quarrel. They hurried out towards the main doors as an alarmed cry reached them.

'*Patrão, Patrão!*'

Macedo cautiously opened the door, his hand still on the bolt in case of a trick. He was astonished to see his houseboy Chico standing there in the rain with his sister, the children's *amah*. They were both drenched to the skin and plainly terrified.

The priest reached out and dragged them both inside, holding the Timorese boy's arm in a tight grip.

'Where have you been? How did you get here? What have you seen?'

'*Djepang* – on the road,' sobbed the boy. 'My sister – we lay hidden, but so many come. They come now, to the house – '

Eva put a hand to her mouth. 'We'll never get out of here alive!'

'Shut your mouth!' Macedo thundered. He grasped her roughly, propelling her towards the staircase. 'Go and get the children. *Amah*, go with *Dona* Eva. Hurry!' He looked back at Chico. 'You lock all the doors and windows. Quickly now, boy, don't stand there staring.' He finally looked round at the priest. 'We must try to find a place to hide the children.'

'Not the cellar?'

'If the Japanese break into the house they will surely look there first.' He hurried through into the drawing room.

'Then where?' asked the priest, following behind.

'Watch the door,' snapped Macedo. 'Let only Eva and the children inside.'

Father Jacinto stood still. 'And what do you expect me to say to the boy and his sister?'

'What you like,' Macedo retorted sharply. 'They ran out on us before. Yes, even those we thought most loyal. So now we must look to ourselves. They must take their chance.' He lost his patience. 'Close the door – and barricade it with something.'

The priest still stood there watching him narrowly. 'Not I.'

Macedo strode furiously back to the door just as Eva appeared with the children and the young Timorese girl. He pulled his wife roughly into the room, the small boy in her arms, and then took his daughter from her nurse. The priest watched as Macedo slammed shut the doors on the terrified eyes of his servants. He drew the bolts and dragged a chair across to wedge the doors closed. They could hear the little *amah* weeping as her brother hammered outside.

'We have no choice,' said Macedo, staring wildly at the priest's accusing eyes. 'If you touch those doors I'll have to prevent you.'

He looked to where his wife and children stood terrified and silent, the little girl clutching at her mother's nightdress.

'You haven't changed,' he declared, staring at her night clothes. 'Why didn't you get dressed?'

'I – I never thought – I – '

'Too late now.' He turned away, his mind distracted by the all-pervading sense of urgency. He knelt and began to roll back the heavy woven carpet. 'Help me,' he hissed at the priest as he began to take up the wooden floorboards below.

The priest went over to him, wondering if he had finally gone mad. But as Macedo worked, he saw a narrow chamber revealed beneath the floor, dark and dank.

'Down there? There is not room.'

'Enough for them,' said Macedo evenly. He met his wife's eyes across the room, imploring her to do as he asked. 'It is the only place, believe me.'

They knelt before the gaping hole and together struggled to bring out an ancient trunk, a cabin trunk covered in cobwebs and grime. The space looked no bigger for all that.

Doubt was in her eyes as she looked from her husband to the priest, but the desperate hammering on the door was enough to convince Eva Macedo. She went to Jaime and silently put his son into his arms. Then, gripping him by the shoulder, she stepped on to the rim of the void. She stretched her neck and kissed him quickly before she lowered herself down into her hiding place.

'Maia, come to me,' she called to her daughter.

The little girl was uncertain, staring at her mother down below the level of the floor. Was it all a game? The strange excitement of the night had somewhat paled. Suddenly she was tired and wanted to go back to bed, back to her own room. The tension in the room made her afraid.

'Come on, child.' The priest swung her down into her mother's arms.

'You must be very quiet, Maia,' Eva told the girl. 'It is a game we are playing. We are hiding, do you understand?' She set the child down in the cramped space beside her. 'Don't be frightened. We're playing a game.'

Macedo still held the boy in his arms. His whole body tensed at the wave of sounds from the compound outside.

'Take the boy now,' he told his wife, passing the child down to her. 'You must be very quiet. If the children make any noise we are lost.' He hesitated. 'I will come for you as soon as they have gone.' He got to his feet, taking up the first of the floorboards. 'It will be dark. Are you ready?'

Eva nodded dumbly, clutching her children as she sat hunched in the black hole. The men lifted the wooden boards and set them back into place, shadowing and finally blocking her from sight.

'Will there be enough air?' asked the priest anxiously.

'Yes, yes, for some hours, at least. More than they will need.'

Father Jacinto wondered if he was being too optimistic. He said nothing, but helped Macedo to set the carpet back into position.

'The trunk! What shall we do with the trunk?'

It stood in the middle of the living room, clearly out of place in that setting.

The door to the hallway was locked. In the shuttered room they had no knowledge of how much time they had left. The rising panic of the *posto* servants could be heard together with running feet outside on the bare boards of the verandah that circled the house.

Father Jacinto had an idea. He took a lace antimacassar from the back of an armchair and began to dust off the trunk, pulling it over on to its side.

'Does it open? Quickly, try to open it.'

'Yes, but I don't see – '

'Take some of those books from the shelves and some china. Anything. Come on, quickly. Try to make it look as though we are packing – '

He threw the soiled lace in a ball under the sofa and wiped his hands. The trunk lay open in the middle of the floor, ready to receive the books Macedo began to pile on the carpet. The priest was still stacking them in the trunk when they heard the girl scream in the hallway outside.

'They are here,' said the priest.

Macedo felt a cold sweat break out down his back. The two men held their breaths, eyes fixed on the double doors that stood locked against the invaders.

There came a sharp staccato of orders given in Japanese. They heard the houseboy Chico crying out in a mixture of Portuguese and Tetum, but his words were lost amid the shouting of orders, screaming and the crash of furniture.

At last there came a hammering on the doors. The wood

seemed to swell and vibrate under the blows of their rifles. The chair rocked and in one sudden continuous movement the double doors burst open.

At the head of the Japanese troops stood the officer Father Jacinto had seen in the town. Now he knew that all hope was lost.

Behind his back, crowding into the doorway, were the ragtag rabble of Dutch native recruits, bearing weapons in their hands.

The two men stood still, facing the newcomers. In his dirty white soutane Father Jacinto stood straight and unmoving, knowing full well that any quick or nervous movements would unsettle the nervous Japanese. But Macedo knew no such thing. His only experience of the Japanese had been their acquiescence when he waved the neutral travel warrants Sassoon had given him under their noses.

He took a tentative step forward, about to open his mouth to speak, when instantly a bullet embedded itself in the wall above his head. Macedo froze on the spot where he stood.

The officer stood in the doorway, his gaze lingering on Father Jacinto. The priest felt the cold eyes on him and was aware of a faint glimmer in that deadly gaze that told him he was remembered.

Major Shimada inclined his head. '*Konnichiwa*,' he greeted the priest ironically.

He carried a Mauser pistol, and a decorated straight sword hung at his side. The steady penetration of his gaze took in the men, the room and the state of feverish packing which had been interrupted.

'So, you intend to leave.' His voice was calm, utterly courteous, , unquestionably dangerous. The words were Portuguese. No translator was necessary here.

Macedo was about to say something but Father Jacinto moved forward, preventing him. His eyes met those of the *shosa* and he lowered his head in a gesture designed to flatter him.

'We are obeying the official order to return to Liquissa,' he said humbly.

A muscle moved in the major's handsome face. He looked about the room with studied calm, returning to the sweating red-faced *chefe do posto*. He barked out a single order in Japanese to the *gunso* at his shoulder.

'*Hei!*'

The troops spread out, pouring through the doorway. The leaders were already heading to search upstairs.

'The Australians will be found,' said the *shosa* ominously.

In the space beneath the floorboards Eva Macedo sat hugging the sleeping boy on her lap, cradling her daughter's head against her knees, her breath shallow with fear.

Dust and grey light filtered thinly through the gaps between the floorboards. They were ransacking the house, pulling her home apart.

She heard boots reverberating overhead, and muffled voices. Straining her ears to catch her husband's voice, Eva felt the pulse beating in her head. The words were in Portuguese but it was not her husband who spoke.

'We have done nothing "subversive".'

She could hear the distinctive pacing of the Japanese officer but his softly-spoken response was lost. With bated breath she waited, scarcely daring to breathe in the confined space. Her eyes met her daughter's and she put a finger to her lips, trying to smile.

All of a sudden she recognized Jaime's voice and a desperate pang of guilt shot through her as she tried to conjure the scene.

'I do not please. I will not tell you anything,' he was saying obstinately as though addressing his native workers. His contempt for the Japanese showed in his voice. 'You have no jurisdiction here. We are neutral Portuguese citizens – '

His rash words were cut short by what was clearly a blow. She heard him sink to his knees on the boards above her head, and pressed her children closer still.

Father Jacinto blamed himself. He blamed himself for staying behind, for not forcing them out of the place at gunpoint. He tried to pray, but the eyes of the officer were on him, cold and unfeeling, watching for contemptible emotion to betray him.

Would that it were I, thought the priest. Lord, let me be the one to suffer.

But the greater torture was Macedo's. Father Jacinto was

obliged to watch as the Japanese soldiers strained Macedo's head back for the third time.

The water torture. It was a distinctively Japanese method of interrogation, but Father Jacinto was haunted by images of the Spanish Inquisition. The room was transformed. It had become a medieval torture chamber, a place of horrors. A cultured race like the Japanese had made this grotesque torture an art form. A cultured race? Surely no human race could be so devoid of human emotion and yet claim to be civilized.

He watched the officer watching Macedo. The *garafão* held five litres. As the last drop forced itself into his straining body, Macedo writhed between his tormentors. The Japanese *shosa*, full of quick impatient energy, began to pace the room again.

Macedo slumped back, his head hitting the edge of the door. His eyes were glazed with pain and he showed no sign of recognition. He did not appear to see the Japanese *gunso* raise the stick before the blows began to rain down on his swollen stomach.

Under his breath Father Jacinto prayed for him and for his torturers, tears unashamedly streaming down his cheeks.

'Eva!'

Below, Eva Macedo heard her name lost on a failing breath. Her daughter began to whisper, sensing her mother's fear, and they trembled there together in the dark.

Macedo lay on the floor, his clothes stained and soaked. When the priest tried to go to him the *gunso* dragged him back and delivered a succession of heavy backhanders across his mouth. Their eyes met briefly and then the priest's head was jerked around. The Japanese major looked deep into his eyes. His head reeled from a blow delivered with the butt of the Mauser. He touched his swollen lips and tasted his own blood.

'One last chance.'

Still Father Jacinto would not talk. Macedo had shown him an unexpected example. They would never learn of the Australians and the women at the villa from him.

'We are the Knights of Bushido,' proclaimed Major Shimada, straightening up. 'We execute at dawn.'

The dawn light was already filtering into the room through the shuttered windows.

'Oh dear God.'

They dragged Jaime Macedo from the floor and, slamming down the lid of the travelling trunk, forced down his head.

Father Jacinto saw the officer draw the oiled blade of his sword. He closed his eyes and his lips whispered some kind of sacred benediction as the prisoner knelt at his feet. The priest was restrained by strong arms and could not do other than pray as he saw the sword raised.

The floor above her head seemed to vibrate suddenly as though a fight had broken out. Furniture crashed directly overhead accompanied by a torrent of frenzied cries in a language she could not and did not want to understand. Feet and screams, hurried movement all echoed on the wooden boards above.

Had they discovered her hiding place? Were they moving the furniture aside to get to her? Would the boards lift at any moment, to reveal their monkey faces staring down at her?

The boy in her arms began to stir, whimpering, and Eva buried her head against him, shielding the children with her own body.

A fusillade of shots rang out some distance away. All over the house there came noises, crashing glass and smashed windows. It seemed the Japanese and their Dutch allies were stampeding about the house, ransacking room after room. Glass and china were smashed underfoot, bullets tore at the plaster walls, exposing the wooden laths beneath. All that was transportable was borne away, the rest smashed to assuage their growing frustration. They hurried though the upper rooms like a savage whirlwind, gathering momentum. Downstairs they found the real prizes, raiding the larders for every scrap of food.

The noise above died away. Eva Macedo dared to breathe again, cradling her children in her lap in the darkness.

For a moment she sat with her head bowed, paralysed with fear as a scream in the distance broke the deepening silence. From the garden or the compound, she thought. No longer inside the house. No, above her all was tranquil, no movement, no voices. Relief flooded through her but was instantly checked by a new fear. She was alone. Alone with her children in this trap. Above her, the house was still.

She knew that stillness could mean only one thing. Looking up as the wetness seeped through the cracks in the floorboards she knew it was the stillness of death.

Chapter Thirty

'No, no, you have to hold it like this.' He moved his arm tighter around her shoulder, correcting the position of the stock. 'If you don't, the recoil will knock your arm out.'

Dede and Jack lay on the cool grass beyond the house, aiming at a row of pine cones set on a ridge. She had not hesitated when he offered to show her how to shoot. The thought of being left up there with no protection helped to make up her mind. Only Jack had any thought for the women once the men had gone. Perhaps because he was in no doubt that they would have to go. Father Jacinto's deadline had run out. They would have to go back to the *posto* to find out what had gone wrong, even if the valley was crawling with Japanese.

She reloaded, took aim and fired. The shot went wide and she waited for Jack's stinging rebuke.

'Not bad, not bad, but if you hold it like this – ' His arm came round her, his face almost brushing hers.

'Yes, I see what you mean.' A smile played around her mouth but she avoided meeting his eyes. She quickly reloaded and tried hard to concentrate, squinting down the barrel.

'Squeeze it. Gently now.'

She squeezed and the bullet snapped the pine cone right off the ridge. She rolled over on the grass and found him grinning down at her.

'I would say, Miss Harriman – '

'Yes, sir?'

'I would say you have hidden talents.'

'So I pass the test?'

'With flying colours.' He was bending his head down to hers

when, out of the corner of his eye, he caught sight of Amy. 'Ah, all well and good.' He stood up abruptly, more than a trace of his former bad humour and irritation coming back. 'But how d'you think you'll do if it's not a pine cone but a bloody Jap?'

Dede sat up, the rifle in her lap, watching as he stalked back towards the house.

'Well, if that doesn't beat all! Now what did I do wrong?'

The dawn brought a flurry of activity outside the villa as the men prepared for their journey down the mountain. Sister Eulalia stood apart and silent, her hands tucked into the sleeves of her habit.

Fielding saw her standing there and went across to speak to her. He was aware that he had lost much of his influence with her since his return from the *posto* without the priest, and wanted to make amends.

'Don't be alarmed, Sister. We'll bring him back safe and sound.'

She raised her grey eyes to his face and looked at him for a long moment. She said nothing but turned away and went back into the house. He was left standing there, his arms hanging loose at his sides, aware of an unspoken rebuke.

'I don't like the thought of leaving you here alone,' Letria told Amy as he helped her to fill the water bottles.

'Don't be afraid for me, Daniel. Things are not as they were. I am accepted again. And besides,' she added with a small smile, 'Jack has given Dede his rifle.'

'Can she use it?'

'She can if she has to.' She saw the sudden alarm in his face and touched his arm reassuringly. 'No one will come here. This place is haunted, remember? The fear of spirits will keep everyone away.' Her grip tightened. She looked up into his strong, beloved face and there was fear in her eyes. 'It is you who are in danger.' She stretched up her hands and drew his head down to hers. 'Come back, Daniel. Come back safe to me. I am nothing without you.'

'I came to say goodbye,' said Jack, leaning in the doorway.

Dede turned slowly to meet him. 'Oh yes, of course.'

They stood two feet apart, not knowing what to say to each other, knowing that the way ahead was full of unknown dangers and that their paths were separating. The unspoken thought between them was that they might never see one another again.

'Well, then, I'm away – ' He looked regretful, turning reluctantly towards the door.

'Jack – '

He stopped and slowly turned back, coming almost face to face with her.

'Don't get yourself killed, Jack.'

Her voice was small and frightened. She seemed suddenly so open and vulnerable that he was deeply moved and afraid for her.

'Don't you worry. They've missed their chance.'

He looked down on her troubled face and suddenly bent his head and kissed her full on the mouth, leaving her wondering.

Their route to the *posto* was doubly difficult. They moved cautiously with their guns at the ready for the first sign of trouble.

The valley was quiet, ominously so. They crouched low as they came in sight of the deserted valley road. They crossed quickly, unwilling to believe the silence. Everywhere there was a strange stillness in the air that put them all on their guard. No birds wheeled in the dusk light, there was no sound at all.

As they reached the far side of the road Jack and Seaton drew up sharp at the edge of the plantation.

'Is that smoke?'

Here they found the first signs of disturbance: hoofprints in the drying mud, crops beaten down. There was not a human in sight. The smoke came from the *posto* outbuildings. As they drew near, moving swiftly between the trees, they saw that the barns were still burning even after the rain.

As they moved cautiously into the open they saw bullet scars on the whitewashed walls and the splintered wood of the doors, which stood wide open.

The compound itself confirmed their worst fears. The *posto*'s plantation workers had borne the brunt of the assault. As he walked between them Fielding felt sick. He passed the burning outhouses and sweat stood out on his forehead. It took a great effort of will not to lose control in front of the others.

'Filthy Japs.'

'Take a look at the head wounds. Made by stone axes.'

'Natives. Those bloody Dutch native recruits from over the border.'

'Father Jacinto saw a whole bunch of the bastards in the town – '

Fielding looked round at them, his lips in a tight compressed line. 'Where is he, then?' he asked in a flat voice.

It was the question in all their minds.

Silently they moved out past the ruins in the direction of the house. Apart from the broken gate and trampled plants in the garden there were no obvious signs of an attack until they reached the steps of the verandah. Then they saw the smashed windows and, climbing the steps, they saw that the front doors had been forced, the door jambs splintered by rifle butts. The wooden verandah and the inner hallway were littered with broken glass. Holding their breaths in dread anticipation, they went inside.

Fielding stopped abruptly on the threshold, hand tightening on his revolver, looking up at the dangling figure.

The others had entered behind him. They stopped to stare at the body hanging from the bannisters at the top of the staircase. The crumpled face, distorted from the rope and twisted grotesquely to one side, was still recognizable as that of the Macedo's houseboy Chico.

'Poor little bugger.'

Seaton and Harrison moved down the hall into the open doorway at the bottom of the passage. It was the kitchen area, with empty food jars overturned and broken crockery crunch-underfoot. Only the cockroaches remained.

Letria climbed the stairs to cut down the hanging boy. But as he straightened, the knife still in his hand, he saw where the nearest bedroom door had been flung wide.

'Ah, no – '

Jack took the stairs two at a time to stand beside him.

'What is it?' Fielding demanded from below, the words catching in his dry throat. 'Is it him?'

Letria came to the ballustrade. His face was ravaged by the sight he had just seen. He said with disgust, 'It's one of the Timorese servants, a girl. Little more than a child, really.' He swallowed hard. 'She's been savagely mutilated and killed.'

Fielding turned away in disgust. 'Get back down here, then.'

He was staring at the passage that led towards the main living room on the ground floor. At the end of the passage the double doors of the drawing room were shut against him. In every part of the house the doors stood wide open, but here they remained ominously closed, keeping their secrets.

Harrison shared none of the captain's inhibitions. He strode straight up to the doors and purposefully flung them back, revealing a scene of carnage and horror.

'Sweet Jesus.'

Across the room Father Jacinto lay in a wide pool of blood that had darkened the carpet on which he lay. His arms were thrown wide and his head was thrown back. The once-white soutane was stiff with life's blood.

Beside him, at right angles, lay Jaime Macedo, half hidden from view by the enormous packing trunk that stood in the middle of the floor.

Jack knelt at the priest's side, turning his face and touching the set features gently. 'Bayonet wound to the chest,' he announced. 'He didn't stand a chance.'

Letria lit one of the lamps and warm amber light spilled out over the scene. Fielding let out a muffled cry of disgust, bile rising in his throat. As Jack turned he saw Fielding's face and looked back to where Macedo's body lay revealed.

'What's – ' the words died in his throat as he suddenly saw the headless corpse of the man they had come to rescue.

Letria was breathing heavily. Sweat stood out on his face in the foetid atmosphere. No, death was not the terrifying climax; it could be a longed-for deliverance.

'But where are the women and the children?'

A terrible fear seized them as they turned their backs on the dead. A pulse beat in Fielding's head and he was filled with panic.

'Perhaps they're upstairs. Perhaps there's somewhere for them to have hidden up there.' His voice sounded hollow in the sweating room.

'Come on, then. Let's spread out and search.' Seaton was halfway to the door already, eager to get out and find some fresh air. But it was Harrison who stopped him.

He stood frozen in his tracks, scarcely believing what he had heard. 'Shut up,' he told them. 'Shut up and listen.'

They were all silenced as the cry came again.

Together they tore at the carpet with frenzied hands, seeing how the stain had spread across the wooden planks of the flooring, seeping below.

'Here, help me!' Jack seized the edge of the floorboard and yanked it up with eager hands, passing it to Fielding.

When two or three boards had been taken up they fell back in astonishment to see the woman with her two small children huddled in the tight space underground.

Fielding knelt on one knee and stretched out a hand to pull her to her feet. She stood in the dank hole, blinking in the light, recognition coming to her face as she looked at Fielding.

Her limbs were stiff and aching from her cramped position. Her eyes hurt in the sudden explosion of light. She stood there as Letria bent down into the hole and grasped the little girl under her arms and swung her up from her hiding place. He cradled her face against his shoulder, talking to her in soft Portuguese.

Harrison took the small boy and then passed him straight over to Jack. Holding the child in his arms, Jack found himself all fingers and thumbs. The boy was wet. He suddenly looked up and saw the unfamiliar and bearded face above him and burst into frenzied wailing for his mother.

Seaton and Fielding between them had fetched Eva Macedo out of her hiding place. She was unsteady on her feet, leaning heavily against the captain for support. Agonized by cramp from hours in her huddled position, she was wearing a dressing gown, filthy from dust and dirt, over her nightdress. Her face seemed drained of all colour, but there was something matting her hair that made Fielding suddenly alert.

'Are you hurt?' he asked her in Dutch, raising one hand to touch the dried blood on one side of her head.

She raised a hand to her hair, finding it marked by blood.

'No, no, not I.' Her voice was barely audible. She ran a hand over her face, as though remembering. Her hair hung limp with sweat, her eyes wild and haunted.

Jack was worried that she would look behind and see what had happened to her husband, but the boy's crying instantly drew her back to her son. She seized him from Jack's arms and began to soothe him with comforting words.

Did she know that her husband and the priest were dead? Jack moved quickly to cover the bodies while she was distracted, but even as he looked back in her direction their eyes met and he understood.

She had heard it all, down there in the darkness. Whatever torture had been played out here, she had been witness to it all, stifling her cries and the fear of her children. She had suffered the full horror for herself.

'Let's get outside,' said Fielding, taking her by the arm and steering her towards the doors. 'Seaton, get some clothes for the children and for *Senhora* Macedo.'

'What?'

'You heard me. Get whatever looks useful. She can hardly travel very far dressed like that.'

Out in the compound they were assailed by the smell. Around the bodies lying in the outer yard were clouds of flies.

'Don't look,' Eva told her children.

'Try to be calm,' said Fielding in Dutch, walking beside her.

She was tall and straight, the boy in her arms, walking past the dreadful sight. The children were too afraid and cowed to do more than whimper at the strangeness. They were clearly terrified of everything, including the wild men with beards and guns.

'Where will you take us?' asked Eva Macedo.

'To the mountains first. Then to safety.'

She nodded, remembering what he had promised that night in the children's nursery.

'Poor cow.' Harrison turned back, hand gripping his rifle.

'Lucky, you should say.' Letria came up beside him. 'The Japanese would not have spared any of them.'

Looking back at the *posto* Jack knew that it was true.

They moved up into the forest slowly. The crowding trees closed protectively about them, moist and clinging in the darkness. Jack swung the little girl up on to his shoulder, grinning in the only language that they shared. She was still hesitant among these strangers, reassured only by her mother's calm acceptance of their company.

They caught a few hours' sleep when they felt safe and far enough from the main road. They chose a place well screened from the trail. Jack took the first watch, passing on to Harrison later in the night. When he awoke, just before dawn, he discovered that Letria was missing. He had gone ahead to scout the area. Something had unnerved him as they came up the shadowed track and he had gone off, moving rapidly and skilfully through the bush in advance of their dawn start.

Fielding and the others did not seem concerned at his prolonged absence but Jack began to look warily around him as they marched, sensing the danger in the air.

After half an hour on the track Jack heard someone approaching before he caught a glimpse of the running figure between the trees. Letria plunged down the tortuous hillside, panting and red-faced, his shirt stuck to his back.

'We can't go on,' he gasped, his chest heaving. 'I have seen horse tracks. I went right up towards the village, but there were no sentries posted. None at all.' He paused, breathing heavily, waiting for his words to have an impact.

'Horses? You mean, Japs?'

Letria turned to Fielding squarely. 'They're here before us, Captain. I went as close as I dared. They have brought the women down to the village. I saw them. They must have caught them at the villa. We're walking into a trap, Captain.'

Chapter Thirty-one

There was no disguising the fact that Mrs Beattie was seriously ill. She was delirious a great deal of the time and seemed to recognize no one. She called out names from the life she had lost in Singapore, names that only caused her more grief and distressed Katherine.

'There's no improvement?'

'No, my dear, I'm afraid not.'

Looking into the shuttered room, Kate watched in silence as Sister Eulalia said her prayers in rapid Portuguese. In the shadows of filtered sunlight the nun knelt with her rosary, smoothing the polished beads between her brown fingers as she prayed.

The sight of the prone figure beyond on the bed confirmed Kate's fear that Mrs Beattie was dying.

Back in her own room the baby was awake and fretful. Kate removed her cover and picked her up. The baby suffered from prickly heat if wrapped up, so Kate took her outside into the cool breeze off the mountain, and sat under the pines.

'One day soon, baby,' she said, 'you're going to have to have a name.' It was a decision she had put off, afraid to open the old wounds of her memory.

The wind stirred the trees. Was that what made her look up? Had she heard their voices drifting, the trees brusquely thrust aside as they pushed on up the native trail?

Kate stumbled to her feet, alert to danger as a wild animal to the huntsmen. She had almost reached the door of the villa as the first Japanese soldiers reached the summit of the hill.

'Dede! Dede!'

The American came running with the rifle at the sound of terror in the girl's voice. Kate huddled against the door, clutching her baby in her arms. From the window Dede saw the Japanese moving through the rich vegetation around the villa.

Their assumption that the house meant safety was entirely mistaken. The Japanese kicked in the door, marching into the room where the women stood huddled close together in the farthest corner.

'Don't shoot, don't shoot!'

The Japanese *gunso* stood in the doorway, eyes searching the room. He took a step forward, gesturing with his rifle bayonet that they should get against the wall. His flat round face betrayed fear and anger as he gestured at them, seeing the rifle in Dede's hand. He grabbed it away from her, seizing it out of her hand, making her cry out in pain.

'*Kura! Lakas!*' He spoke in short, erratic bursts. None of the words he barked at them made any sense and their blank terror only seemed to anger him further. He moved closer, threateningly, snapping out another staccato order. Only the words '*tuan cataus*' meant anything.

'*Tuan cataus*,' Sister Eulalia repeated and shook her head vehemently.

The *gunso*'s eyes widened slightly as they made contact. '*Ah so-ka? Kura!*'

Sister Eulalia obediently took a step forward. Kate wondered at her directness and courage. She held the gaze of the Japanese before dropping her eyes with seeming respect. Kate was astonished to see the nun make the most cursory of bows, but the gesture seemed to appease the Japanese. He looked at her, head tilted.

'*Gaijin* – '

'*Português*,' said Sister Eulalia. She turned to include the other women. '*Todos Português*,' she lied. '*Tuan cataus pigi-pigi. Tuan cataus pigi-pigi Lolotoi – dis-sana*.' And she shrugged as though she could not care less that they were gone so far away. But she hoped that the mention of Lolotoi, a town far away to the south near the Dutch border, would mean something to him.

The *gunso* seemed to pause to consider this, obviously

finding the heady mixture of Portuguese and Tetum dialect beyond him. He pulled the nun across the room, looking at her face accusingly, and then herded all the women down the corridor before him. He forced Sister Eulalia to open each door they came to, pushing her before him, as though he was afraid of an explosion of bullets from some unseen Australian.

But the explosion was in Japanese when the *gunso* discovered Mrs Beattie on her sickbed. The soldiers poured inside, overturning the bed as they ransacked the room.

'Oh, no – '

Sister Eulalia's protest was cut short by a vicious slap to the face by the furious Japanese sergeant. Mrs Beattie had been thrown on to the floor, striking her head as she fell. She lay in an ungainly crumpled heap with her head twisted to one side. The Japanese finished their fruitless search and stepped over her inert body as if unaware of her existence.

Sister Eulalia ran across and lifted Mrs Beattie from the floor, holding her head in her lap. There was a dry rattle in the back of the Englishwoman's throat and her eyes were glazed.

Kate met the nun's eyes and saw the compassion there.

'It's no use, it's too late. She's gone.'

Sister Eulalia began to pray. '*Ego te absolvo a peccatis tuis* – '

Dede stood in the doorway, her face white with rage. 'She's dead and you can't hurt her now.'

The *gunso* looked directly at her, his narrow eyes glinting. He had to crane his thick bullish neck to stare up into her face because she was so much the taller. Without the slightest comprehension of what she said he struck her heavily on the side of the head, a blow which sent her reeling.

Amy caught her as she crumpled, barely conscious and with blood pouring down her cheek. She looked up at the *gunso* and suddenly she was speaking, not in English but in her mother's own tongue.

It was hard to say who was more surprised, the *gunso* or the other women in the room. He went across to her, lifting her face between his short stubby fingers. He examined her features closely, his small eyes burning with malevolence as he snapped out a series of sharp questions.

Amy answered him quietly, her Japanese fluent and smooth

as Dede lay unmoving in her lap. The Japanese soldiers in the doorway looked at one another in surprise and speculation. Their sergeant barely concealed his astonishment. He seemed ill at ease, suspicious of the soft-spoken young woman kneeling at his feet.

Sister Eulalia saw that Amy was asking him something, pleading with him in her eloquent Japanese. The nun met Kate's eyes and saw her admiration for the girl's bravery.

The *gunso* lifted his hand, and for a moment Sister Eulalia thought he was going to strike Amy, but instead he pulled the girl to her feet and snapped out instructions to her to leave Dede alone. Then he turned and stalked towards the door, leaving a guard on the threshold.

'Please don't be angry with me,' Amy said slowly. 'He would have hurt Dede.' The American was now sitting up, holding her head and looking around her, still dazed.

'What are they going to do with us?' Kate whispered, more afraid for her child than for herself.

'Whatever it is,' said Sister Eulalia without taking her eyes from the guard in the doorway, 'they've left us in no doubt what will happen if we refuse to do as they say.'

'Yes, they were going to kill us,' said Amy in the same steady voice she had used before. 'Now he will let his officer decide.' She looked round the circle at their faces. 'He says we have ten minutes to pack before they take us down to the village.'

Chapter Thirty-two

The walk down to the village was long. In the heat of the day there seemed no end to it. The Japanese used bamboo staves to force them forward through the bush.

Kate found the easiest way to carry the baby was to perch her on her hip as the native women did. She felt tired very quickly with the unaccustomed exercise, but she knew that to stop would mean a beating from the leering Japanese guards.

Arriving in the village she was haunted by the look in the dark eyes of the natives who had helped them. They watched the arrival of the women with fear, knowing their connection with the missing Australians.

All the natives had been herded together in the central square of the village. The Japanese had already demonstrated their power over life and death. The body of Sha Nana, the village chief, lay sprawled before the *lulic* poles with his wives mourning around him. Seeing their grieving, terrified eyes, Sister Eulalia made a move to go to them. The sudden movement alarmed the Japanese. A soldier thrust a bayonet at her, his shout merging with Kate's cry for her to stop.

Above the commotion, Dede heard another voice, more authoritative than the others. The crowd around the women parted, suddenly quiet. They turned and saw a young Japanese officer with his sword at his hip standing before the chief's house.

He rasped out an order and his troops immediately moved to herd the women prisoners away from the local Timorese. A contingent of native men, terrifying in appearance with their curious weapons and painted faces, began to beat the villagers away towards a hut on the opposite side of the square. Dede saw the difference between them and the local Timorese and judged that these must be the Dutch native recruits working for the Japanese. They had clearly been drinking from the chief's own stock and appeared to take a particular relish in maltreating their countrymen, using their weapons to subdue all opposition. There was a desperate wailing and screaming as they were pushed and kicked into the area where the Japanese wanted them.

'What are they going to do with them?'

The question that was in everyone's mind hung unanswered in the air.

The guards discouraged them from talking by jabbing their bayonets at them, herding them towards a hut where one of the Japanese collaborators stood at the ladder. He wore a headband and seemed better dressed than the others. From his lank straight hair to the clothes that he wore, Sister Eulalia thought him an Indonesian. As his eyes flicked over the women she read a cold-hearted suspicion in his face that boded no one any good.

'Not you.' He had singled out Amy, grasping her viciously by the arm and drawing her out of line.

He began to speak to her in rapid Japanese, having obviously heard what had happened at the villa. He looked her up and down insolently. His dark eyes were dull and heavy, reflecting little light. Suddenly he grabbed at her again, pushing her before him. Amy screamed and Sister Eulalia grabbed hold of Amy's arm.

A number of guards ran over, bayonets flashing, followed by the officer. They parted and drew aside in deference. But Sister Eulalia did not let go of Amy's arm. He cast one look in her direction and then ordered his men to take Amy from her.

'No!' cried Dede. 'Don't hurt her!'

The officer turned round and stood before her. In his gaze she saw that he was shocked by her intervention.

If it had not been so alarming, Dede might have felt absurd. She was by far the taller, at least a head above the Japanese officer. As his eyes met hers she saw that he did not enjoy her physical advantage over him one little bit. She knew he was going to make her pay for outfacing him before his men.

'You English woman?' His English came as a surprise. A faint flicker of hope rose in her, inexplicable in the circumstances. He took his time looking her over. 'English,' he repeated with apparent distaste.

'No. I'm an American,' she told him, head up.

He looked back at her as satisfied as though she had just confessed a crime to him. '*Gaijin*.'

In his gaze she saw that he regarded her as his inferior, a base creature, a woman from an alien race. She knew very well that women in his country were conditioned to be subservient and obey a fixed standard of feminity and submission to their men that would be abhorrent to western women. In his eyes she was less than his own women because she did not know how to behave. She was beneath his contempt. Her dress and her behaviour, to say nothing of her extreme size and strange appearance, could only reinforce his disgust.

He cast a sideways look at Amy, as though comparing the two. Standing between the Japanese guard and Sister Eulalia, she looked very young and vulnerable. He went and lifted her chin, looking at her delicate features with an appraising eye.

Dede saw the look and knew she had to intervene.

'She's English,' said Dede quickly, afraid of him suddenly. He came and stood next to her again, a faint expression of distaste on his mouth.

'Why lie? *Gaijin* lies. Colonial woman.' He looked from Dede to Sister Eulalia with undisguised loathing. 'You have no respect.'

She read the cold severity of his gaze but knew she had to speak. 'You cannot touch her,' she told him brazenly.

He hit her a stinging blow across the face with the edge of his hand. He was not used to being contradicted, least of all by an alien woman.

She stumbled under the blow but quickly regained her feet. Her whole head throbbed and she was unsteady as she stood there. Her head lifted with sudden defiance, her eyes bright with will, not tears.

'The Imperial Japanese Forces are kind to women,' he said abruptly and took Amy by the elbow, propelling her across the square towards the ladder of one of the huts.

The *gunso* pushed Sister Eulalia and Dede back into line

with Kate and her baby. With the butt of his rifle he motioned them away, forcing them into one of the stilt houses. They climbed the ladder and collapsed in the darkness together. The sago-leaf walls were woven close together but light still filtered in. They crouched together on the rush matting, Dede clinging to Sister Eulalia as tightly as Kate clutched her baby, quivering with fear.

Outside, the village had fallen strangely silent as the line of armed Japanese took a step back from the villagers.

'What are they going to do with them?'

The villagers were herded into the chief's house under blows from their Dutch counterparts. When they were all inside, the Dutch natives began to pile branches and dry grass under the stilts of the house. The Japanese soldiers watched them, bayonets fixed.

Sister Eulalia had risen to her knees, looking down through the entrance to the hut. 'No, no! They cannot do it!'

The other women crowded around her, staring through the gaps in the atap wall.

'Please God, no – ' but no sooner had her words fallen away than two soldiers moved forward and set the grass and wood alight with rags doused in petrol.

Sister Eulalia began to pray softly, rapidly under her breath. Her rosary beads clicked between her restless fingers as the flames caught and began to surge up the sides of the dry-thatch house. The fierce crackling of the fire almost drowned the terrible crescendo of screams from inside.

'Everyone.' Dede was rigid with shock. 'Even the children.' She began to cry, twisting and wringing her hands. 'Amy, where's Amy?'

Sister Eulalia put her arms around her, stroking her hair away from her bruised and bleeding face. She clung to the nun desperately, whimpering like a small child.

The trees formed a steamy canopy overhead. Lying in the grass in the heat of day, they were all bathed in sweat. Jack could feel it trickling down between his shoulder blades while only feet away he watched two Japanese sentries relieve themselves where they were without self-consciousness. Jack had been greatly tempted to put a bullet through their heads, but in the peace of the grove the noise would have alerted the main Japanese force and ruined everything.

Dusk now bathed the compound in a crimson haze. The Dutch native recruits were drunk on rice whisky and slaughter. The smoking ruins of the chief's house stood testimony to their wanton brutality. It was clear that the Japanese had little control over their local cadres. The relationship between them was in a delicate balance, at best a dangerous alliance. The Japanese officer had imposed a strict segregation on his men as they ate their rations and turned in for the night.

'Right, it's time.'

Bending low, keeping their heads down, the Australians ran out of the shelter of the treeline and out along the bamboo stockade in the cultivated gardens of the village. They took great care not to tread on the dry branches underfoot to betray their position to the Japanese sentries posted at either end of the village compound.

Fielding went first, doubled up as he ran, clutching his carbine between sweating palms. Harrison and Seaton moved in behind, eyes darting across the village for signs of danger, as wary as hunting tigers. Crouching in the long grass, Jack and Letria waited their turn. They each had twenty rounds of ammunition left, Jack using Letria's rifle and the Portuguese with Fielding's revolver.

As the captain signalled for them to follow, Jack suddenly saw the unmistakable figure of Amy appear in the entrance to the hut of the Japanese officer. He pointed her out to Fielding and they all froze where they were, watching as she made a silent descent of the ladder.

As she made her way across the compound she was lightfooted and cautious, hesitating each time one of the Japanese guards seemed about to turn and discover her. She approached the hut where the other women were being held, watching the Japanese guard who sat slumped over at the foot of the ladder, cradling his rifle in his hand.

In the shelter of the low stockade Jack and Letria sat on their haunches taking deep breaths. Jack's strong square hands clenched about his borrowed rifle, his finger ready on the trigger if Amy put herself in danger. He watched as she went up and spoke to the guard, but he would not move aside for her. They saw her gesture in the direction of the officer's hut, but the guard was suspicious. Instead of going alone to obey the summons she brought, he seized her by the wrist and started to drag her across the square with him, while she struggled.

The whiplash crack of a rifle spun him backwards. He fell, flinging back his head as the bullet took him full in the throat, blood spraying over Amy as he fell.

'Got the bastard,' said Letria with satisfaction.

All at once flashes of fire exploded around the village. Jack's arm jerked with the recoil as he took deliberate aim and fired at the other Japanese sentry. Bullets drilled and splintered the wood and palm leaves of the atap houses. Japanese troops and Dutch native recruits poured out of the houses, many being caught before they could even climb down to the ground. The Dutch natives ran in all directions, their primitive weapons useless, relying on the Japanese for their defence.

Kate, Dede and Sister Eulalia had hidden their faces on the floor as the first shots rang out. But exhilaration soon replaced fear as they realized who was behind the attack. Chips of mildew and moss came scattering down around them as bullets whined over the compound with a rising inflection. Looking down they could see the body of the Japanese sentry at the foot of the ladder. Blood ran down to form a pool on the earth at his feet. Amy's dress was stained with splashes of blood but she did not hesitate. She seized the guard's rifle with both hands and crouched beside the ladder, using his corpse as a shield.

'Come on,' she called up to them. 'Come down now, quickly.'

Dede was first down the ladder, pulling Sister Eulalia after her. Kate came last, her baby held against her breast, climbing down the ladder one-handed. She almost tripped over the sentry on his back in the dust, eyes wide to the heavens.

The Japanese troops and their allies were too preoccupied in a firefight with the Australians at the edge of the village to notice the women's escape. But the Japanese officer had appeared in the entrance of the hut he had shared with Amy, hand on the Mauser at his belt.

'Drop the bastard,' cried Jack, but before he or Letria could take aim, Amy had twisted round and fired. The recoil slammed back against her shoulder, but she fired again. His uniform jacket erupted as the bullets caught him in the chest. He swayed and then plunged down from the hut and landed heavily in the dust underneath.

Disgust clawed and caught in her throat, but she swallowed down the horror of all that had happened to her in the last twenty-four hours. She had to concentrate on getting the other women out of danger.

'Make for the trees. Hurry, hurry!'

Sister Eulalia began to run, her habit held up in handfuls, hearing the gunfire behind them. Amy pushed Kate with the baby before her and followed Dede as she ran between the tall thatched houses away from the fighting.

'Come on, Amy, come on – '

Dede turned, waiting for the girl to catch up. Amy seemed not to hear her. She stood, wavering, the rifle still in her hands, unwieldly and out of place.

'Amy – '

Dede couldn't understand why she seemed to have stopped dead. She turned back, but suddenly the girl raised a hand as if imploring her to go on. Her strange blue eyes were enormous with pain as she beseeched her to go.

Suddenly she collapsed on to her knees, dropping the rifle. With both hands she clutched her dress as an obscene scarlet stain turned the faded silk wet.

'Amy!'

Behind the body on the ground she saw the Japanese *gunso* fire again, the bullet pumping into lifeless flesh now beyond his reach.

Plunging into the long grass beyond the village, Dede expected a bullet in her back at any moment. She could hear gunfire and screaming. Behind her the compound was on fire. Her own breath sobbed in her ears as she fled the horror.

She reached the cover of the bush and collapsed, her legs giving way. But the instinct for survival was too well tuned. She began to crawl towards the shelter of the trees, aware of Sister Eulalia in front of her and Kate a long way ahead urging them on.

They collapsed together, panting, their breath hammering

in their ears. The bush was around them, hiding them, but Letria had seen them and called out, some distance away.

'Are you hurt?'

Sister Eulalia shouted back in Portuguese, '*Não estou nada ferida. O sangue é dos cabrões japonês.*'

His harsh laughter echoed back across the grass, cheering them as they moved to join them. But the laughter stopped as he realized there was one of their number missing.

'Come on, come on,' said Seaton, appearing from the trees. 'Let's move it out of here.'

They moved on between the trees, using every twist and turn of the forest trail. The Japanese had seen them go. As Jack and Letria brought up the rear with covering fire, a fusillade of bullets struck the trees above their heads. The chase was on.

Chapter Thirty-three

They retired into the friendly shelter of the forest, striking deep into the bush to avoid the Japanese pursuit. Night closed about them like a cloak, shrouding the trees in dark shadows. Fear sat heavily on the group as they lifted weary feet over the tangled roots and creepers in their path. They were all in shock from the events of the past days.

When at last they dared to stop, Fielding would permit no fires. No one knew how far away the Japanese might be.

They huddled together under the cover of thick foliage to exchange their stories. Fielding began, as always, but it was left to Jack to complete the account of what they had found at the *posto*. The women sat in taut silence, looking at Eva Macedo and her children. When Jack spoke of Father Jacinto, Kate looked at Sister Eulalia but her face remained calm, resigned, as she absorbed the shock.

'So he is dead.'

'I'm sorry. He was a fine man.' It was the captain who spoke. 'A brave man.' His voice was leaden with sorrow.

'I suppose I knew it all the time.' She looked up, meeting his soft blue eyes. 'How did it happen?'

Fielding exchanged a look of horror with Jack, and Jack it was who took pity on him and told her the rest. At length she leant forward, her hands pressed close together in her lap expressing all her suppressed tension.

'Don't these people fear God?'

Her eyes were red with fatigue. She got slowly to her feet, steadying herself with a hand on Kate's shoulder. Suddenly she seemed an old woman. Kate looked after her fondly, sharing her bitter grief.

Katherine heard her softly praying long after they had all turned aside and tried to get to sleep. She lay there in the moving darkness, listening to the nun's faint liturgy against a background of bird calls and night noises. The forest seemed infested.

Unable to sleep either, Dede joined Letria, who had volunteered to take the first watch. He stood with his back against a tree trunk, cradling his rifle in his arms. He spun around, hearing her approach, the gun pointed at her stomach. She was appalled to see the tears staining his cheeks.

'I'm sorry,' she said softly. 'I came to tell you about her – '

He nodded slowly, lowering the rifle, and she went forward to join him under the giant tree.

He had known, of course, the moment he saw that only Dede, Kate and her baby, and Sister Eulalia had reached the safety of the bush. But the full realization of his loss did not hit him then. It was no time for personal grief. His mind had suddenly been crystal clear, his aim ruthless, all his hatred and vengeance channelled into killing as many Japanese as he could find as they broke out of the village.

'She saved us all.' Dede did not attempt to check her tears any longer.

'It was quick?'

She nodded dumbly, her face washed with tears, knowing she lied. For she had seen Amy die, had seen her corpse jump as the bullets hit her, her hand outstretched like a claw, her eyes half-shut staring up at the dark sky. That memory she kept secret and hoped one day to live to forget. Letria's pain was great enough.

She made a promise to herself as she left him there. She had seen death at close quarters, had seen Amy robbed of her future. Who knew if there would be a tomorrow for any of them? From now on she would value each day as it came, live each day to the full – for who knew if it might be her last?

At first light they moved on, careful to cover any trace of their camp from possible pursuit.

'We have to go faster.'

'We have to think of the children.'

'Carry them.'

Eva Macedo let the men take her children for her. She took it as her right. She was neither grateful nor gracious and walked on without a word. Kate had only seen her talk to Fielding and that in her own Dutch language. She supposed Eva must still be in shock, unable to take in the brutality of her husband's death. But then they were all shocked and exhausted by everything that had happened.

It was plain to Kate that the little girl Maia was confused about their sudden hurried departure from home, but Eva made no move to comfort or reassure her. She only ever seemed to pay attention to her young son.

Jack and Letria took turns in carrying the little girl. Letria at least could talk to her in her own language. She appeared amazingly resilient, seeing their journey as an adventure, as some kind of complicated game for adults.

There was a sense of timelessness in the depths of the green forest. The air was dense and wet with the cloying perfume of exotic tropical flowers. The sunlight fell through the rich emerald foliage, lighting dust spirals in the air. Deep greens, sapphires and turquoise formed a canopy of leaves. The air was filled with the drone of insects, the sudden shrieks of the hornbills and the flap of escaping wings.

'Where are we going? Do any of you have the least idea?'

They stopped, turning to stare at Eva Macedo where she had sat down, fanning herself with a huge leaf.

'Save your breath,' said Seaton brutally. 'You'll need all your strength. Get moving.' He hauled her to her feet unceremoniously.

'Here,' said Harrison, 'you take the kid. He's your son after all,' and he dumped the little boy back in her arms.

The temperature soared. Sweat streamed down their backs as they moved on again, plagued by flies and clamouring mosquitos in the deep green shadows.

'*Australie!*'

'What was that?' They stood rooted to the spot in the middle of the forest.

'I didn't hear – '

The cry came again in that instant, sending waves of terror through each one of them.

'*Australie! Australie!*'

The cries came from the depths of the forest, from somewhere above on the mountain.

'It's the Japanese! They've found us!' Eva cried in despair.

'Shut up, you stupid bitch!' Seaton put a restraining hand across her mouth but she fought him off.

'How dare you touch me!'

The cry came again, eerily in the midst of the forest, and they fell silent. Wet with sweat they listened to the mocking, taunting calls, unnerving in the stillness of the mountains.

'How far away, do you think?' Letria asked Fielding in a hushed urgent whisper.

'It's hard to say.'

Letria flashed a look of exasperation at Jack, furious that he could never get a straight answer out of the captain.

'Sounds travel very far,' said Sister Eulalia. 'But if we stand around here they will soon find us.'

'You're right, of course,' said Fielding grimly. 'Let's get going.'

There was no time to think, although they were all scared out of their wits. They knew they had to keep on moving or the Japanese would be on them. They had all seen what the Japanese could do. Escape was the only thought in their heads.

They plunged further into the forested hills, but the Japanese catcalls continued to mock their progress.

Through a jade-green mist they passed down into a deep defile between the fern-clad mountains. The dappled light played tricks with the path and Eva slipped at one point and fell.

'I cannot go on. You must leave me here.'

Jack passed the little Macedo girl over to Letria and went across to her mother.

'Now look, lady, you can bloody well do what you like but you're not going to put the rest of us at risk.'

Eva stared up at the wild figure with fierce eyes. 'Well, really!'

'So just keep your mouth shut and get moving. Or don't you want to go on living?'

She looked to Fielding in appeal. 'This is intolerable.'
'Aw, dry up,' said Jack.
They kept up the pace deep into the afternoon. If they stopped at all it was only for water. They were all bone weary, driven only by fear.
Kate had only one thought in her head. She had to save her baby. She had become Kate's sole reason for living, for surviving.
Amy had given her life to make sure they all escaped. She had sacrificed herself for Kate and her baby.
Suddenly it came to Kate to call the child Amy. The idea delighted her, it seemed so right. She looked down at her daughter thinking, Amy, little Amy, and could not wait to tell the others.
Each of them made their own reasons to survive. Kate had Amy, and that was enough.

Jack sat beside Dede on the edge of the grass bank, remembering the tension between them, each waiting for the other to talk first.
'Surely now we've lost them?'
'For the moment.' He looked down at her feet. 'I reckon your shoes have about had it.'
'I don't care. I'll go barefoot if I have to.'
'I didn't know you were so tough.'
Dede looked round at him and had to smile. 'Neither did I. I guess they'd never recognize me back in Pasadena – '
'Do you care?'
'Not a lot, no.'
They both broke into laughter, heads touching together.
'We're bloody fools, you know that?'
She looked up into his face, suddenly serious now. 'If you had died I don't know what I'd have done.'
'You've got more guts than any woman I've ever met.'
They gave each other courage to go on. Just being together gave them strength, knowing that the other was there. When the going got really tough, there was someone to rely upon, someone who cared.
Amy's tragic and heroic death had made Dede realize how short their time together might be. Letria's grief had made her

open up, suddenly vulnerable to the emotions she had buried for all manner of reasons now forgotten. She realized how precious this time together had become to her, how much she cared. There was no time to waste in bickering and hiding their true feelings for each other when each day could very well be their last.

Chapter Thirty-four

The fierce sunlight was in his eyes as Jack caught up with Letria and Fielding.

'Any idea of where we're going?'

'Not a hell of a lot, no,' Letria said bluntly.

'Does this path lead down into the next valley?'

'It must,' Fielding stated.

'But does it?' Jack demanded. 'You have the bloody map.'

The captain looked at him, his face yellow with sweat. Unfortunately, he had no idea where they were. 'It's my guess that it does.'

'Your guess? We can't go on your guesses, mate.'

'I know, I know!' Fielding exploded and thrust the map at Letria. 'You bloody well sort it out if you're so clever.' He stalked on up the path, wiping the sweat from his forehead, more riled than Jack had ever seen him.

'He won't listen to anyone any more.'

'Yeah, but is he right, d'you think?'

Letria pored over the map, frowning in concentration. Finally, exasperated, he folded the mildewed paper and shrugged. 'I keep my eyes on the sun. As long as we're heading south we ought to be all right.'

Great, thought Jack cynically.

The countryside was all alike in that place. They had no sooner descended one ridge of the hillside than they were faced with another rise, even more steep than the last. The sun beat down upon them in dappled spotlights between the thick foliage. They waited for the afternoon rains with burning anticipation.

It came of a sudden with a rush of wind. The rain began to spot the swaying giant ferns and hung like tears from the fat green leaves. Wild orchids glowed vibrantly against the vivid emerald of the branches.

The dense sky unloaded its leaden burden of water upon the land. The thick syrupy splashes turned the dust-dry ground underfoot to squelching ochre-coloured mud in seconds.

They camped that night in a clearing, too tired to talk. Their faces were pinched with exhaustion. They shared out the remaining food with growing awareness that there would not be sufficient to last out the journey to the coast.

'We need food urgently,' Sister Eulalia informed the captain.

'Don't you think I know that?' snapped Fielding curtly.

Seaton met Jack's gaze, sharing the same thought. He got up and went across to the captain, hands on hips.

'Well, Letria's spotted a village on the map,' said the sergeant. 'We've talked it over and we want to give it a go.'

Fielding looked up, breathing heavily. 'It's too dangerous.'

'Come off it! We've got no choice.' Seaton turned away, summoning the support of the others.

'What's wrong now?'

'Don't blame me, mate. He won't chance it.'

Harrison got to his feet, glaring furiously at the captain. 'It's the only bloody village in the area.'

'I say we should give it a go,' Jack added quickly.

'If it's the only village in the area,' said Fielding, 'then the Japanese will be there.'

Seaton threw him a scathing look. 'Christ! A captain's supposed to lead by example.' His livid face poured scorn on the younger man.

Fielding turned red as a schoolboy caught out in some mischief. He seemed fairly apoplectic with rage.

'We should at least make a recce,' Jack said, stepping in to offer some sort of compromise that would avoid a fight. 'Give it a go, will you?'

'You don't have to come with us, Captain,' sneered Seaton.

The captain looked up into the circle of accusing faces. He knew he had no choice if he was to remain their leader.

'We'll go tonight,' he said.

The tropical night fell like a curtain. Letria had been delegated to stay to guard the women and children. The others took most of the ammunition they had left and prepared to set out by the light of the vast yellow moon.

Dede watched Jack cleaning his rifle with a growing sense of foreboding. Ever since the horror of the village deaths she had been acutely aware of the danger closing in upon them. The Japanese were getting closer every day. How long could they keep just one step ahead?

She wanted to talk to him, to tell him to take care, to watch out for himelf. But the proximity of Seaton and Harrison stopped her from approaching him and she missed her chance. As they set out she was left behind, afraid for him, aware that if one loved one also feared.

It was eerie walking at night in the moonlight. The deep shadows were deceptive, hiding their path more than a few feet ahead. Jack Ford brought up the rear of the straggling line, constantly on guard, his rifle at the ready for any movement in the shadows.

They emerged out of the trees and began to slip and slide their way down the spine of the ridge, shaking loose the scree. A rapid stream fed by the rains lay between them and the small settlement in the valley, its rushing noise obscuring their approach. Lying in the long grass on the marshy riverside, Seaton and Harrison considered their chances. They were the undoubted expert raiders, the ones who had put into practice what the others had only been taught on courses at Wilson's Promontory.

'What d'you think, mate?'

The full moon played tricks on their eyesight. It was impossible to reliably judge the terrain. The bland colourless light created shadows full of unseen dangers.

'I don't know,' said Seaton slowly, cagily. 'Let's get in closer and take a look.'

They waded the fast-flowing stream and dripped water down the track in the direction of the village. At the edge of the bush they stopped again, convinced now that something was wrong.

Seaton was a chancer, an improviser. He was exhilarated by danger and by the risks he took. There was no one better to lead such a foray. The others took their cue from him, even Fielding. They trod in his footsteps to the village boundary, stopping again as the sergeant crouched in the dust.

'I don't like the look of this.'

There were no guards posted, no sign of life at all. In every other village they had seen on the island there had always been some sign of activity, always fires that burnt night and day.

As they entered the stockaded area they realized their mistake at once.

'We're too late. They've been here already.'

It was the smell that alerted them. The smell of death and decay. They froze on the spot, aware of the dead lying in the shadows all around them.

To his dying day Jack Ford would remember the stench as he entered that wasteland. The evil odour of rotting flesh poisoned the air. The houses had been ransacked and burnt. The ruins had long since cooled down, the ashes grown cold. The villagers had either been slain or seized for Japanese forced labour. Corpses lay spreadeagled between the skeleton timbers, bloated and covered by clouds of insects.

The strangers stood in the middle of this scene of carnage, silent and shaken. They had come all this way only to find that the Japanese were one step ahead of them.

'What are we going to do? We still need food.'

'You won't find any here now.'

The simple truth was bitter to hear. The whole night's business had been a waste of time.

'Let's get the hell out of here,' said Jack in deep distaste.

The way back was made twice as tortuous by the knowledge that the Japanese could not be far away. The bodies in the village had been cold, but the heat of the day had not had many days to work upon them.

They're still here, somewhere, Jack thought with a hot memory of fear. Our luck isn't going to hold out much longer.

They redoubled their efforts but progress uphill to the treeline was slow. They were all weary and disheartened, resenting their lack of a night's rest and their failure to return with food. They marched in silence, keeping their thoughts to themselves, leaving Fielding to retrace their steps the way they had come.

Of course the path was the same. One part of the hill looked just the same as any other, that was it. But why then did Jack begin to feel uneasy, looking at each tree as though to confirm his growing suspicions?

The clearing opened suddenly before them, with the waterfall dropping straight from the sheer rock face. They stood there on the edge of the glade in silence as the realization struck them that they were lost.

Even as they turned accusing eyes to Fielding, the silence was shattered by the reverberation of two shots, loud and very close at hand. A bird flew up into the air with a piercing cry.

'Near,' whispered Seaton.

'Yes, near.'

They stood where they were, unwilling to move and show themselves.

'Jesus.'

The sounds of movement through the rustling undergrowth were distinctive now, punctuated by the staccato of a language they all recognized.

The first Japanese stepped into the clearing just twenty yards away. He saw the Australians in the same instant as they saw him and cried out as they all dived for cover.

The alarm had gone up and they suddenly saw a whole patrol running towards them between the trees with fixed bayonets. They spread out, moving swiftly.

The first bullets took Seaton full in the back as he ran for cover. Jack heard him grunt, his mouth agape, eyes starting as he staggered and then fell headlong. He lay only yards away, his hands clawing at the grass.

Jack leant with his back to the tree and reloaded. He had a clear view in both directions but he could hear the Japanese fanning out between the trees. Seaton was dead. There was no help for him now, but Jack knew the rest of them had to get out of there while they still could.

'Come on, come on.'

Jack pulled Fielding along with him as they plunged into the bush. Rifle in hand, he dragged him slipping and sliding through the thicket, down a bank of ferns and thorn bushes.

Harrison was right alongside at one moment, but as they dropped into the dense undergrowth on the far side of the thicket he was nowhere in sight.

'Where the hell – '

Fielding was up on his knees about to go after him, but Jack pulled him down by the shoulders. 'You mad bastard – '

He wrestled Fielding to the ground and lay half across him, smothering his protests with the side of his hand. The captain was down and stunned, only his eyes eloquent in the half-light of the forest dawn.

Harrison was running through the bush away over to their left. Somehow he had lost the others, frantically searching the trees ahead for his friends, but they seemed to have vanished into the earth.

He awoke from the dream of horror to the reality of the hunt. Behind him he heard the yells of pursuit. He ran through the bush, his legs snagging on the thorns. Ran until the breath was choked in his throat and his head pounded. The trees and branches slashed at his face as he stumbled through the thicket, his legs almost failing him. The air around him was full of cries of pursuit. They were almost on him –

Suddenly he crashed headlong into a yawning gully that opened up beneath his feet. He rolled and crashed down the steep slope and into the scrub at the bottom. His head spun as he tried to pick himself up, but he could not find the strength. The trees around him on the high banks stood in silent mockery.

He clambered to his knees, uncertain which way to run. The uncanny silence of the gully unsettled him. He turned each way, feeling oppressed, growing more terrified with every moment. In that split second of silence he knew that he was going to die.

The trees wavered. He saw them move. There was someone up there, watching him. . . .

His scream rent the air above the bush.

Jack felt his mouth grow dry. There had been no time for fear before. Now it was different. He lay with his face just inches from Fielding's. He saw Fielding's eyes start wide at the terrible scream, the single shot. The captain's boyish face was laden with guilt, his voice full of nervous hysteria.

'We're done for. They'll find us.'

'Shut up and keep down,' Jack whispered, ruthlessly pushing Fielding back on the ground.

'I should have gone to help him. He thought he could trust me.'

So did I, thought Jack, so did I.

Chapter Thirty-five

It was late in the morning before the two survivors found their way back to the camp. Letria heard them coming through the bush and stood at the rise of the hill, his rifle at the ready.

'Thank God, thank God!' Relief was all over his face. He helped Fielding up the slope and then looked beyond Jack, waiting for the others.

'Seaton – Harrison?'

'They won't be coming,' said Jack sharply.

His face was lined with dirt as he turned to look straight into Dede's eyes. She was shocked to read the message in his eyes.

'We ran into a Nip patrol,' he said shortly.

Sister Eulalia rapidly crossed herself. The tension in the small group was more acute then ever.

'But the food,' cried Eva Macedo. 'You brought us some food?'

'No food either,' Jack announced and pushed roughly past her. The death of two men mattered nothing to her compared to the thought of food for her children.

He collapsed into the grass, every limb throbbing with pain from the long fruitless trek. All he wanted was to get some sleep, but Dede had followed him, kneeling beside him, her dark face anxious and concerned.

'What happened, Jack?'

He raised weary eyes to her and said, unsmiling, 'I don't think you want to know.'

No words were strong enough. There was nothing he could say to tell her the full horror of what he had seen or the full measure of what he felt over Fielding's actions.

'You could have been killed!' Dede whispered desperately.

'Don't doubt it. It seems to me,' he told her quietly, 'the longer this bloody business goes on, the more it pays to know who your friends are.'

She followed his narrow glance in Fielding's direction. 'You don't trust him?'

'Not a hell of a lot, no,' he retorted cynically.

Dede said, 'You've seen some terrible things.'

He knew it but his mind was on other terrors – the dead at the village, the bodies at the *posto*, Macedo's headless corpse. It was more than just Seaton and Harrison who had been sacrificed.

You don't know the half of it, he thought bitterly. He stared across at Fielding with open resentment. He was more than an irritation to Jack now. Fielding had become a liability, even perhaps a positive danger.

'Don't let yourself be fooled,' he told her sharply. 'Nothing is ever worth getting yourself wiped out for, understand? That man's blunders have cost lives. Don't you be next.'

He lay curled up, asleep in a short time. She knelt there beside him for some minutes, watching him as he slept.

Letria had no more luck with Fielding. The captain sat hunched on the grass, breathing heavily, his sun-bleached hair stuck to his damp forehead. He shrugged away all questions, too tired to speak, the dense humidity wrapped around him.

He could feel the soft grey eyes of the nun surveying him and shifted uncomfortably. He was deeply disturbed by the events of the morning, shocked by the senseless waste of Seaton and Harrison.

Their loss lay heavily on his conscience. He could have saved them. They had looked to him as their leader. They had expected him to have all the answers.

His eyes narrowed as he looked across to where Jack Ford lay on his back, already asleep. It was Ford's fault, preventing him from going to help them. Ford had stopped him and they had died. He would not easily forget that.

He lay back, utterly drained and exhausted. They ought to press on, there was no time to waste. Between the high trees the sun burnt down on them and he knew it was impossible to go on until they were rested.

He was still aware of the old problem there in the background. It had not gone away at all. It lay at the back of his brain, dormant perhaps but just biding its time for the right moment to strike again.

He was not well. He knew it inside, even if he would not acknowledge it to anyone else.

He could not permit himself to give in to it. If he became sick, who was going to lead them? No, he could not afford to be ill, he had to battle against it.

The sense of not being in control, of feeling this sickness slowly taking over, was now with him constantly. It was as if some outside force were manipulating both mind and body, and it terrified him.

Moving out along the forested cliff-face the monstrous shadow of the mountain offered some shade, but the character of the landscape was changing. Before long they emerged on to the exposed edge of a twisting gorge into the direct sunlight.

They were short of breath and gasping in the thin air at 9,000 feet, the sweat running down their legs like tepid oil into their boots and shoes. Dede touched her dry, cracked lips, feeling the cotton shirt hang saturated from her shoulders. Sweat ran down her arms and through her fingers. She had never felt so drained.

They had been following the track of the spiny ridge for hours now. They had learnt not to take the most obvious tracks for fear of walking straight into the arms of a Japanese patrol. They knew now that nowhere was safe from the enemy and their collaborators. The island had been split asunder by gangs of bandits and mercenaries in a war stirred up by the Japanese. Smoke from burning villages could be seen in the valleys and dead bodies had been found in the rivers. Only yesterday they had come across a crumpled cigarette packet dropped by a Japanese.

It was almost noon when the air was suddenly full of the low surging sound. It seemed oddly familiar to Dede but it was not until the Japanese Zero fighter appeared down the valley that she remembered where she had heard the sound before.

Everyone stood rooted to the spot watching the plane in the gully thousands of feet below them. Its aero engine droned in the still mountain air. Although they knew they could not be seen at that height, they were still rigid with tension, the sweat gleaming on their faces.

They had not gone more than another mile when Fielding and Letria came to a sudden halt, and there appeared on the track ahead of them a small band of native hunters.

From their clothes and feathers they were local to the area and not part of the contingent from Dutch Timor. There were no signs of the painted markings they had seen on the native recruits working with the Japanese. A wild surge of hope shot through the refugees. Was it possible that they had finally got ahead of the Japanese? In their race to the coast they could scarcely be more than a few miles apart.

The two groups stood and stared at each other without speaking. Father Jacinto's tragic loss was now very evident and only Sister Eulalia had even a smattering of local dialects to help them communicate. She went forward bravely, a strange bedraggled sight in her stained white robe hitched above her boots. The usual greetings were exchanged.

'*Diac-lai?*' Sister Eulalia's first priority was food.

'*Lai eiha.*'

It was the expected response. Food was the most precious commodity these days. Even if the war had not yet reached their village they must surely have heard its warning rumble from the mountains.

She discovered that half the food of the village had been given to another party of refugees, *tuan cataus* and Portuguese, who were heading for the coast. They had talked about *tuan cataus* boats and a long journey.

'*Mana mau pigi?*' asked the hunter, chewing betel nut.

'*Pigi pigi Same,*' replied the nun.

The Timorese exchanged dubious glances about the wisdom of this. Their rapid discussion in dialect was too fast for Sister Eulalia's translation skills and they looked on helplessly.

Fielding was nervous, his lips pressed tight in a thin line. He could not abide being on the outside, not knowing everything that was said. It was clear that he suspected the natives would sell information about them to the Japanese. He was very reluctant to tell them anything, least of all where they were going.

'They say the Japanese are already in Same,' Sister Eulalia told the others. 'They have heard they are also in Betano, on the south coast.'

Fielding shook his head, clearly disbelieving.

'Come on,' Jack said sharply, 'the boongs know what's what.'

There seemed no option but to follow the Qualan River, avoiding Alas and all other large settlements, making for the coast. The news of an Australian ship fired them to press on.

Sister Eulalia struggled valiantly with her basic knowledge of their dialect, emerging eventually with several bunches of *hudi mean*, the succulent red bananas of the region. They made their farewells to the huntsmen and set off southwards, travelling for more than an hour before they dared to stop.

They rested at last as the first leaden drops of rain splattered in the dust. Immediately everyone tried to fill their water bottles from the ready torrent running off the huge leaves all around. Only Eva Macedo made no attempt to help. She stood with her face upturned, letting the water run in rivulets through her short hair, soaking her clothes. She was used to having nursemaids and servants to look after the children and see to her every need. She could not or would not do a thing for herself.

'I've never met such a selfish bitch,' Dede said to Kate.

'She's not used to it – '

'Who is? She had damn well better get used to it just like the rest of us.'

Sister Eulalia divided their rations. 'For the food we are about to receive, may the good Lord make us truly thankful.'

In the leaf-green shadows of the palm fronds they sat around eating the tasty pink fruit. Kate noticed that the nun was more than usually quiet.

'Is there something wrong? Is there something you haven't told us?'

'Oh, Katherine, you are so perceptive.'

From the pale sickly young woman she had once been, Sister Eulalia now saw in Kate a woman of strength and sensitivity, a mother with her child to protect and fight for.

'You have enough on your mind,' the nun said gently, but Kate was not to be deterred.

'Why won't you tell me?'

The two women and the baby crouched together under the spreading shade of the low palms. Sister Eulalia shook her head sadly.

'It should not surprise me any more. I, who have seen so much evil in this world.' She met Kate's troubled eyes. 'I no longer know what to think.'

Kate knew she had been severely shaken by the death of Father Jacinto. They had been such close friends and colleagues for so many years. She was no longer a young woman. At her age such losses came hard. What happened at the *posto* was only the first indication of what could happen to any of them on this terrible journey.

The harsh cry of the forest birds sent a thrill of terror through the silent camp. With head bowed Sister Eulalia told Kate what she had not dared to tell the others. The natives had spoken of new acts of retaliation against Portuguese who helped the Australians. Two missionaries and a *deportado* like Letria had been seized and locked in a church soaked in petrol and then set alight.

'My God,' whispered Kate, cradling her baby closer.

'God?' responded the nun, her voice taut with emotion. 'Do you believe in God, Katherine? A God who permits the death of His own servants? Who permits women and innocent children to be burnt alive, to be tortured for giving us food and shelter? – and brave men to be beheaded?' She shook her head violently, her wise eyes bright with unshed tears. 'No, no, child, I see no hand of God here.'

The dripping forest was rent by a long jagged streak of forked lightning as the dense thunder cracked overhead. The heat of the day had gone and lightning flashes lit up the steaming bush as they huddled together for warmth.

Between the racing storm clouds the cold light of the moon lit up their faces. Their sodden clothes clung to their backs. Water dripped from their chins and the men's beards and pulled down their arms and legs. Shivering under the canopy of trees they endured the deluge for more than an hour.

'We need a fire,' Sister Eulalia told the captain as the full force of the storm died away. 'We will all be sick if we cannot dry our clothes.'

'It is out of the question.'

She stared at his stony face in astonishment. 'But the children – '

'There could be Japanese in the area,' he said sharply. 'We cannot take the risk.'

Letria heard him and sought a compromise. He offered to make a reconnaissance of the area, to see if it was safe to light a fire for an hour or two at least.

While he was gone resentment burned in the eyes of the women as they looked at Fielding. One by one, thought Dede, he had alienated them all.

Letria reappeared looking grim, his voice unusually low. 'We've got company.'

He took Jack, Fielding and Dede with him to the rise of the bank where they lay in the wet grass on their stomachs.

They stared in shock at the moonlit ribbon of road twisting down the edge of the mountain. All the time they had been only yards away from one of the main roads that bisected the island. And coming up the road was a column of slow, grinding military vehicles with their headlights shining in the rain. The Rising Sun pennant flew from the leading car.

'This whole bloody island is a trap,' said Jack as three open trucks passed below them filled with Japanese troops.

In the cruel moonlight they saw a party of twenty or thirty Dutch natives herding a greater number of men, women and children along the road like cattle. The natives wore headbands and bristled with weapons, but carried no guns.

The Japanese and their captives passed only yards away from where the fugitives lay in the long grass. In the moonlight the Portuguese captives were clearly visible, bound for the north and the concentration camp at Liquissa.

Chapter Thirty-six

The rain continued relentlessly. The sky was leaden with the threat of more to follow. The swollen river had turned the lowland into a swamp. Limpid green pools of still water lay across the land.

After the afternoon rains the bush was like a hothouse. Clouds of insects hovered in the shafts of light between the trees. The flowering trees and shrubs had taken on new life. On every side magnolias, eucalyptus and frangipani blossomed in luxuriant new growth in the moist earth.

'Get down, get down!'

A swarm of Zeros circled in the high blue sky.

'Don't move, anyone.'

They had plunged into the cover of the undergrowth. Through the fringed leaves they saw the enemy planes droning in the patched stillness, looking so innocent.

No one talked until the Zeros had disappeared. Jack rolled over on to his stomach under the riotous, almost obscene colour of the overhanging flowers. Above him the brightly coloured tropical butterflies glinted like jewels between the thick fleshy stems.

They realized that their only hope was to leave the open track and follow the bend of the river in the shelter of the trees. Along the river the she oaks reminded Jack of Australia. Parts of the forest were rich with tropical tree ferns, elephant ears and liana vines, but where the mountains cut away, the land lay bristling with scrub and gum trees just like the outback.

Walking along the riverbank they spread out in a long line.

They had not gone a mile when suddenly the little Macedo girl screamed.

Her mother knelt at her side, lifting the girl's leg.

'What is it?' asked Fielding impatiently, coming back to see what was going on.

'She's been bitten by something,' said Eva, white-faced and shaking, 'by a snake or a spider.'

Dede had seen no snakes but the spiders were the size of tea-plates. She shuddered at the thought of such a bite.

Sister Eulalia took the little girl's leg on her lap and examined her foot. An angry red rash had appeared already and Maia Macedo was crying from the pain. She looked round at her mother, her little face crumpling.

'Please don't let it hurt!'

'She's been poisoned!' cried Eva in horror. 'She'll die – '

'Keep quiet! You're frightening the child,' said Sister Eulalia, pressing the girl's foot with her fingers. Suddenly she gave a smile of triumph, producing a bloody thorn some three inches long from the sole of the foot.

'No snake, no spider,' she told the girl's astonished mother, 'just a sago thorn.' She carefully wiped the child's foot and improvised a bandage to hold a pad in place against the wound. 'No disinfectant, I'm afraid. We are in the dark ages again. It will do very well in a day or two. Try to keep it dry.'

After the rains there was mildew everywhere. All their things were contaminated and slowly rotting. Even their bodies had begun to suffer. Little running sores and blisters developed and spread from the damp heat.

The night clouds raced in the rising wind as they made camp in the thick bush. The treetops swayed, glistening with rain in the lurid storm light. The first heavy drops stung their faces and they were wet to the skin in seconds. The rain came violently with a rustling of leaves as the skies emptied themselves over the land.

The rain drove across the earth in long straight lines. The trees sobbed under the weight of water.

Sleep did not come easily. The nights were long and after the rain the trees dripped on for hours. Fielding lay on his side, a little distance from the others, listening. He was drenched with sweat and his throat felt parched and swollen, but he still trembled with the damp. He could barely contain the surge of rage he felt at his own inadequacy. He could see his body shaking with weakness. Grotesque! Inexcusable! A fine leader he was! How they must all despise him. How could they follow such a leader? Had they not all seen his failures?

He had always been healthy, quite unaware of his good fortune. He had blindly pushed himself physically as well as mentally at university and after he volunteered. But now, when he needed all those faculties most, he was being denied.

He lay there, tormented, the hours slow to pass. Letria and Jack Ford turns on watch. His thoughts roamed wildly as he waited for sleep to come and claim him. He was haunted by memories of the sand hills at Avalon where he had camped as a boy. In his mind he could see the Middle Harbour and its boats, so familiar, so real. Spit Hill and the house. Above all, Miriam. Miriam who, by now, had surely forgotten him. He had failed her, too. He had failed them all. There was no disguising the truth. He could feel them all looking at him, their eyes watching him, whispering about him behind his back.

Dawn raised mist spirals from the low valley and he sat up. From his burning eyes he saw the face of Sister Eulalia, like a wraith, watching him.

For some time now she had been observing Fielding with the growing awareness that a crisis was coming.

'He's not well,' she confided to Katherine out of earshot of the others.

'It's malaria again.'

'No, it's more than that. He's not just ill. He's changed. His whole attitude is different.'

Kate shrugged. 'He's just exhausted – we all are.'

But the nun was persistent. 'He's been trying to hide it from us.' She turned back to look at the captain where he sat under the trees. 'He's afraid but he doesn't want us to see it.'

Kate looked too, seeing the sudden weight loss, seeing for the first time the hollows under his cheekbones. She got up and took him some of the fruit left over from the night before.

'You ought to eat something. You had little or nothing at all yesterday.'

The eyes that looked up at her were bright with fever. 'Don't start feeling sorry for me – '

She retreated, stung and more than disturbed. She sought out Jack who was washing at the stream.

'I don't like the look of the captain. I don't think he can take much more of this.'

'I can't help that. He'll have to. It's the same for all of us.' He saw that she was seriously concerned, but he had to be honest. 'Look,' he said flatly, 'I don't care. I don't care as long as he keeps up. Nothing is going to stop us from reaching the coast and finding that ship out of here.'

They grew ingenious at coping with the basic necessities of life on the move. The rains had brought benefits as well as problems. Riverbeds and pools that had been barren and dry were now filled to overflowing. The deep cool waters were inviting and they took to bathing in their remaining clothes, washing away the mud and filth of the journey.

Red-faced and sweating, it was a delight to wade into the emerald pools. They made a strange sight in their mixture of native clothing and Australian army issue. Jack had lost everything but his shorts and boots. He was tanned a deep brown and his beard was now full, changing the shape of his face. Letria had gone quite native and with his dark skin and black beard he could easily have passed for a Moslem trader except for his startling pale eyes. Even Fielding had now discarded the torn army jacket he had worn for so long.

The leaves and lianas formed a green canopy over the limpid waters. Dede sat on the bank, her wet clothes moulded to her back and her hair sculpted to her cheeks. She sat staring at her hands, at the torn nails and rough weathered skin. She thought how much she had changed from the ambitious research student who had met Warren Brandon in LA. Another world. Another lifetime.

She looked up and saw Jack swimming across the pool towards her. He moved languidly in the water, the skin of his arms and shoulders burned dark as teak. He pulled himself out of the water, droplets clinging to his smooth brown skin, and sat beside her on the bank.

'Isn't the water wonderful? I feel like a new woman,'

laughed Dede, running a hand through her wet hair.

Jack grinned at her, his full mouth soft, his green eyes bold, holding hers. The laughter died slowly from his face as he looked at her, their heads very close together. He reached out a hand towards her and she drew close, the smile gone from her lips as their eyes locked.

His hand slid across her bare shoulder and came to rest on the nape of her neck. He leant towards her and laid his mouth against her throat. She took his head between her hands, water still rolling from his dark hair and beard, and kissed him. His mouth opened for her, drawing her down, promising an untapped well of passion.

But it had all become suddenly too intense. They sat up, drawing briefly apart, yet still touching, their eyes entranced.

She was different. She had softened and changed from the woman he had first known back at the convent. He traced her face with his finger, wondering at the change in her.

'I don't know where I learnt to be so tender.' Her breath was soft on his cheek. 'After everything that's happened, we choose this time and place to fall in love.'

'When this war is over,' he told her, 'everything is going to change. But now I've found you, I'm never going to let you go.'

Chapter Thirty-seven

They began a descent of the mountain, torn and grazed by the sharp rocks. The rains made the tracks into mudslides, treacherous underfoot. It had taken far longer than they had calculated. The going was becoming increasingly harder and they were all exhausted, weakened by sickness.

'How much further?'

'Not so far now.' Letria passed Jack the map, soft and faded from the damp and humidity.

They were descending towards the valley of the Qualan River. Swollen by the rains, it cut a tortuous path out of the mountains and into the swamplands of the southern coast.

'You all right? You look crook,' said Jack, coming alongside Fielding as they marched. His words were meant as a gesture towards reconciliation, but the captain did not take Jack's concern well. He turned ferociously upon him, eyes bright in his feverish face.

'Don't you worry about me, Corporal. You look to yourself – '

Jack's patience was on a short fuse. 'To hell with you then, mate,' he retorted, falling back to rejoin the others.

'He's cracking up,' he told Dede in an aside as they paused together overlooking the valley. 'Once we've crossed the river it will be easier going, I reckon.'

Letria, coming up behind them, looked cynical. They could already hear the roar of the torrential river pounding through the gorge below.

'When we cross the river,' he repeated ironically.

The gully at the foot of the fern-clad rocks had been turned into a seething whirlpool of ochre mud and high white foam. A native rope bridge of vines and creepers hung limply across the swollen river, barely inches from the fevered waters.

'We have to cross that?' said Kate in a small voice.

'There is no other way.'

'You're out of your mind!' said Jack, face to face with the captain.

'We're going on,' said Fielding, squaring his shoulders. 'I am the officer here, and that is my decision, do you understand?' His eyes flashed dangerously at Jack. 'What's the matter, Corporal? Are you afraid to join us again?' He had still not forgotten Jack's stand against him at the villa. 'Are you such a coward, Corporal?'

Jack stared at him, his green eyes narrowing, a flicker of bitter resentment barely held in check in their depths.

Without a word Fielding turned and stalked to the edge of the path. 'If we cannot cross here,' he announced, 'we don't stand a chance of escaping.'

Down at the river's edge the roar of the flood waters made conversation virtually impossible. They stood on the rocks, wet and slippery underfoot, watching the rope bridge taking a battering from the tempestuous river. Under normal conditions it must have hung clear of the waters, but the recent storms had released a floodtide down the narrow gorge and the centre of the bridge now hung well below the white waves.

'All right, then,' said Fielding authoritatively. 'We must get ourselves organized. We will have to carry the children across and we need someone on each side of the river to help the women.' He took a deep breath, looking away towards the foaming river. 'I'll go ahead and test the bridge first.'

Jack caught him by the arm. 'Don't play the fucking hero here, mate.'

The captain stopped abruptly and they faced one another. 'Understand one thing,' Fielding warned him, 'I am leader here.'

'No one is disputing it,' said Letria hurriedly, 'but Jack has a point. Let one of us go first, then should anything – '

His words were left unspoken. One look at the rope bridge was enough to raise doubts about anyone making it across.

'I'll go.' Jack took off his rifle and gave it to Dede. 'Just in case,' he said, his hands briefly covering hers.

She watched in silence as he stepped on to the seemingly fragile construction of vines. At the very first step his weight caused the bridge to sway violently. He gripped the higher ropes and tried to steady himself.

The vines were wet underfoot and each step required intense concentration. The farther he moved out over the swirling yellow river, the closer he came to sinking into its dangerous waters. By the time he had negotiated his way to the centre of the bridge his boots were well under water. The white foam threatened to throw him off balance.

On the shore the watchers held their breaths, unable to take their eyes from the swaying figure. Dede stopped breathing, gripping his rifle with white-knuckled hands, aware of Sister Eulalia at her side whispering prayers. Even Eva Macedo was entirely caught up in the drama, holding her son and daughter by the hands.

'He's made it! He's there!'

A sigh of intense relief went through the little group and tears sprang to Dede's eyes. They waved excitedly to Jack on the opposite bank. Their euphoria was somewhat dashed when Fielding, breathing deeply, turned next to Dede.

'You go next,' he told her.

Her wide eyes briefly met Sister Eulalia's but she did not argue. Jack was on the other side waiting for her. She slung his rifle across her shoulder and moved towards the bridge, setting her foot on the trembling rope.

'Keep your eyes straight ahead,' Letria advised her. 'And don't look down.'

It was a strange sensation to stand quivering on the vines just inches from the explosive roar of the river. She took Letria's advice and did not look down, certain that if she did she would lose her balance and fall. She kept her eyes fixed on the opposite shore where Jack stood ready to catch her. She felt like a tightrope walker she had once seen in a circus back home.

She moved her hands one at a time out along the rope, feeling her centre of gravity shift, then bringing her feet into line. The rifle weighed heavy on her back, slipping occasionally to add to her fears. But the nearer she came to the shore the more confidence she gained, and when she was only yards from safety she almost ran the final part of the rope, falling into Jack's waiting arms. They both broke into spontaneous laughter and relief, holding each other in a tight embrace.

'Come on!' she cried out to the waiting women on the far bank, although she knew they could not hear her.

Across the water Sister Eulalia was worried about the children. 'Kate, can you manage the baby?'

Kate nodded, her eyes fixed firmly on the far side of the river. She took little Amy and tied her tightly with her shawl across her back, in the native style. As she stepped out on to the rope, both her hands were free.

She took a moment to steady herself, very conscious of her baby awake and gurgling on her back. It was not only her own life at stake but that of her child as well. For the first time in her life she had responsibility for another person and a reason to keep on living. With greater confidence she began to edge her way out on to the bridge.

Dede watched her from the other shore with a hand at her mouth. She was even more terrified for Kate and her baby than she had been out there on the rope herself.

'It's all right,' said Jack, 'she's doing it.'

They were both ready to catch her as she stumbled over the last few feet of rope into their arms. The baby was perfectly content in its secure seat on Kate's back and seemed to have enjoyed her first real adventure.

But across the river some kind of argument had broken out. Eva Macedo stood on the rope bridge, shouting at Sister Eulalia.

'I don't care! I'm going next – '

She had her son balanced on her shoulder but he looked far from safe. Surely she was not planning to cross the bridge with only one hand free? But she was, and everyone stood in silence watching her progress.

Kate was forced to admire her skill as she negotiated the rope bridge with her extra burden. She pulled herself along by one hand, holding the boy safe with the other. She never hesitated and never took her eyes off the way ahead. Her face was set in a mask of avid concentration as she came closer step by step. But when Jack and Dede caught her at the end of the bridge she stood shaking uncontrollably, on the verge of tears.

'Maia!' She turned her back on them, looking across the river to where her small daughter stood, her hand in Letria's.

But it was Sister Eulalia who was sent across next. She looked very frail and unsteady on her feet as she took to the bridge. Her soiled and shabby clothes were hitched high of her legs but the fierce waters still caught her, sucking the fold of her habit around her sturdy boots.

'She'll fall!' cried Kate, grasping Jack by the arm, and for a moment it seemed that the nun would indeed fall as she stopped dead in the middle of the flood, swaying violently on the rope.

'Someone should have gone with her,' said Jack, wondering if the bridge would bear his weight.

'Stupid old woman,' breathed Eva Macedo. 'If the bridge breaks now how will my daughter get across?'

But Sister Eulalia had regained her strength, balancing once again as she stepped forward, her face grim with determination and running with sweat. Kate stood at the end of the bridge to meet her as she struggled ashore, ignoring the impatience of the Macedo woman who waved her arms for Fielding to send over her daughter next.

But of course the child could not negotiate the bridge alone and unaided. It was Fielding himself who insisted upon taking her, leaving Letria to stand on the far bank alone.

The captain took the girl high on his naked shoulders, her small legs dangling on either side as she clung tightly round his neck.

The extra weight was evident from the start. As he stepped on to the rope bridge the bottom dipped perilously below the surging river. By the time he reached the lowest part of the bridge he would be in the water almost to his waist. One false step would mean drowning for them both.

Eva Macedo was almost beside herself with fear. She stood at the end of the bridge and Jack had to forcibly restrain her from clutching at the ropes and making the bridge swing, causing the captain to lose his balance.

As he plunged deeper into the water, the little girl gripped his neck tighter. They saw his face red from exertion, half smothered by his young passenger.

Then, all at once, he was down, on his chest in the floodtide, with the little girl still clinging to his neck and screaming wildly, echoed by her mother shouting from the shore.

Jack pushed Eva roughly aside but even as he went to step out on to the bridge he saw that Letria was there before him. The Portuguese moved cautiously towards the middle of the river where the captain clung with both hands to the upper rope, pounded by the fierce torrent.

The bridge rocked violently, bearing a greater weight than before, torn and dragged from side to side by the pounding waters. Letria struggled to join them in the middle of the river, talking in his own language to the child, trying to get her to release her stranglehold about Fielding's neck.

At last they saw Maia swung up onto Letria's shoulder as he held on to the rope with one hand. By careful manoeuvring he circumnavigated Fielding and moved out across the final section of the bridge with the little Macedo girl.

Jack was there to help him, taking Maia as he reached the bank and ready to help the Portuguese ashore. But Letria was looking back to see what was happening to Fielding and before Jack could prevent him he had turned about and was heading out across the river again to help the captain.

Exhausted and weakened, Fielding had not the strength to pull himself out of the water and regain his foothold on the bridge. It was all he could do to hold on to the swinging rope until Letria reached him. His hands were numb from the water. His body had taken a merciless pounding against the rocks under the water.

Letria stood above him, one foot on either side of the Australian, keeping one hand on the upper rope. He stretched with his free hand down towards Fielding, shouting instructions above the roar of the water. But the captain had no strength to raise himself, unable to release even one hand from the rope that was his lifeline. It was left to Letria to bend down to try to pull him bodily free of the river suction, getting his arm around the captain's shoulders.

The rope bridge swung uncontrollably as they struggled together in the midst of the flooded river. The watchers on the shore were shocked into silence at the spectacle. Letria dipped bravely into the deep swirling waters to retrieve the captain, dragging his weary body like a dead weight from the river.

Yet at the very same moment that Letria got Fielding safely on to the bridge in front of him, the Portuguese seemed suddenly to lose his balance.

Perhaps the bridge could not bear the weight of two grown men. Perhaps the ropes had been weakened by the fierce current. But as Fielding struggled upright, with only a matter of yards to go to reach safety, his rescuer slipped and plunged backwards into the raging waters, striking his head violently on one of the jagged rocks as he went under.

A fearful scream went up from the shore. As Fielding staggered ashore and fell forward in an exhausted, shivering huddle, they watched as Letria was swept away in the white-capped torrent down the gorge until his body disappeared completely beneath the waters.

Chapter Thirty-eight

The sun burst over the horizon. After the storm the dawn was stifling, promising another hot and exhausting day. As always when the rain ceased the insects came to plague them. The dappled forest trail was clouded by mosquitos, hungry for blood. They whined in their faces and got caught in their hair. Kate wrapped a corner of the shawl over little Amy's face to protect her as they walked on.

The tall kunai grass was still wet and before they had gone a few yards they were all soaked again. Down in the lowlands the character of the island changed yet again. The swollen rivers snaked between a landscape of silent forest and grassland swamped by sheets of mirrored water. Above all was the stench of rotting vegetation.

Here the trees were dense, obscuring the light, eerily silent. Grim and unsmiling, the survivors moved with leaden steps through a network of streams and twisting creeks. Exhaustion and despair made them all listless. According to the map the tributaries of the fierce Qualan River would lead them down to the coast. They were so near now and yet so far.

The ancient rotting trees provided a tangled labyrinth of roots and slimy branches over the evil-smelling mud. Clouds of vicious insects hung over the brackish water, yellow and oily in the slanted light of the sun. The high vaults of the trees gave some protection from the heat, but the shade was dark and foetid with decaying plants in the undergrowth.

Sister Eulalia stumbled and almost fell sideways into the foul mud of the swamp, but Dede caught her and steadied her in time. The nun trembled with horror.

'Where are we, in the name of God? What is this terrible place?'

They felt certain that they would come upon other refugees and perhaps even remnants of the Australian commandos. But in that dark and twisting maze of waterways they could have passed within half a mile and never even known they were there at all.

'At least we ought to be safe from the Japs,' said Jack. 'We'd have to literally fall over the bastards to be found.'

But if that was one advantage it was clearly outweighed by enormous disadvantages. Their progress slowed right down. It was not only the swampland but their general poor state of health. They were now short of food of any kind, fresh food being a thing of the past. They were shorter still of water, ironically enough. The dank green pools of the forest had been bad enough, leading to some diarrhoea in the Macedo children, but here the flooded waters were choked with weed and stagnant with pollution. Bilharzia was the least they would get from drinking from the standing waters of the swampland. Only such rainwater as they could catch kept them going as they strived to put one foot before another.

Quicras proved to be a pathetic settlement of abandoned huts set deep in the mangrove swamp. How long it had been deserted they could not tell. The stench of the place and the decaying thatch alive with insects offered no hope. In the swamp everything before long rotted down to a dank jungle of weeds. It was hard to believe that anyone could have survived in such a place for long.

From Quicras the land slid away to the sea in a tight tangle of mangroves in foetid, shifting mud. A flash of forked lightning brilliantly lit up the glassy river. The backwater was a sinister, silent morass of foul mud and dense banks swarming with pestilent flies and mosquitos.

The heat of the day turned the tunnel of vegetation into a steamy hothouse. They had a hard time just keeping their feet in the tangled undergrowth of creepers and tree roots. Jack carried the little Macedo girl on his shoulder, leaving the boy for his mother to hold. Dede kept a close watch on Sister Eulalia, afraid that she could slip again, and called back to Kate from time to time to see that she was all right.

But Fielding, parched and dying for water, slipped as he tried to get to the river. He was immediately sucked into the slime and stinking ooze almost to his chest. As he sank, his cries brought the others hurrying back to him. He was sinking in the mud before their very eyes.

As he was sucked down under the shifting surface of the green-crusted swamp, Jack and Dede struggled to pull him out. He was sinking deeper and deeper as they seized his arms, struggling to pull him free before he sank altogether under the thick slime.

Choking and spluttering, he was pulled clear, dragging his filthy legs free of the powerful force on to the bank again. Maia screamed out in horror, clinging to her mother, cringing away at the sight of him.

'Holy Mother.'

'It's disgusting,' cried Eva.

Fielding was covered in clinging leeches from the foetid swamp. He writhed as he looked down and saw his own body, shivering anew with fever and calling on the others to get them off.

Even as they watched the black leeches swelled with his blood, clinging with tenacious jaws to Fielding's skin. The slug-like leeches stuck fast to his legs, chest and stomach. Dede shuddered with horror. Leeches were the things of nightmare. She knew that if they tried to pull the filthy creatures away, their heads would remain buried in his flesh. They could go a year without a bite, it was said, so whenever they happened to latch on to a piece of flesh they literally made a meal of it. They swelled black, gorging on Fielding's blood.

'Wait,' said Sister Eulalia, 'I know what to do.' She began frantically searching in their packs, finally producing the small quantity of salt they had carried ever since leaving the convent. She took handfuls to sprinkle over the shivering captain as he twisted and shied away. The damp salt appeared to work an instant miracle. The leeches dropped off one by one as the salt touched them. They fell on to the dank ground and burst with a disgusting squelch, spurting fresh blood over those standing near.

Fielding's teeth were chattering uncontrollably. He was covered in weed and slime from the swamp. As the leeches dropped away they revealed a quantity of raw triangular wounds where they had bitten. The wounds bled profusely, the blood running down his legs. The leeches had injected an anti-coagulant that meant the wounds could bleed for up to an hour afterwards.

'We can't stay here in this foul place.'

'He can't go on.'

Fielding tried to object but Jack held him firm.

'Save your breath, mate, okay? We'll go on when you can make it.'

The place was infested with leeches. Soon they were all afflicted. The little monsters crawled up their clothes and over their feet, searching for any opening. Unless flicked aside before they could batten on, they would drink blood until satisfied. Jack discovered one crawling in through the eyehole of the laces of his boots and knocked it away, but the creature attached itself to the soft flesh between his fingers. After applying salt he was left with a painful bleeding puncture mark. Like Fielding's wounds it eventually clotted, leaving behind a distinctive purple scar.

'Let's get the hell out of here before we're eaten alive,' Jack told the others.

He helped Fielding to his feet, feeling the heat from his body and yet the captain shivered uncontrollably. There were no dry clothes he could put on that would help.

Half-supporting, half-carrying the captain, Jack led the little group out of the leech-infested swamp. For more than an hour they fought their way between the dense undergrowth, warily treading a path between the mud and the river.

There seemed no end to the swamp. They reluctantly decided to make camp for the night, finding a place above the level of the water. Dede finally succeeded in starting a fire to boil a little of their water to make tea, but the steam caught the clouds of mosquitos and they fell into the boiling water by the dozen.

They were all so weary it was an effort to share out their remaining food rations and eat. Sister Eulalia passed food to the Macedo children but Eva would not take anything for herself. She put a hand on her forehead.

'No hot or cold spells? No shivering?'

Eva shook her roughly away. 'Leave us alone.'

Sister Eulalia rejoined Kate, seriously concerned. 'I don't like the look of her.'

'All she needs is a good night's rest. Like all of us.'

But a night's rest was more than they could expect in those conditions. The dense night was unbearably long and steamy amid the dark backwaters. As dusk fell like a curtain between the trees the insects descended to feed. The air grew dense with clouds of flies and mosquitos which bit into the skin like red-hot needles.

The insects were more numerous than they had seen anywhere before. The night was filled with their persistent whining and buzzing.

In the cold dawn Dede woke from a fitful, feverish sleep, cramped and shivering. She watched the white mist drifting across the surface of the river, wraithlike, sinister. It was growing lighter at every minute. From the mists the trees materialized like ghosts, dank and silent, breathing the poison of the atmosphere.

'This place is no good to us,' said Sister Eulalia, waking to sit at her side. 'It is a place of malaria.'

Fielding awoke burning with fever. Emptying his water bottle he took the last of the quinine, well away from the others.

He was soaked with sweat and yet shivering uncontrollably. He felt no guilt any more that he had hidden the supply. He needed it more than the others, after all. He was their leader. It was up to him to make the decisions, to get them through this and safely to the coast.

He stood with his head resting against a tree, almost too weak to keep upright. Soon, soon it would take effect. He had his back turned, hiding the worst as long as he could, but his frustration choked him. Soon, soon it must take effect.

'Fielding, you ready?'

The captain seemed suddenly to stagger, the blood rushing to his head. He felt dizzy and took a moment to steady himself.

'I need some time,' he called out.

But Jack was there beside him, taking in the look on his face. 'What's wrong? Are you ill?'

Fielding mopped his face, shivering wildly. 'I can't go on any more,' he admitted, his voice cracking. 'I can't keep up the pace.'

Jack stared back, astonished at Fielding's admission more than the sight of his yellow, feverish face. 'Well, you have to, mate,' he said bluntly. 'You don't have any choice.'

Fielding met his steady green eyes and saw compassion as well as irritation. After a moment he nodded abruptly, trying to straighten up. Jack watched him with genuine concern. He saw that Fielding was really ill, his mind eaten up with the fever.

'That's it, mate, you'll do fine.' He refrained from offering an arm to steady him, aware of the narrow line he was treading.

At the first opportunity Jack went to talk to Sister Eulalia. 'Is there any quinine?'

She shook her head. 'Ironic, isn't it? The East Indies are the source of quinine – and yet I have none I can offer you.'

'It's not for me, Sister, it's Fielding.'

'Yes, I know.'

'You know?'

'For some time now. I recognized the signs.' She looked back at Jack. 'But he has his own supply.'

'He what?'

'Don't blame him, please. He was so very ill back at the convent. Remember that was why he was left behind.'

The captain was weak on his feet but his fever seemed to have somewhat abated, leaving him drained and sallow. The flesh of his face looked gaunt, all its boyish youthful fullness vanished. Jack stared at him with a growing presentiment as the ragged line set out at last, moving south.

Chapter Thirty-nine

When they stopped at last to rest they found themselves in an area of grassland and free-running water.

Their sweat-drenched clothes never seemed to dry and clung uncomfortably to their bodies. They had all lost a lot of weight and bore the marks and scars of their journey. Prickly heat, sores and mosquito bites like pockmarks marked their legs and arms. Fielding's score of leech-bites had formed small ulcers all over his body.

He had a temperature of 105 degrees, with pains like rigour in his back and limbs. He lay on his back in a delirium of thirst. Jack searched him but found no more quinine. Fielding must have finished the supply. But his teeth chattered although the sweat poured down his aching limbs in streams. He had a racking headache and groaned as he tried to sit up.

'I have never seen anything like this,' said Jack, watching his convulsion-like spasms.

'I have. Just once,' said Sister Eulalia, her face grey with anxiety.

Fielding began to writhe on the ground, whimpering and groaning, totally unaware of his companions. Maia Macedo was now terrified of him.

'What can we do for him?'

'What is it? What's wrong with him, Sister?' asked Dede.

Sister Eulalia bit her lip and looked away. She had no desire to make a diagnosis, to condemn him out of hand. Perhaps she was wrong, perhaps it was not as bad as she feared after all.

'Come on, Sister,' said Jack impatiently. 'You said you'd seen a case like this before.'

In the continuing silence Eva Macedo stepped forward. 'So have I,' she announced. 'It is malaria.'

'We know that,' snapped Jack.

The look she gave him was intimidating and the small group fell silent again, allowing her to continue.

'Then you also know that there are many different kinds of malaria. Benign, tertian – the last stage is the worst. It comes when the fever reaches the brain.'

Dede stared at her hard and then turned round to look at Fielding where he lay in semi-conscious delirium.

'What happens then?' Jack was asking.

'You die.'

Jack and Dede both looked at Sister Eulalia, hoping she would deny it, but the nun slowly shook her head.

'There is nothing I or anyone can do for him.' She put a hand to her face, weary beyond measure. 'I saw it there, written in his face. I saw it once before. The fever and the headaches, the desperate longing for water. And now the delirium and convulsions.' She looked up at them. 'She is right. It is cerebral malaria. There is no cure.'

Fielding's temperature was rising. They could try to keep it down by immersing him in water, but once his temperature reached 107 degrees he would sink from delirium into coma. At 110 degrees it would be too late, his brain would fry.

There was a terrible ringing silence, broken only by Fielding's tortured cries.

Sister Eulalia emptied the contents of her small roll of possessions, searching for anything which could help him. So few things left. All the medicines she needed had been left behind for the Japanese at the convent or the villa. She began to put them back in despair when her hand came upon the morphine.

'Sister – '

She looked up sharply, her hand briefly holding on to the tube of tablets.

'We have to get on,' said Jack. He had calculated that they were a day or more away from the coast.

Sister Eulalia held the tube in her hand. Should she tell them what she had found? Half a grain would not help him, no, he would need more than one tablet again and again.

'Sister – '

'Yes, yes, I'm coming.' She quickly put away all the supplies as she struggled to her feet.

'How can we go on?' Dede was asking. 'Just look at him.'

Jack ran a hand through his hair. 'Well, if he can't walk then I'll just have to carry him.'

'Jack, you can't!' cried Dede, going to him.

'It's impossible,' Kate agreed fiercely. 'You'll kill yourself before we've gone a mile.'

'Well, what else do you suggest? We can't leave him here for the Japs to find.'

They could not argue with him. They were all desperate to be on their way. They were so near now to their goal. The coast was virtually in sight. There was only a coconut plantation stretching down to the shoreline and then they would surely be safe. They would rendezvous with the other Australians and get off the island.

'There's no other way.'

Dede proposed that they remove their shoes and boots to avoid leaving a trail for any Japanese patrols in the area.

'That way, at least, if they see our footprints they may take us for Timorese.'

It was a relief to tread barefoot on the soft mud and grass. Their feet were already covered in sores and blisters. They could fare no worse unprotected.

As Jack lifted Fielding on to his back he struggled to control the surge of bitterness he felt towards the sick man. He knew that if it had not been for Fielding more of them would have lived to reach the coast. If it had not been for Fielding they might already be there and safe.

The children were enjoying the walk barefoot. They kept up a bright chatter as the party set out until Dede suddenly hissed, 'Shut up, all of you!'

She was standing stock-still, her head cocked slightly to one side, listening.

Beyond the trees they suddenly all heard it.

There was scarcely time enough to pull one another into the shelter of the tall grass before a patrol of Japanese appeared, calling to one another among the coconut palms.

Kate crouched low, cradling the baby in her arms. Little

Amy stirred and began to whimper. She put the child to her breast to quieten her, sick with fright.

Jack lay beside Fielding as he writhed in delirium. Sweat poured down his body as the fever mounted. He moaned, shivering, and began to cry out. Jack met Dede's terrified eyes as he clasped a hand tightly across the sick man's mouth just as the group of Japanese passed by within yards of their hiding place.

Chapter Forty

The coconut plantation had thinned into bare scrub. As they moved with nervous caution between the wavering palm trees they were all aware that they were increasingly visible and exposed to danger. The mottled expanse of bush and scrub beyond was barely adequate to hide their approach down to the coast.

Jack stopped and released his hold on Fielding. He lay on the ground beside Fielding, his face gleaming with the exertion of carrying the captain.

Dede offered him the last of their water. 'You're exhausted, Jack. Let's make a stop here.'

'No, we've got to get on. We'll never make it if we keep stopping.'

'Just for an hour or two.'

He looked around, thinking that actually this was the best area of ground cover they would find before reaching the beach. It could not be more than a mile or two now. Perhaps they could take a rest now, and then press straight on. With luck they ought to reach the shore by nightfall.

'You get some sleep,' Dede told him gently, touching his face. 'We'll watch the captain.'

Jack took himself a little way off and curled up in a small hollow under one of the palms. Eva Macedo and her children lay down together without a word, too weary to argue about the lack of water, while Kate fed her baby.

Fielding lay on the ground between Dede and Sister Eulalia. His breathing came in great gasps that shook his whole body. His skin was yellow and shining from sweat that poured out after the convulsions that shook him at intervals without pity.

'Can't you give him anything for the pain?' Dede asked the nun, haunted by the bright starting eyes that seemed to beseech her wordlessly. 'We're so near now, so near – '

Sister Eulalia looked at her drawn face, etched with lines of exhaustion and despair. She knew that Dede was afraid they would never make it, not with Fielding. She put a reassuring hand on her shoulder. 'I'll sit with him. You get some sleep now.'

Dede met her eyes and then looked quickly away, afraid to acknowledge the doubts she read there. She crept quietly away to lie down beside Jack, to fall asleep and shut out all thought.

Sister Eulalia mopped the captain's brow, soothing her patient as best as she could without words. He had changed so much from the boy she had reasoned with back at the convent. That seemed so long ago now. The childlike softness of his face had gone. His youth had deserted him. She clutched his hand as the cramps seized him once again. He writhed and tossed in her grasp, his slack mouth distorted by pain.

Watching him, Sister Eulalia could only pity him, sharing his torment, knowing that his bitter struggle could only lead inexorably down to death.

She unrolled the bundle and laid out her things on the grass. She was deeply pensive, touching each item with her fingers, returning always to the small metal tube. Each tablet contained half a grain of morphine hydrochloride.

In the stillness while the others slept, she examined her solitary conscience. Had Dede suspected what she meant to do?

Dede was right. They were so near now, and yet Fielding's illness could still prevent them all from reaching safety. There was no denying it. Jack was exhausted, killing himself to carry a full-grown man in these conditions, in this place. There was no way that he could continue.

Ever since they had set out from the convent she had had doubts about the young captain, doubts about his ability to lead them. He was so young, so inexperienced – and apprently unwilling to take advice from those who knew the island: Letria and Father Jacinto.

Ah, dear God! How it hurt to remember! If only he had not

gone down there that day. If only Fielding had refused to leave him behind.

But was it his fault? Father Jacinto's untimely death, his fault? She had seen Letria's death for herself, so wilful, so unnecessary. But Sergeant Seaton and Harrison, they too had died. Were their deaths his fault, as Jack Ford plainly seemed to think?

The sick man whined piteously. Looking down at his stricken face she could not bring herself to lay the blame on him. He had brought his death upon himself, that was burden enough. God's will. Was she to be His instrument in this? Offering blessed mercy at the end?

The savage doubts which racked her during their journey had made her question her very calling. The horror, the sinful waste of all she had seen and heard shattered the safety of her past convictions. How could God allow such suffering? Where was God when such terrible things were happening? The whole world was at war, there was suffering and death in every corner, and yet God apparently let it all happen. Was it as a result of evil? Were they being punished for their sins, was that it? But no, the Lord had rejected such thoughts and so must she. She had been weak and given way to doubts. She had not learnt from all this suffering, she had been blind.

Sweat rolled down her back. This was no place for a personal crisis. She had to be resolute and strong.

Her rosary lay in a pool in the palm of her hand. Perhaps she had been led this way for a purpose. Perhaps she had been meant to make this journey.

God was testing her and she had failed in her duty to Him. Until this moment. As her hand fastened securely about the morphine lying in the grass, she saw at last the hand of God offering mercy.

She could hesitate no longer. Her work was sanctified.

Stirring as the wind rose in the fading light, the sleepers sat up one by one. The first drops of rain splattered into the dust about them, signalling a sudden deluge that rapidly engulfed them.

Kate bent over Fielding where he lay. 'So he slept at last,' she said.

'Yes. Now he sleeps,' said Sister Eulalia.

Dede met her eyes and knew at once that Fielding's calm sleep would not be disturbed. She stood over him in silence, noting the dilated pupils before she knelt and quickly closed his eyes. In death he looked like a golden child with his hair falling across his face.

They buried him in the bush in the soft sandy earth. Jack took his dogtags and emptied the contents of his pockets, turning over a crumpled letter in his hands. As he smoothed the faded paper a tiny snapshot fell out on to the grass. He retrieved it quickly before it got damp from the rain and stood a while to wonder at the black and white photograph. A woman stood on a whiteboard porch with a dark-eyed labrador dog at her heels. She was smiling out at the photographer with love radiant in her eyes.

'Who is she?' asked Dede softly at his shoulder.

'I don't know. He never mentioned having anyone waiting back home.' He turned the letter over in his brown fingers and saw that it was only half written. At the top of the page Fielding had written, 'Darling Miriam – '

'I'll take it back with me,' said Jack abruptly, getting to his feet. He was surprised and moved at the loss. 'Somehow I'll see that she gets it.'

The scrubland reached down almost to the high tide mark on the beach. Clumps of bamboo and dwarf nipah palms littered the sandy flats, strong with the scent of wind and water. In the night the rolling breakers beat upon the dark shore. The glistening water shone black and silver in the faltering moonlight.

They were challenged by a voice out of the darkness as they first set foot on the beach. The sentry stood out against the black expanse, an alarming silhouette with rifle raised.

For a moment they were seized with fear. Had the Japanese arrived before them?'

'Who goes there?' His voice quickly dispelled their fears.

'Friends! Don't shoot us, mate!'

He lowered his rifle, his mouth open in surprise as Jack plunged forward over the sand towards him with a shout of relief.

'You'll never know how pleased we are to see you, mate!'

The sentry stared at the bearded, emaciated figure in a pair of faded army shorts and caught him in his arms.

'Reckon you're a sight,' said the sentry, steadying him. 'Who's that you've got there with you?'

'Women and children. Refugees. English, American, Portuguese and Dutch. We thought we'd never make it before the Japs.'

'Only just, mate. You must have the bloody luck of the Irish. Get yourselves down the beach and find the major. We're waiting for a ship out this very night.'

Beyond him they saw quite a crowd gathered on the grey sand. The night clouds raced in a strong wind off the shore. The moonlight was fitful at best. They hurried forward down the beach.

Their arrival was greeted with surprise and astonishment. The group on the beach was composed mainly of Australians and Dutch in various states of undress and ragged uniform. Many of the men sported beards their grandfathers would have been proud of. There were also women and children, all of them Portuguese, who had lost their husbands or reluctantly left them behind in the mountains to continue the war against the Japanese. There were also two nuns from a Dutch order who had crossed the island from the far west with a priest with a broken leg borne on a valiant pony.

The beach rang with strange mingled languages. There was laughter as well as tears as they exchanged stories and shared food and water with the new arrivals. Kate and her baby were the centre of attention.

'God has been with us,' concluded Sister Eulalia.

In the darkness the Australian troops began to light signal fires to guide the ship waiting offshore. There was a lamp to flash out a message to announce that it was safe to send boats ashore.

Watching with Jack just beyond the breaking surf, Dede felt a greater tension than ever before as she watched and waited. Should a Japanese spotter plane fly over now all their hopes of rescue would be gone for good.

'There it is,' breathed Jack, the excitement clear in his voice as the first return signal flashed out of the black night.

Across the rolling breakers the signals bounced on the rippling waves, spelling out the good news.

'Well, mate, we're finally going,' said a wounded Australian at their side. 'Seems they nearly didn't get through. Nip fighters strafed one of the convoy off Betano.'

We're really going, thought Kate, hugging little Amy.

'We would never have made it without you, Sister,' Kate told her.

Sister Eulalia's eyes were moist with unshed tears and she hugged Kate as the first small boats swept in on the tide. 'God's ways are wonderful, child. I felt, in my heart, that we would be captured, but He has brought us through.'

Together they had seen death, destruction and the birth of new life. They were as close as two people could ever be.

All around them on the beach the refugees were suddenly full of activity as they started to move out towards the waiting boats. On the shore Jack held Dede back as the water lapped their feet.

'Dede,' he told her urgently, looking into her face, 'Dede, I'm not going with you.'

She stared at him, uncomprehending, her nails biting into his arm.

'I can't, don't you see? I've got to go back with the others, as long as they're staying.'

The realization of what he was saying suddenly struck her and she shook her head wildly.

'No, no, Jack, you can't! You can't do that! It's too dangerous, you'll be killed – '

'Not if I can help it.'

'It's happening again, just like Warren.' Her eyes beseeched him, her voice an urgent whisper. 'Don't let it end here. I don't want to lose you.'

Her eyes held his as the dark waters swirled and surged about their legs.

'This isn't the end,' he told her. 'This time it's going to be different. I'm coming back to you.'

He bent his head and his mouth fastened on to hers as she came into his arms, unaware of the others around them.

'I'll wait, I'll wait for you for ever,' she promised, savouring his closeness, reluctant to let him go.

'I'll keep you to that,' he said solemnly and with a final snatched kiss he let her go.

Sister Eulalia saw Dede turn towards the boat and passed the small Macedo boy to her to carry into the sea. Dede passed the child into his mother's arms where she sat in the bow of the first boat. As Eva took him, her face broke into a spontaneous smile and she stretched out her hand to pull Dede on board.

As they sat in the cramped little boat, the banter of the Australian crew masked their mixed emotions. Kate saw Dede looking back at the dark vastness of the island, still and silent across the water.

We have survived, thought Dede, looking back to the land, thinking of its dangers, thinking of Jack still standing there on the shore. Against the brooding skyline the jagged mountains of the interior stood out black and full of memories.

Memories of Letria and brave Amy who had given her life to save them. Of Mrs Beattie left unburied back in the villa in the heart of the mountains. And Father Jacinto, who had died so bravely with Macedo, face to face with his Japanese executioners.

Jack, Jack, will we ever be together again?

Before them lay the dark waters of the Timor Channel and five hundred dangerous miles to Darwin in Australia.

Kate looked down at her baby in the circle of her arms. She, too, was thinking of the future and the new start to come.

The lowering clouds of night were already fading in the east, heralding the coming of the dawn. Another new day was about to begin.